"Touch me, Miri."

"Kiss me back. I've been dying of thirst for you all my life without even knowing it. You can't deny what we do to each other, Miri."

"It's unfair of you to torment me this way," she wailed softly, shamefully aware of his steely hardness. "Your experience arms you with knowledge that turns my own body against me!"

With a growl, he rolled her to her back, his hand cupping the indentation of her waist, one knee insinuated between her thighs. "If your lovely body was all I wanted, I could have had you that first night . . ."

DEVIL'S MOON

SUZANNAH DAVIS

AVON BOOKS ◆ NEW YORK

AVON BOOKS
A division of
The Hearst Corporation
105 Madison Avenue
New York, New York 10016

Copyright © 1991 by Suzannah Davis
Inside cover author photograph by Terry Atwood
Published by arrangement with the author
Library of Congress Catalog Card Number: 90-93394
ISBN: 0-380-76127-0

First Avon Books Printing: February 1991

AVON TRADEMARK REG. U.S. PAT. OFF. AND IN OTHER COUNTRIES, MARCA
REGISTRADA, HECHO EN U.S.A.

Printed in the U.S.A.

RA 10 9 8 7 6 5 4 3 2 1

For
Tim Nelson and Kevin Nelson,
my brothers, my friends

"Oh, swear not by the moon, th' inconstant moon."

—*Romeo and Juliet,*
Act II, Scene ii

DEVIL'S MOON

Part I

Prologue

A tremor shook the old woman's wrinkled hands, disturbing the design of tea leaves floating in the bottom of her coconut shell cup. It did not matter. She had already seen enough in those murky depths to frighten even a priestess of her undisputed mystical talents.

Outside the tiny thatched hut where she sat, long-tailed monkeys screamed in a clattering bamboo thicket, and the night howls of a hunting tiger echoed down the surrounding hills. The giant cat did not worry the old dukun. Whenever they chanced to meet, whether in the lush steaminess of the jungle or on the hard-packed trails that bordered the shimmering rice paddies, she always addressed the noble feline respectfully, calling him Grandfather, and thus satisfied, he left her in peace. On this island, set between the warm ocean waters belonging to the Goddess of the Southern Sea and the northern lands whose peoples still worshiped in Shiva's temples, the forces of man and nature formed a delicate matrix in which all might coexist peacefully—except on nights such as this.

3

With a muttered incantation, the old woman spilled the amber liquid from her cup into the clay bowl of a coconut oil lamp, dousing the floating banana fiber wick. The silver fire of moonshine poured through the open doorway. Painfully the ancient dukun rose, then paused in the low opening. In her hands she held a broad banana leaf heaped with the offerings of rice and fruit meant to appease the capricious spirits that roamed the world this night.

The shining face of the goddess looked down on the old woman, an enormous sphere that filled the sky, bright and pure as the blossom beloved of the deities. Only once in a great while did the moon rise with such grace and fullness, heralding a time of signs and portents. On such a night, demons frolicked, and mortals had best beware of their mischief-making, for magic reigned, ghosts walked, and the unwary were bewitched into desperate acts.

In the coastal city below her mountain, the blue-eyed conquerors of the dukun's golden-skinned people did not understand the necessity for such precautions. Those who sat beside the old kings and decreed the new laws of commerce and justice scoffed at the ancient wisdom, walking unprotected, without benefit of amulet or charm to keep them safe from their own folly.

Shrugging her stooped shoulders, the dukun dismissed the white-skinned intruders. Let them court disaster as they might. She would never be so foolish.

Bathed in the cool silver light, the old woman carefully placed the offering before her threshold. She shivered, even though the air was warm and fragrant with the perfume of night-blooming flowers. The signs she'd read in the bottom of her cup marked this moon-rising as a time of powerful endings and beginnings, and she was anxious for herself and for those who depended on her guidance to put this night safely behind her. But for now all she could do was wait and remember and . . . watch.

Tales of heroes and gods arose in her mind, stories she'd recounted many times in the hope of arming the child of her heart with their powerful protection for just such an *uncertain night as this. As the power of the old tales filled her, the* dukun *made a final gesture to ward off demon-magic, then carefully shut her door against the cool and mysterious beauty of the Lotus Moon.*

Chapter 1

The Preanger District, Java
August 1721

Whether he wanted it or not, he had company.

Anthony Benedict, Marquess of Bentley, master of the *Mirage*, and adventurer *extraordinaire*, squelched his irritation by taking another swig of the fiery Javanese gin that his ebullient host had pressed on him all evening. The liquor burned down his throat, and he scowled at the feminine figure crossing the moonlit terrace that separated his chamber from the dense tropical gardens surrounding the sultan's *kraton*.

After all, there were limits to what a man must accept in the name of hospitality, and he had already declined Lord Palu Tanah's offer of female companionship more than once during the course of the evening's protracted entertainments. Even now the drums and gongs of the *gamelan* orchestra continued below in the main courtyard, a weird and discordant—at least to English ears—accompaniment to the shadow-puppet play he'd left to the rest of the sultan's enthralled guests only moments before.

Standing in the shelter of his doorway, Tony narrowed

his slate blue eyes in watchful suspicion at the maiden's stealthy, almost furtive approach through the checkered shadows of the bamboo-latticed arcade. It wasn't that he did not appreciate the offer of a night with one of the slender beauties in Lord Palu's service, he thought.

Perhaps the excesses of his youth that had won him notoriety as the infamous "Wastrel Lord" were responsible for the restless boredom that had blunted his appetites of late. A year and a half ago he'd made peace with his lifelong enemy, then set out on this quest to the East. There had been little time and less inclination for fleshly pursuits since then. Besides, as an English merchant whose welcome from the Dutch authorities monopolizing the Java spice trade would be less than enthusiastic should his true purpose be revealed, despite the treaties that bound their two homelands as allies, he must be cautious. Establishing a rich market for his family's Free Indies Shipping Company was a goal he'd vowed to attain despite the risk, and now it was within his grasp. As soon as he completed his negotiations with a certain unscrupulous Dutchman in league with Lord Palu, Lord Anthony Benedict could add another title to his collection—that of smuggler.

So, he reminded himself with the cynicism of thirty-three years, it was wise for a man to know exactly what was expected in return for a favor who appeared in silken slippers and sarong, especially when she came from the most powerful man in the province. Which was why Tony intended to turn down whatever the girl had to offer.

Setting aside his chased metal cup, he stepped onto the terrace and was instantly blinded by a slash of brilliant moonlight. A soft gasp whispered in his ears, and he turned toward the sound, blinking against the dazzle. For an instant there was a dizzying, disturbing sensation of vertigo. Frowning, he took another step, focusing with difficulty on the figure halted mere feet away. The words of rejection died on his lips.

Parallel bars of silver fell through the arcade roof, capturing the maiden in a prism of light, holding her motionless. Her attitude was as startled as Tony's, but even in the mottled texture of light and shadow, he could see that she was beautiful.

Large, almond-shaped eyes whose pale color Tony could not name were framed by finely arched brows, and her features were delicately carved. The high cheekbones, straight nose, and lushly curved mouth held none of the flat broadness he'd seen in so many of the Javanese people, but rather an aristocratic elegance. Her dark hair was pulled back from her face, dressed in an elaborate looped style, crowned by a headdress of fresh flowers. Blue and brown flowers were repeated in the batik design of her floor-length sarong and the breast cloth that left her honey-tinted shoulders bare in the manner of traditional Javanese court dress.

An irrational but undeniable sense of recognition stunned Tony, and he knew she felt the same shock. She was lovely and exotic, but it was not her beauty that touched his hardened core and melted it with a single glance. Her expression was so vulnerable, her lovely face so innocent, that Tony's heart hurt to look on her. A longing strong and elemental stirred him, as if he glimpsed a part of himself long missing and mourned for and now suddenly restored. Unable to stop himself, he moved forward like a man in a dream.

The dream was shattered by the strident chatter of an angry servant. The sudden appearance of the wiry man dressed in sarong and turban severed their mute connection, and both Tony and the girl jumped. Ishta, the majordomo in Lord Palu's household, bore down on them, black eyes snapping, hands striking the air like serpents, his guttural words a heated chastisement. Grabbing the girl by the bare arm, he jerked her roughly, wringing a gasping protest from her in rapid Javanese.

"Release her, sirrah!" Tony's voice boomed over the distant cacophony of the *gamelan*, and he started forward, a primitive, possessive anger filling him. His fists clenched and his muscles bunched in readiness as he prepared to come to her defense, but her soft words froze him in his tracks.

"Please! I must have the Englishman!"

Good Lord! His beauty spoke English, too. The possibility of a real conversation in this heathenish land was an enticement in and of itself, and all the more reason to indulge his temper.

"Take your hands off her, by God!" he ordered again.

Ishta cast him a searing, contemptuous glance, growled something further at the girl, and shoved her back in the direction she'd come. Her reply was unintelligible to Tony, but he had heard her desperation and saw the anguished glance she flung his way.

With a speed belied by his size, Tony seized the servant, cuffed his ears so soundly his turban flew off into the darkness, then pitched him bodily into a nearby clump of banana fronds. Although he did not understand the savage shrieks Ishta emitted as he struggled free of the bushes, Tony knew without doubt that he was being roundly cursed. Placing his fists on his narrow hips, Tony threw back his head and roared with laughter.

This action only incensed the humiliated servant all the more. With an evil glance, Ishta scurried off into the moon-spangled darkness of the long terrace.

"You have made an enemy, sir."

The soft, melodious voice recalled Tony, and he turned to the slender figure who hovered uncertainly in the shadow of a wooden pillar. With a flourish admired in the best London drawing rooms, he swept her a courtly bow worthy of his most lavish satin coat. It was an elegant gesture even in his plain white linen shirt and fitted, fawn-colored breeches, and it spoke volumes regarding his breeding and heritage.

"Your servant, mistress." Tony cast a disparaging glance after the retreating majordomo. "He will not interfere again."

"Sir, I fear that is not so," she contradicted him in an anxious tone. "You have dared to touch his head. In this land that is the veriest insult. He will return."

"Then I shall treat him to more of the same, should he dare lay hands on you again against your wishes."

"For this courtesy, I thank you." She folded her hands beneath her chin and returned his bow. "But Ishta meant only to preserve your solitude as you requested."

Tony moved a step closer, but her expression was masked by the dappled light. "You knew this, yet you came anyway? Had I foreseen such a delightful visitor, I would not have made it necessary for you to be so bold."

She looked away in confusion, and Tony wondered if she had followed his flirtatious remark. After all, though her English was good and curiously unaccented, it held a not-unpleasing foreign cadence that suggested her tongue was not accustomed to the language. In a gentler voice, he complimented her.

"Your English is lovely to my ears. I confess, though I've had skilled interpreters in my business dealings here, I've missed the sound of the King's English in general speech."

"Thank you, sir." She bit her lip, hesitating, and Tony sensed an urgency and agitation about her that made him frown.

"What is it, my dear? Though I did violence to that insolent servant, you have nothing to fear from me."

Her breath shuddered in a long sigh, and her words were a murmur. "You are most kind, sir. You make the task before me easier."

Unsettled by her hesitancy, Tony's mind raced. There was no mistaking her distress. He could feel how she quivered, pressing ever deeper into the shadows. What desperate fix had led an apparently well-educated woman of her obvious standing to seek him out unless . . . unless Lord Palu had ordered it?

A part of Tony, that small boy inside who had been spoiled since birth, cried out in frustration and anger. For one perfect moment in the moonlight, he had known the rightness of being with this woman, had been caught up in an illusion that had no substance. Now her words recalled reality, and he inwardly railed at a sense of betrayal and disappointment that cut deeply into the hidden core of his heart. His head told him such a notion was insanity, and he tried to shake off the unreasonable feelings, focusing on the facts. If this maiden had come to him on Lord Palu's

command, why should it trouble him? The inescapable fact
was that it did. Unbearably.

"What is your desire, mistress?" he asked cautiously.

"My desire . . . ?" she echoed, puzzled.

"Surely there was some purpose to your coming here
tonight?"

"Oh! Yes—" Her eager voice was stilled by the sounds
of activity on the lower terrace. She darted back, her movements skittish and nervous. "It is Ishta, returning to send
me away."

"I can deal with Ishta." Tony's tone was annoyed.

"No! I mean . . . we cannot speak at length here, sir."
She held out her hand to him in appeal. "Quickly! Come
with me. We will seek a place where no one will disturb
us."

Tony could hardly believe his ears. So she meant to go
through with the assignation? Anticipation mingled with
disappointment in himself, in her. Again he shook off the
surprising emotional confusion and tried to concentrate. Perhaps he should attempt to discover just what Lord Palu was
up to. The rhythm of marching feet along the terrace decided
him. Placing his large hand in her much smaller one, he
followed her into the darkness.

There was a strange, breathless stillness in the garden
under the roof of palm trees. Night sounds were muffled,
and the music of the *gamelan* faded, became a rhythmic
heartbeat more felt than heard. Like two shadows, they
darted beneath the spreading limbs of a banyan tree, followed a narrow path through a rustling bamboo grove, then
crept through a shoulder-high border of ferns and fragrant
night-blooming jasmine. Tony followed docilely until this
point, then brought his companion to a halt beside a crumbling brick wall overrun with pale-hued orchids that caught
the moonglow and threw it back heavenward like a thousand
shiny trumpets.

"This is far enough," he said. There was an opening in
the wall, partially hidden under a mass of creepers. Dropping her hand, Tony pushed aside the vines to reveal an
ancient, iron-hinged door. "What is this place?"

"I do not know." Her voice held a tremor.

"Surely you have some idea. You brought us right to it."

With a suppressed shiver, she crossed her arms over her breasts. "I've never been within the *kraton*'s walls before."

Tony shrugged, then reached for the handle.

"No!"

Her sharp cry stopped him. "What is it?"

She shook her head, staring at the dark door, and white petals drifted from her headdress to settle like snowflakes at her feet. "This is a temple. Perhaps a shrine. We shouldn't—"

"I've had enough of your games, my girl," Tony snapped, suddenly impatient. He grasped her arm and hauled her forward, pulling open the door at the same time. "We'll speak here."

Helping her across the threshold, Tony surveyed the simple windowless room. Red brick walls rose to two full stories like a medieval tower. The moon peeked through high window slits, glinting off strings of brass temple bells that hung silent in the lifeless air. A low platform covered with bamboo matting and cotton cushions stuffed with rice straw and kapok lined one wall. In the center of the room was a round stone with a scooped-out place in the middle that Tony guessed was a hearth or a place to burn offerings and incense.

"See? Nothing so awful," he began, turning to the girl, then stopped. She stared at the opposite wall, where a crude drawing was revealed by the slanting beams of light. The figure, daubed in red ochre, was grotesquely obese, with bulging eyes and a comic turn of expression.

"Semar," she murmured.

"Who?"

"You do not know the ways of this land, Englishman. This place is sacred to Semar. He is a fallen god, yet powerful. In the time of Buddha, he was brother to Shiva the Destroyer. We'd best begone."

"He looks like some kind of clown."

"You recognize him from the shadow-puppet play you

attended. He is sometimes playful, yet at midnight it is Semar who fights the forces of destruction. In the end he rises from a pyre to regain his true god-form.''

Tony was not impressed with the story of the play. He was more interested in the fact that she had so closely watched his movements. Had she been a member of the sultan's audience, too?

"I don't think this demon will mind our visit,'' he said. ''I have questions . . .''

"Of course." She nodded. "But first, I have brought an offering.''

Turning away from him, she fumbled in the folds of her sarong for a moment. Tony's mouth went suddenly dry, and his heart took up an erratic rhythm. The offering she referred to could only be herself. A few twists of fabric and her sarong would be free.

But, disappointingly, when she turned back to him a few seconds later, she was still modestly clothed. With hands clasped before the gentle swell of her bosom, she slowly unfurled her fingers, opening them like the velvety petals of a lotus blossom.

Tony's jaw dropped in surprise. Lying warm and satiny against her palms was a lustrous pearl the size of a quail's egg.

"Where did you get that?"

She shrugged. "Does it matter, Englishman? All that is important is whether you like it.''

"Me?" Totally confused, Tony hesitantly poked the shiny white globe with his fingertip. A wry laugh shook his massive chest.

She bit her lip uncertainly. "What humor do you see in this? The offer is honorable. Perhaps it is not enough?''

"Ah, lady, if you only knew." Again Tony chuckled, and his smile was enigmatic. "Pearls have always played rather an important role in my life.''

"I do not understand.''

"Never mind. It's an old story." Suddenly Tony's mouth tightened and his chin grew taut, nearly erasing the deep cleft in its center. Firmly he folded her hands closed over the pearl. "The question here is what you intend to get for your pearl."

"I told you. It is an offering."

"A gift to Semar?"

"No." Her voice was soft, her eyes pale and luminous. "To you, Englishman."

The words were scarcely out of her mouth when a great gust of wind exploded through the upper reaches of the tower, setting the temple bells to jangling fiercely. The gust swirled about them, and at their backs the heavy door slammed shut, leaving them in a well of darkness broken only by the high bars of moonlight. The woman gave a soft, startled shriek, and instinctively Tony pulled her into the protective circle of his arms.

She trembled like a doe, and her bare skin was warm and satiny smooth beneath his callused hands. Her fragrance rose to his nostrils in intoxicating clouds of sweet frangipani and sweeter woman. She was slender and supple as a reed, and he held her gently, with a strangely possessive tenderness.

"It's only the wind," he murmured.

His chin brushed against the blossoms in her headdress, and he realized she was taller than he'd thought. Though still dwarfed by his English stature, she was not so tiny and doll-like as most Javanese women, and this pleased him. She stirred against him, pushing away, he thought, a bit reluctantly.

"I beg your pardon, sir. It—oh!" With a little cry of distress, she fell to her knees, and her shadowy outline bobbed as she patted the dirt floor. "The pearl! I dropped it."

"Do not alarm yourself. We'll find it." He moved toward the door. "A bit more light will help our search."

But when he pushed the handle, he met resistance. Frowning, he pushed harder, then set his broad shoulder to the massive planks and used all his weight to force it open. Stubbornly, it refused to budge.

"I still can't find it," she said, almost frantic. "Will you not open the door?"

"I'm afraid I can't, my dear. It appears something—or someone—has blocked it."

She gasped. "What?"

"Perhaps Ishta has found a way to repay the insult," Tony suggested dryly. He tested the door once again, found it immovable, and gave up. "We're locked in."

She was motionless for a long moment. When she spoke, her words were strangled. "You mean we're trapped?"

"It seems so. At least until morning. Perhaps when the palace stirs, then a gardener will hear our calls from this remote corner."

"But I can't stay the night!"

Tony crossed the small chamber, squatting down in front of where she knelt, trying to read her shadowed expression. His voice was too silky. "You have someone waiting for you, perhaps?"

"My—my sister," she whispered, drawing back from the menace in his tone. "She will worry if she wakes to find me missing."

"No one else?" he demanded sharply.

The shadowy outline of her head wagged back and forth in denial. "We have only each other now."

Tony did not acknowledge the swift surge of relief that no man waited at home for her, but his posture relaxed, and he was once again sympathetic. Orphans, he mused. There was no guessing what dire circumstances had led this maid to seek him out. The incongruity was the magnificent pearl. She had means, at least of a sort, but apparently could not use them. What hold did Lord Palu have over her and her sister? "Is that why you came here tonight?" he asked gently.

"Yes, it is for my sister's sake, you see." Bending forward again, she stretched out her hands. "Oh, where is that wretched pearl?"

Tony knelt down to join her search, grunting in pain as his kneecap hit a hard, round object. "I think I've found it."

"You have it? Where?"

He shifted, picking up the gem. "Here. See?"

In the darkness she could see little, and so her fingers closed over his. Finding the pearl by touch, she then heaved a heartfelt sigh of relief.

Tony smiled, amused. "Since you seem to have no—er, pocket in your garb, let me keep it for you in mine so that we will not have to play this game of hide-and-seek again," he offered.

"Yes, of course. You must keep it."

"I'll put it here." Guiding her hand with his own, he showed her by feel the narrow pocket slit at his hipbone, tucked the gem within it, then hesitated when her fingers lingered on his side. His hand covered hers, pressing her palm against himself, and a sudden flare of mutual awareness burned between them, unseen in the darkness but bright as day nonetheless. Tony's other hand slipped unerringly beneath the heavy weight of her hair looped at her slender nape.

"Sweet one, what are you doing?" he asked huskily, bending closer.

Her voice was faint. "I—I do not know."

"Nor do I."

Slowly he dipped his head, settling his mouth against her trembling lips. She was soft and sweeter than the most exotic nectar, and he had to stifle a groan of protest as he forced himself to end the kiss. He wanted more, so much more, but he was confused by the inexperience he sensed. Again he wondered at Lord Palu's intentions, and at this innocent's actions. He took a deep breath.

"What are you called?"

She came out of her daze with a jerk, ducking her head in embarrassment, standing and pulling away from Tony in a swift, agitated movement. "Oh, sir!"

"Your name," he insisted, holding her wrist firmly as she strained away.

"M-Miri," she stammered, twisting free of his grasp. She fell against the stubborn door, rattling its handle and beating at the unresponsive panels with her small fists. "How can this be locked? There must be some way out!"

Rising, Tony went to her, turning her gently to face him.

"Not unless you can scale these walls, Miri. I assure you Ishta was thorough in his methods. We will remain until someone comes to release us." A smile curled his lips, and he chuckled, trailing a knuckle down her cheek in a brief caress. "Ishta little realizes the favor he has done me."

Backed against the door, she gulped, "Sir . . ."

"My name is Anthony Benedict—Tony if you will so honor me."

"I—I know."

One sun-streaked brow lifted. "You know much about me already."

"Only that the English sea captain with golden hair touched with a sunset's fire comes to Lord Palu's on the night of the Lotus Moon. I have been waiting."

"So have I, Miri." He bent closer, brushing her lips with his own, and his voice held a strange note of wonder. "Maybe all my life."

"This is Semar's doing," she protested breathlessly. "You are bewitched. Pay no attention. Instead, think of your return to England. Will you sail through the Strait of Sunda?"

Tony smiled at her tactics but humored her. "As a matter of fact, that is my plan. Do you fancy a sea voyage?"

"How far could I go for the price of a pearl?"

"As far as you care to, my dearling."

In the silvery darkness his fingers mapped the shape of her round chin, the slenderness of her neck, the pulse that beat erratically at the base of her throat.

"You are exquisite," he murmured, and felt her start of surprise. "What? Has no one ever told you that you are beautiful?"

She shook her head. "Never. You are the first to tell such a lie to my face."

"And modest, too," he chuckled.

His exploration took his hand to the soft swell of her breast, and she gasped at his brazenness and tried to lunge away. Catching her shoulders, he easily forestalled her, his voice suddenly sober.

"Are you afraid of me?"

"N-no."

"Then why do you run from me when it was you who sought our meeting?"

"Because . . ." He kissed the shallow hollow behind her ear, and she moaned.

"Yes?" His mouth was muffled against her neck, and he could feel the shivers that coursed over her skin.

"Oh," she whispered, "you chase every thought from my head . . ."

"I don't want you to think of anything but this, of anyone but me, Miri. You enchant me like no woman I've ever known." He paused, his hands tightening on her. "Is that crazy? Can you understand what I'm feeling?"

"Yes, I understand—" Her hands clutched at his strong forearms, and her whisper was tremulous with a desperate hunger that echoed his own sudden, overwhelming need. "—because I fear I am bewitched, too."

Then she was in his arms completely, reaching for him eagerly, her body melting against his as their mouths met and clung. Tony had never experienced such instantaneous arousal in himself, nor such sweet and complete response from a woman. Madness rose in his brain like bubbles in a wineglass, and he crushed Miri to him, his hands moving avidly down the elegant curve of her spine and tangling in her hair. Pins slid free, and the headdress fell to the floor as her hair cascaded down her back in a sheer, heavy fall of woodsy-fragrant silk.

Breathing heavily, heart thumping painfully, Tony traced the ribbon of her lips with his tongue and was immediately rewarded as she opened her mouth fully to his fevered exploration of its intimate depths. Boldly he delved her secrets, tasting her essence, and a thrill of pleasure shot through him when her tongue joined in the play, timidly at first, and then with more assurance as he groaned his encouragement.

Somehow her hands were beneath his shirt, tracing the washboard of his rib cage, teasing the hard nubs of his nipples, threading through the pelt of soft reddish gold chest hairs. Tony reverently cupped her breasts, exulting in the perfect weight and fit of the small, soft globes in his palms.

An exploratory twist of the breast cloth and sarong, and the rectangular sheets of fabric that were her only garments fell to the floor, leaving her totally nude.

If there had ever been any restraint in Tony, it was gone now.

Picking Miri up, Tony carried her to the low platform and followed her down. Awed at her delicate beauty, her tiny waist and slim thighs, the subtle indentations and valleys of her satiny skin, he worshiped her with hands and lips in all the ways he knew until they were both wild with need. Leaving her only long enough to tear off his own clothes with a haste born of near-insanity, he joined her on the rude couch, only hazily aware that he had completely lost control.

There were no words, no rules, no courtesies, no promises to keep. It was only the two of them, striving together for a primeval ecstasy. The round face of the Lotus Moon disappeared from the window slits, leaving only a faint silver reflection to illuminate their trysting place, but they were past the point where sight was necessary.

When Tony urged her thighs apart, Miri opened gladly, stretching her arms over her head luxuriously, totally free and wanton. When he entered her, there was only momentary resistance, noticed by neither in their dual sighs of pleasure. Then there was only the wild, pagan ride to completion, a crescendo built by the *gamelan* orchestra, heard only distantly before but now seeming to fill the room with its pulsing, complicated beat, as the ancient, internal tempo of passion brought Miri and Tony both to sighing, shouting climax.

And at that same instant, high above their lovers' bed, the metallic laughter of the temple bells chimed in the still and windless night.

Tony opened his eyes, then closed them again, squinting and blinking at the glare. The moon had been replaced by the searing, white-hot globe of the noonday sun, and the burning tropical rays beat down on him through the window slits above his head. His mouth tasted like ship's tar and bilge water, and his head pounded so evilly, even his scalp hurt.

Groaning, Tony tried to sit up. He made it on the third attempt. Gingerly holding his aching head in his hands, he tried to bring his muddled mind into focus. What the hell was he doing here? He lifted his head for another bleary-eyed look around at the crumbling ruin of a room, and sweat popped out all over his naked body at the effort.

Naked? An alarm went off in his brain. Miri!

Tony whirled around, but her place on the cushioned platform was empty. So was the room. Cursing, Tony surged to his feet, only to immediately regret it as the walls swam before his eyes, and his ears rang.

Damn it! What was the matter with him? He hadn't been this guzzled from drink since he and Angus had tested the native brew in Madagascar. Javanese gin was more potent than he'd bargained for. And now—blast it all to hell and back—Miri was gone!

In fact, there wasn't a sign that she'd ever even been here. The thought stopped Tony in his tracks, and the hairs on the back of his neck quivered. No forgotten garments intertwined with his twisted clothes on the floor. No flower headdress wilted in a corner, discarded hastily in the throes of passion. Not even a single crushed blossom dusted the floor to mark the tale of seduction and surrender. It was as if she were an Arabian *houri*, some spirit from a moonlit paradise now returned to her rightful place.

"Goddamn it! I did not make her up!" Tony told himself out loud.

How could he have invented anything so real, so absolutely perfect? He'd be crazy indeed to have fabricated a memory that rivaled a tale of his own *supposed* exploits. Not once, but many times, they'd come to each other during the night, hardly coming down from one plateau before one or the other was reaching out yet again, then leading the climb to the peak by yet another route.

Tony stumbled to the door. It creaked open with the touch of one finger, its planks thin and rotting in the tropical humidity, and certainly no barrier to a determined assault.

There was no sign of Miri in the garden. Cursing without truly considering the source of his anger, Tony staggered back inside. He grabbed up his shirt and breeches with a gesture that bordered on violence, wondering briefly at the brownish stains on his hands, then jerked his pants on.

By God! Did she think she could leave, just like that, without a word—after the miracle they'd shared? Didn't she have any idea how unique their joining had been? He'd had to travel nearly around the world to find a woman who pleased him so well, whose essential femininity complemented everything in him that was masculine. He'd never felt so protective or possessive about one of his lovers, not even when he'd thought himself half in love with his brother's wife-to-be. How dare Miri walk away from that!

His fingers faltered on the buttons of his breeches, then dug in the high pocket at the hard knob stretched beneath the fabric. Withdrawing his hand, he opened his palm, then sucked in a hissing breath.

Miri's pearl gleamed in his hand, sitting beside his favorite snuffbox, a tiny work of art in jade, carved with the outline of a lotus blossom.

Tony's fist clenched around the two objects. She was real, as real as everything that had occurred between them. Mysterious as the moon, she might be, but Miri was *his*. If he had to search every inch of this pagan island, *nothing* would keep him from finding her.

Chapter 2

S he'd failed.
And sinned.

But worse than that, she'd turned her back on duty.

Miri ducked her head under the cool green waters of the bathing pool and scrubbed mercilessly at her long, straight hair, but she feared no amount of washing would ever erase her shame. Straightening, she pulled the wet mass over one shoulder and squeezed the moisture out of the ash blond strands. It had been necessary to use the juice of the racu root to darken it in order to enter the *kraton* the previous evening, but she could not have guessed then what consequences would result from her rashness.

Miri swallowed hard, her clear gray eyes staring sightlessly across the narrow lowland river that divided her village from the rolling foothills and, higher up, the smoking mountain that dominated the lush tropical landscape. The cool water lapped at her thighs and plastered her plain cotton sarong to her lithe form, but Miri was oblivious to the familiar scenery, to her own shivering discomfort, to every-

23

thing but the memory of the madness she'd shared with the Englishman.

Her wantonness made her skin heat, just as it had the moment he'd touched her. In a land of dark-eyed, golden-skinned people, Anthony Benedict's fairness had stunned her, even in the moonlit darkness of the sultan's garden. She had not been prepared for a man of such beauty, from the hard strength of his square jaw with its charming cleft and his lean, tanned features, to the piercing blue of his eyes and the blaze of fire in his sun-streaked hair. But more than that, she'd been mesmerized by the strength he radiated, a magnetism that drew her to him with promises of fulfillment not only physical, but spiritual, a man in whose arms she had nothing to fear. They'd come together with explosive passion, but even at his most ardent, she'd sensed his inherent gentleness. She'd felt protected and cherished even as she'd experienced for the first time the pleasure a man and woman could give each other and the addicting freedom of total abandonment.

"Miri! Miranda!"

Her stepsister's call jolted Miss Miranda Agnes Langford from her dangerous reverie with a breath-stealing surge of guilt. Turning, Miranda watched Rija's rapid progress down the steps carved into the steep and overgrown riverbank below the thatch-roofed huts of their village. Only fourteen, the young Javanese maiden was small and slight, yet agile and graceful as a gazelle, descending the stairs with an anxious expression etching her patrician features. Miranda suddenly felt much older than her own twenty-five years.

At sunrise, reality intruded into her enchanted garden, and she'd fled the *kraton* in a panic, though the Englishman had slept on as one drugged. She hadn't even wondered until later why the blocked door offered her no resistance. Upon reflection, she decided he'd tricked her into believing they were trapped, the better to work his seductive magic. And fool that she was, it had worked beautifully.

Yes, she'd abandoned everything with—here her mind balked, refusing to call him Tony, even to herself—with the Englishman. Caught up in a dream, a nightmare, she'd been moonstruck, surrendering her virtue and her mission without protest or demur. Nay, she'd *gladly* given the Englishman everything he wanted, while forgetting the reason she'd risked her life to invade the sultan's domain. The English sea captain was their last hope of rescue from Lord Palu's horrifying edict, but shamefully, she had been too bemused by the spell he wove to even tell him what she wanted!

Miranda waded slowly toward the riverbank, where Rija waited. In the brilliant sunshine her failure was all too clearly revealed, and she longed to curse her weakness of character, but her English was too rusty from disuse to form the words. The heavy weight of guilt and failure lay in her chest like a lump of stone.

"You have risen with the sun." Rija greeted her sister in Javanese, her dark brown, almond-shaped eyes wide with inquiry. The girl handed Miranda the dry sarong she'd left in readiness on the bank, eager questions tripping from her full lips. "Why did you not wake me, sister? Is it done? Did you see him? Will the sea captain take us in his ship to the English fort at Benkulen? When do we leave?"

"Such a barrage of questions!" Miranda remonstrated gently, stalling for a moment. "Is this the dignity of a princess?"

Rija bowed, accepting the chastisement with a dimple in her cheek. "I beg your pardon, sister. At times like these it is terribly difficult to remember my exalted position."

Smiling fondly at her stepsister, Miranda automatically took the sarong, arranged it around herself, then loosened the wet one beneath it to drop at her feet. She'd had ten years practice at the appointed morning and evening bathing times of her adopted country to perfect the maneuver that kept her modestly clothed at all times. She was glad that when her sea captain father had married Rija's mother, the widowed Princess Sura of Cirebon, he had been too practical to demand that his English-born daughter adhere to the heavy British style of dress in this climate. Miranda retrieved her wet sarong, then led the way back up the staircase carved into the bank.

"Miri?" Rija's tone held exasperation, but she followed her stepsister, hiking up the hem of her sarong in a manner that would not have pleased her royal mother had she lived. "You have not answered my questions."

Reaching the top of the bank, Miranda offered her hand to help Rija up, her expression solemn. "That is because I have no answers to give you."

"He refused?" Rija's eyes widened in dismay.

Miranda looked away. "Not exactly."

"But—"

"Come into the house to talk. It's many miles to the *kraton*, and I am weary, and hungry, too."

"Of course! Forgive me for my thoughtlessness!" Rija urged Miranda forward, and they ducked through the low doorway of the airy hut that had been their home since Captain Richard Langford's untimely death.

The walls were made of flattened bamboo, woven into panels that afforded privacy without curtailing the flow of the cooling river breezes, and the roof was thatched with palm fronds. The hut had several rooms, and floors of brick tiles, as befitted a princess of the province, and it was furnished with simple bamboo cots and tables as well as a heavy ship's chest, an English chair and desk, and a small, glass-fronted cabinet that housed Miranda's precious supply of books in Spanish, English, French, and Dutch, a legacy of her lifelong travels.

Rather than leave his only child behind in England when Miranda's mother died, Richard Langford had kept her with him on all his many voyages, seeing to her education himself. An early facility for languages earned Miranda an important position on her father's merchantman, and she had conducted business for him in ports as far-flung as Cairo, Cartagena, and Calcutta. But for the past six years, Miranda's language had been most often high and low Javanese as she raised the young stepsister she'd come to love as her own daughter.

Rija quickly took Miranda's damp sarong, hung it on a peg to dry, then called to Noppa, their wizened manservant, to fetch a platter of cold rice and fruit. Miranda seated herself in the English chair and pulled a bone comb through her drying hair, binding the fair, almost silvery mass at her nape with a bit of coconut hemp string, then smiling her thanks as Noppa shuffled in with her breakfast. Rija squatted on her heels, waiting for Noppa to leave and Miranda to begin, forcing herself to contain her curiosity, though impatience and anxiety haunted her dark brown eyes. Miranda knew she could not put her off any longer. With a sigh, she set aside the comb and reached for the platter.

"We will have to find another way to reach Benkulen," she said, taking a bit of rice between her fingers and eating with dainty, efficient movements. "I—I could not arrange our passage to Sumatra with the Englishman."

"But the time draws near," Rija said, gnawing her lower lip. "I cannot wed the murderer of our father! But if I do not, Lord Palu will have me killed, and perhaps you and all the villagers as well."

"I know." Miranda's appetite deserted her. She pushed aside the platter and rubbed her throbbing temple. "I promised your mother that I would always take care of you. I swear I will find a way for us to leave Java, at least until this danger is past."

"It is an honorable alternative. Even in the time of Buddha, when the great temples were built, entire villages sometimes fled to escape the hardships of forced labor."

"I have heard the teachers speak of these temples." Miranda tried to smile to encourage Rija. "Perhaps when this is over, you and I will make a pilgrimage of thanksgiving to one of these holy places."

"I will have many prayers and offerings to make, for I have surely been blessed with the best of sisters," Rija said, her liquid eyes serious. "Even when our father found a husband for you, you would not abandon me."

Miranda shrugged. "I have no regrets on that account, you know. You needed me more than that fat Dutch planter did."

Rija's finely arched brows drew together in a worried frown. "Yet if you had accepted the offer, you would now be safe in a home of your own with babies at your feet. I fear I have brought you nothing but sorrow, Miri. If I could free you from this charge my mother made, I would. You know that I would bow to any marriage Lord Palu arranged but this.''

"I know." Miranda gripped Rija's hand fiercely, and her expression darkened. "I will not allow Lord Palu to give you to Steef van der Djink, no matter what alliance he wishes to make with that murdering Dutchman."

"If only we could prove Djink attacked Papa Langford's merchantman, then perhaps Lord Palu—"

"Lord Palu cares naught for an unimportant English sailor whose death occurred more than six years ago," Miranda said bitterly. "Djink did him a service by so ruthlessly removing Papa as a threat to the Dutch East Indies Company's monopoly and Lord Palu's portion of the profits. And I underestimated Lord Palu's deviousness."

"In what way, sister?"

"Foolishly, I thought his allowing us to live here in this village under his protection was an act of mercy. I realize now he was biding his time, waiting until you were of age to seal the alliance between himself and the Dutch East India Company by linking your royal line and hereditary rights with the outsiders. We are both no more than pawns in his game of power with the Dutch."

Rija nodded, her eyes glowing with anger. "I fear that as regent-by-marriage, Djink will demand my people plant more sugar and coffee to meet the Dutch quotas while he lines his own pockets at our expense." She rose, her posture regal and dignified, every inch a princess of the royal blood. "I swear my people will not suffer for their love of me, not even if I must fling myself into the burning mountain to prevent it."

"All is not lost yet," Miranda said with a half smile at Rija's dramatic vow. "We will travel across the mountains to the coast and hire a small prau to take us through the straits."

Rija shook her head. "The way is long and slow. Lord Palu's men will surely stop us before we reach the summit."

"We will use stealth.''

"Lord Palu's spies are everywhere already, trying to locate the bandits led by Virat Amang."

"Surely Lord Palu has little to fear from Prince Amang? The son of the deposed sultan cannot even raise an army and is forced to live as a fugitive in the jungle."

Rija shook her head. "The *dukun* says only the prince will be able to avenge his father's death, and Lord Palu heeds her warnings by doubling the patrols. Because of this, we would find no safety in the hills. If only the English captain had agreed! Then we could go swiftly, before Lord Palu was aware of our intent! Tell me, sister, weren't you able to see the Englishman?"

Miranda felt a flush creep up her neck. "Ah, well, yes—"

"Then why would he not heed the plight of one of his own?" Rija asked. "You said yourself when Noppa brought the news of his visit to the *kraton* that it was like a gift from Allah in our time of need."

"I—it was not as simple as I thought. Things happened so swiftly, I couldn't explain . . ." Miranda gulped, then forced briskness into her voice. "But after meeting him, I'm certain he wouldn't serve our purpose. We can devise some other plan . . ."

"But why must we?" Rija interrupted. "Go to him again and make him listen to our plea. He cannot refuse us if he knows the truth."

"The English are an unpredictable race. Besides, it would be impossible for me to return to the *kraton*," Miranda said weakly. "I was able to slip inside the gates only because so many guests had come to the feast of the Lotus Moon. Anyway, now that the celebrations are over, he will go back to his ship."

"The vessel is anchored in the harbor of Batavia, is it not? Why can't we go directly to the ship? That would be even better." Rija's expression became animated as she warmed to the idea. "If we are already aboard when you give him my mother's pearl, then greed, if not honor, will force him to accept us as passengers."

"The pearl!" Miranda gasped, and the blood drained

from her face as the horrifying realization struck her full force. In her haste to leave the scene of her disgrace that morning, she had abandoned Rija's pearl!

The giant pearl had been the last of Rija's mother's gems, their only source of support over the past years. Though they'd lived quietly, frugally, studying in the village school with the Muslim *kiai*, laboring in the rice paddies beside their neighbors, their resources were nearly exhausted, and now she'd squandered the last of it! They wouldn't even have enough to hire a prau should they be fortunate enough to reach the western coast!

The pulse at Miranda's temple threatened to explode, and she pressed her fingertips against the pain. "Oh, Rija, forgive me! I—I don't have it anymore."

"You lost it?"

Miranda's voice was faint. "The Englishman has it."

"Then that is perfect!" Rija exclaimed, delighted. "He cannot refuse to help us now that he has accepted our offering. That would be dishonorable."

"He didn't understand," Miranda began, dread building within her heart.

How could she face Anthony Benedict again? Unbidden, her breath faltered and the secret depths of her body throbbed with the memory of passion and pleasure. Ruthlessly she thrust the seductive thoughts deep into the hidden recesses of her mind. In her insanity, she'd succumbed to temptation at the Englishman's hands, and it had afforded her nothing. Survival depended on her doing her duty, but she could conceive of no greater humiliation than having to meet him again after what had transpired between them.

"It would be useless to approach him again," Miranda said hoarsely, her eyes not meeting Rija's.

"You can make him understand," her stepsister insisted. "Please help me, Miri. I will die before I wed such an evil man as Steef van der Djink." Her voice dropped, and she shuddered fearfully. "Though many find him very fair to look upon, it is whispered he is unbearably cruel to his women."

Miranda's heart melted. With a wordless murmur, she

gathered Rija close. How could she deny the only family she had left? Rija was so young and innocent, and there was no one else to protect her. What was a brief embarrassment when so much hung in the balance? Besides, to a man like Benedict, their encounter meant little and would be soon forgotten.

But as for me, how will I ever forget the night of the Lotus Moon?

Angrily Miranda again buried the betraying thoughts. She must concentrate on convincing the English captain to take them to Benkulen. With luck, Captain Benedict would accept the obligation that went with the pearl, but if he expected anything more, he would be sorely disappointed.

"Don't worry, little sister," Miranda said, stroking the shiny black skein of Rija's hair. Her touch was loving, but her fingers trembled uncontrollably. "For you, I will even face the Englishman again."

The late evening sun was a hot red ball that hovered on the horizon over Batavia, turning the canals of the Dutch capital of Java into fetid, steaming ditches. Even on the busy harbor wharves the air was still and thick, with no cooling breeze blowing over the water to ease the sweltering city. Traffic congested both the harbor and the narrow, squalid streets of the waterfront. Vendors' cries, sailors' curses, and water buffaloes' bellows increased the cacophony to fever pitch as tempers flared with the heat.

Miranda walked along the warped planks of a pier, holding a lace-edged, perfumed handkerchief against her nose to ward off the noisome stench. Rotting fish, carrion, and human waste floated in the water, polluting the humid atmosphere with an unbearable odor. Beside her, Noppa, his shoulders stooped under his best collarless jacket, and his bandy legs covered by a sarong batiked by the Princess Rija herself, wrinkled his nose with a countryman's disdain for the city but said nothing.

Miranda paused to catch her breath, exhausted by lack of sleep and the hurried trip she and Rija had made downriver in the village *kepala*'s, or headman's, outrigger boat.

Rija now waited safely in the market stall of Sintu, a distant relative of the *kepala*'s, while Miranda sought out the means of their escape from Java. The closer she and Noppa came to the dock where the Englishman's vessel was moored, the harder her heart pounded.

Beneath the high neck and long sleeves of her old tan linen traveling gown, Miranda's skin was drenched with her own perspiration, partly from the oppressive heat, partly from nervousness. The dress was an outdated style that had once fit but now hugged the fuller, more mature shape of her breasts a bit too snugly, making it even harder to breathe the soupy air, and her petticoats clung to her legs in damp, sticky clumps. For a brief moment she thought longingly of the sarong she'd left with her baggage at Sintu's, then resolutely put it out of her mind. She'd come on the most urgent errand of her life, and this time there was no way Captain Anthony Benedict would mistake her for anything other that what she was—a proper English lady.

Miranda stuffed her handkerchief into her bodice, then adjusted the strings of the conical woven bamboo hat she wore as protection against the sun. She vainly pushed back the pale straggling wisps of hair that had worked loose from her tightly braided chignon, but the strands kept falling into her eyes and sticking to her damp, flushed cheeks. A bright-eyed fisherboy mending his nets at the foot of the dock gave her directions, and Miranda bade Noppa to wait for her by the boy's small turtle-shaped boat, then continued up the dilapidated pier alone toward a figure lounging near a moored rowboat.

"I beg your pardon, sir," Miranda said stiffly. "I wish to see a Captain"—her throat constricted, and she had to swallow hard—"Benedict. Can you direct me?"

The old seaman she addressed had a grizzled strawberry mane faded by the sun, salt water, and age. His knobby features were tanned the color of teak, and silver stubble glittered on his jaw. He wore a plain, worn-to-softness shirt and a pair of tarred breeches. Squinting at her carefully, he spit into the bile-colored water, and then creaked to his feet.

"Aye, ma'am. I can direct ye, for all the good it'll do. English, are ye?"

His Scots burr and blunt question took her aback. "Why, er—yes."

The old sailor's craggy face split into a grin. "It's a right pleasure to greet another of King George's subjects so far from home! Angus Pratt, ma'am, at your service." He swept Miranda an awkward but heartfelt bow that would have made her smile if she hadn't been so nervous.

"How do you do, Mr. Pratt? I am Miss Miranda Langford." She dipped a curtsy in return, grimacing at the unaccustomed constriction of her stays. "If you please, Captain Benedict?"

"You have business with the master?" Angus eyed her consideringly.

Miranda blushed, her face going beet red on top of her heat-flushed cheeks. She could guess what Angus was thinking. Only a woman of injured morals would seek out a man on her own.

"I—I must secure passage to Benkulen with Captain Benedict." She pointed to a sleekly trimmed vessel at anchor not far away from the end of the pier. "Is that his boat?"

"Ship, ma'am," Angus corrected, but his expression was dubious. "Aye, that's the *Mirage*, all right, but I ain't heard word one about this Benkulen."

"You probably know it as Fort Marlborough. You've heard of that? Just across the straits to Sumatra."

"Aye, I know the place now, but the captain ain't partial to passengers."

"He'll take my sister and me, I'm sure," Miranda replied in a grim tone. "Will you take me aboard the *Mirage* so I may speak with him?"

"Sorry, Miss Langford, but he ain't here, and I don't reckon he'll have much of a mind to talk to anyone, not judging by the tearin' mood he's been in all the blasted day. I told him to stay away from those heathenish doings, but would he listen? Faughh! He's as stubborn as his brother, he is."

"But I must speak to him," Miranda began anxiously. "You see, I—"

A huge black cat jumped onto the dock behind Angus, and she broke off with a soft, startled cry. The cat was the largest she'd ever seen, with evil yellow eyes, but it was the very dead, very mutilated water rat he held between his sharp teeth that made Miranda's gorge rise.

Angus whirled about, then chuckled loudly. "And what have you brought me today, matey? Ach, ye're a rare hunter, ye are."

Miranda shuddered as the feline pranced proudly toward them, tail held high, the unfortunate rat leaving a trail of its life's juices on the bleached boards. "Is—is this your animal, Mr. Pratt?"

The old salt scratched his chin while ruminating. "Well, miss, Beelzebub here is the kind ye can't rightly say belongs to any man."

Miranda took a hasty step backward. "At any rate, kindly see that he keeps his distance with *that*."

As if following the conversation, Beelzebub paused, cocked his head to one side, and narrowed slitted yellow eyes at Miranda. Without warning, he bounded gracefully to her feet. Setting his prize down before her, he uttered a scratchy yowl that demanded she congratulate him for his accomplishment, too.

"Mr. Pratt!" Miranda gasped. The infuriating animal was rubbing himself in unadulterated pleasure back and forth against her threadbare skirts!

"Well, look at that," Angus said in wonder, then stared at Miranda with new respect. "Only one other person I ever seen him take such a liking to, miss, and she's halfway 'round the world from here."

Miranda gaped at the now loudly purring feline and wondered how to extricate herself from the animal's untoward affections without offending the old man. She was not at all certain a creature that had mangled its prey as badly as this one had could be trusted. Clearing her throat, she tried to lift her skirts out of harm's way.

"Er, Mr. Pratt, please—"

"Ach! On yer guard, lassie!" Angus interrupted. "Here he comes!"

Beelzebub arched his back, hissed loudly, then shot off the pier to disappear underneath a thwart in the rowboat. Miranda whirled to see what had frightened such an intrepid hunter, and her heart leapt to her throat at the sight of the tall, elegantly dressed man striding down the dock toward them with an escort of a half score of weather-beaten sailors. If she could, she would have hidden, too, but she stood frozen in her tracks, her face burning. Disconcertingly, Anthony Benedict stormed past her with barely a glance.

"Get ready to cast off, Angus!" Tony barked.

"No luck, Cap'n?"

"No goddamn thanks to any of these pinheaded lubbers!"

The captain of the *Mirage* was in a rage, and his entourage of sailors hung their heads and rapidly climbed down into the rowboat. Tony glared at them, hands on his hips, his expensive eggshell satin jacket bunched carelessly at his side. His handsome features were distorted by angry frustration, and sweat dripped from the short auburn locks that curled at his nape and forehead. Beneath a lace cravat, his damp silk shirt clung like a second skin, delineating every rippling muscle in his powerful back and shoulders. Miranda's breath caught at the sight, and her stomach somersaulted alarmingly.

"I tried to tell ye it was hopeless, didn't I?" Angus asked in a genial tone. "Like finding a needle in a haystack. Fergit the wench, boy, ye've other fish to fry. Fill our hold with cargo first, then tomorrow we can raise anchor and leave this hellhole for good."

"You needn't remind me the Dutchman's on his way, old man. I may be half-mad, but I haven't forgotten why we're here." Tony looked down at his feet and scowled. "Christ's blood! What is this filth?" he roared, kicking Beelzebub's prize into the harbor with a vicious swipe of his booted toe. "What are you waiting for, you old curmudgeon? Let's get the hell out of here."

Miranda listened to the exchange in utter horror. Where

was the man whose gentleness had won her, body and soul, at least for one mysterious, magical night? This vulgar, blaspheming, bad-tempered individual held no resemblance to the tender, generous man who'd given her a glimpse of paradise.

With a blinding flash of shaming self-revelation, Miranda saw that her reluctance to face Anthony Benedict again had been in part fear that an estimable man would look at her with contempt for giving herself to him like a common prostitute. And if he was truly as wonderful as she feared, it was possible she'd fall under the spell of his irresistible magnetism again, forgetting once more her duty to Rija.

Evidently her concerns had been totally misplaced, and disappointment and disillusionment shattered her. The interlude they'd shared had been nothing special, merely a sordid coupling between two strangers. She caught her breath on a gulp of repugnance for both herself and Benedict, a revulsion a thousand times greater than even what she'd felt for Beelzebub's dead rat. Her swiftly indrawn breath drew Angus's attention back to her.

"Wait, Cap'n," Angus said, grabbing Miranda's elbow to tug her forward. "This here lady's wantin' to have a word with ye."

Anthony Benedict flicked a glance over the wilting woman, taking in the inferior quality of her gown, her sun-reddened complexion, the mud-colored eyes with the dark, bruised half-moons of fatigue beneath them, and instantly dismissed her. "Well?" he demanded rudely.

He doesn't know me. The realization shocked Miranda into speechlessness.

"It's passage off the island Miss Langford wants, Cap'n," Angus hastily interjected.

"Impossible. You know the *Mirage* doesn't carry passengers," Tony snapped. His dark blue eyes looked right through her, and his lip curled. "Especially women."

Deliberately he turned his back, ending the exchange, and Miranda saw Rija's last chance slipping through her fingers. She had not been prepared for this eventuality, but she shouldn't have been surprised that he hadn't recognized her. After all, in her incongruous native hat, with her fair hair falling down into her face like a witch's, clad in the unbecoming gown, she supposed she looked very much like a dried-up spinster, a female too long in the colony, withered by the sun like a piece of copra, and hardly the type of woman to interest a man like Benedict.

A wild desire to laugh tickled the back of her throat. Why, until last night, that was exactly what she'd been! She'd been so busy caring for Rija these past years, she'd neglected her own feminine nature. Perhaps that was why she'd reacted so strongly to the courtesan's disguise she'd used to enter the *kraton*, luxuriating in the sensations of being totally female—attractive, desirable, and, for a short time, even beautiful. Why should Tony Benedict be expected to recognize the transformation he'd wrought within her when she didn't recognize it herself? Squashing back the urge to hysteria, she forced herself to think of Rija. To protect her sister, she would do anything, even reveal the cosmic joke that had been played on both her and her unsuspecting lover by some mischievous demigod.

"Sir!" Miranda caught Tony's sleeve, and her voice was imperious. "You must hear me out!"

His gaze was glacial, and frost seemed to drip from his soft but steely words. "Must I, indeed, madam?"

She released his shirt as though burned by some unbearable cold. "I—that is, you and I—we're countrymen ... You *owe* me this." She faltered badly at the growing tautness around his mouth but stumbled on. "I must leave the island and ... and I came to you because—"

She found it impossible to say the words that would destroy the remaining shreds of her dignity. Desperately she reached for the ties of her coolie hat. If she couldn't tell him the truth, then she'd have to *show* him!

But Anthony Benedict was a man whose limited patience had been exhausted. Grabbing Miranda's upper arms before she could remove her hat, he hustled her back to Angus's side, ignoring her shocked gasp.

"Angus, escort this female off the dock," Tony ordered, his voice tight with irritation. Miranda spluttered in pure outrage at being handled so peremptorily, as if she were of no more importance than a sack of rice or a side of goat meat.

"The *Mirage* hires out to no one, madam," he continued roughly, shoving Miranda into Angus's arms. "I have no time to entertain the ridiculous demands of hysterical women."

"I am not hysterical, sir!" Miranda shouted angrily. "If you would just listen—"

"Madam, there must be a hundred other ships in this harbor. I suggest you seek out one of them."

"I can't!" Miranda said desperately. "I haven't the means since you—"

"So it's charity you want as well?" Tony demanded in disgust. He dug in his pocket, flipped Angus a golden coin, then turned toward the rowboat, throwing his final instructions over his shoulder. "Give her that and get rid of her, Angus. Van der Djink is coming, and I must ready the tallies or the deal will never be made."

The deadly name choked off Miranda's nearly incoherent protests like a noose around a convict's neck. Horror widened her eyes under the brim of her hat, and for an instant they lost the muddy brown color reflected off her gown and became a pure, pale green.

Steef van der Djink, here? And dealing with the Englishman? Dear Lord, if Djink should see her, he would surely recognize his betrothed's English guardian! Who knew then what damaging conclusions he would draw, what tales he would carry to Lord Palu's ears? Pearl or no pearl, she could not risk discovery!

Ducking her chin, Miranda jerked free of Angus's hold. Grabbing up her skirts, she scurried down the dock, the old salt gamely keeping pace at her side.

"I'm sorry, miss," the old man said. "I knew there weren't much chance he'd take ye on at the start."

"It's all right, Mr. Pratt," she replied, white-lipped and breathless with fear.

"You mustn't mind the Cap'n, either," Angus advised, puffing a little. "He's just a bit on the outs, ye see. Normally

he's as smooth as cream with the ladies. Has quite a way
with them.''

"I understand. Really, Mr. Pratt." She paused at the end
of the dock, wishing he would leave her, then stuck out her
hand in an effort to hasten their farewell. "You did what
you could. Thank you."

Angus gingerly squeezed Miranda's fingers and pressed
the coin into her hand. "Sorry it weren't more, miss. Next
time you come to old Angus, mebbe I can do better for
ye." A dour smile twisted his ruddy features comically.
"After all, any friend of Beelzebub's is a friend of mine."

Miranda smiled weakly and tugged free of his grip, too
distracted to care that she had accepted Benedict's money.
"Yes, I'll remember. Thank you again, Mr. Pratt."

Then she called in rapid Javanese to her manservant, and
the two of them hurried away, disappearing within moments
into the bustling crowds of the dockside marketplace.

Angus scratched his jaw thoughtfully and wondered why,
in this hell-blasted heat, a lady like Miss Langford would
run as if the devil himself were after her.

Chapter 3

If Lord Anthony Benedict had been in London, he'd have known better than to sit across a gaming table from Steef van der Djink. As it was, Tony merely reflected that if a smuggler couldn't be choosy about his partner, he could at least be careful.

Tony narrowly watched the tall, elegant blond Dutchman over the remains of an exotic but surprisingly tasty meal Angus had served them in the master cabin of the *Mirage*. Unless he'd lost all of his considerable talent for assessing character, Tony knew Steef van der Djink had the cunning of a jackal and the instincts of a cobra. In the presence of so formidable an individual, it was wise to maintain one's own defenses, so Tony affected the foppish mannerisms of the English court that were second nature to him in order to hypnotize the cobra into complacency.

Indicating a cut-glass decanter, he smiled blandly across the littered table at the Dutchman and lifted one eyebrow in polite inquiry. "More brandy, perhaps?"

"No. I have imposed on your excellent hospitality far too well already this evening."

The Dutchman's unrelieved black garments were a perfect backdrop on which to display the golden perfection of his face and form. His features were exquisitely handsome in all respects, but no warmth was reflected in his ice blue gaze. Though Tony knew his own looks had never failed to turn a feminine head, he felt decidedly lackluster next to the austere, almost angelic beauty of this man.

Tony shrugged, poured himself another dram, then replaced the crystal stopper. "You'll not mind if I indulge, then? This far from home, a man must at least keep up the semblances of civilization. Tell me, Steef, do you not miss polite society?"

The Dutchman bowed his closely shorn, gilt-colored head and smiled coolly. "There are compensations."

Tony snorted and gave an airy wave of his hand, exposing the fine lace dripping from his cuff. "In this stinking hole?"

"Batavia is an unfortunate mixture of many cultures, but you saw the countryside when we met at Palu Tanah's palace. It is a beauteous land in many ways." Steef's chilly eyes gleamed with a cool and calculating avarice. "It is there that a man may still live as a king."

"If he's careful." Tony laughed, setting aside his goblet. "My friend, the sultan would have your head, as well as certain other essential body parts, if he knew what you were doing."

"He will not miss the paltry sum we skim from this season's harvest."

"And your employer, the Dutch East India Company?"

Steef shrugged, his narrow mouth twisting. "It was the Company who introduced the coffee plants to the natives and encouraged their cultivation barely a decade ago. Now they panic because the production exceeds the quota, and there is talk of limiting cultivation. The fools in Europe cannot be convinced such tactics are shortsighted, but you and I, Captain Benedict, will reap the benefits. My producers are anxious to be rid of their surplus. It will be profitable to all involved."

"As you say," Tony replied, feigning a bored yawn. "I suppose I may as well return to England with *something* in the *Mirage*'s holds, if nothing else but to justify my voyage to my mother and her bookkeepers. You wouldn't be able to get your hands on something a bit more exotic, say silks or ivory?"

"Unfortunately, no." Steef's thin lips tightened.

Tony gave another negligent wave. "Well, no matter. We can use the ballast, and I suppose I can give these coffee beans away to my friends." He pushed back from the table and rose, then went to a large sea chest resting at the foot of the comfortable built-in bunk. "Shall we deal with this boring business now? I believe the agreement was half your price in advance and the remainder on delivery?"

The Dutchman stood and accepted the heavy leather money pouch with a slight bow. "That is correct, sir."

"And where am I to take on this cargo?"

Steef took a square of parchment from his breast pocket and unfolded it on the table. He tapped his index finger on a spot on the ink rendering of the Javanese coastline. "After your ship's empty holds are inspected by the harbor authorities and the Company is convinced you are not abusing your welcome by trying to take on contraband goods, you will be free to leave. My holdings are here. Be there at dusk, two days hence."

"And if I am delayed?"

"Then we will both lose. Fear of the sultan's wrath makes the natives skittish. If you miss the rendezvous, they will take it as a bad omen and sell your cargo to some other source."

"I'll make certain we arrive on time, then!" Tony said with a wry laugh. "Is everything on Java decided on the basis of omens and signs?"

"Nearly always. It can be most inconvenient, for even though most are nominally Muslim, elements of Hindu, Buddhist, and religions even older still permeate this culture. There is a superstition for every occasion. Often even beatings will not convince a native to return to work if the signs are inauspicious." Steef's eyes were cold with disdain. "Java is a backward country in all respects. It will take a leader with vision to bring forth its potential."

"A vision that will no doubt render great rewards to the individuals with the courage to pursue it," Tony commented dryly.

A knock sounded on the cabin door before the Dutchman could reply, and Angus's grizzled red head appeared. "Ach, excuse me, Cap'n. I was just after yer dishes, is all."

"Come ahead." Tony motioned Angus forward, then cast an inquiring glance at the Dutchman. "I believe we have concluded our business."

Angus nodded and set about noisily clearing the dinnerware from the polished table that was also the captain's desk. Steef tucked the pouch in his pocket and handed Tony the refolded map.

"I know that our little venture will be successful, Captain Benedict. If you find yourself next year with another ship with an empty hold, perhaps you will return."

"Who can tell what one will be doing in a year's time, Steef?" Tony asked, clapping the other man on the back. "But I will bear it in mind."

"Since the night is still young, perhaps I can return your hospitality?" Steef suggested.

The offer was such an incongruous footnote to Steef van der Djink's rather austere personality, Tony was instantly intrigued. "In what manner?"

"There is a certain . . . house . . . with which I am acquainted where you may find some amusement, sir. I will direct you if you wish?"

Tony grinned. "No doubt in this house one can meet ladies who have an hour or two to while away with a weary traveler?"

"Indeed. Ladies skilled in the Indian ways of pleasure or pain. You will agree that the two can be opposite sides of the same coin?"

"Without doubt." Tony strove to keep his features in an expression of vaguely bored curiosity, but something about Steef's manner chilled him. He knew instinctively which side of the coin the Dutchman preferred. "Perhaps another time."

"Mayhap you do not care for the local women?" Steef asked seriously. "Such tastes can be a hardship to a man in a locale where there are so few white women. One must make adjustments. I, myself, will soon wed a local princess."

Tony raised one sun-lightened eyebrow. "Then I must congratulate you, it seems, on your good fortune and your shrewdness. A link to a royal household will surely enhance a man's vision."

"Yes, sometimes in order to reach a larger goal, one must be willing to make sacrifices."

"If your betrothed is as lovely as some of the local beauties I have seen, then it will scarcely be a sacrifice," Tony said with a touch of acid in his voice.

The remembered scent of frangipani and a woman's exotic softness rose within him, and with it came the profound sense of frustration he'd tried to hold at bay all evening. Despite all his best efforts, he'd been unable to find Miri. Neither Ishta nor any of the other *kraton* servants knew her, nor was she to be found in the palace village, nor even in any of the exotic brothels in Batavia itself. Except for the pearl now securely locked within the *Mirage*'s strongbox, he would indeed begin to believe she'd been some sort of Javanese sprite sent to taunt him for the emptiness of his life by showing him for one brief span how full it might be. With an effort, he set these thoughts aside, but Steef van der Djink's disdain of native women—even his own wife-to-be—rankled Tony's already overstretched sensibilities. To prevent his irritation from erupting, he forced a jocularity into his voice he was far from feeling.

"Indeed, my friend," Tony continued, "you may be most fortunate in your choice of bride, for it is clear from the hag I met today that our own women do not wear well in this climate."

"Cap'n, belay that!" Angus snorted angrily and banged a plate onto his tray. "She was a real lady, she was."

"A European?" Steef inquired idly.

"English, I believe. And what a harpy!" Tony chuckled and screwed his face up as though he sipped vinegar.

"Perhaps I am acquainted with her. There aren't that many in Batavia, as you know."

"She was no rare prize, that's for certain. What did she call herself? Leonard? Lavender?" Tony's handsome face brightened. "I have it! Langford!"

"I've heard of her," Steef said carefully. His next question was too casual. "How did you meet?"

"She wanted to arrange passage off Java or some such business, but I hadn't the time nor inclination, much less such a tendency toward self-abuse as to have such a fright aboard my *Mirage!*" Tony said, laughing.

Steef's half smile was serene, but his eyes were frozen orbs of icy blue. "If you're certain you will not join me, Captain Benedict, I will take my leave."

"Alas, I must see to other matters, Steef. Thanks all the same."

"Your servant, sir." The Dutchman bowed his way out of the cabin, and in moments Tony heard the muted sounds of his departure aboard his own longboat.

"Well, Angus, what do you think?" Tony demanded, turning to the old man.

"Stick yer hand in a weasel's burrow, ye're bound to get bitten," Angus returned sourly, stacking dishes.

Tony laughed, his gaze affectionate. "Look, you old sea dog, I know you think my head is full of cotton wadding, but you have to admit I've been a fair pupil in your school of practical seamanship. Why, I'll bet Kit didn't do half so well!"

"For such a young pup, ye're certain full of yerself," Angus retorted. "And yer brother learnt twice as fast 'cause he wasn't spouting foolishness every blasted second of the day and night!"

Tony didn't take any offense. After a rocky beginning, he and Angus had developed a unique relationship based on mutual respect, friendship, and insult hurling. When Tony's brother, Kit, married and retired from the sea to take up life as a merchant in the Carolina Colony, he'd passed on to Tony the *Mirage* and Angus Pratt. What the Marquess of Bentley hadn't known about seamanship when they'd left Charles Towne and then, later, England, Angus had soon pounded into him on this ambitious voyage to find new Eastern markets for the Benedict brothers' Free Indies Company. After all, Tony grinned to himself, if Angus wasn't a friend, why would he put up with such abuse?

"Come now, Angus, be fair," Tony cajoled. "I haven't done so badly this time, have I? A fair cargo, and promise of the same next year if I want it. Do you know what a shipload of Java coffee will bring on the London market? Why, enough to pay off all the liens against the Bentley estates and more than half again!"

Angus snorted. "You and your grand schemes! It's right glad I am to be heading home again, but we'll be lucky if the Dutch Company doesn't blast our arses right out of the water! I'm getting too old for this kind of tomfoolery, and that's a fact!"

"Don't worry, everything's taken care of." Tony picked up the map and waved it. "All we have to do is show up at the appointed place in two days time."

Angus's rheumy gray eyes held a gleam of skepticism. "And what about this female ye've been howling about? Had the whole crew, almost, out combing the countryside for yer light-o'-love. Tell me that's good business!"

"I don't have to explain myself to anyone," Tony snapped, showing a flare of the temper that matched his flaming locks. Arrogance shuttered his expression, and he scowled darkly, tapping the map absently into the flat of his palm.

"No, ye don't," Angus agreed, watching the younger man with a puzzled look of concern on his lined visage. "What's so important about this woman, anyway, lad?"

"Damned if I know." Tony's scowl faded, and his mouth quirked in a lopsided, self-mocking grin. "Never mind me, Angus. You know I'm 'tetched.' I fear last night the moonshine transformed me into a lunatic."

"But—"

Tony silenced him with a wave, his expression suddenly

pensive. "Just ask the first mate to see me, will you, Angus?"

Angus carried the loaded tray to the cabin door. "Aye,
Cap'n. I'll send Mr. Tassel to ye directly."

When the door closed, Tony stripped off his elaborately
styled coat and cravat. In the not-so-distant past, finery such
as this and the next moment's entertainment were all that
would have filled his head, but things had changed. After
all, fighting the Spanish in the Caribbean and renewing
bonds with a brother that had been dead to him were heavy
matters. It made a man take a look at his life. And when
the self-assessment came up lacking, a man made changes.

Such as installing a new steward at his English estates to
end the waste and oversee the needs of his neglected retainers. Such as facing up to the debts he'd accumulated
with dissolute living. Such as accepting the fact that his
mother wasn't the woman he'd thought, but to confront her
would profit no one. And finally, setting out on a voyage
whose purpose was twofold: to fill again the Benedict coffers
with the profits of the Free Indies Company and to discover
for himself if there was anything worthy or laudable in Lord
Anthony Christian Benedict's character.

Tony gazed through the small porthole at the lights flickering around the rim of the harbor, and heaved a sigh. *The
verdict is still out on that one*, he mused.

The fact was, the *Mirage* had a fair chance at being one
of the first ships to reach England this season with a cargo
of coffee. He would receive a premium price, and he hadn't
been overly optimistic in his boast to Angus. This one shipment could save him financially, if he made the Dutchman's
rendezvous on time.

And he couldn't do that if he continued to look for Miri.

Feet braced wide apart, hands linked behind his back,
Tony stared at the water, his mind full of images of Miri.
He was hollow with longing for her, and he laughed softly,
bitterly, that he—the Wastrel Lord, the conscienceless se-
ducer, the heartless lover—should be reduced to this impotent position.

He'd found the one woman in the world who touched his

most hidden needs, then lost her. To find her, *if* he could find her, he'd have to renounce the reason he'd come so far. It boiled down to a simple choice: redeeming the Benedict name and clearing his debts by taking his cargo to England at the earliest moment, or giving everything up for a woman who'd made it clear by her very flight that she didn't want him.

Tony's jaw tightened even as an almost unbearable sense of loss enveloped his soul. There was no choice. He'd used past hatreds and imagined wrongs to excuse the excesses of a wastrel's life and to ignore his responsibilities long enough. If he was a man of character, then it was time to forget personal desires and perform his duty to his family and himself.

There was a brisk knock on the cabin door. Tony didn't bother to turn around. "Come in, Mr. Tassel."

The first mate, a competent man with a pug-dog face, entered and waited attentively. "You wanted to see me, sir?"

"Ready the crew, Mr. Tassel," Tony said. When he turned to his first officer, his eyes were bleak. "We sail at first light."

"Miri! Miranda, wake up!"

Closing her eyes tightly, Miranda tried to hang on to the last sweet vestiges of sleep, ignoring the hand that shook her shoulder. It wasn't fair, she groaned inwardly. She'd only laid her head down on this simple pallet moments ago!

"Miri, please!"

Something in Rija's voice penetrated Miranda's fog, and she sat up abruptly.

The tiny, cluttered storeroom in the rear of Sintu's shop was lit only with the oily flicker of a small coconut oil lamp. Rija knelt next to the pallet, her dark eyes large and frightened in the wavering yellow light. In the narrow doorway, Noppa held the lamp, his wizened visage pinched with concern.

"What is it? What?" Miranda demanded, automatically reaching for her tan gown and pulling it over her shift.

"We must go. Now." Rija swallowed hard. "Sintu's cousin brought word from the *kepala*. The Dutchman knows we are in Batavia and why. He is looking for us."

"God in Heaven!" Miranda struggled to her feet, fastening her gown with trembling fingers.

"Sintu's cousin says Djink is so angry, he intends to wed me by force tonight!" Rija quavered shrilly.

"Hush, all will be well," Miranda soothed, shoving her feet into her shoes. "You're dressed? Good. And our things? Thank God we had some warning—"

From the front of the shop came shouts and a crashing as someone broke down the flimsy bamboo door. The loud voices and angry demands could be heard clearly through the plaited bamboo walls. Miranda clutched their small bundle of possessions against her breast and looked frantically around the room. They were trapped!

Rija slumped. "It's too late."

Noppa's sudden movement made them both jump, and their eyes widened in horror at the short, curved blade he held high above his head. The knife whizzed through the air, slicing down between the two frozen women, slitting the bamboo wall behind them.

"Go now, Princess," Noppa said urgently, withdrawing the knife, a decorated ceremonial *kris* of great spiritual power that he'd made himself. "Allah will protect you."

"Come on, Rija!" Miranda hissed, roughly pushing her stepsister through the opening. "You, too, Noppa!"

The old man shook his head. "No, lady. I stay for honor. Now, go quickly!"

Miranda opened her mouth to protest, but it went unspoken. Screams mingled with the sounds of destruction as the intruders' search of the shop brought them ever closer. She looked at Noppa again, understanding the enormity of his sacrifice. The old man smiled encouragingly at her, serene with his destiny, and turned with his knife to wait. With a sob, Miranda ducked through the slit, grabbed Rija's hand, and raced down the squalid alley.

Tears streaming down her cheeks, her breath soughing raggedly in her throat, Miranda ran for her life, ducking and twisting through the narrow back alleys, dragging Rija through the darkness. She did not know where she was going, only that it was away from Sintu's shop, away from the angry shouts and feet pounding in pursuit, and away from the strangled sounds Noppa made as Djink's men murdered him.

Dogs barked at their passage, and beggars sleeping in the lanes cursed when they stepped on them in their haste. At any sign of movement, Miranda turned away, taking a labyrinthine path. Soon she was completely disoriented, but at least they had lost the dangerous shadows that followed them. Knowing that they were just as likely to be running straight into Djink as away from him at this point, Miranda finally drew Rija to a halt near the open arcade of the deserted produce market to catch their breaths.

Rija wept quietly into Miranda's shoulder. "Noppa, oh, Noppa . . ."

"You must be brave, little sister," Miranda whispered brokenly. The old man had been dear to both of them. "Noppa would want that."

"What will we do? What can we do?" Rija hiccuped.

Miranda had no answer. They could not return home, and to seek shelter with anyone was only to invite the slaughter of other innocents. They had nothing with them but the clothes they carried, and thanks to Captain Benedict, no means to pay for passage on another ship. Miranda frowned, remembering, and her fingers felt for the heavy lump of the gold coin she'd tied into the hem of her shift. It might be enough to induce someone to take them at least out of the harbor, and unless her nose deceived her, she knew which direction to take. Already the sky was growing gray in the east. They must hurry, for without the blessed cover of night, they would be all too easy for Djink to find.

"Come on," she murmured.

Hand in hand, she led Rija from post to corner to doorway. The city was beginning to stir. Morning activities brought life to the streets, and the odors of smoke and cooking food floated in the humid air. Miranda knew that in her European dress she was highly conspicuous, but there was no time to change into a sarong now, so she kept going until she began to recognize her surroundings.

"I know where we are," Miranda said at last, peeping around the edge of a dilapidated shop. The wharves stretched out in front of them, already bustling with the early preparation of native fishermen. In fact, they stood not thirty feet from the very dock with the same little fisherboy with his turtle-shell boat where she'd met Anthony Benedict just the day before.

Miranda squatted down with her back against the shop wall and tried to gather her thoughts. If Djink was willing to kill to find Rija, then it was certain he would not give up until he found them. They had to leave or at least hide someplace, but where? How? Miranda racked her brains, willing herself to *think*.

Voices nearby startled her, and she pulled Rija down, huddling in the lee of the run-down building. Straining her ears, she realized the men spoke in Dutch. She released a sigh when it became clear these were not Djink's men, but officials of the Company apparently conducting business. Her attention caught again when they addressed "Captain Benedict."

Peeking cautiously around the corner, Miranda could see several figures silhouetted against the rapidly brightening sky. She caught a glint of red in the tallest man's hair, and her lip curled with loathing. Benedict! This was all his fault!

She noticed that Mr. Pratt flanked Benedict. If only he had been the one to make the decision. She was certain Angus Pratt would have helped her if he could. One of the men pointed to the *Mirage* and then down the narrow track to the customs building. Straining her ears, she caught pieces of the rather heated conversation between Benedict and the two officials.

". . . ready to sail . . ."

". . . sign the documents . . ."

". . . miss the tide . . ."

". . . procedure . . ."

". . . goddamn it!"

At last the group moved, with Benedict stalking off in the lead, headed for the customs house.

Miranda's glance lifted to the outline of the *Mirage* waiting silent and serene in the harbor. A plan formed in her head, so desperate and unexpected, it made her catch her breath at its audacity. She jerked back to her place beside Rija, her hand pressed against her pounding heart.

"I have an idea," she said.

"Angus, what the hell is that damn cat yowling about?"

"Derned if I know, Cap'n. Want me to check on him?"

"I'll do it." Tony waved the old man back to his seat on an upturned water keg and stalked across the *Mirage*'s rolling deck toward an open hatch. Tassel had just relieved his watch, and a fair wind filled the sails above his head, as it had for the past two days. Squinting at the angle of the brilliant sun, Tony judged they would make landfall at Steef van der Djink's holding by late afternoon. Time enough to kick a certain fat, bad-tempered cat from here to Kingdom Come, he thought with a wicked grin, then swung himself down the steep companionway ladder.

It was at least twenty degrees warmer on this level. No wonder the men preferred to swing their hammocks topside, he thought, wiping beads of sweat from his brow and following the sound of Beelzebub's abrasive but plaintive screeching. The sound came from the after hold, the deepest part of the ship, where their cargo would be stored, and Tony wondered if Angus's precious Beelzebub had gotten himself trapped by a shifting hogshead barrel. Although no love was lost between Tony and the cat, Angus doted on the animal, so Tony climbed down into the stifling hold after him.

"Beelzebub! Come on, you no-good hair ball," Tony called, stooping to keep from bumping his head on the low crossbeams. "Where the hell are you?"

Feeling a bit foolish, Tony crept through the dim hold, peeping around stacks of empty casks. "Here, kitty."

Beelzebub sailed from behind a hogshead, howling a protest, then shot through Tony's legs. Startled, Tony jerked

upright and banged the back of his head soundly against a
beam. Holding his lump and cursing a blue streak, he circled
in place, looking for the feline.

"Goddamn you, cat! I'm going to use your guts for harp
strings! You—"

Tony broke off, puzzled to see the animal disappear behind a line of large, upright barrels, only to fly back out
again, ass over ears, the next second. For a shocked instant,
Tony hesitated, wondering what sort of monster rat could
whip an old soldier like Beelzebub. A stealthy rustling issued from behind the huge cask. That was no rat! Lunging,
Tony reached behind the barrel and came up with a fistful
of pale blond hair.

"Ouch!"

"No, you don't!" Tony gritted. Grappling with the
squirming stowaway, he hauled in his prize, then stared in
slack-jawed astonishment into the irate face of none other
than that pasty-eyed English biddy, Miss Langford. "You!"

"Let go!" She struggled, shoving at the fist still clenched
painfully in the straight, heavy skein of her long hair. Before
he could comply, another female figure popped up from
behind the barrel, shrieked, and threw a punch at his head.

Tony ducked instinctively, and for a single blinding moment he thought the second woman was his Miri. But no.
Although dark-haired and beautiful, this girl was too short
and sloe-eyed. The level of his disappointment was reflected
in his roar of rage. Grabbing the two women by the arms,
he dragged them from behind the barrel.

"Be still!" he bellowed, giving them each a shake. They
both subsided, the Javanese maiden in a cowed manner with
her eyes lowered to the deck, Miss Langford with her chin
up and her delicately carved nostrils flaring with temper.
Tony eyed the pair grimly. "What the *hell* are you doing
here?"

"I believe," the Langford woman said coldly, "that we
were taking an ocean voyage—for our health!"

Tony snorted. "Aye, and you look it, too."

The two women were pale and weak, their cheekbones

flushed with spots of crimson from the nearly unbearable heat. Tony frowned suddenly.

"How long have you been down here? Since yesterday? Never mind!" He dragged them toward the ladder. "It's a wonder you both haven't been boiled to broth by now. Don't you have a grain of sense, woman?"

"My name is Miss Miranda Langford, and this is my stepsister, the Princess Rija." Her voice was stiff with chilly hauteur, but she gasped when he grabbed her hips and basically boosted her up the ladder. "Sir! I'd be obliged if you'd keep your hands off my person."

"*Miss* Langford," Tony said between clenched teeth, lifting the younger girl out of the hold, "you'd best be grateful for my forbearance, for my first inclination is to beat you soundly for your misdeeds!"

The commotion they were making had suddenly gained them a curious audience of off-duty hands. Tony ignored the incredulous faces and wide grins, dragging his two prisoners toward the next ladder. In the hatch above, Angus's face popped into view.

"What's all the ruckus? I—Holy Mary! Miss Langford!"

Tony manhandled the two women up the steep stairs. A black shape streaked past them, flying beneath the Langford woman's tan skirts. She shrieked, then all but stumbled onto the main deck into Angus's arms.

"That dratted cat!" she said, gasping. Beelzebub pranced back and forth, proud as a Queen's escort, purring loudly. "Can't he tell I don't like him? If it hadn't been for his screeching—"

"You might have both perished from the heat down there." Tony scowled as he half carried the nearly swooning Javanese girl. "Come on, Angus. Help me get these two to my cabin." He looked around at the circle of gaping sailors. "Don't any of you have anything to do? Carlisle, bring some fresh water to my cabin, and then perhaps somebody can tell me how these two got on board *without anyone seeing them!*"

Guiltily the crew hastened back to work. With a disgusted snort, Tony escorted his guests across the quarterdeck, then through the narrow companionway to his cabin. He set Rija on the bunk and thrust Miranda Langford down in a chair.

"All right!" he barked, making them both jump. "I want some explanations."

"If—" Miranda broke off, swallowing harshly. "May we have some water first, please?"

Angus quickly dipped two cups from the water cask, passing the first to Tony for Miss Langford, then kindly helping Rija with hers. Rija gulped the liquid thirstily, but when Tony handed the Englishwoman her cup, he noted she forcibly restrained herself, taking dainty sips until her thirst was slaked.

Tony watched her narrowly, his arms folded across his chest. With her hair loosened and falling about her shoulders in a pale sheet, Miranda Langford looked much younger than he'd assumed. Of course, she was still such a twig of a proper British spinster, he could practically hear the starch crackle in her stays. He frowned. Still, something wasn't quite right . . .

She sighed deeply, closing her eyes for a moment when she finished drinking. Her lashes were long and dark against her honey-colored cheek, and they fluttered like butterflies as she took a bit of moisture on her fingertips and dampened her temples, the hollows behind her ears, the slender line of her neck. Tony stiffened, watching her unconsciously sensual movements. She drew her damp fingers across the vee at the base of her throat, then downward, following the front opening of her ugly gown, unfastened just far enough so that he could see the shadow between her breasts.

Tony straightened abruptly. "Had enough?"

She opened her eyes, meeting his truculent gaze, then wet her lips and looked away. Placing the cup on the table, she folded her hands in her lap and nodded. "Yes, thank you."

"Now perhaps we can have the truth. How did you get aboard my ship?"

"I paid a fisherboy to row us out, then we waited until everyone was busy and climbed up the ladders."

"Remind me to have a talk with the crew, Angus," Tony

said sourly. He leaned over the table, forcing Miranda to look up at him. "But that's no explanation. I thought I made it clear that I wasn't in the market for passengers."

"Do you think I *wanted* to come back to you after . . . after . . ." She flushed, and her fists clenched in her lap. "I had no choice! We couldn't stay in Batavia, and this was the *last* place Steef van der Djink would look for us!"

"Steef? What's he got to do with this?"

She jumped to her feet, swaying unsteadily, but there was real heat in her clear gaze. "Everything! And it's all your fault, Captain Benedict!"

"Mine?" He drew back, thinking the woman was crazed by her ordeal.

"Yes, yours! I figured it out. You told Djink I'd been here, didn't you? That's the only way he'd have known we were in Batavia."

"I may have mentioned your name, but I still don't see—" He broke off as Rija dissolved into copious tears. Angus looked uncomfortably at the weeping girl, but Tony's exasperation was plain. "Now, what's wrong with her?"

Miranda went to Rija, hugging her shoulder protectively. "Rija's English isn't very good, and she's afraid you're going to send us back."

Tony ran a hand through his copper-hued curls and looked up to heaven as if for strength. "Actually, I think the customary punishment for stowaways is simply to pitch them overboard. *Which I'm tempted to do right now!* What have you to do with Steef van der Djink?"

"Lord Palu has decreed that Rija is to marry Djink."

Tony's face registered his surprise. "This is Steef's betrothed?"

"Please, understand me. We are fleeing for our lives," Miranda said urgently. "When Djink heard our plan, he sent his men for us, and our servant was killed."

"A runaway fiancée deserves drastic measures."

"I will never allow the union," Miranda said stonily. "There is a blood feud between us and Djink that cannot be forgiven. If only we can reach Benkulen, then the English authorities will help me."

"I'm not going to Benkulen."

"Then whatever is your next port of call." She forced a humble tone, and he could see what it cost her. "Captain Benedict, I beg you to accept my apologies. Your help, although unwilling, has been a great boon. At least we're out of Djink's reach."

"Not exactly." Tony shot Angus a wry look, but the old man just scowled.

"Wh-what do you mean?" she wavered uncertainly.

"Miss Langford, I make it a practice to stay out of local squabbles."

"Oh, but—"

Tony raised a hand to silence her. "Furthermore, I'm engaged in important dealings with Steef van der Djink. In fact, within just a few hours, we'll be docking at Steef's plantation."

"Oh, no!"

Ignoring her panicky cry, he smiled. "Miss Langford, I ask you, what better wedding gift could I bring my business partner than his own bride?"

Chapter 4

❦

"Put on your hat, Tiktik," Teacher said.

"No." The little black-eyed girl, no more than four and naked except for her *kabaya*, stomped her bare feet in the shallow waters of the rice paddy, then lifted her chin defiantly. *"I don't want to."*

Teacher hid a smile, knowing this little one's feet were already on her destined path. Still, even a princess needed to learn the lessons of life. "Did I ever tell you about the only ghost who dares to come out during the bright light of day?"

Tiktik's eyes grew wide. "N-no."

"The Banaspati leaps out of the ground at exactly noon, runs swiftly on his hands like the Old Man of the Forest, chasing and devouring any child he sees who does not wear her hat!"

Tiktik squealed in fright. "Sister!"

Sister poked another rice seedling into the flooded paddy, then straightened, placing a hand to the ache in the small of her back. "Don't tell her these tales," she said sharply,

59

her eyes like the sun on the surface of the paddies. "They frighten her and give her nightmares."

"Which is worse, sunstroke or bad dreams?"

"Just tell her the truth." Sister picked up the bamboo cone and set it on Tiktik's head. "Wear that or your head will get too hot."

Teacher stared at Sister. "We both said the same thing, but which truth will she remember?"

Miranda stared at the Englishman, horror-stricken at his calm pronouncement. "You'd turn us over to Djink? Even after what I've told you?"

"And what is that, madam?" Tony questioned mildly. "You must admit your story is most improbable. It is merely my duty to return fugitives to their rightful master."

"Duty!" Positioning herself protectively between the Englishman and Rija, Miranda curled her lip in contempt. "Do not befoul the word with this prating nonsense! It is your greed that blinds you to common decency. From what loathsome hellhole did you spring that you could contemplate such cruelty?"

Tony scowled. "Perhaps I don't care for an interfering woman sticking her long spinster's nose where it doesn't belong."

Miranda colored hotly, but before she could phrase a retort, Angus stepped forward.

"Begging yer pardon, Cap'n," the old salt interjected, his gravelly tone placating, "mebbe we oughtn't be too hasty. All we're after is them coffee beans, ain't it? Letting the ladies go on their way ain't no skin off our noses as long as we get what we came for."

"If you please, sahib," Rija faltered, wiping her tears. Her soft, girlish voice and halting English lent an exotic musicality to her words, and the movements of her hands were graceful and stylized as a *wajang* dancer's. She pointed to Tony. "Prince Amang has coffee, if . . ." She touched her own breast, then Miranda's.

"What does she mean?" Tony demanded, frowning suspiciously as the sisters conducted a rapid exchange in whispered Javanese. "Who is this Amang?"

"Virat Amang," Miranda answered, "the rightful heir to the sultanate of Preanger." She surreptitiously wiped her damp palms against the folds of her skirt, steeling herself into a lie of desperation. "My sister is right. If we are seen safely into the prince's care, his followers will fill your holds with coffee many times over."

"A likely tale," Tony snorted, irritably rubbing the lump on the back of his head. "Palu Tanah is sultan of that region."

"Only by deceit and murder!" Miranda countered angrily. "Amang is the true sultan, and he will soon take his rightful place. The *dukun* has foreseen it."

"Miss Langford, you astonish me." The smile on the captain's lean, patrician face was faintly taunting. "Surely you do not place credence in the mumblings of some native seer?"

"She is a very wise woman," Miranda said defensively. "Prince Amang will return from the jungle to claim his inheritance and—"

"And mount a rescue on your behalf by filling my holds with coffee?" He gave a half smile of disbelief, one sunbleached auburn eyebrow cocked at a sardonic angle. "Quite a feat for a man driven into hiding, Miss Langford. Have you any notion how I'd go about finding this remarkable individual, should I decide to pursue his generous offer?"

Miranda felt a rush of color stain her cheeks. "N-not exactly. But I know he will honor my sister's noble blood, and his forces are rumored to be everywhere, so—"

"I've heard enough of this far-fetched tale." Tony straightened with a gesture of annoyance. "Miss Langford, I find your predilection for deceit exceedingly tiresome. Perhaps you'll be more forthcoming with Steef van der Djink. Angus, take these two below, and don't let them out of your sight for a moment."

Miranda gasped. "Nay!"

Wailing and pulling her hair, Rija raised her hands to the heavens in tearful supplication.

"Ach, see here, Cap'n . . ." Angus began, his Scots burr accentuated by uncertainty.

From underneath the table, a mournful feline howl joined the cacophony.

"Quiet!" Tony roared, exasperated. "God's bones! Can't a man have a moment's peace on his own ship?"

"Sir, I beseech you!" In her panicky distress, Miranda clutched his forearm, shivering at the feel of warm flesh and taut sinew beneath the silk of his sleeve. "Rija must be protected from the Dutchman. I will do anything you ask—anything!"

There was an instant's charged stillness between them, an awareness that hung in the air like the faint scent of frangipani. Something flickered in the depths of Tony's slate blue eyes, instantly squelched as he swept a lazy, examining glance from her bedraggled head to her soiled hems. His tone was nasty with insinuation.

"Just what are you suggesting, madam? Frankly, you have little to offer."

Mortified, Miranda snatched her hand away as if scorched. It took all her resolution to meet his gaze.

"I am well aware of my shortcomings, sir," she said, hating the tremor in her voice, "but it is abundantly apparent that I am no weeping, hysterical maid. Our plight is mortal. If you allow Rija to fall into Djink's hands, you will certainly be sending her to her death!"

That startled him. "What? How?"

"The princess has vowed to take her own life rather than let that villainous Dutchman use her against her own people. He would make them little more than slaves in their own homeland, for his barbarism is well known."

Tony hesitated, frowning. The young Javanese maiden sniffling in terror before him was a mere child. Picturing her with Steef van der Djink made his gorge rise. What defense would the girl have, wife or not, against a man of his persuasions? Tony realized his antagonism for the English harpy and his annoyance at her unwelcome and complicating intrusion into his plans were overshadowing his better judgment. As if sensing his chain of thought, the Langford woman pressed her case.

"Captain Benedict, I appeal to you! Though Rija and I do not share the same blood, she is as dear to me as my own flesh. Surely you have family that means as much to you as she does to me? Someone you'd die for—your mother, a sister or brother?"

"Yes," Tony said slowly, "I have a brother."

"Then—"

"Enough, Miss Langford." With a gentle hand, Tony caught Rija's small chin and lifted her face for his examination. Miranda held her breath while his mouth twisted with a small, self-derisive smile. "Never let it be said I vent my spleen on innocents. I suppose what the Dutchman doesn't know won't hurt any of us."

"Then we may go?" Miranda went limp with relief. "Oh, sir!"

Tony released Rija and turned to Miranda. "But I'll not take you a pace farther than the Dutchman's wharf, is that clear? I suppose I can find a fisherman with a prau who'll take a couple of stowaways off my hands for a coin or two. Then whether you decide to head for Benkulen or to seek Prince Amang will be no concern of mine."

"Yes, of course. Thank you. That would be entirely suitable," Miranda agreed, the grateful words tumbling from her lips.

With a small glad cry of understanding, Rija dropped into a squat, balancing gracefully on her heels. Bending forward in a low obeisance, she placed her forehead on the toe of Tony's polished leather boot. His expression was disconcerted.

"Nay, child," he protested, catching her elbow to help her up, "do not humble yourself before me."

Ignoring his words, Rija immediately resumed the same position at his feet. Tony shot an uncomfortable glance at the pale, silent woman standing beside him. "Why does she do this?"

"The *dodok* is a sign of homage to a superior," Miranda explained softly. "Rija is expressing her gratitude."

"And you, Miss Langford?" A teasing grin curved his lips. "Are you not also grateful?"

Miranda stiffened, gritting her teeth at the man's insufferable arrogance, but unwilling to risk Rija's safety by antagonizing him with the scathing words she longed to hurl at his head. Bottling up her pride, she folded her hands beneath her chin and began to sink into the *dodok*—only to be jerked upright by a hard hand on her upper arm.

"Get up!" Tony growled. "I prefer your defiance. That at least makes us equals."

Astonishment widened Miranda's silver-gray eyes. Releasing her, Tony stepped around Rija's prostrate form.

"See to your sister," he said shortly, motioning Angus out of the cabin ahead of him. "You may rest here until we anchor, but I promise I'll see the last of you both before the moon rises this night."

"I still don't trust him," Angus said, his grizzled expression ominous.

"Relax, old man," Tony ordered. "Your years betray you."

He leaned in languid ease against the railing of the *Mirage*, idly watching the late afternoon shadows move across the palm- and palmetto-lined riverbank. The Dutchman's plantation bordered a sheltered harbor at the mouth of a minor tributary that brought goods and produce out of the interior. The small fleet of praus bobbing at the foot of a wharf would soon be transporting Tony's precious cargo of coffee from the plantation's bamboo storehouses to the *Mirage*.

"Steef couldn't have been a more cordial host," Tony continued. He absently rubbed the face of his lotus-carved snuffbox between his fingers. It was an unthinking gesture of long standing, an automatic habit whenever his mind was preoccupied, but he caught himself now, aware the tiny object had become almost a talisman in recent days. With a small snort of self-disgust, he shoved it into his pocket and continued to regale Angus with the details of his visit.

"Even your ancient palate would have appreciated the array of delicacies presented at Steef's table, though the walls of his dining room were covered with enough gilt to blind a man!"

Angus snorted. "What's he think he is, a King?"

"In this land, being a Dutch regent is the next best thing. But no, I believe he is merely a man who surrounds himself with beautiful objects. It caters to his vanity, but it is an expensive obsession."

Angus's bushy gray brows drew together in a scowl. "Ambitious men bear watching, boy."

Tony flashed a wry grin at the old sailor's sour grimace. "You're too suspicious. Steef may be a dangerous ally, but we've taken every precaution. You know what to do if there's trouble. Steef is a businessman, after all, and as eager to profitably conclude our business as we are. Besides, I played the role of obnoxious, self-important fop to such perfection, he's heartily sick of my company and anxious to see my back."

In his best London finery of brocade coat, knee breeches, and silver dress sword, topped off by a carefully coiffed and powdered wig, Tony was the epitome of dandyism, and certainly no threat to the elegant Dutchman's peace of mind. And that was exactly what Tony had counted on as he'd endured his partner's interminable hospitality at Djink's sweltering whitewashed mansion, a pretentious European monstrosity rising incongruously out of the lush tropical jungle setting. Let the Dutchman think him a fool. All that mattered was keeping the cobra at bay until they'd loaded their cargo and safely left Javanese waters.

"So what's holding things up?" Angus demanded. "We could have had the holds half-filled by now."

Tony shrugged. "Perhaps the natives are waiting for a good omen."

Angus shuddered superstitiously. "Well, the sooner the better, I say. Ain't you ready to leave this heathenish country?"

Unbidden, a face caught in an aureole of moonbeams rose in Tony's memory, and his throat ached with an unfamiliar tightness. To leave Java meant leaving a part of himself behind—that part he'd given a girl called Miri.

Abruptly angry with himself, Tony felt his jaw throb with tension. It was madness, this torment of loss he felt over a mere female. Even if he found Miri, how could he take his native mistress home to England? If he made her his wife—no, the idea was ludicrous, impossible. His mother and her coterie of titled friends would make short work of such an innocent. Not even the Wastrel Lord could be forgiven for such a breach of propriety.

Tony released a sigh. Obviously he was suffering from some tropical fever that had affected his brain. Angus was right. The sooner they left Java for good, the sooner he'd recover from this soul-sickness, this obsession with a dream. He scowled at the exotic mental vision of Miri, desperately willing the image that haunted him to leave him in peace, and in his mind's eye Miranda's features shifted, dissolving into another face . . .

". . . sorry to bother you, sir, but I wish to know . . ."

Miss Miranda Langford's words trailed off uncertainly at Tony's transformation into fashionable gentleman. A pale braid fell over one of her shoulders, and her strained features and the violet half circles beneath her eyes marked her fatigue. When he continued to stare at her, nervousness made her voice grow suddenly tart.

"I realize you are not overly fond of me, Captain," she said with some asperity, "but *must* you scowl at me so ferociously?"

Tony came back to reality with a jolt that bordered on shock. God, he *was* half-mad if he could confuse this old maid with his sweet Miri! The thought did nothing for his already frayed temper.

"I lay no claim to a honeyed nature," he snapped irritably. "Why have you left your cabin, madam?"

The soft curve of Miranda's mouth thinned into a tight, annoyed line. Beside this strutting peacock, she knew she appeared as insipid and colorless as an English sparrow.

Her dirty, mud-colored gown and the old batik sarong she'd tied shawl-style across her shoulders was ample disguise despite the disconcerting flash of distant recognition in Tony's eyes. Thankfully, his bullheaded, arrogant disposition made him see only what he wanted to see.

Miranda shuddered to think what his wrath might be if he realized the truth. Her mortification would then be the least of her worries. It was imperative she and Rija be on their way before anything so disastrous occurred, so she ignored his ill temper, lowering her eyes with feigned meekness.

"I only wish to inquire if arrangements have been made for us to leave your vessel."

"Such impatience, my dear!" Tony chided, taking perverse pleasure in goading the woman. He peeled off his sumptuous jacket and stripped out of his waistcoat, smiling inwardly at her outraged look at such familiarity. "Are you not enjoying our hospitality?"

"I care not for your trifling humor, Captain Benedict," she returned stiffly, looking away from the rippling expanse of chest muscles revealed by the clinging, sweat-dampened silk of his shirt. "You are the one so adamantly eager to be rid of us."

Now, why should that statement of fact needle him? It wasn't as if he owed her anything, was it? Still, her demeanor left him feeling somehow worthless and smallminded.

Scowling, Tony dragged off his wig and handed it and his discarded garments to Angus. Irritably running long fingers through his short-cropped coppery-gilt curls, he decided his unease was because he couldn't quite peg this Langford harridan—so straitlaced one minute, so unexpected and outlandish the next. His lips quirked involuntarily. Imagine, stowing away with a Javanese princess! Well, they wouldn't be his problem much longer.

"You're right, Miss Langford," he said abruptly. "We've wasted enough time. Your prau is waiting opposite the Dutchman's dock. Gather your sister and I'll escort you myself."

"That isn't necessary," Miranda murmured, taken aback. The less time spent in Captain Benedict's company the better!

"Let me be the judge of that. I'd thought to transfer you to your boat during the confusion of loading my cargo, but if we delay further, you'll miss the tide." He shot a glance at Angus. "I'll see the ladies safely away, then roust Steef's lazy workers into action. Tell Mr. Tassel to be ready on this end. By God, they'll load cargo by moonlight if necessary!"

"Are ye certain the ladies will be all right?" Angus asked.

"We'll be fine, Mr. Pratt," Miranda said quickly.

"Well, it's good luck I wish to ye." The old man's face fell into rather sheepish lines. "It's been a right pleasure knowing ye, lass."

Touched by his kind words, Miranda smiled around a sudden thickness in her throat. Tony gave a disgusted snort, but even his disdain couldn't vanquish her pleasure at the old man's simple friendliness. She reached for his gnarled hand and shook it.

"Thank you, Mr. Pratt. I'll always remember your kindness. I'll go get Rija now, and—oh!"

She stumbled, tripping on the large black cat that had suddenly materialized at her feet with a strident yowl. Tony caught her arm, steadying her automatically. Just as instinctively, she jerked free of his touch.

"I'm all right." Flustered, she looked away from his puzzled frown. Beelzebub continued to howl mournfully, and she took an uneasy step away from him. "What evil spirit has possessed this animal that it should persecute me so?"

Angus scratched his grizzled head. "He don't mean no harm, lass. Cats are fey creatures. I suppose he knows ye're leaving us, him having taken such a fancy to you. I don't suppose you could pretend to like him just long enough to bid the poor ole bugger farewell?"

"Well . . ." Biting her lip, Miranda bent, gingerly stretching out her fingers to the feline. Beelzebub sniffed them once, then broke out in a loud, rumbly purr, rubbing his broad head and battle-scarred ears against Miranda's palm and closing his yellow eyes in ecstasy.

"Ach, I dunnae ken what magic charm ye used, but ye've tamed him, lass." Angus chuckled.

"Poor old thing," Miranda murmured, gently stroking Beelzebub's thick coat. Her voice was soft with unexpected tenderness. "All he wanted was a loving hand."

Tony gazed in hypnotized fascination at the woman's pale hands moving in slow, sensual caresses through the cat's midnight black fur. A flicker of recognition hovered tantalizingly on the edge of his consciousness, some distant but familiar memory. Despite the humid, oppressive heat, a sudden chill shivered down his spine.

"We have no time for this foolishness!" His words held a harsh note that he couldn't explain. He took a swipe at the animal. "Begone, you misbegotten son of Satan—"

In the blink of an eye, Beelzebub sprang, sank his sharp teeth into the back of Tony's hand, then leapt away, hissing.

"Goddamnit!" Tony's curses peppered the air. Holding his bloody hand, he kicked at the animal, but Beelzebub was too fast, disappearing down an open hatch with a final defiant hiss. "Vicious bloodsucking bastard! I'll feed you to the crocodiles!"

"Ach, Cap'n, did he hurt ye?" Angus asked anxiously.

"Hell, yes! Why, he damn near took my arm off—" Tony broke off, glaring at the woman whose soft gray eyes danced with mischief and whose hands pressed against her lips could not quite conceal her mirthful grin. "So you find this amusing, Miss Langford?" he demanded.

"Of course not," she squeaked, struggling to bring her features under control and not quite succeeding. *Pompous ass!* she thought. *'Twas no more than you deserved!*

Instead, she cleared her throat and offered her advice. "You'd best clean the wound with spirits, sir. Putrefaction sets in swiftly in this tropical clime. Shall I assist you?"

"I suspect your ministrations would not be the tenderest," Tony returned sourly, wrapping his handkerchief around the hurt. Unbelievably, a self-deprecating smile twitched the corners of his mouth. "Well, just don't stand

there, madam! Fetch your sister before any other calamities
befall me!''

Something in the bottom of Miranda's heart went weight-
less at that smile, and she caught her breath in panic. Nay!
She could not allow this handsome, unprincipled scoundrel
to seduce her unwary heart again! Shame at her own weakness burned her cheeks, and she ducked her head and hurried
to get Rija.

A few short minutes later, Miranda sat with Rija and their
meager belongings in the prow of the *Mirage*'s longboat.
Two broad-shouldered sailors rhythmically dipped their oars
into the gradually darkening waters of the sluggish tributary,
shooting them rapidly toward the shore opposite the Dutchman's wharf. Tony himself manned the tiller, guiding the
boat into position beside a small, square-sailed prau moored
at the edge of the thick underbrush.

The prau was manned by a single brown-skinned native
whose filed teeth were black from chewing *siri*, a mixture
of betel nuts and lime. It was a common sign of beauty in
both men and women among the Javanese, but somehow
their boatman's blackened grin filled Miranda with unease.

"I've paid the fellow well, Miss Langford," Tony said,
vaulting over the side into calf-high water, oblivious to the
damage to his expensive boots. He caught Rija under knees
and shoulders, making her giggle as he lifted her easily into
the waiting boat. "He'll take you wherever you wish."

"Can you take us across the straits to Telok?" Rija asked
the boatman in Javanese.

He lifted his broad, flat paddle in assent and nodded,
grinning and jovial. "Yea, my lady. It is but a small
matter."

"Very well." Some of her nervousness at being so near
Djink's territory began to uncoil. She found Tony's inquisitive gaze upon her and hastened to explain. "From
Telok we can make our way to Benkulen by foot if necessary. I—I thank you again for your help, Captain Benedict, however unwilling it may have been."

"Prettily said, madam." A muscle ticked in Tony's jaw,
and he felt a twinge of misgiving for the first time. "But

perhaps this is not the safest solution to your dilemma after all . . .''

"It will do," she said in a rush. "I would not burden you further."

He accepted that with a brief arching of his brows. "As you say." He extended his arms. "Then if you'll allow me . . . ?"

It took her a moment to realize he was offering to lift her as he had Rija. Heat flooded her at the thought of being in his arms again, and her limbs trembled betrayingly. She shot to her feet, her hands knotted in her skirts.

"I—I'm perfectly capable of taking care of myself, thank you!"

Looking up at her as she stood in the gently rocking boat, Tony shook his head. "As Angus would say, 'Ach, ye're a stubborn lass!' "

"I assure you—"

Tony broke off her protest by sweeping her into his arms. She landed soundly against his chest, evoking approving chuckles from his two oarsmen. "Save your assurances for someone who'll believe them, my dear."

Off balance, Miranda gasped and clasped his neck as he stepped across the space separating the two boats. A chilly voice pierced the dusk, freezing them in their tracks.

"Ah, Benedict!" Dressed in black, Steef van der Djink materialized like an avenging angel amid the dark underbrush on the muddy riverbank. A squad of burly natives armed with swords and European muskets appeared at his side as if by heavenly magic. "I see you've brought the rest of my payment as promised!"

"W-what?" Shocked into immobility, Miranda's unbelieving gaze flew to Tony, but his lean face was expressionless. She was convinced he'd planned this betrayal all along, and her rage exploded. Her hand cracked across his cheek. "You *bastard!*"

Kicking and pummeling his chest, Miranda fought for freedom. Tightening his grasp, Tony controlled her struggles easily, then leaned over and dropped her unceremoniously into the bottom of the prau, where Rija cowered in terror.

"Quiet, wench, or I'll wring your scrawny neck," he ordered in a tight voice. The only sign of tension was the pulse that jumped in his square jaw.

In a flurry of skirts and petticoats, Miranda scrambled to her knees, shrieking, "You black-hearted devil! I'll see you in hell for this perfidy!"

On the bank, Steef threw back his golden head and laughed. "Ah, my friend, I had no notion you played nurse-maid to such a fishwife! I do extend my sympathies."

Turning his back on the woman, Tony sloshed toward the Dutchman, one steadying hand on the prau's mooring rope. "Not my usual choice of feminine companionship, I assure you, Steef. But you've spoiled my little surprise . . ."

"There are no secrets, neither here nor in Batavia, which I do not know." The Dutchman's icy blue gaze fell on Rija, and a smile that was not a smile twisted his perfect face. "You've done me a service, transporting my little princess to me."

"Murderer!" Miranda screeched. She pushed Rija behind her, groping in the bottom of the boat for the extra paddle as though she were a knight arming for battle. "You'll not have her!"

"The deed is done, madam," Steef informed her calmly. "I've made the walk to the temple with the holy man, and spoken the wedding vows before him, as prescribed by the customs here."

"What? That's impossible!" Frantically Miranda's gaze flicked over the densely overgrown riverbank, the impassive faces of the native soldiers, and the uneasy expressions of Tony's oarsmen, searching vainly for some way out of her predicament. Heart sinking, she knew they were trapped.

"Quite possible," Steef contradicted. "All that's left to complete the ceremony is the wedding feast. 'Tis a pity neither you nor Captain Benedict will live to enjoy it."

Miranda sucked in a frightened breath at the threat.

"I always knew you had the heart of a pirate, Steef," Tony remarked with a cool, feral display of white teeth that held no humor. "So you intend to take her without even a by-your-leave?"

Miranda shot him a startled look. Was he coming to their defense after all?

"Of course," Steef replied with a shrug. "Why should you make all the profit when I have need of your *Mirage?*"

As Tony's mouth went grim, hysterical laughter bubbled in Miranda's throat. The blackguard! It was his damn ship he'd die for, not her and Rija!

Tony snarled at the Dutchman. "You'll have to kill me to take my ship."

"As you wish," Steef agreed with a laugh. "Seize him!"

Steef's men charged down the bank. Tony drew his sword and shouted to his men, "Hodge, Barry—defend yourselves!"

But instead of facing the onslaught, he turned, slashed through the mooring rope, and set his broad shoulder against the prow of the prau. His intense blue gaze locked with Miranda's astounded eyes. "Try to get back to the ship—hurry!"

With a mighty shove, he sent the shallow vessel sculling swiftly into the river's currents, and Miranda's befuddled mind into total confusion. Things were happening too rapidly for her to sort out truth from lie. Were they all victims of Djink's treachery? As he stood on the bank, the Dutchman's sculpted features twisted into a mask of ugly rage, and he drew a pistol from his sash.

"Tony, look out!"

Her warning cry came too late. Tony spun awkwardly in the knee-deep water just as the Dutchman fired point-blank. The force of the blast knocked Tony backward in a spread-eagled splash, and he was gone, instantly swallowed up by the dark river.

Searing pain tore through Miranda, and her agonized scream echoed over the water. A volley of musket shots rang out from all sides, and she threw herself over Rija, covering her sister with her own body, grief and terror and rage filling her heart to bursting.

The two sailors in the longboat sprawled half-in, half-out, either wounded or dead. A half dozen of the Dutchman's henchmen splashed through the shallows, occasionally slashing at the water with their swords. Miranda caught her breath on a deep, painful shudder. Anthony Benedict's courageous attempt to save them had demanded the highest price. A terrified glance over her shoulder revealed an attacking flotilla of praus bearing down on the *Mirage*. Of immediate concern, their native boatman was paddling madly—intent on sending them straight back to the riverbank and the waiting Dutchman!

"Not that way, you fool!" Miranda cried, pointing frantically. "To the ship!"

To her dismay, the little man merely grinned his black-toothed grin and continued to paddle. Too incensed to think, she jumped to her feet, swinging her oar into the side of the man's head. The blow knocked him sideways into the water, but the inertia of his fall rebounded, making the little boat rock too far in the opposite direction. Off balance, Miranda pitched headfirst into the river as the prau capsized, rolling Rija in after her.

Coughing and spluttering, Miranda surfaced to a world gone mad. Thunder exploded over her head, and banshee screams whistled from the banks. Giant palm trees splintered into kindling, and lightning and the smell of gunpowder filled the air. It took her several confused seconds to realize that the noise and destruction was round after round of cannon fire coming from the *Mirage!*

"Rija!" Hampered by her long skirts, Miranda treaded water frantically, breathing a sigh when Rija bobbed to the surface beside her.

"Sister!" Rija gasped.

They kicked to the side of the overturned prau, scrambling for handholds, cringing at the deafening cannon salvos. It took only a moment's futile attempt for Miranda to understand they stood no chance of righting the capsized boat. Now the Dutchman's minions swarmed both banks of the river. It took only another split second for Miranda to realize their only hope lay in reaching the *Mirage* before Djink's attacking fleet.

"Swim for the ship, Rija!" Miranda ordered. Though they both were strong swimmers, in the diminishing light and the confusion of the fight, the risk was enormous. But there was no other way. "Angus will help us!"

"But, Miri—"

"Swim, I said!" Miranda screamed, pushing the girl. "I'm coming."

With a wide-eyed nod, Rija obeyed, diving like a porpoise and disappearing beneath the surface. Cursing her clinging garments, and knowing that whatever slim chance she stood would be eliminated by their weight, Miranda fumbled to free herself. Just as the last bodice button popped open, something brushed her leg, then clamped down hard.

The murky depths of the river closed over Miranda's head, and her startled shriek died in a gurgle of terror.

Chapter 5

Her lungs on fire, Miranda fought the unseen force that dragged her down. Disoriented, she struggled for the surface, clawing to be free of the aquatic monster. At last she burst again into the blessed air, flailing and choking.

"Stop it, you silly bitch! It's me!"

Tony's ragged, gasping words surprised her so much that she went under again. A hard hand tangled in her sleeve and jerked her back, thumping her into the side of the overturned prau. Coughing, she kicked hard to stay afloat this time.

"I thought they'd killed you," she croaked over the clamor of the pitched battle going on all around them.

He groaned. "They damn near have."

His hair was plastered against his skull, and his hands scratched weakly at the rough boards of the boat. The light was nearly gone now, but the torches on the Dutchman's praus and the intermittent flash of cannon fire illuminated features twisted in pain. Losing his grip, he sank lower into the water, and Miranda's panic returned.

"Don't you dare!" She grabbed a handful of his shirt. Seeing him "die" once had been horrifying enough. She had no intention of letting it happen again, but how could she keep an injured man afloat? The hull of the prau bobbed in the freshening breeze. "Take a breath," she ordered.

"Huh?"

Without bothering with further explanations, Miranda put her hands on his shoulders and pushed them both under again, kicking so they surfaced this time in the nearly pitch-black air space beneath the capsized prau.

Tony's weak curses echoed hollowly. "Goddamn it, woman! Are you trying to finish what the Dutchman started?"

His profanity almost made her smile. If he could still swear, there was life in him yet. Miranda explored the underside of the vessel by touch, blindly feeling the outline of neatly coiled lines and fishnets lashed into place, a long, canvas-wrapped pole, and finally a supporting thwart. She placed Tony's hand on the brace. "Hold on to that."

Water lapped about their shoulders, and the smell of dead fish was overwhelming, but the momentary respite gave them a chance to catch their breath.

Tony's voice was a husky rasp. "Got to get . . . to the *Mirage*."

"I know. Where are you hurt?"

"My side."

"Is it bad? How do you feel?"

"Like I'm going to puke."

"There's no time for that!" Miranda snapped. "Can you swim? I'll help you."

"I'd rather go by boat."

Being scared to death made Miranda furious. "This is no time for stupid jokes!"

"Who's joking? Help me turn this thing over."

"I can't. I already tried."

"Can you touch bottom yet?"

"What—" She realized he'd been pushing at the boat the whole time they'd been under it. Dropping her legs, she felt her toes sink into the slimy ooze of the riverbed. "Yes, I can."

"On three, then. And better make it count," he grated. "I've only got one good try left in me."

It was a superhuman effort, but it worked. The muffled security of their dark haven disappeared the moment the prau rolled upright, exposing them to the clamor of the battle and the rising wind.

"Oh, sweet Jesus." Tony's voice was thick with pain and defeat. "The mainsail's afire."

Barely sparing a glance back at the beleaguered *Mirage*, Miranda pushed him after the prau, which was drifting inland on the incoming tide. The thick foliage lining the riverbanks loomed over them like a black tunnel. There was no sign of the Dutchman, but all activity centered on the docks now, where additional praus cast off and men ran for cover under the artillery barrage. No one noticed them and their tiny boat.

"Get in, get in!" Miranda urged.

Shoving and prodding him, Miranda helped Tony hoist himself painfully into the boat, then with trembling limbs, dragged herself over the side and fell in after him in a tangle of sopping skirts. Levering himself halfway up, one arm flung over the gunwale for support, Tony squinted through the clouds of smoke at the outline of the *Mirage*.

"Cut it loose, damn it, cut it loose!" he muttered. "Lord, Kit will murder me if I lose the ship!"

Dripping wet and trembling, Miranda scrambled to his side. Now that they were in the boat at last, she was uncertain what to do next. In this turmoil, how could they reach the *Mirage* intact without even a paddle?

There was a loud crack, and Miranda gasped. The *Mirage*'s mainmast twisted, its sail totally engulfed in flames, and it fell in slow motion over the side, smashing into a quintet of the Dutchman's praus that were too slow or too unlucky to clear away in time.

"Good man, Mr. Tassel." Tony chuckled weakly.

Shrieks of the dying mingled with a renewed volley of cannon fire, and in the brief flare of light produced as the flaming sail set fire to the demolished boats, Miranda saw a small, feminine figure being hauled up the *Mirage*'s bow on a rope.

"Rija!" Relief left her breathless. "Rija's safe!" She turned joyfully to Tony just in time to see him slide into a heap in the bottom of the prau. "Captain Benedict!"

Heart pounding, Miranda felt for a pulse under his jawbone. To her relief, she found it, thready but present nonetheless. Then her glance fell on the growing pool of crimson staining the side of his shirt. Pulling up his garment, she stared in horror at the ragged gouge of bloody flesh striping his ribs. "Oh, my God!"

"Stop your wailing, woman," he muttered, his eyelids fluttering. "I'm not dead yet."

Not knowing whether to laugh or cry infuriated her. Whipping off the sodden sarong still knotted about her shoulders, she wrung it out and pressed it hard against the wound to staunch the flow of blood. Fortunately, the ball hadn't pierced his chest, but it had careened through hard muscle, skidded along his ribs, then exited at his side, leaving a path of mutilated flesh from below his right nipple to just above his kidney. "Curse you, Anthony Benedict! Don't frighten me like that!"

"Easy, damn it! That hurts!"

"Damn it, yourself!" She was practically weeping with fright and fury, but her hands were busy tearing at the hem of his shirt for a strip to bind the makeshift bandage to his torso. "Get up, you blackguard! We're not out of this yet!"

"I wouldn't even be in this mess if it weren't for you and your noble sister!" Tony ground out, gritting his teeth with the effort to sit up.

Miranda quickly wrapped the strip around him, securing it with a tidy knot. "No, you'd merely be dead, murdered for your ship, you—you smuggler! So keep your accusations to yourself while we figure out a way to reach the *Mirage*, because while you've been lying there in a maidenly swoon, we've been drifting *the wrong way!*"

"Just as well," Tony grunted under his breath. Shaking his head to clear the grogginess, he gauged their growing distance from the battle. Looking around, he noticed the long, canvas-wrapped pole lashed along the inside of the prau. "Here, help me with this sail."

"A sail? Why didn't you say so?"

Between them, they untied the thongs, then set the end of the pole into a notch in the pointed prow. Tony sank on unsteady legs into the stern of the little boat, holding his side and breathing hard, his face pasty as he took the tiller. Miranda unwrapped the tattered canvas, then handed him the sheets.

"Can you turn us around? How will we get through? What if—"

The wind filled the little lateen sail at that moment, and with a jerk of his wrist, Tony sent them scudding before it into the heart of the river's darkness.

"Wait!" she cried, frantic. "What are you doing?"

"Saving our skins, if we're lucky."

"But the *Mirage*—"

"—is retreating. Tassel finally unfurled the fores'l, thank God. They'll make it now."

Miranda jerked around, her eyes widening at the ship's diminishing outline. "But they're leaving us!" she wailed.

"They have their orders—save the ship first." His laugh was raspy and harsh. "Besides, they don't even know if we're still alive."

"Oh, God, you're right! Rija—"

"Angus will take care of her."

"But how will I find her again?"

"Calm down! Mr. Tassel had orders to put in at Bantam if anything went wrong."

"We've got to follow them!" She glared at the shadowy figure in the stern. "I demand, sir, that you turn this boat around immediately!"

"Use your head, woman," Tony countered painfully. "We'd never catch the *Mirage* in this thing, and if we run the Dutchman's gauntlet and fail—well, do you think he'll have any qualms about killing us both after this debacle?"

"Maybe he thinks we're already dead, too."

As if to refute her words, an excited flurry of alarm cries

rang out from the opposite bank, followed by a series of musket shots. Tony ducked, caught Miranda's shoulder, and slammed her into the bottom of the boat so hard her ears rang.

"Get down, and stay there!"

Swearing roundly, he adjusted the sail to catch every bit of the warm night wind. The little boat bucked and soared ahead into the winding darkness of the river, outdistancing the tiny band of pursuers crashing through the undergrowth. As their shouts grew fainter, he released a shuddering breath.

"There's your answer. Someone knows we're out here, and this is Steef's country. That bastard will be after us the minute we show our English faces."

Miranda struggled cautiously to a sitting position beside him. Though they were both soaked, she took unconscious comfort in his warmth. Shaken, she spoke in a ragged whisper. "What shall we do?"

"Try to put as much distance between us as we can . . ." The wind jerked the lines he controlled, and he stifled a deep groan.

"Then what?" Miranda questioned anxiously. "Go overland to the coast to Bantam? I don't know this country, but it might be possible . . . Captain Benedict?"

Tony leaned heavily against her, his head lolling, and the ropes slid though his hands. "Take them," he muttered, his words slurred and weak.

Alarmed, Miranda grabbed the lines before they slipped completely free. "I don't know how to sail this thing!"

"Just keep us to the middle course . . ."

He slumped forward, and Miranda managed with great difficulty to hold on to the sheets while rolling him to his back so that his head rested in her lap. Panting with exertion, her heart pounding with renewed panic, she pressed her fingers against his face, talking to him softly, urgently.

"By the Goddess of the Southern Sea, don't do this to me! Captain Benedict, can you hear me? Please . . ."

But there was no answer except the lap of water against the prau and the snap and rustle of the wind in the sail.

Touching his side in the darkness, she felt the warm stickiness of blood seeping from his wound. Bending her head, she pressed her lips against the damp curls of the man she held, whispering a heart-wrung prayer.

"Don't die, Tony. Oh, sweet Jesus, please don't let him die . . ."

The urgency of the voice drew Tony from the darkness toward the light. Reluctant at first, a half-forgotten hunger and the memory of sweet surcease changed that reluctance to eagerness, and he sought the sense of the words . . .

". . . got to wake up. Oh, please, Captain Benedict. Someone's coming."

It was a supreme effort to open his eyes, and the face above him was fuzzy and indistinct, haloed by the gray-white light of an overcast dawn. Reaching out, he grazed the softness of a cheek with his fingertips, exploring the contours of the face by touch like a blind man. The unformed question in his hazy mind was resolved, and he relaxed. He knew her, and knew he was both safe and loved.

"No, you can't go back to sleep! Wake up!"

Tony's lids fluttered in confusion, and he struggled to remember something, anything that would explain her urgency. He could only think of one thing.

"What is it, love? Has your husband come to roust me from your bed?"

There was a hiss of indrawn breath, then she shook him roughly. "You're dreaming, you scandalous rake! Get up at once!"

Raw pain scorched his side at the unexpected movement, and the haze evaporated from his brain. With a vile epithet, he levered himself up to a sitting position in the bottom of the prau. At some point in the night they'd lost the wind and were now moored to a low branch overhanging the riverbank. Slender fingers of gray fog curled over the surface of the water, undulating and flowing like something alive. He glared at the object of his enmity through bleary eyes.

"Good God, it's you again."

"You needn't bother to thank me for keeping you alive, Captain," Miranda said sarcastically.

Involuntarily he touched his side, then realized he was neatly bandaged with strips of what could only be her petticoats. Even Beelzebub's bite had been tended, tied up with a scrap of lace-edged linen. He had to hand it to her, she was efficient and innovative, but what a viper!

"If you intend for me to save what's left of your worthless hide, sir," she continued in a voice that sliced through his aching head like a rapier, "then I suggest you make the effort to rise. Someone's approaching from the river, and it could well be the Dutchmen!"

"Why didn't you just say so?" he grumbled. "Or does it please you to inflict pain on the helpless?"

He was rewarded by a contemptuous look and a toss of her long pale braid. "I should have known better than to expect courtesy from such a miscreant knave!"

In a fair snit of temper, she whipped down a stretch of mud-colored fabric that had protected his resting place from the fine rain misting the humid air and settling like silver dew on her fair head. With a start, Tony realized that all the proper Miss Langford wore was the blood-stained sarong she'd used to bandage him initially, and a shapeless linen shift with a drawstring neckline that covered a surprisingly fine pair of breasts. But he didn't have the opportunity to consider her sacrifice of her clothing for his care or the indisputable fact that she was slender and delicately curved beneath the native garment before she was at his side berating him again, her voice echoing hollowly against the encroaching walls of fog.

"We can't stay here!"

He was suddenly aware her unease was not completely due to their imminent discovery. "What is it? What's wrong?"

Shivering, she crossed her arms and rubbed her fingers against the gooseflesh prickling her skin. "I don't know . . . the fog . . . can't you feel it?"

He snorted derisively. "Don't go all silly and superstitious on me now, woman. The only thing sinister out there walks on two legs. As a matter of fact, I'd as lief believe some benevolent genie has sent us his aid just in the nick of time.''

She looked thoughtful, and some of the tension in her strained face drained away. "Mayhap you're right. But we still must hurry! Can you walk?"

"If God preserves me from tyrannical women, I can do anything I please.'' With a grunt, he rolled over the gunwale into the shallows, then watched her bundle her dress under her arm and do the same. "The question is, walk where?"

Miranda pointed into the jungle. "That way, west into the hills, then we can go north to Bantam. If we keep to the jungle and avoid the rice paddies, no one should see us.''

"All right. Untie the boat.''

She sent him a harried glance, then did as he said, giving the little vessel a push that sent it far out into the green center of the river, where it caught the current, bobbed, then began a stately progress back down the stream, disappearing into the creeping fog bank as if it had never been.

"If we're lucky, they'll have no idea how far we got before we abandoned ship,'' he said.

Swallowing, she stared after the prau, clearly uneasy at giving up the mode of transportation that had seen them safely through the night. "And if we're not?"

He shrugged and turned to climb the bank. "Then we'd better keep moving. Come on.''

Leading the way, Tony pushed through the thickest part of the lush undergrowth, knowing that within a few feet they would be swallowed up, invisible to any casual observer on the river. Ignoring the pain in his side, he walked automatically as the foggy air cleared, stumbling from time to time, aware that the woman followed him through the thicket of face-slapping vegetation, but offering her no other consideration. The third time he slipped on the wet grasses, he fell to one knee, grimacing at the pain that lanced through his side like a hot brand.

"Stubborn, bullheaded man!'' She was instantly at his side, her mouth clamped in an angry line, hauling his arm around her shoulders. "Lean on me, sir! You'd risk breaking open your wound again rather than admit you're weak as a kitten."

"I can make it—"

"Hush! Listen . . ."

They held their breaths, keeping perfectly still. Excited voices drifted from the direction of the river.

"Damn! They must have found the boat. Can you understand what they're saying?" Tony whispered. His mouth was against her ear, and he inhaled the flowery fragrance of her hair, vaguely recognizing the sweetness of frangipani.

She strained to hear, shaking her head. "Only a portion . . . they're going on . . ."

"When they don't find anything, they'll be back," Tony said grimly.

"Then you'd best let me help you so we can make better time."

"I'm too heavy for a slip of a female like you."

"And I'm stronger than I look."

Tony snorted. "And determined to have the last word, aren't you, Mistress Nurse?"

"I've no intention of falling into the Dutchman's clutches because of your male vanity," she returned tartly.

Tony took a deep breath to refute that assertion, and immediately regretted it. Teeth gritting, he stifled a groan, then, panting and pale, gave her a sheepish grin.

"Perhaps you're right, for now."

Her radiant smile at this small victory transformed her, and Tony blinked, stuck by how pretty she could be under the right circumstances. While he preferred his women vibrant and earthy, with her hair down and a pleasant expression lighting her face for more than two seconds, Miranda Langford might even be considered beautiful in a pale, colorless, almost ethereal way. With unusual acquiescence, he allowed her to serve as his crutch, more and more conscious of her softness and her sweet scent even though the effort to keep moving made his jaw knot and sweat pop out on his brow.

Stoically he tried to think of anything but his discomfort,

only half listening to her occasional murmured words of encouragement. In the gradually brightening daylight, it occurred to him that he'd never seen anything so green as this topical paradise.

From the broad leaves of banana plants to the feathery fronds of the tall palm trees, everything was oversized and bursting with life. Liana vines, jasmine, and orchids flourished in every color and size, from the tiniest crimson blooms to platter-sized alabaster flowers dripping with nectar. Long-tailed monkeys scolded from the treetops, and small, unseen animals scurried underfoot in the rich compost. In the overhead canopy, birdlife abounded; parrots and doves and peacocks fed on a colorful array of glistening fruits and myriad iridescent insects.

Tony lost track of how long they walked, merely counting one step at a time in their halting progress through the dense growth. Finally Miranda stopped, gasping for breath.

"I'd like to rest a minute," she said, carefully unlooping his arm from her shoulders.

His ears buzzing, Tony reached for the trunk of a nearby palm to steady himself. The rain had stopped, but every leaf and frond dripped, and they were both still wet through and through. Wisps of pale hair had worked loose from her braid and waved softly about her head. He was not so far gone he didn't notice the intriguing shadow of her nipples pressing against the thin, damp fabric of her chemise, but her flushed face made him frown in concern.

"I've worn you out. Why didn't you say something sooner?"

"Why didn't you? You're white as a specter."

He grunted, gingerly lowering himself to a seat on the ground. "I'm all right."

Tucking her blue and brown flowered sarong around her calves, she squatted on her heels. She watched him anxiously, then lay her palm against his forehead. "Nay, you're not. You've a fever."

"Hardly surprising," he said dryly, dragging her hand down his strawberry-stubbled cheek, luxuriating in the coolness of her touch. "I've been shot, you know, and I think I've cracked a couple of ribs as well."

Licking her lips, she tugged at her captured hand. "I'll get you some water."

"No, wait. Maybe it wouldn't hurt so damn much if I was bound up tight. Think you can do it?"

"With what?"

He jerked his head at her bundle. "Why not contribute what's left of that horrid gown of yours? No woman should have to wear anything so ugly, and besides, I find your sarong very flattering."

Looking extremely uncomfortable, she snapped, "My wardrobe—or lack of it—is certainly none of your concern, Captain Benedict! However, for the sake of our common endeavor, I'll gladly offer the gown."

"What a turn of phrase you have, Miss Langford," Tony said, a wry smile twisting his mouth. Releasing her hand, he gave the long, champagne-colored braid hanging over her rounded breast a quick, mischievous yank. "Common endeavor, indeed. Does this mean we may be friends after all?"

"It means that I need you to reach Bantam alive, sir," she said stiffly, unfolding the gown. "If I just had some way to cut it . . ."

Reaching into his boot, he drew out a slim dagger. "Use this."

Turning the deadly blade over in her hand, she cast him a speculative look, then inserted the tip in the skirt of her gown and began to rip. When she had a pile of strips prepared, she knelt next to him again, not meeting his eyes.

"As long as we're at it, I should check your bandages, too. If you'll remove your shirt . . ."

Tony sat forward and allowed her to help him slide the ragged silk shirt from his shoulders. Her hands were gentle as she untied the knots holding the makeshift bandage in place, and he watched the play of expressions cross her face as she peeled the bandage free, the tip of her pink tongue touching her upper lip in worried concentration. She sucked in a little ragged breath at the sight of the scabbed and puffy gash, just beginning to show pink signs of inflammation at its edges.

"At least it's stopped bleeding," she said in a shaky voice.

"Calm yourself," he said, " 'tis no great hurt. I've suffered far worse and survived."

She glanced up, her gray eyes wide as she met his dark blue gaze. "You have?"

"On numerous occasions." A deep, humorous slash appeared in his long cheek, more devastating to unwary female hearts than any mere dimple. "Usually in a duel over a woman."

She pinkened. "That, sir, does not surprise me in the least!"

"You think I'm a scoundrel, don't you?"

"I *know* what you are."

To be so thoroughly dismissed by this haughty stick of a woman disgruntled Tony no end. He caught her chin, smiling at her in knowing challenge.

"Don't be too certain of that, Miss Langford. I might try to change your mind." She jumped to her feet, only to be forestalled by his hand on her wrist. "Where are you going?"

Flushing, she gestured vaguely. "The *dukun* taught me the ways of her people. There are herbs in the jungle that may ease your wound."

He let her pull free, then closed his eyes and wearily rested his head against the palm trunk. He had to admit he did feel like hell, but he was strong and healthy, and he knew from experience he'd recover his strength quickly. Still, it was pleasant to have someone worry over him, even if she was a spinster with no sense of humor. For the duration, they were allies, however reluctant. Perhaps, for harmony's sake, he shouldn't bedevil the Langford woman with his teasing.

Arrogant, wicked devil of a man! Miranda's hands shook as she gathered the jungle's bounty. How dare Anthony Benedict take such relish in unnerving her, after all she'd done for him! Why, she ought to leave him where he sat. It would serve him right if he wandered around in circles for years.

Over her head, ring-tailed monkey chittered at her intrusion. Miranda took a deep breath and fought for calm, smiling slightly at the little creature's acrobatics. The little men of the jungle were good luck. Indeed, to kill a monkey was the worst of omens. Perhaps this little one's presence was a sign that things could only get better. In spite of herself, Miranda's mood lightened.

No, she couldn't do anything so un-Christian or uncivilized as abandon Tony, no matter how he tormented her. Besides, if she helped him, when they reached Bantam he'd be so indebted, he'd have to take her and Rija to Benkulen. With that thought firmly in mind, Miranda returned to find Tony dozing against the palm tree.

Without volition, her sympathy rose again. He was desperately hurt and had hardly voiced a complaint, despite the agony she knew he suffered with each step. That, at least, deserved her admiration. She touched his broad shoulder, and he came awake instantly.

"Let me tend to this," she said softly.

Kneeling again, she bent to her task, crushing the herbs she'd gathered and packing them around the wound. With the knife, she cut another strip off the hem of his shirt to use for a bandage, and bound the injury.

"Your touch is tender," Tony murmured wryly, "but that was my best silk shirt."

"It will serve you better this way," she returned briskly. "Now lean forward, and I will bind your ribs."

Nodding, he lifted his hands to his ears to provide her access. The broad expanse of his well-muscled and hair-dusted chest was mere inches from her nose as she passed the torn strips behind his back. His musky scent filled her nostrils, and the warmth of his skin radiated through her sodden garments, making her shamefully aware of his masculinity and her vulnerability.

"Make it as tight as you can," he warned.

"I know how to do it!" Miranda snapped.

"Must you take exception to everything I say?" Tony complained. "I'm no happier about our situation than you, yet I don't leap on your every word as if it were a mortal insult."

"No, you merely ridicule me unmercifully about everything, conduct no true gentleman would condone!" Mouth compressed in a mulish line, she jerked the bindings tight. He gritted his teeth on a soft moan, and she was instantly contrite. "Oh, I'm sorry! Did I hurt you?"

His fingers stopped hers before she could release the bindings. "No, leave it. It feels better already. You are an able nurse, Miss Langford. What puzzles me is how you come to be in this hellhole."

Concentrating on tying the knots, she answered absently. "My father was a merchant captain such as you. I grew up on his ships, acting as interpreter until he married Rija's mother."

"Interpreter?"

"Yes, I conducted his business in Spanish, French, German, and a host of pidgin tongues and dialects."

"You are a linguist, then? How extraordinary to find another learned woman. My sister-by-marriage is a scholar, too."

She shrugged. "I can take no credit for my gifts. My travels have been my education, and I've had the good fortune to see many marvels, Captain. But I've grown to love this 'hellhole,' as you call it, in the ten years it has been my home. Java is a land of many mysteries."

"Ten years? How old are you?"

She glanced up, annoyed. "Certainly old enough not to have to answer such an impertinence!"

He laughed, chucking her under the chin. "And certainly too young to be called spinster by the likes of me, eh? Come on," he cajoled, "your secret's safe with me."

The irony of his words made her smirk. Controlling her expression with difficulty, she said, "I'm twenty-five, if you must know. How old are you?"

He reached for what remained of his shirt and slipped it

on. "An old man compared to your tender years. Thirty-three by the calendar, a thousand and three by experience."

Miranda's mouth cinched in a disapproving moue. "Due to all those eager ladies and their irate menfolk, no doubt."

"Do I detect a hint of censure?" he asked with a chuckle. "You would not be so quick to judge if you knew my tragic history, my dear. I'll admit I squandered my youth in lustful pursuits, but I've reformed, I swear."

"I find it hard to believe," she said, her tone chilly. So he was a liar, too! Their first encounter was more than enough evidence of his continued profligacy, and herself just another of his conquests. The conclusion was bitterly galling.

"What do you question?" he asked. "That a rake could reform or that I've had some success with the fairer sex?"

"Well, of course, a man of your looks may have his choice—" She broke off at his pleased laughter, chagrined she'd revealed that she found him handsome. She lifted her chin in an effort to maintain her dignity. "Physical beauty in no way excuses a philandering libertine's behavior, sir!"

He grinned, his eyes sparkling wickedly. "You are too harsh. 'Twas only because of my unhappy boyhood and misunderstood youth that I sought solace where I might."

"You look for sympathy from the wrong person, sir. Others no doubt have suffered similar hardships, yet still manage to live honorable lives."

"Perhaps, but to grow up knowing you can never win your own father's favor is a heavy burden. Since I could never please the old man, after a while it seemed better not to even try. Got myself kicked out of quite a few snobby schools, the best London clubs, the lowest dives, and a succession of boudoirs along the way." His grin grew even wider at her shocked expression. "Damned good fun, too, most of it."

She made a small, irritated sound and stood, uncertain if his words were all braggadocio or if they held an element of truth. "You mock me."

His expression sobered. "Nay, I mock myself. Only in recent times have I come to terms with what I'd become

and determined to make improvements." He spread his
hands, gesturing at himself. "You see what my determination has wrought. I've lost my ship, my crew, and the
cargo that would have redeemed my honor and"—he
grimaced wryly—"brought ease to my mother's old
age."

"Oh." Miranda's eyes were wide and troubled. "I did
not realize . . . That is, I've been so caught up in my own
concerns, I neglected to consider yours. I beg your pardon.
But all is not lost, for when we reach Bantam—"

"Yes, the Dutchman will have much to answer for."

The deadly gleam of vengeance that shone in his blue
eyes chilled her to the core. "Are you thirsty? Hungry?"
she asked nervously. "I brought water and fruit."

"Thirsty," he answered.

She brought him a broad banana leaf in which she'd
gathered silver globules of fresh rainwater. "You must
drink as much as you can. It will help keep the fever
down."

His first attempt to drink off the leaf was a dismal failure,
the droplets skittering across the slick frond, missing his
open mouth altogether, and splashing down his strong neck
to wet his shirt and trickle through the mat of reddish-blond
hair on his chest. His annoyed expression made Miranda
giggle.

"No, no! Like this." She demonstrated, holding the leaf
in a vee so that the water ran in a stream directly into her
mouth. "See?"

His second attempt was no better. He cursed and irritably
scrubbed circles in the moisture dribbling down his chest,
the gesture making Miranda feel strangely light-headed.
"Try again," she said huskily.

This time he covered her hands with his own, guiding
them so that she held the leaf for him. Miranda watched as
he drank deeply, mesmerized by the movement of his throat
muscles and the firm strength of his touch. She was nearly
overcome with a powerful feeling of protectiveness, as a
mother nourishing her child, and at the same time, a surge
of such intimate awareness that her breath choked to a stop

and her heart threatened to pound from her body. Somewhere in the distant recesses of her mind, temple bells
chimed in the wind.

Tony raised his head slowly, startled by the electricity
suddenly generating between them. There was a surprising
flash of green in the depths of her wide, equally startled
eyes. He had the impression someone was trying to convey
a supremely important message, but he was too slow and
dull to catch its meaning. Closing his hands, he pressed
hers together, crushing the leaf in between, and he felt her
tremble.

"What is it about you?" he muttered to himself. His gaze
focused on the petal-soft curve of her mouth, and he swallowed harshly. Why did he feel so mysteriously compelled
to this woman? "I don't even like you."

His words broke the spell, and she jerked away. "Nor
I, you! 'Tis the fever making you feel so queer. Can you
eat?"

With jittery movements she poked finger-sized bananas
at him while wolfing down a few herself, but he shook his
head and got stiffly to his feet.

"I'm not hungry. We'd better go."

The hours passed in monotonous plodding, broken only
when Miranda urged Tony to rest. His fever raged off and
on, making him a bit incoherent at times, though with her
help, he kept the pace. After their earlier exchanges, now
they passed barely half a dozen words between them, concentrating their energies on getting as far from the river by
nightfall as possible. Though neither voiced it, both feared
if they stopped for too long, they might not be able to start
again.

As they struggled though the enveloping undergrowth,
more footsore and weary with each step, Miranda occasionally plucked pieces of fruit—thumb-sized berries, mangosteens, a lemony starfruit, the ubiquitous bananas—and
stowed them in a sling made from the remnants of her gown.
Dinner would be welcome when they finally found a stopping place.

At one point a sudden crashing in the upper canopy followed by a resounding *thump!* caught Miranda's attention.

"Hold this," she said, shoving her sling into Tony's arms. "Wait here."

She disappeared into the foliage before Tony had a chance to protest.

"Wait! Come back here, Miss Langford. What the hell . . . ?" He scowled and started after her, only to have her reappear, smiling broadly, carrying an evil-looking brown globe studded with vicious thorns.

"What the devil is that?" he demanded suspiciously.

"Durian." She hefted the fruit, judging it a small one of only seven or eight pounds. "They only fall when ripe and fully fermented. We're lucky to find one so late in the season."

"Phew!" Tony made a face. "Not only would that thing kill you if it hit you, it stinks of rancid cheese and chamber pots."

She looked slightly indignant. "It is a great delicacy in this region, a favorite among men and all manner of beasts."

"*I'm* not eating anything that smells like *that!*"

Laughing softly at his expression, she tucked the durian into her sling. "You'll feel differently later. Hunger is a great seasoning."

"We'll see." He was dubious. Then his expression changed. "What's that?"

Miranda followed his glance, seeing nothing, then discerning the regular shape of several overgrown mounds, lined up one after the other and leading off into the jungle. Tony brushed away the crust of dirt and vegetation on a portion of one, revealing the pocked and crumbling surface of a limestone block.

"It's man-made," he said, running a hand over his sweaty brow and frowning.

"And old," she added. "Mayhap a marker of some kind?"

"Let's go see."

Another forty minutes hike found them standing, open-mouthed in wonder, on the perimeter of an overgrown ruin. Time and nature had worn the once ornate stone carvings to barely visible shadows and tumbled the pointed arches and vaults of a magnificent Hindu temple so that the area resembled a set of blocks abandoned by some cosmic child. The jungle had taken over in places, tilting walls and crumbling massive cubes of stone, but here and there a wall or a spire stood intact and a few paved spaces were still open, not even the jungle's tenacious growth able to penetrate solid rock.

"It is a sacred place," Miranda whispered. "Holy ground."

"Are you willing to risk the wrath of these old gods for a dry place to sleep?" Tony asked.

"Dare not to mock what you do not understand," she said severely, then relented. "I can't go another step, either. Only the very brave—or the very desperate—would dare intrude here."

"And which are we?" He was practically swaying with fatigue, and his pallor under his deep tan alarmed Miranda.

"Both, Captain. Come, we should be safe for a while."

They explored the ruins, passing under the watchful eyes of the gods peeking from the weather-worn bas-reliefs carved into the walls. Some of their poses were meant to teach life's lessons, others to depict a portion of the epic Hindu mythology, but some were blatantly erotic, gods and mortals in the varied aspects of love, both spiritual and physical.

Tony caught Miranda's eye after passing a particularly explicit carving, and he laughed at her blush. "These pagan gods seem to have an overactive interest in a very human activity."

"Your mind is a sewer of depravity, sir," she retorted. "These depictions are simply an allegory to a—a higher level of being."

He merely snorted, holding his side. Pointing at a portion of wall that formed a corner and seemed relatively intact, he asked, "What about there?"

The paving was cracked, but moderately clean and dry,

and free of hiding places for snakes and other unsavory vermin. Miranda set her sling down, eyeing the cant of the broken walls as Tony gingerly lowered himself to the ground with a gusty sigh of relief.

"It will do," she agreed. "I'll gather some banana fronds for thatching, and we'll have a snug haven should it rain again."

"I'll help." He made a move to rise, but she restrained him with a hand on his shoulder.

"No, Captain. 'Tis but a simple matter, and you need to rest more than I. Lend me your knife and I'll return anon."

"Why do women love to bully men?"

She couldn't help a tired smile. "Because we so rarely get the opportunity."

Chuckling, he handed her his knife. "Be careful, all right?"

With his comradely warning warming her, Miranda nodded, then set off to fetch their "roof." Sometime later, her arms loaded with banana fronds, she again made her way through the shadowy ruins, her mind on nothing more than rest and perhaps, if they could manage it, the luxury of a fire to dry their clothes.

A sudden stirring of foliage brought her up short, listening warily. She took another hesitant step, then froze in terror. Not twenty feet away, a huge golden-eyed tiger crouched, his long striped tail lashing the air impatiently.

"Don't move," came Tony's quiet command. "As you value your life, don't move."

But it was too late. At Tony's words, the tiger sprang. With a cry, Miranda dropped her armload of fronds and ran for her life. In the next instant, Tony charged past her toward the beast, bellowing at the top of his lungs, then hurled the thorny durian right at the tiger's nose!

The odoriferous durian bounced once at the big cat's paws, then the animal grabbed it between its massive teeth, turned, and disappeared back into the underbrush with hardly a ripple of a leaf. Thunderstruck, Tony could only stare after it.

"You fool! You utter fool!" Miranda flung herself at him, furious and shaking. "You could have been torn to pieces!"

His arms closed over her involuntarily, his expression still mystified. "By Old Nick's garters! I thought we were both dead! Did you see that?"

"'Tis my fault!" Miranda gulped, choking on hysterical laughter. "Tigers adore durians even above fresh meat, for the fruit makes them drunk. The smell led him right to us. Thank God you had the nerve to give him what he wanted."

"Hell, woman," he roared, " 'twas the only weapon I could find!"

They stared at each other. Tony's lips twitched. Miranda giggled. Sudden hilarity overtook them, and they threw back their heads and howled. Holding each other, they gave their merriment free rein in a release of tension that had Tony holding his battered side in protest. But then in an abrupt turnabout, Miranda's laughter changed, and covering her face in her hands, she dissolved into uncontrollable sobs.

Nonplussed, Tony swore darkly. Urging her back to their corner, he pulled her down to the ground beside him, holding her close, trying to soothe her.

"Hush, now, it's all over. Please, Miss Langford! You've been so brave through all of this, completely admirable. You're really a wonder."

"I was s-so s-scared," she said, choking on her tears. Her hands found his face, and she touched him as if to reassure herself that he was indeed unharmed. "And then you . . . and I thought . . ."

His mouth nuzzled her temple, then trapped a tear at the corner of her eye. "It's all right," he murmured, calming her the only way he knew, "it's all right."

His lips brushed hers in a feathery kiss, and he drew back, smiling slightly, gently pushing her fair hair back from her flushed face. His smile faded slowly, and his gaze intensified.

"Dear God," he muttered.

She heard the strangeness in his voice and gazed up at him through tear-drenched eyes, her mouth parted and vulnerable.

"I am a fool," he said, his voice thick with emotion. "I am without doubt the greatest fool in all of Christendom. Dear God—*Miri!*"

And then his mouth covered hers.

Chapter 6

The kiss was rapacious, demanding, hungry—so wonderful and at the same time so frightening, Miranda trembled violently, her lips clinging to his even as some distant part of her panicked brain shrieked that this discovery was nothing less than total disaster.

Rolling her beneath him and pinning her against the paving stones with his body, Tony finally released her mouth. His slitted eyes were bright with fever, and his voice was harsh.

"I could kill you."

There was nothing loverlike in his tone, nor in the pressure of his hands. Miranda knew that the blood-chilling fear she'd experienced during the tiger's attack was but a pittance compared to the absolute terror she felt now. She made an involuntary movement toward freedom, but he pushed her flat with barely controlled violence.

"No, don't try to pull away or I *will* throttle you!" he ground out. "Was this your idea of a game? Some kind of test?"

"I—I don't know what you're talking about," she managed, only to strangle on the rest of her protest as he mauled her mouth with a punishing assault, his tongue invading and stealing what was left of her breath.

"Don't lie to me!" He fumbled with her braid, loosing it, threading his long fingers through its heaviness, then crushing a fragrant handful to his nose. "The color's different, but the scent is still yours, still sweet . . . Damn you, woman, you put me through hell!"

Blood thundering in her ears, she gasped, "It's not what you think—"

"Then explain it to me! By God, I'll have your explanations!" Framing her face with his palms, he held her still for a minute inspection of each feature. "It is you! Miri Langford . . ."

"Miranda," she whispered rashly.

His mouth ravaged hers again for that impudence. "*Miri*. Don't ever deny it. And don't ever deny that you're *mine*."

"Stop, please, Captain Benedict," she gulped, her head spinning.

His thumbs pressed her cheekbones, and his words were a furious growl. "*Tony*. My name is Tony, damn you. Say it!"

"T-Tony." Her throat was tight with tears, and his weight crushing her breasts made it impossible to breathe.

"Why did you leave me that night?" he demanded. "Why?"

"I had no other choice!" Her head moved restlessly from side to side in confusion. "I was afraid, ashamed . . ."

"Of what we shared?" His ferocious expression was suddenly tempered with pain. "Christ's wounds, Miri! It was exquisite!"

"But I'd never . . . experienced such wantonness . . ." Her voice choked on her misery. "I don't know how it happened."

"But it did." It was not a question, but a demand, a challenge to deny the truth if she could or dared.

A hot tear trickled from the corner of her eye and splashed against his fingers. Her voice shook. "Yes . . ."

Tony released a shuddering breath and buried his face in the tender curve of her neck, reveling in the scent and texture of her skin. "I nearly went mad."

Shivering with the delicious sensations of his mouth nuzzling her, but more frightened than ever, she slanted her fingers into his sunset-colored curls. She'd meant to push him away, but her traitorous hands lingered, delighting in the crisp, springy texture. Appalled, she dropped her hands to his shoulders and pushed urgently.

"I'm sorry, I never meant it to go so far, but I was desperate."

He drew back slightly, frowning. "Was that your plan all along—to sell your virtue for passage off the island?"

"No, no! To buy it, with Rija's pearl! You have it yet, do you not? The other . . . just happened, and in my shame I forgot my mission."

There was a hint of masculine satisfaction in the faint curl of his mouth now. "Yes, the pearl. So then you came to the dock." He shook his head. "I was churlish and blind, I'll admit, but I was nearly insane by then, for I'd searched the entire countryside and all of Batavia in vain for you."

Amazement clouded the quicksilver of her eyes. "You had?"

"How could I not, after knowing you?" Tenderly he drew an outline of her lips with his fingertip. "You are the cruelest of women, Miri. Why didn't you tell me who you were?"

"I did," she pointed out, swallowing hard. "But then with the Dutchman on his way to see you, it seemed a gift from God that you did not recognize me."

"Or the trick of some demon," he growled, and again, there was that faint flicker of hurt behind his eyes. "I would have helped you, Miri."

"How could I be sure?" Her lower lip trembled. "And later, you were so harsh and angry . . . I'm not even certain I can count on your help now."

"You can count on much more than that, if only you will. There was magic between us that night. Something

extraordinary happened to me, but apparently not to you—
at least not enough to trust me.''

Alarmed by the bitterness in his words, Miranda tried to
explain. "Rija's safety was paramount. What was I to a
wastrel like you? Just another woman to bed. I couldn't
take any chances. I still can't!''

His jaw flexed at her unknowing use his infamous ap-
pellation, and the shallow cleft in his chin nearly disappeared
with the tension. "You're not just any woman to me. When
we made love—''

"It was a mistake!'' she cried, struggling beneath him
as her panic and humiliation returned full force.

"Nay, sweeting, never that.'' A high color washed his
cheekbones. "I'd call it fate or the hand of God, if I believed
in either. Saving that, 'twas destiny, at least, that brought
us hence to make the sweetest love ever known.''

"You are shameless! Let me up, you knave!'' she cried,
breathless with the images his words recalled. "I forgot my
duty once with you, but it shall not happen again!''

His low laugh mocked her. "How can it not, Miri? Even
now you feel the tug of forces that bind us—as I do.''

The hard ridge of his manhood pressed intimately against
her. Suppressing a shameful excitement, she glared up at
him in defiance. "Liar! You deceive yourself. Now release
me, before you do yourself a harm.''

"What's killing me is not having you again,'' he muttered, nibbling at the delicate angle of her jawbone.

She twisted, straining away from the scratchy-soft rasp
of his red-gold stubble and the supple seduction of his lips.
"You have no right!''

"After the hell you've put me through, I have every
right!''

Fending off her hands, he leaned forward to suckle and
nip at the peak of one rounded breast through the thin covering of her chemise. Her back arched, and she moaned in
response to the fiery tingle that ignited low in her body.

"Don't!'' She flailed wildly, and her elbow connected
with his injured side.

With a hoarse cry, Tony jerked and rolled off her into a

ball, his knees drawn up and his face contorted in pain. Miranda scrambled to her knees, appalled at what she'd done.

"Oh, my God! I'm sorry!" She hovered anxiously over him, afraid to touch him, shocked by the whiteness around his mouth. "What can I do? Are you all right?"

After an interminable moment, he finally sucked in a ragged breath and managed to open one eye. "You damn viper! Do I look all right?"

Her lower lip quivered. "It wasn't intentional. If you hadn't—"

"Oh, hell, I know." Taking a careful breath, he slowly uncurled from his fetal position and held out a hand. "Help me up."

Warily Miranda assisted Tony so that he rested with his knees bent and his back against the crumbling wall. He clutched his bound side, and his face was still unnaturally white.

"I'm sorry," she repeated, biting her lip. "Are you bleeding again?"

"I don't think so." He focused on her worried features, and his lips twisted in a pained half smile. "Stop blaming yourself. It was no more than I deserved."

That admission startled her. Settling herself a short distance away, she gazed at him with wide, troubled eyes. "I did not mean to hurt you."

"I know. Forgive me for frightening you. I fear my passion for you o'erpowered the thimbleful of good sense I have left."

A wave of delicate color rushed up her neck and darkened her cheeks. "You should not say such things."

"Why not?"

She glanced away. "Because it's not seemly and . . . and they're untrue."

"Miri, you and I escaped all the bounds of propriety the night of the Lotus Moon. And there is no greater truth than what we shared."

"Oh, stop!" She buried her flaming face in her hands,

and humiliation made her words a mumble. "I just want to forget it ever happened."

"I won't let you."

His surprisingly grim tone made her look up in alarm. "We must."

Frowning slightly, he shook his head. "I don't understand. A chance like ours comes but once in a lifetime. Why else would I go nearly insane trying to find you again? You don't willingly sacrifice the kind of perfection we shared."

She shook her head in denial, her voice barely a whisper. "That night was a dream only, a fantasy wrought by Semar that had no basis in reality. Nameless, faceless—we acted without conscience, ignoring our obligations and responsibilities. In the pure light of day it is impossible."

Chuckling softly, he reached for her hand, folding it between his own. "Improbable, but not impossible, now that I've found you again."

"I don't understand what you want from me! 'Tis simply the mystery of our first meeting that produces this obsession." Agitation made her eyes darken to a turbulent shade of pewter. "You don't know me at all. How can you say you desire Miri now when only moments ago you despised Miranda? Whatever happened before, I'm not your harlot, and you have no claim on me!"

"Sweeting, I know your innocence full well," he murmured. The color was returning to his face, though his eyes were still overly bright with fever. "I don't understand all that's happened either. But I do know that we shared something beautiful. After lying in my arms, how can you be shy of me?"

"It's different now . . . now that I know who and what you are," she said, blushing with embarrassment. "You are not honorable in the ways I expect a gentleman to be. You're a scoundrel and a womanizer and not at all the kind of man I'd choose to know under normal circumstances."

His eyebrows lifted mischievously, and he brought her hand to his lips, kissing her fingertips. "So you resist because you despise what you see? Or because you like it all too well?''

She gasped as this barb struck too close to home. Jerking her hand away, she stumbled to her feet. "Conceited jackass! You *are* mad to think I'd ever willingly have anything to do with you. What happened was a . . . an aberration, a momentary weakness, and since it shall never happen again, there's nothing further to be said about it!''

He scowled darkly. "I can think of plenty.''

"Restrain yourself, sir! Our situation is dire indeed without added complications, and this revelation changes nothing.''

"The hell it doesn't!'' Stiffly, using the wall for support, he pushed himself to his feet. In the distance, thunder rumbled as he tried to reconcile his sweetly yielding dream lover to this prickly, intriguing, absolutely infuriating female. "By God, you're a stubborn woman!''

"One of us has to be sensible!'' she insisted. "We must reach Bantam, the Dutchman's minions aren't far behind us, you're sick and hurt, and now there's a *drunken* tiger out there . . .''

Her voice had become a wail, and to Tony's amazement, her face crumpled, and fresh tears streamed down her cheeks. Remorse pierced him. On an overwhelming surge of protectiveness, he pulled her resisting form back into the circle of his arms.

"Poor Miri! What a waterworks you are! And with just cause, saddled with such an ungrateful, cantankerous companion!'' he murmured.

He stroked her long, straight hair and found its fairness as subtly shaded as a moonbeam. How could he have ever thought of her as colorless? he wondered. She was multifaceted and as endlessly varied in both beauty and spirit as a flawless diamond, and he wanted both her fire and her sweetness with an ache that fairly tore him asunder.

"I'm a bastard to force the issue when you're so weary and confused,'' he said in apology. "Are you tired, sweetheart?''

Sniffling, she nodded, knowing herself a weak-spined

fool to allow him such liberties considering their circumstances, but too needful of solace and a strong shoulder to lean on—just for a moment—to deny herself the luxury.

"Then perhaps we should call a truce," he suggested.

She wiped at her tears. "Truce?"

"You're right about the precariousness of our situation. Suppose we refrain from hostilities until we reach our destination? We shall be comrades, compatriots—" he smiled charmingly "—even cronies, if you will."

Her answering smile was tremulous with relief. "Yes, of course."

"It's a pact, then. Friends we'll be, until such time when we shall discuss our relationship in a calm and leisurely manner."

Suspicion clouded her eyes. "That smacks of a seduction, sir."

"You cut me deeply with your mistrust, my dear!"

"After such a sample of your expertise in that quarter, I have reason to be wary," she admitted.

Her honesty thrilled him. So she was not unmoved by his touch, merely confused and cautious and so very innocent. His crooked smile was tender. "I can but live in hope of the future, Miri."

She looked away and eased from his embrace, her voice husky. "There can be no future for us, sir—ever. Once we reach Bantam, you will return to England, and I must take up my duties as the Princess Rija's guardian. Better for us both to have no regrets when that time comes."

Straightening her shoulders, she took a steadying breath. "Now, I must fetch a new roof, for unless my ears deceive me, the monsoon will blow another rainstorm our way very soon."

Tony watched her move away to her task, chilled by his fever and the calm certainty and eminent sensibility of her words. But the Wastrel Lord had never let anything so mundane as being sensible stand in the way of what he wanted. Perhaps he was obsessed, but a part of him that he had no control over yearned for a renewal of the intimacy and communion they'd shared on that special night.

So they'd gotten off to an unusual start, taken the cart before the horse. He could be patient, hard as he found it. Every woman deserved to be wooed, and Miri was no exception, although between her embarrassed modesty and her everlasting notions of duty, she was a considerable challenge.

Tony grinned to himself. Who'd have ever thought he'd be grateful for his wastrel past? But he was, for now he could bring all of his experience to bear to win this beguiling, entrancing woman. He suspected Miranda Langford was the key to what he so desperately needed to fill the restless emptiness of his existence. The problem would be convincing Miri that to find happiness, sometimes it was best to forget about being sensible. Ignoring the ache in his side and the ball of pain throbbing behind his eyes, he went to help her.

By the time the sun set, they had erected a thatch of woven banana fronds covering the right angle of "their" corner, and laid out two separate piles of fronds as beds. With flint and steel from Tony's breeches pocket, they built a small fire to keep away any nocturnal visitors, then wearily settled in to make a meal off the remainder of the fruit.

Tony found out how low his reserves of strength were when he tried to take off his damp boots. Cursing his weakness, he struggled with the stubborn leather until Miranda took pity on him.

"Here, let me help," she said, straddling his outstretched leg and tugging at his boot heel. Casting a glance over her shoulder, she smiled at his dubious expression. "Go ahead. I know the procedure. I often helped my father this way."

Shrugging, he placed his other foot on her sarong-covered bottom and pushed. The boot slid off in Miranda's grasp.

"I must admit a female valet has its rewards," he said with a twinkle as they repeated the maneuver. He'd never considered the flat of one's foot a person's most erotic zone, but placing it on the softly rounded buttocks of a scantily clad and attractive woman had definite possibilities. "I suppose I have your father to thank."

"He died about six years ago," she said. Squatting in

front of Tony, she continued her valet duties with unself-conscious and unselfish grace, peeling off his sodden stockings and laying them before the fire to dry. "Steef van der Djink murdered him."

"What!"

She nodded, holding his long bare foot, warming his cool flesh between her hands. "You see now why I cannot allow Rija to wed such a monster."

"She must be very important to him that he would go to such lengths to have her," Tony said thoughtfully. He sighed with pleasure as she shifted her ministrations to his other foot.

"With her hand comes power, land, and the obedience of her people. He could order them to grow many times the VOC's—the *Vereenigde Oostindische Compagnie*, or Dutch East India Company's—coffee and spice quotas, forcing the natives to neglect their rice crops. Many would starve."

"While the Dutchman fills his coffers, there would be nothing to fill their bellies."

"Exactly. That is why this marriage must never come to pass."

New respect showed in his expression. "You're very courageous to flight such a powerful man by yourself, Miri."

"For Rija's sake, I can do no less." Their eyes met and a current seemed to pass between them, centering on the point where her fingers lingered on his lightly hair-dusted instep. At that moment, a dark, winged shape swooped through their little camp, and they both jumped.

"What the hell was that?" Tony demanded.

Flustered, Miranda hastily released his foot, laughing nervously. "Just a *kalong*, a flying fox. Hundreds of them sleep in the treetops by day and hunt by night."

Tony took off his ragged shirt and lay down, eyeing the dark sky above them uncertainly. "Hunt for what?"

With a smile, she rose and went to her own pallet. "Insects, mostly. A flying fox is a rather large bat, you know."

"Bats—ugh!"

"They're harmless, Captain."

"Tony, remember?" he corrected. "We're friends now."

"Then good night—Tony," she said in a hesitant voice. "I'll be close by should you need me in the night."

Tony shifted uncomfortably and stifled a groan at her choice of words. What he needed was her under him while he loved her into insensibility. He grimaced at the heat rising in his loins and laughed at his own folly. He was too sore and feverish to do a woman justice, and they both knew it. Still, he wished she'd finish with whatever tantalizing adjustments she was making to her native skirt.

Watching her through the fan of his sandy lashes, he jerked when he realized she'd deftly opened the sarong, holding it like a screen between them, unaware that in the flickering firelight her chemise-clad silhouette fell on it like one of the shadow puppets of a *wajang* play. With a snap of her wrists, she spread it over herself like a blanket and lay down.

"Good night," he said in a strangled voice, trying to ignore the mental vision of the luscious curves and valleys that lay beneath the patterned sarong. "We'll move on again at first light."

She made a drowsy sound of assent and gave a quiet sigh that set Tony's pulse to racing and increased the pounding in his head. Cursing his body's response, he determinedly shut his eyes. He'd be a gentleman and keep his distance while she became accustomed to him, but when they reached Bantam, she'd better be on her guard!

"Jimmy!"

Miranda shot bolt upright, startled from a deep, exhausted slumber by Tony's strangled shout. Only a few glowing coals remained in their fire, but it was enough for her to make out his broad-shouldered outline thrashing on the rude pallet. Outside their makeshift shelter the night was still black, filled with mysterious sounds and the patter of more soft rain. Unmindful of the fact that she was clad only in her knee-length shift, she clambered to his side.

"What is it? Tony, are you all right?"

"Bloody Spanish bastard tried to kill Jimmy!" he muttered.

"You must have been dreaming," she soothed. She touched his bare shoulder, then gasped, and her hands sought his face, his forehead—he was burning up with fever! "Oh, no!"

"Miri?"

"Yes, I'm here. I'll get you some water."

When she fetched him a banana frond cup, he was sitting up, swaying slightly. "The whole world's spinning," he muttered.

Miranda helped him drink, her brow pleated in worry. "Your fever's much higher."

He handed her back the frond, shuddering violently. "Damn, it's cold."

"It's a chill." She snatched up her forgotten sarong and wrapped it around his shoulders, then urged him back down. She had no notion what to do next. Chuckling, he surprised her by catching her around the waist and drawing her down beside him, snuggling her into the bow of his body.

"I'm always causing you trouble, aren't I?" he murmured into her hair.

"Well, we certainly aren't going to reach Bantam with you in this condition." There was a tremulous, breathless note in her voice. "Let me up."

"Keep me warm, Miri. Just for tonight."

"Tony . . ."

"Humor me. I'm not a well man, you know."

"How can you make jokes?" His forearm lay across her waist, and her hands moved restlessly over the taut muscle and too warm skin. The darkness invited confidences, admissions of weakness she could not have spoken earlier. "I—I'm frightened."

"Of what, dearling?"

That you'll tempt me to forget my duty, an inner voice whispered. *That, charming deceiver that you are, you'll steal my heart, then break it without a thought, leaving me nothing.*

But aloud she said, "That Djink will find us. That we'll both die in this jungle. Or that your wound and this fever will kill you, and I'll be alone."

"I won't leave you, Miri. After so much trouble to find you, do you think I'd let you out of my sight again? Even death quails before my determination. Besides, I'm a Benedict, and we're much too spoiled and stubborn to die."

Shivering, he drew her closer still. Through the thin stuff of her chemise, Miranda felt the heat radiating from his body, and an answering warmth that was another kind of fever began to burn her skin. Despite that, she felt curiously comforted by his words, and some of her anxiety melted. She felt him shift, and quietly asked the question that had been in her mind. "Who is Jimmy?"

"Hmm?"

"You called for him in your dream."

"My brother, Kit. Christopher."

"Why do you call him Jimmy?"

"An old pet name from childhood. We're twins, you see. Gemini. Gemmy became Jimmy."

Miranda could hear the affection in Tony's voice. "You're close to him, then?"

"Now. We were . . . raised apart. We only found each other again two years ago during the Spanish threat."

"What an extraordinary story. Are you much alike, you and your brother?"

"Perhaps not in temperament, but in appearance, yes, though he is more blond than red, and—well, feel for yourself." He drew her hand back, guiding it to his left ear to explore the small brown mole on his lobe. "The mark I bear here is found on Kit's right ear, making us mirrors of each other."

"I truly fear for the women of this world knowing there are two of you in it," she murmured, half-teasing, half-truthful.

Tony chuckled. "Kit and his wife live in the Carolina Colony. Knowing how Kit feels about Lexa, I'm probably an uncle by now."

There was a certain wistfulness in his tone that she could

not overlook, but whether it was due to a special feeling for his sister-in-law or envy over his brother's apparent happy marriage, she couldn't guess. "Are you warm enough yet?"

He tightened his grip, preventing her from moving away, and smiled against her ear. "No, stay. I assure you I feel like utter hell, so you are perfectly safe, but I am a notoriously bad patient and must have my way in order to recover speedily."

He was as conniving as a mischievous little boy, and it made her laugh softly. "That, I can believe."

"Then kiss me, love, for you are the only medicine I need."

Catching her chin in gentle fingers, he turned her head to meet his, and his mobile lips moved over hers softly, tenderly. With a sigh, he released her, settling back down, his arms encircling her possessively, protectively.

"Rest now, Miri," he murmured. "Your sweetness is a certain cure."

Shaken more than she would admit, Miranda stared into the darkness, wondering again what manner of man was Anthony Benedict. There'd been nothing threatening about that kiss, but its very gentleness coiled new ribbons of emotion about her heart, weaving around the cords forged by his passion and braiding them into something totally new and strong and enticing. She knew she had to be very careful, but weary and worried, she could not bring herself to leave the haven of his arms, telling herself it was only to comfort him that she stayed.

When Tony woke, he was drenched in his own sweat, a sure sign that his fever had broken in the night.

He was also very much alone.

"Miri!" Every muscle and joint protesting, he rose from the bed they'd shared, leaving their shelter to stand blinking in the brilliant light of another steamy day. He called her name again, but there was no answer, and a terrible sense of déjà vu squeezed his heart with icy fingers.

She'd vanished just as completely as she had the night

of the Lotus Moon, but this time his head was filled with awful images of disaster. Where was she? Had she abandoned him again? Had his overeager advances frightened her away, or was she hurt somewhere, perhaps a victim of that tipsy tiger or some venomous reptile?

Heart pounding with dread, he staggered barefoot through the sinister silence of the ruined compound, searching for any sign of her, his throat too dry to do more than croak her name. Sweat rolling from every pore, he climbed over a broken wall onto a low hillock, then came up short.

A paved terrace lay below him, bounded by an intricately carved wall of bas-relief scenes containing a multitude of figures in various positions. But it was the flesh-and-blood female figure holding a banana frond while making the traditional *dodok* that made his breath catch.

"Miri!" Unmindful of anything but reaching her as quickly as possible, Tony plunged headlong down the grassy embankment.

Miranda looked up in alarm. "Tony, be careful!" She was on her feet, running to meet him, by the time he skidded, scraped and bruised, to the base of the hillock. "What is it? What's happened?"

He grabbed her bare shoulders in a furious grip. "Don't *ever* do that again!" he bellowed.

Fresh from her bath, she smelled sweetly of crushed flowers, and her wet hair had been worked into an intricate knot at her nape. She wore only the sarong knotted about her bosom with a single peach-colored blossom tucked into the shadow between her breasts. Bewildered, she stared at him, her full lips parted in amazement. "Don't do what?"

"Leave me like that!" With a desperate groan, he caught her neck and kissed her savagely, as if he could brand her as his own in this manner so that she would never again forget it. When he lifted his head, he was breathing hard. Her eyes were closed, and she hung limp and docile in his arms.

"Miri? Did I hurt you? I'm sorry, dearling. You scared me to death—"

"I think," she said in a shaky voice, "that you must be feeling somewhat better."

"What? Ah, yes, I am."

"Good."

The open-handed blow she landed against his jaw rattled his teeth and made his ears ring. Dumbfounded, he held his cheek as she wrenched free, her eyes sparking glints of green.

"Why'd you do that?" he asked, a bit plaintive.

"If you persist in grabbing me as the mood moves you, *Captain Benedict*," she said icily, "then I shall be forced to smack you soundly each and every time!"

With a toss of her head, she pivoted and marched back to her forgotten banana frond. Disgruntled, Tony rubbed his jaw. Then his lips twitched. Damn if she wasn't right. His usually urbane manners were in a shambles due to her. But could he help it if the primitive emotions she aroused in him so easily were turning him into a barbarian? He'd better gather his control and apologize quickly or she'd write him off as a madman for good.

He strode after her. "Miri, you're absolutely right. I humbly beg your pardon and—what the devil are you doing now?"

Squatting, Miranda calmly arranged several choice pieces of fruit on the banana leaf, made a low obeisance, then sat back on her heels. The look she gave him was bland.

"Why, witchcraft, of course."

Chapter 7

"**Y**ou can't be serious!" Tony's long face expressed his shock.

She shrugged. "Are you so sure? You must admit you scarcely know me."

"I know you're no witch!"

"Really? The *dukun* taught me much, including the preparation of love charms. Who's to say this strange passion you profess is not a spell I cast over you?"

For an instant he was unsettled, then he shook his head firmly. "This is a dangerous jest, Miri."

Suddenly she laughed. "Perhaps so, but your consternation is ample reward."

"Paying me back?"

"As you so richly deserve." Rising, she dusted her hands.

"I'd rather you box my ears again than risk such blasphemy." His eyes narrowed as he glanced between her offering and the pendulous figure carved into the wall before them. "I know this demon. Semar again, is it not? What are you about, Miri?"

A faint color rose over her cheekbones, but she was unrepentant, even quietly defiant. "You may find it silly or even repugnant, but it is the way in this land. Like the ancient Greeks, the Javanese believe everything on the earth—the plants, the rocks, the sea—is endowed with a semidivine life."

"They believe these things have souls?" he demanded, incredulous.

"Of a sort. It is an imponderable force, invisible, but with the capacity for great good or great evil, so they endeavor to propitiate it with libations, prayers, and offerings."

"Is that what you're doing?"

She shrugged. "If we offended the spirit of Semar and started all of this trouble, then is it not practical to ask for his influence to restore the balance in our lives?"

Bemused, Tony grinned. "Miri, you are a pagan!"

"I am a Christian, sir," she retorted with quiet dignity. "But in this country, there are many names for God. Some call him Shiva; others, Buddha, Allah, Jesus. It is well to remember that to no man is revealed everything under heaven."

"So you're a philosopher, too."

"Nay, I am merely open to life's questions. Nothing here is absolute. Paradoxes fill all the stories and myths of gods and men. There are always twilights between night and day, good and evil, reality and possibility. Can you explain what began under the Lotus Moon? I certainly do not know who is the pagan here."

Her candor and unusual outlook delighted him. "I've never known a woman with such insight and perception."

She accepted the compliment with grace. "I pride myself on seeing the realities."

"Realities!" he scoffed. "You are as much a dreamer of possibilities as I am."

"I merely adapt to my situation as best I can. For example, I know that my wearing native dress would have me banned from most polite European communities, yet in this tropical country, I find it positively asinine to torture myself with too many layers of clothing.''

"If our countrywomen thought for a moment they could look half as beautiful as you, then I'm certain the styles would change instantly,'' Tony said, favoring her with an appreciative glance that made her blush. ''I'm sorry more haven't your good sense, for it tries a man's patience to contend with hoops and laces and petticoats, I assure you.''

''I daresay it does,'' she said dryly. ''But you misunderstand. While the sarong is practical here, in England I would just as quickly assume standard dress in order to function unobtrusively.''

''What a disappointment,'' he teased. ''It seems a shame to cover even an inch of so practical a woman.''

''You are outrageous, sir, by any standards.'' She took a step closer, inspecting his haggard features. ''However, I'll forgive you this time, for my instincts tell me you should not be up yet.''

''I'm fully recovered. We should have been on our way hours ago.''

''Hogwash. You're too weak to walk ten paces.'' In a manner-of-fact way, she touched his forehead, testing the temperature of his skin. ''At least the fever's gone, but this must be a day of rest for you to gather your strength, or we'll never reach Bantam.''

''Quite the little general, aren't you?'' he asked, amused at her taking charge of the situation.

''This is my world, Tony. 'Tis best you let me be your guide.''

''Perhaps you're right. You've done an excellent job as my guardian angel so far. Dare I believe it's because of your growing affection for me?''

''You delude yourself, sir! Mere human decency required it. Besides, to insure my sister's safety, I would have done as much for any rogue. Now, enough of this faddle! Are you hungry? I've gathered coconuts.''

''I'd rather avail myself of whatever bathing pool you

found first." He wrinkled his nose. "I stink of my own sweat."

"Many Englishmen would hardly find that a reason to endanger their health with the risk of total immersion," she said with a small smile.

He snorted. "I'm a progressive, Miss Langford, a man ahead of my time. Bathing holds no terrors for such an intrepid soul as I!"

"You buffoon!" she said, laughing. "Very well. This way."

Miranda led Tony through the maze of ruins and then followed another line of those curious marker stones into the dim and shady jungle, down a natural slope that ended in a slow-moving stream. Palmetto and giant ferns covered the banks, and flowering vines twisted into a lacy arbor overhead.

"Any crocodiles?" he asked humorously.

"Probably not, but you could see a snake." She couldn't help a smile at his dismayed expression. "Usually harmless, of course, though I wouldn't take any chances."

He looked at the green water and swallowed. "Thanks for the advice."

She plucked a small globe from a leafy shrub at the edge of the stream and handed it to him. "Crush this to work up a lather. It's a soap tree fruit."

He broke open the milky-fleshed fruit and sniffed it. "How curious. Wait, where are you going?"

"To give you some privacy, or do you expect me to supervise your toilette?"

He grinned and drawled, "The idea crossed my mind."

"I think not." Turning, she started back up the slope.

"Could you give me a hand with these bindings first? I can't quite reach . . ."

She knew it was a ploy, but rolling her eyes heavenward, she relented. He stood docilely enough while she fumbled with the stubborn knots, then unwrapped his chest. Her careful examination of his wound heartened her.

"It looks better," she murmured, her fingers gently probing the area. "How are your ribs?"

"I'm breathing easier, thanks to your nursing."

"You were very lucky." Solemnly she lifted her gaze to his. Her breath caught at the intensity shining in his slate blue eyes.

"Yes," he said in a husky tone, running his knuckles down her cheek in a feathery caress. "Yes, I was very lucky."

Shivering, she took a hasty step backward, breaking the electric contact, alarmed at her body's singing response to such a simple act. "I—I'll wait for you at the top of the rise. Just don't get your hurt too wet."

"But what if I fall? What if I have a dizzy spell?" he cajoled. "You can turn your back and preserve my modesty while simultaneously keeping me company. Come on, Miri. I may need you."

"Infant! All right, have it your way," she said, turning around with an exasperated flounce. "You spoke rightly about being spoiled. Have you always gotten everything you want?"

"Almost always," he admitted cheerfully, stripping out of his breeches. Grinning at her stiff back, he noticed she wore his dagger tucked under a fold of her sarong at her waist like a native's *kris*. Deftly slipping the blade free with one hand, he kicked his pants into a heap at her feet.

"I may as well scrape off this prickly hedge on my face as long as I'm at it," he said, wading into the stream. "Now, don't peek."

"As if I would!" Miranda sniffed disdainfully. She was acutely conscious of his state of undress, and her heart pounded in an erratic rhythm, but she strove for nonchalance. "You greatly overestimate your appeal."

"So beautiful and yet so cold," Tony mocked, making a huge production of splashing and scrubbing, all the while remarking loudly about how good it felt. "You're certain you wouldn't like to join me?"

"Captain Benedict, you forget yourself!"

"Ah, yes, our truce. Damned inconvenient, that." Another massive splash, and he said, "You can turn around now. I'm perfectly decent."

Miranda took a cautious look over her shoulder and found him sitting waist-deep in the opaque water, his wet hair curling at his temples, and the lower half of his face obscured by suds. He whistled between his teeth while he removed his beard with the edge of the dagger, pulling his cheek this way and that, then tilting his chin skyward to attack his thick neck and prominent Adam's apple.

"Careful you don't slit your own throat with such tomfoolery," she managed, dragging her eyes away from the sun-warmed expanse of his chest and shoulders. She picked up his discarded breeches, suddenly intent on dusting and brushing off as much accumulated soil as she could. "These are ruined, I'm afraid."

"My tailor will be devastated." Cupping his hand, he splashed water over his face, then, like a large and contented lion, shook his sun-streaked auburn mane, spraying the vicinity with an arc of iridescent water droplets.

"Perhaps I could rinse them out for you," Miranda said, kneeling at the stream's edge. She patted the small side pocket, drawing out the contents—the flint and steel, a coin—before she washed the garment. "They'll dry soon enough in this heat—"

Her words trailed off as she removed the final item, a jade snuffbox carved in the shape of a lotus blossom. The green gemstone felt warm against her fingers, smooth and hard, yet almost alive, evoking impressions of a man's hard, smooth flesh beneath her hands.

"It's lovely, don't you think?" Tony asked.

Miranda's head jerked up. "Yes, beautiful."

Still sitting in the water, he propped his elbows on his knees, slowly tapping the flat of the dagger against his palm. "I've quite a collection of these little baubles, but this one has always been my particular favorite for some reason. Peculiar, isn't it?"

Her fingers trembled on the snuffbox. "We all develop affection for certain items from time to time."

"No, it's more than that. Just touching it seems to bring me peace. I think perhaps it came into my possession for a purpose."

Miranda wet her dry lips and tried to laugh. "You're being fanciful."

He lifted his bare shoulders in a slight shrug. "Perhaps I'm a victim of the mysticism that pervades this region. Whatever, I'm convinced that carved lotus was a signpost, pointing me to you."

Her laugh was shaky. "How absurd."

"Is this the woman who makes offerings to Semar? How can you believe in one sign and not another?"

"I never said I believed exactly," she protested, unsettled by the blue flame that flickered in his eyes.

"I'll tell you what I believe," he said, suddenly fierce. "People said I was mad to set off on this voyage, but from the moment the plan first came to Kit and me, it was as if the idea was burned into my brain. I would let no one gainsay me, not my friends, my lawyer, not even my own mother. I told myself it was so I could recoup my fortune, but there was a restlessness in me, a wanderlust that could be quieted no other way. I was meant to come here, Miri, because I was meant to find you."

Breathless, she shook her head. "I don't know what to say."

"Say you feel it, too. From the moment I saw you standing in the moonlight, something touched me in a way I'd never guessed was possible." He held himself motionless, yearning and an uncharacteristic vulnerability etching his lean features. "I knew you and recognized you in my heart from the first, and I thought you felt the same magic. Tell me I wasn't dreaming."

How could she respond to his honesty with anything less than her own? "You weren't dreaming," she whispered.

He heard the reservations in her voice. "But?"

Miserably, she shook her head. "We've been over this before. I'll confess my weakness and my shame and still admit I'm grateful for one perfect night to treasure, but our circumstances—"

"Damn the circumstances!" In a rush of water, he was on his feet, nude and male and utterly magnificent. Rivulets of moisture ran down his chest, disappeared into the dark, curled nest of his loins, and trickled through the sandy dusting of hair on his sinewy legs. His knuckles were white on the forgotten dagger, and his blue eyes burned.

Clutching the lotus box, Miranda rose, too, her breath catching on a gasp as he stepped inexorably closer. She couldn't have looked away if her life depended on it. "Tony, don't!"

"You really don't understand, do you?" he asked, his throat working. "I don't want your gratitude, I want you!"

Lips parted, she stared wide-eyed, shocked and mesmerized by the desperation in his eyes. He took a step, another, his gaze raking her features, searching for the answers he wanted, then his glance flicked beyond her, and his expression changed.

Like lightning, he grabbed her arm, jerking her roughly behind him. He crouched, dagger ready, his face a snarling mask.

"Tony, what—?" She choked on her words.

Up the slope stood a group of native soldiers armed with swords and spears. The leader, a short, burly man in a dark blue sarong, waved his spear and called out in Javanese.

"Run, Miri," Tony said grimly, sweeping his dagger menacingly from side to side. "I'm bound to get a couple of these bastards before they get to me."

"No, Tony!" Peeking around his broad shoulders, she reeled off an answer to the intruders in Java's melodic language. The burly native nodded in reply.

"Do what I say, damn it!" Miranda's sudden laughter rankled Tony's tense nerves, and he scowled incredulously. "By God, Miri—"

"It's all right!" she said. "We are delivered." *In more ways than one*, she thought, caught between relief and hysteria.

"What the hell are you talking about!"

Tony's astounded expression and unself-conscious nudity produced several snickers from the assembled troop. Blushing to the roots of her hair, Miranda shoved his breeches at him.

"Clothe yourself, sir! His Highness, Prince Virat Amang,

commands our immediate presence, and I, for one, do not
intend to keep him waiting!''

The day-long trek to Prince Virat Amang's temporary
camp would have been impossible for Tony except for the
sturdy mountain ponies produced by Pak, the burly leader
of the scouting party and the prince's second-in-command.
Still, by the time they'd traveled through the jungle into
cultivated territory, skirted the terraced, mirrorlike rice paddies, and arrived at the green and secluded hillside compound of a small *desa*, or peasant village, Miranda was
again concerned by the fatigue and strain that etched Tony's
face.

Their arrival in the village of palm-thatched and plaited
bamboo huts created no small sensation, bringing forth
every villager, from the oldest wrinkled dowager to the
youngest round-eyed infant, to ogle the strange white-
skinned visitors. Pak brought them to a simple dwelling,
then left them in the charge of the young matron of the
house, instructing them to refresh themselves while he informed the prince of their arrival and made preparations for
the *selamatan*.

"What the devil is that?" Tony asked a bit later. He
joined Miranda on a bench in front of the hut after their
hostess had provided them with perfumed wash water and
fresh clothing.

"A *selamatan* is a ritual meal that marks any important
occasion in Java," Miranda explained. Her hair hung loose
and straight down her back, and she wore an intricately
patterned gold and ebony sarong that fell to her ankles, and
matching *kabaya*, or short-sleeved blouse. Despite the exotic attire, she appeared completely at ease, as cool and
regal as a sultana.

"Our presence must be an omen the prince does not intend
to take lightly," she continued.

"And an excuse for more offerings?" Tony asked, fid-
geting with his newly donned *bajoe*, a boxy shirtlike affair
that had replaced his own ragged silk garment. Unfortunately, Tony was much taller and broader than the typical

Javanese male, and his shoulders and arms were nearly bursting the seams of the *bajoe*. He had adamantly refused to exchange his breeches for a sarong.

"It is their way, as I said before," Miranda replied quietly, and looked away.

She was still wary after Tony's impassioned outburst at the stream. His well-remembered words stirred her strangely, yet she found his sentiments hard to believe. What use would a charming rogue like Anthony Benedict have for a plain woman like her except for the passion of the moment? It was better to avoid any return to such a topic, she decided. Still, his haggard expression brought her compassionate concern to the forefront yet again.

"Are you certain you feel able to meet the prince after our arduous day? I could make your excuses."

The lines in his face softened with indulgent humor. "What a mother hen you are! And how I delight in all your clucking over me!"

Her lips pursed in annoyance. "Never mind! I regret I bothered to ask."

"Your care for my welfare is balm to my battered ego, Miri. I thank you for it, but I'm certainly not going to refuse the invitation of a man who is our best chance to leave this region intact. His interest hints that we may be valuable in some way to him."

Miranda nodded in agreement. "Because we fought the Dutchman, who is allied with Prince Amang's sworn enemy, the Sultan Palu Tanah. The prince's network of spies is formidable indeed to have brought him word of our plight so soon."

"Or else Steef himself mounted such a campaign for our heads that no one in this region has not heard of it," Tony remarked, the line of his mouth becoming grim. "I would know what bargaining power we have with this prince of yours. Besides, I'm starving."

She laughed softly. "Then you are indeed feeling better."

"Not if I have to sup on weird fruit again," he groused. "Is there no man's food in this country? I could eat a haunch of venison right now."

Miranda hid a knowing smile and rose as Pak arrived to escort them into the prince's presence. "Rest assured, sir, you will not go hungry this night."

With Pak in the lead, they followed a stone path through the village, then crossed a stream by way of an arched bamboo bridge wondrous in the intricacies of its architecture and construction. Finally they came to a large stone hut set alone in a grove of palms, with two huge banyan trees in the front whose multitude of branches dipped to the ground to root into a tangle of auxiliary trunks. Pak bade them to wait on the overhanging porch, then disappeared into the house.

"Waringins," Miranda offered, catching Tony's curious eye on the unusual species of tree.

He shook his head, half in wonder, half in distaste. "I'll take good English oak over such any day."

Miranda felt a pang at the sudden reminder of Tony's true home, and his imminent departure from Java. Annoyed at herself for the unreasonable stab of loneliness this thought provoked, she frowned at him.

"Waringins are a princely symbol in this land, an indication of nobility."

"Monstrosities," Tony pronounced. "A suitable home for fairies and goblins."

Miranda smiled mischievously. "You're very astute. The *Pontianak* haunts these trees, a cruel sprite who lures unsuspecting men to their deaths with her beauty and her song."

Tony gave her a skeptical look. "And what makes this spirit so malicious?"

"Some say she is the soul of a dead virgin who never knew love, but would fain win it yet. But if a man kisses a deadly *Pontianak*, he is doomed, so beware, Captain Benedict."

"This sprite has all the earmarks of a discarded mistress," Tony remarked dryly, humor curling the corners of his mouth. "Is there no defense against such a vindictive fiend?"

"If a man is quick-witted and courageous, he might seize

a lock of the *Pontianak's* hair. Even so much as a single thread is a mighty talisman, and whosoever has it will live to a great age, rich, honored, and happy, the husband of a sultan's daughter and the father of princes.''

"What a fairy tale! I'll wager you actually believe it, too," he said with a laugh.

She gave him a mysterious look through the veil of her lashes. "The question is—do you?"

He stepped close to her, inhaling her ever-present fragrance of frangipani, and idly wrapped his index finger around a strand of her silvery-fair hair. "Perhaps I do, at that," he murmured.

With one swift movement, he pulled his dagger from his boot and neatly clipped the lock, holding it up in front of her startled eyes before she could even gasp her surprise. "Now I'm safe from your spell, eh, Miri? Or is it already too late for me?"

Involuntarily her fingers felt for the shortened place in her hair, and astonishment and fury made her splutter incoherently. "You . . . I . . . why, you—"

"A token only, my dear. Something of you to keep close to me always." Grinning, he pulled out the tiny jade snuff-box, dumped its contents, then carefully curled the lock inside and poked it back into his pocket slit. "I pray this charm brings me the prize I most desire."

The sudden heat in his gaze made her blush. "You're truly insufferable! I pray that you have enough sense to cease your foolishness, especially in the prince's presence. As you say, he is our best chance to reach Bantam, Rija, and your ship, and I sincerely hope you do not offend him and spoil our chances!"

"My dear, I can pull my forelock with the best of them, but I'll be damned if I'll make a *dodok* to this heathen. I'm an Englishman and the Mar—"

"In this land that means nothing! Hush, Pak's coming for us," Miranda interrupted. She gave Tony a severe look. "Just follow my guidance. Is that clear?"

Tony gave a short nod of assent, then followed her inside, inwardly cursing his loose tongue, thankful she'd interrupted his inadvertent slip. He'd always been proud of his heritage and wielded his power as the Marquess of Bentley to suit his own purposes, but he did not want his title to influence Miri in any way. Rather, he wanted her feelings to flow as honest and uninhibited as the night they met. The prideful fancy made him grimace sourly, but that was simply the way he had to have it.

Coconut oil lamps burned in the corners of the whitewashed room they entered, the perfumed oil blending with the pungent and spicy odors of food. Surrounded by retainers, a young man stood on a small raised platform before a low table spread with the numerous dishes of a magnificent feast. As Pak presented them, and Miranda responded to the formal introductions, Tony realized this youngster was not what he'd expected.

Prince Virat Amang was no more than twenty, and his dark, aquiline features revealed the Arabic blood in his aristocratic lineage. He wore a small turban, and his *bajoe* and sarong were fine quality but modest in color and design. Experience beyond his years and the gleam of powerful determination burned in the prince's black eyes, signifying a charismatic leader and a man to be reckoned with. When Miranda made a *dodok*, Tony thought it no more than expedient to show his respect, and swept the young prince his best courtly bow.

The prince gestured for Tony to take the right-hand place at his side at the *selamatan* table. Tony cast Miranda a questioning glance, and she nodded, then knelt down gracefully in the place next to Tony.

"I don't understand," he muttered. "Aren't we going to discuss anything?"

"It would be inauspicious now." Miranda smiled. "First, we eat."

For the next three hours, Tony and Miranda endured a courtly ceremony of pledges and toasts, and a meal of a seemingly endless number of elaborate courses. As they ate, Miranda quietly named the various *sambels*, side dishes that accompanied the mountains of rice that were the primary course. Tony gamely sampled *saté*, or meat grilled on green sticks, roasted goat, fish in all forms, sweets made from colored rice and palm sugar, stewed foul, salted duck eggs, chutneys, and highly seasoned sauces reeking of cayenne pepper.

"Tell me this is the last of it," Tony pleaded in a whisper when the servants finally brought in steaming bowls of hot tea and sweet comfits made from coconut and palm syrup.

Miranda laughed softly and took a dainty bite of her confection. "You did say you were hungry, did you not?"

"I'm as stuffed as Fairhaven's Christmas goose!" he groaned.

Her brows arched in a question. "Fairhaven?"

"The, ah . . . country house where my mother lives," he said lamely, knowing "house" was a misleading term when describing the stately mansion and lands that were the seat of the Bentley title and the Benedict family fortune. "It lies near a little village by the same name."

"My father's people lived near Bristol, but there was only Cousin Letty left the last we heard," Miranda said with a small sigh. Pak clapped his hands for attention just then, and she sat up straighter, murmuring to Tony, "Now we begin."

The young prince rose and made an oration of welcome, which Miranda quietly interpreted for Tony. When Amang had finished, Tony rose also, bowing to his host and the assembled personages. Then he caught Miranda's elbow and raised her to his side.

"Tell the prince I bring him greetings from the powerful and benevolent King George of England," he instructed her. "Extend our best wishes and our everlasting gratitude for his timely help and ask how we may repay his generosity."

Surprised at Tony's eloquence, Miranda relayed the message, then interpreted the prince's even reply. "Prince Amang says his greatest pleasure is to thwart Lord Palu and his allies in their every endeavor."

Tony glanced at her. "Have you fully explained our situation? Will he help us reach Bantam?"

Miranda again conducted an exchange with the prince,

her manner respectful and polite, yet very much self-assured. The prince nodded once, still listening intently. Smiling to himself, Tony absently pulled the lotus box from his pocket, stroking it for luck as he allowed himself to be impressed by Miri's diplomatic abilities.

He'd seen glimpses of her wit, her intelligence, and the capacity for passion that lay beneath her quiet reserve, and each new layer of her personality that was revealed only tantalized him further. How many other secrets lay beneath her composed facade? It would take a lifetime to discover them all, and he knew he'd never grow bored with her as he had with other, lesser women.

Barely listening to Miri's indecipherable conversation, Tony chewed the inside of his cheek, disturbed at the direction of his thoughts. Was he really thinking of a lifetime commitment, of marriage? Had he, the Wastrel Lord, the perennial bachelor, been mortally smitten by a pale slip of a girl with unorthodox views? His fingers moved even faster on the jade snuffbox. Perhaps he *was* bewitched. He only knew that for the first time since he'd lost his virginity, he was at a loss how to proceed with a woman. He almost wished the prince would delay them here so that he'd have the time he needed to woo and win her, but as Miri turned to him, smiling, he knew he'd lost the opportunity.

"Prince Amang will provide us safe escort to Bantam," Miranda explained, her gray eyes shining. "He is most pleased that Rija escaped the Dutchman and offers his protection, but it still may be safer to continue to Benkulen, especially since I received the impression that the prince is gathering his forces."

Tony's gaze sharpened. "For an assault on Lord Palu?"

"It must be."

Tony chewed on that for a moment, aware that the prince watched him closely. Deliberately, he stuck the jade lotus back into his pocket, then faced Amang again, hands on his hips and feet spread wide in a purely male stance of pride, one warrior to another.

"Tell the prince that I, too, know the burden of vengeance. To destroy the usurper and wreak havoc on that scurrilous Dutchman, I offer shot, black powder, and six of my ship's cannons to aid in his quest for justice.''

"You know well how to play this chess game of revenge," Miranda said softly. ''The prince would not have asked for supplies, and your offer places you in a special position of favor.''

"Just tell him.''

When Miranda relayed the message, the young prince's finely carved features relaxed imperceptibly and took on a look of satisfaction. He spoke again, and Miranda's eyes widened. She turned back to Tony.

"The prince accepts your gift, and begs you to receive, as a token of his great esteem, a hundred bags of rice and coffee, which he will send with us to Bantam, and his assurance that the Dutchman will not prosper.''

Tony smiled and bowed deeply. "He is most gracious.''

"And you are very sly, Captain,'' Miranda murmured.

"Until I can see to matters personally, I'll take any opportunity to strike at Steef's black heart, my angel. Perhaps I am beginning to understand the Eastern mind at last.''

The prince spoke again, and for the first time that evening, a smile lit up his features. Listening to him intently, Miranda flushed.

"What did he say?'' Tony demanded.

"It's nothing. A compliment.''

"Miri . . . ?''

Exasperated, she gave a little huff of breath. "If you must know, he offered you a position as a general over his troops. He thinks any man who has the courage to protect his . . . a woman when he's naked and virtually unarmed must be either a great warrior or a madman. He could use both when he attacks Lord Palu.''

Tony laughed, shaking his head while the prince and his retainers chuckled along. "Decline the offer, quickly, Miri, before I take complete leave of my senses and join his noble cause.''

"I think the prince understands our desire to reach Bantam.''

"Then wish him good luck for me. I hope he succeeds.''

Miranda made a *dodok* and spoke quietly. The young prince bowed once.

"*Insya Allah*," he said.

"*Insya Allah*," Tony repeated, surprising Miranda. "Yes, *God willing*, soon we all will meet our destinies."

Chapter 8

*T*eacher smoothed Sister's pale hair, helpless to soothe
the girl who shed bitter tears into her lap. Of all her
students, only this stranger, this fair, quiet child, had found
such a place in Teacher's ancient heart, but now there was
naught she could do to assuage the girl's grief.

"How can this be?" Sister sobbed. "Oh, Father . . ."

"Courage, my daughter," Teacher said. "Death is a
part of life, and we have no choice but to accept it."

"Why must evil triumph?"

"Do you not remember the Mahabharata tales? Life is
not a battle between good and evil, where there must be
winners, but an acknowledgment of the perpetual ebb and
flow of darkness and light."

"I don't want to accept it!" Sister scrubbed angrily at
her tears, but they fell unchecked.

"Think on Semar's death, little one."

"Prince Arjuna's comical servant?"

"Yes. Only we Javanese have given Semar and his sons
a special place in the epic tale brought centuries ago from

India. Only we place Semar in the center of the wajang, *for he was sent to earth to perform a special mission as friend, helper, and wise mentor of the Pandawa princes and all men."*

"But he was murdered, just as my father," Sister said bitterly.

"No. Arjuna was bewitched by Shiva into promising to kill his beloved servant, but to ease Arjuna's dilemma, Semar stood in a bonfire. Instead of dying, he revealed his true god-form and defeated Shiva. Your father now has shed his earthly form like Semar, and in the paradox of life and death, where dawn is dusk, and sunset is daybreak, his poignant might and compassion are set free."

Moisture streamed down Sister's pale cheeks. "But, Teacher, I shall miss him forever. How can I endure it?"

"You will, my daughter, because you must. And that is just another paradox."

"There must be a better way," Tony grumbled.

"Not in Java."

With a smile, Miranda continued to plod down the rutted track that bisected a verdant rice field. They followed a creaking two-wheeled cart loaded with sacks covered by a canvas and hitched to a lumbering, flop-eared water buffalo. To their rear, another equally slow-moving cart and nearly a dozen sturdy ponies made up the rest of their small caravan. Several of Prince Amang's soldiers and a half dozen peasant drovers formed their escort.

"It'll take us a month to reach Bantam at this rate!"

"When we took our leave, Pak said six days," she corrected. "That means only three more days now. If the rains continue to hold off."

Tony wiped his sweaty forehead with his sleeve and squinted at the sun hovering on the lip of a lofty green mountain rising like the back of an elephant to the southwest. A thin wisp of smoke rose from the mountain's cratered center, an indication that the volcano was merely resting. Three days on the road at this snail's pace and the frustration of being denied the privacy he craved with Miri by her own elusiveness and their escort's impassive but unwavering scrutiny had made Tony's temper as uncertain as the volcano's.

"How can you be so damn complacent?" he demanded. "Aren't you anxious to see your sister?"

Miranda's lips parted in surprise. "Of course I am. But wailing about our progress will not help her, and I've no wish to call the Dutchman's attention to us by galloping through the countryside. Besides, you were the one who agreed to trade cannon for cargo."

"Perhaps a strategic error," Tony murmured, then sighed. "At least Tassel will have sufficient time to replace the mainmast."

A flicker of trepidation crossed Miranda's face, an involuntary revelation that she was not as calm about their situation as she appeared. "And after that? How long will he wait in hope of your return?"

"Long enough. I wouldn't be surprised if Angus is planning to mount a rescue back to the Dutchman's holding. There's nothing the old man loves more than a good fight."

"I hope he knows better than to risk Rija!" Miranda said in alarm. "Poor thing! I know she's frantic with worry."

"Calm yourself, Miri. Your pretty little sister is safe. Angus may bark like a woman-hater, but he's really soft as goat cheese when it comes to helpless females. He'll take good care of her."

"She's so young, barely a child," Miranda said, her white teeth worrying the soft swell of her bottom lip.

"Young, perhaps, but fully a woman," Tony replied. The cart driver turned and spoke just then, and Tony stifled a groan. "Not again!"

"Another village. Quickly, under the tarp!"

Tucking up the hem of her borrowed sarong, Miranda scrambled onto the rear of the swaying cart, motioning for Tony to join her. Together they settled into a hollow space between the sacks of rice and aromatic coffee beans, then pulled the canvas over their heads.

"Do you think this is really necessary?" Tony asked, trying to accommodate his long legs within the confined space as the roll and tilt of the cart shook them like dried peas in a pod.

Miranda sat opposite, her arms folded about her knees to leave him as much room as possible in the shadowy hole. "Pak thought it a wise precaution. If we are seen, news could travel quickly to the Dutchman."

"I thought this was Amang's country."

"The populace is divided. Amang's is the stronger claim to the sultanate, but Lord Palu rules with fear, and his army is strong. It is the younger men who despise Lord Palu's oppression who slip into the jungle to join Prince Amang's cause. I fear the conflict will be long and bloody when it comes."

"Civil war often is."

"That's why I think it best that Rija and I go on to Benkulen." She hesitated, licking her lips. "Tony? I know I have no right to ask, but will you take us there?"

He felt his stomach sink. She was talking of their parting, and the fact that she could mention it without even a tremor in her voice cut him deeply. Forcing an even tone, he replied, "Why stop there? Why not come back to England with me?"

"Oh, I could not!" The cart dipped alarmingly as one wheel hit a hole, and her breath caught on a little gasp. "I could not expect Rija to leave her country, her heritage."

"Your love for your sister is admirable, Miri," he said, "but you cannot live your life for her. What happens when she marries? You'll end up alone."

"She's much too young to think of marriage," Miranda protested faintly.

"Not from what I've observed in this country. Girls even younger than she bounce their babies on their hips. Your duty as guardian must include making her a suitable match." His mouth twisted in a wry grin. "Take it from me, as one experienced in such matters, it isn't always an easy task."

"How do you know?"

"Have I not told you Lexa was my ward before she married Kit? A merry chase she led him, too." He shook his head ruefully. "At any rate, if the Princess Rija were already married—perhaps to someone as suitable as Prince Amang himself—then you'd have truly foiled Steef van der Djink in the cleverest way.''

"Mayhap you're right," she said slowly. "Though Prince Amang is not a suitable choice, for he may get himself killed if there is an uprising! Still, marriage for Rija might be her best protection . . ."

"Then what's wrong?"

Miranda sighed. "The duty of matchmaker is an onerous one indeed. I must weigh the realities sensibly to provide her a good and upright husband, yet still I wish Rija might find happiness and her heart's true love.''

"And what of you, Miri?" Tony leaned closer, his voice husky, and laid his hand on her knee, rubbing it through the thin stuff of her sarong. "Do you want the same heart's desire for yourself?"

She shook her head, shifting uncomfortably. "I'm too old for daydreams like that.''

"Nay, your hopes for Rija reveal your own romantic nature.''

His hand slid under the weight of silvery-fair hair at her nape, and suddenly their faces were so close, she could feel the warmth of his breath feathering across her lips. It was the first time he'd touched her in days, but she realized the defenses she'd tried to rebuild were as insubstantial as smoke in the face of his magnetic attraction.

"Don't, please," she whispered desperately.

In the dim, diffused light, his eyes were the blue of midnight. "What scares you about true love, Miri? The possibility that it exists at all? Or the fact that you can't admit you've already found it?''

"I haven't. You're mad—"

His lips dammed up the surge of her protest, capturing her soft whimpers and consuming her denial. Lying back against the stack of sacks, he used his strength to pull her on top of him. One hand tangled in her hair, holding her still for his foraging mouth, while the other splayed possessively in the small of her back, pressing her pelvis into the cradle of his thighs.

"Touch me, Miri," he pleaded. "Kiss me back. I've been dying of thirst for you all my life without even knowing it."

"This is crazy!" she panted, arching away, her hands planted on his shoulders. "You just can't—ah!"

Her movement gave him clear access, and he buried his nose in the valley between her breasts, pushing aside the overlapping sides of her *kebaja* to burn her skin with the wet rasp of his tongue. A shudder of pleasure rippled through her, and he smiled against the soft swell of her flesh.

"You can't deny what we do to each other, Miri." The pressure of his hand on her spine coupled with the rolling gait of the cart rubbed their bodies together in a most suggestive and pleasurable manner.

"It's unfair of you to torment me this way," she wailed softly, shamefully aware of the steely hardness of his manhood against her most sensitive folds. Even their clothing did little to quell the mounting excitement. "Your experience arms you with knowledge that turns my own body against me!"

With a growl, he rolled her to her back, his hand cupping the indention of her waist, one knee insinuated between her thighs. "If your lovely body was all I wanted, I could have had you that first night in the temple."

"You insufferable goat . . . That's a lie!"

Grinning wickedly, he ran his hand up her rib cage to cup one breast, then insolently flicked the hard pebble of her nipple with his thumb through the thin fabric of her *kebaja*. "Is it, my sweet?"

Frantic to stop the stab of piercing pleasure racing from her breast to her loins, Miranda covered his hand with her own. "Cease, you rogue! Can you not control your lust? Or must you complete my humiliation by forcing me to couple with you here?"

Looming over her, his expression darkened. "When I love you again, it will be only you and me with time enough to prove the depths of what we feel."

His intensity both thrilled and frightened her. "Unhand me! You're trying to confuse me with your wicked talk."

"Lord, why did you bless me with such a stubborn wench?" he demanded rhetorically.

"Anthony Benedict, you blackguard! Release me, you low-down—"

Bending, he fitted his mouth to hers, kissing her breathless, sweeping the sensitive corners of her mouth with his tongue as if to taste her essence and then coming back for more. When he lifted his head again, Miranda was dizzy, her bones molten, and somehow her hands had found their way around his neck.

"At last, a way to still your shrewish tongue." He laughed softly. "It feels so good to touch you again."

"It's wrong of us," she murmured tremulously. "A sin . . ."

"Nothing is sinful that feels this right, Miri. You're a part of me, and what we share will always be an act of love."

Tentatively she touched his face, running her fingertips down the hollow of his lean cheek, stroking the corner of his mouth. Though her brain warned his sincerity was suspect, her heart received another message, and suddenly she had no will or desire to fight him—or herself—any longer. Her eyes were full of a dawning wonder. "I shouldn't believe you, but . . ."

He swallowed. "But . . . ?"

"But, God help me," she whispered, "somehow I do."

Releasing a breath he hadn't been aware he was holding, Tony smiled crookedly. His voice was thick with tenderness. "Then I can be patient for the rest of it, Miri, if only you'll kiss me now."

With a shyness he found utterly endearing, she cupped his face with her palms, letting her fingers brush the burnished curls at his temples. Her hesitant glance roved over his face, as if impressing each feature—each tiny line crinkling the corners of his eyes, the arch of his sun-streaked brows, the finely carved jut of his nose, and the charmingly sculpted indentation of his chin—into a mental book of remembrance. When finally she was satisfied, she tugged him closer, the dark semicircle of her lashes fluttering down against the sun-kissed ivory of her cheek. Tony watched her until her soft lips met his, then his eyes closed, too, and he was lost in her sweetness.

It was the first kiss she'd freely bestowed since the night of the Lotus Moon, and its innocence mingled with the passion humming below the surface of their skin. Destroyed and reborn in the same instant, Tony exulted, knowing again the joy of her touch. When the kiss ended, he drew back with a groan to find he was shaking.

"See what you do to me, love," he murmured, pressing her palm against his pounding heart. "You have more power than you yet realize."

"I knew from the start I lacked the strength to resist your brand of madness." Her wobbly laugh tore at his heart. "This is hopeless, you know. It can't survive."

"I refuse to accept that. And you know us Benedicts, stubborn and—"

"—spoiled," she finished with a soft gurgle of laughter. "Dreamer. You think this is your own personal fairy tale, complete with the happy ending of your choice."

"I'll make it come true for both of us," he said, and she laughed again at his arrogance and self-confident assurance even while a thrill of foreboding arrowed down her spine.

"If only you could," she breathed, and gasped as his warm hand stroked her thigh. The look she gave him was one of such pure invitation that he missed the hint of desperation locked in its depths. "Mayhap we should take happiness as we find it."

"Here? Now?" That devastating slash appeared in his cheek at her abrupt turnabout. "You witch! First you lead me around in circles, then, even in surrender, you want to pipe the tune! Though you're as tempting as a goddess, I agree this cart is hardly suitable for the loving I have in mind with you. I want us to be somewhere we'll not be interrupted."

"Then when? Tonight when we camp?" Her fingers pressed urgently into his shoulders. Her decision made, she wanted him with the single-mindedness of a child, for as long as he might be hers. To delay even a moment longer seemed intolerable.

"Yes. Tonight." His voice was hoarse with the images of anticipation. He caught her lips again, savoring her flavor, and she responded eagerly, moaning a protest when he suddenly froze, then lifted his head to listen. Someone called out, and the cart's cadence changed.

"What is it?" Tony murmured. "Why are we stopping?"

Panicked cries and a sudden scream of pain made Miranda struggle upright, gasping. "Bandits!"

In the next instant, the tarp was dragged free, exposing them to air and daylight and flights of arrows splitting the blue sky. The cart driver slumped backward, a feathered shaft through the center of his chest.

"Stay down, Miri!" Tony pushed her back, then came face-to-face with a brown-skinned bandit climbing into the cart with a drawn sword.

Grabbing a heavy sack of coffee, Tony used it like a shield, then hurled it down onto the bandit's head with a blow that sent the man sprawling unconscious onto the dirt highway. Looking up, Tony saw their small caravan scattering in all directions, the nervous ponies bolting, several bodies lying motionless in the track, the rest of the panicky peasants hieing for safety across the rice paddies toward the distant jungle. Amang's soldiers scrambled to draw their swords, but the ambush had been carefully planned, and the superior numbers of the attacking force made the outcome inevitable. One frenzied pony's lead rope was trapped beneath the cart's wheel.

"Get ready! We'll have to make a run for it," Tony barked at Miranda, and pointed to the animal. She nodded in understanding. On horseback, there just might be a chance they could escape, too, leaving the plunder of rice and coffee to these bandits.

Pulling the dead driver's sword from his belt, Tony swung it over his head with a fair imitation of Angus's Scottish war cry, then leapt down into the fray. The dagger from his boot dispatched one surprised would-be assailant, and

Tony fought through the bloody melee, felling one opponent after another with his ferocious slashing. His hand closed over the pony's reins the moment Miranda screamed. Whirling about, Tony choked on a terrified shout. "Miri!"

A wiry bandit stood in the cart, holding Miranda from behind with one arm, and pressing the curved point of a *kris* against the base of her throat. A killing rage burned in Tony's blood. Involuntarily he took a step forward to protect his woman, but Miranda's captor spat a guttural order, and a cordon of soldiers surrounded Tony, encircling him with a menacing ring of blades. Snarling low in his throat, Tony parried and thrust, disarming one, drawing blood from another, his one determination to reach Miri. The man holding her shouted again, then jerked the blade even closer to her slim throat. Tony froze instantly, the meaning of the threat abundantly clear.

"All right, all right!" Tony said hoarsely, casting his bloodstained weapon aside. Immediately he was seized by rough hands, his arms jerked behind him and bound. "Miri, are you all right?"

"Y-yes." Her captor pushed her out of the cart, and she stumbled on the muddy track.

"Leave her alone, you whoreson!" Tony growled, and was instantly smashed in the in the gut with the butt of a spear. He fell to his knees, doubled over and gasping.

"Tony!" Miranda lunged for him, but her ebony-eyed jailer held her fast.

"Jesus!" Tony swore between gritted teeth. "What do they want? The coffee? Are they going to kill us for it or hold us for ransom? Ask him."

Miranda spoke hesitantly. The leader's grunted reply made her face go chalky.

"They're the sultan's men!" she whispered. "Oh, my God, Tony! Lord Palu wants *us!*"

Lord Palu's urgent command to find and return the English sea captain and Princess Rija's stepsister had evidently impressed their escort, for he spared neither his mounts nor his prisoners during their hurried hundred-mile journey cross-country to the *kraton*. Three days after their capture, Miranda and Tony stood before the sultan's empty dais, dirty, hungry, and staggering with fatigue.

"Are you all right?" Tony murmured, disliking Miranda's pallor. They'd hardly been allowed a word together during their arduous pilgrimage, but with his hands bound in front, he couldn't take her in his arms to comfort her as he wanted.

"As well as anyone can be who's scared to death," she replied with a wan smile. "I only wish I knew what Lord Palu intends to do with us."

"We can take a good guess." Tony's expression under his sandy-red growth of beard was grim. Quickly he assessed their position.

Immediately upon their arrival within the sultan's gates, they'd been half led, half carried through the open halls and arcaded passageways of the *kraton*, finally reaching the upper terraces of a marble-floored *pendopo*, a formal receiving area surmounted by tall carved pillars and a tiled roof. Colorful and sumptuous silk drapings floated in the cool southern breezes captured by these upper regions of the royal residence, and plump, kapok-stuffed floor pillows and satin settees completed the furnishings. The area was actually more covered porch than traditional room, with pierced half walls and balconies overlooking the lower courts, including the one where Tony had once been a guest at the *wajang* performance. Well-armed guards wearing turbans and identically patterned sarongs and *bajoes* were stationed at every doorway and opening, silent and watchful sentinels. Even a full-scale attack of King George's finest infantry would find the going difficult here. Escape appeared impossible.

Tony could almost hear Kit, in his guise as the Dandy, one of Carolina's most infamous privateers, giving his advice on their apparently hopeless situation. *When might fails, rely on guile.*

"On your knees, infidels!"

The English command caught Tony by surprise, as did the blow across his back that knocked him to the floor.

Cursing, his ribs stinging, he tried to rise, but the guard's foot in the small of his back and Miri's frantic hand on his arm prevented him.

"Tony, please! Stay as you are," she whispered, her own forehead pressed to the cool marble. "The sultan!"

Face contorted in pain and rage, Tony peered up at the dais, where a servant held the royal golden parasol over the round and happily Buddha-like figure of the Sultan Palu Tanah, resplendent in red and purple robes and a most un-Buddha-like scowl. And next to him, dressed in elegant black as always, was the golden and angelically handsome Dutchman.

Tony's breath hissed between his teeth. "Steef!"

Steef van der Djink merely lifted one pale eyebrow and smiled.

Lord Palu mounted the dais, planted himself on an armless settee, then gestured his retainers into place below him. The group of older men with impassive expression and obsequious demeanors shuffled to the foot of the dais, but one hovered at the sultan's shoulder, and Tony recognized him as the official interpreter. Lord Palu spoke sharply.

Hesitantly Miranda sat back on her heels, then gave Tony her arm. "We may rise."

"How very gracious," Tony said dryly.

"Best watch your tongue, Englishman," Steef advised. "If you displease Lord Palu, he may take a notion to cut it from your head."

"How incovenient. Then I couldn't tell him you meant to cheat him out of his coffee duties with a little behind-the-back smuggling," Tony told his erstwhile partner.

The Dutchman's perfectly formed features tightened into a hard mask. "I should have finished you over your soup."

Tony's grin was insolent. "And bloodied your expensive carpet? I knew you wouldn't risk the mess."

Lord Palu's bellow for quiet could not be mistaken in any language. His angry tirade and vigorous gesticulations left little open to interpretation—he was ill-pleased with everyone. The interpreter bowed and translated his master's message for the foreigners.

"Lord Palu grows tired of these childish games. Is this how you repay his kindness, Englishman? By tempting his regent to cheat and betray his master? Fortunately, my lord's Dutchman is too smart to play such a fool, and brought the knowledge of your crime to Lord Palu immediately."

"I'll bet!" Tony snorted, subsiding only when Miri put her trembling hand on his arm. The interpreter continued.

"The upstart Amang is but a gnat against Lord Palu's might, and he loves his people too well to lay waste to the land. In his wisdom, Lord Palu decrees a blessed marriage between a daughter of his heart and his trusted regent to bring his subjects peace. But out of her wickedness, the jealous sister has hidden his jewel away. What say you, woman?"

Eyes on the floor, Miranda stepped forward, addressing the overlord in flawless Javanese. "This lowly servant regrets any offense, most gracious sovereign. Forgive my ignorance, but since a match between my sister and her foster father's murderer must be an abomination before almighty Allah, I knew the scheme was none of yours."

"You are clever, lady," Lord Palu grunted, "but it will avail you nothing if my wrath falls fully on your head. Now, speak! Where is the Princess Rija?"

Raising her eyes, Miranda feigned her surprise. "Indeed, my lord, I do not know."

"What evil trick is this, you serpent?" the sultan roared.

"No trick, my lord," Miranda protested. "See my grief, witness my tears, hear my wails of sorrow! Your greed-filled regent wrongfully attacked us when the Englishman had taken pity on our lowly state. In the confusion, both Captain Benedict's ship and my sister were lost. Truly, I would welcome your help in restoring her to my care."

"Your loyalty stinks of monkey excrement, lady. How came you to be that traitor Amang's hands?"

"The Englishman was badly hurt, my lord, and my debt to him was one of honor," she said, gesturing to Tony, whose expression registered his puzzlement. "Even now, he suffers with his wound. Forgive me, my lord, but when

kindly folk offered their help, I did not stop to ask which
master they served.''

"Foolish woman! Your failure will buy you a traitor's
death!''

Miranda sank to her knees. "Your pardon, lord, I beg.''

"Then tell me where the princess is!''

Hanging her head, Miranda knew her life hung on the
balance, yet she could no more turn Rija over to Lord Palu
and the Dutchman than she could have walked the valleys
of the moon. Since she wasn't exactly certain Rija was still
aboard the *Mirage* or that the ship had even made it to
Bantam, it was only a small lie when she whispered miserably, "I do not know.''

Lord Palu's face grew purple under his natural dusky
color. "Perhaps your memory will improve if I have my
men remove your Englishman's ear?''

"What?'' Miranda gasped and blanched. Involuntarily
her gaze swung to Tony, then focused on his left ear and
the tiny brown mole that was suddenly so precious.

"Perhaps his right hand?'' the sultan speculated idly. "Or
his genitalia?''

"My lord, you would not be so unjust!'' she cried, aghast
and panic-stricken.

"Miri, what is it?'' Tony demanded. "What's he saying?''

"He—he says he'll have you tortured unless I reveal
Rija's hiding place,'' she choked, eyes brimming.

"I'd take the threat seriously if I were you, old friend,''
Steef said, laughing. "I've seen his people slice a man to
ribbons while he still lived.''

"And no doubt you enjoyed every minute of it,'' Tony
sneered. "What a choice! Do you hope for such a treat
again, or must you settle for the princess?''

The Dutchman shrugged. "Why not both?''

"Monster! Unnatural creature!'' Miranda's hands balled
into white-knuckled fists. "Rija is better off dead than wed
to you!''

"That can be arranged as well.''

Lord Palu spoke again in a booming voice. "Well, lady? Have you no answer?"

"My lord . . ." Miranda began, her tone pleading.

The sultan pointed at Tony. "Take him."

"Nay!" Frantic, Miranda prostrated herself on the floor at the base of the dais and pressed her forehead against the sultan's plump, sandal-clad foot.

"My lord, you must not!" she begged in utter terror. "The Englishman was my dupe! He had no knowledge that Rija and I came aboard his ship, nor any inkling that helping us would offend you. Have mercy, O Mighty One! Make me a slave, anything! But for justice's sake, spare him!"

The sultan halted the approaching guard with a single lifted finger, and his gaze was speculative. "Your love betrays you, woman. Speak, or see your lover die."

"Miri, don't . . ." Not quite understanding her obvious distress but reluctant to see her humble herself before this tyrant, Tony drew her to her feet and pulled her to his side. She stared at the sultan in shocked horror.

Of all the nightmares in the universe, this had to be the worst—to choose between the sister whom she loved and this man whom she adored with all her heart. She was forced to admit it to herself now. How she'd dodged and parried, trying to deny the truth that had been born between them the night of the Lotus Moon! But the veil was stripped, and all revealed. She'd loved Tony unconditionally from the moment she'd seen him, trapped in a band of silver moonlight, and everything that had happened since had been merely a slow revelation as her soul unwrapped the mystery of Anthony Benedict.

But what a dilemma! Could she sacrifice honor and loyalty and duty for Tony's sake? What of her love for Rija? But Rija was safe for the moment a hundred miles away, and Tony—sweet, spoiled, magnificent man!—was here and at the mercy of an angry monarch bent on revenge or worse.

"Bantam," Miranda gasped on a piercing breath that was all naked betrayal and giddy relief. "They took the *Mirage* to Bantam, and Rija went with them."

Satisfaction spread over the sultan's jowly face. "Dutchman?"

"My men in Bantam already have their orders," Steef said. "They will be found."

"Miri! What have you done?" Tony had followed enough of the conversation to catch its drift, and his expression was thunderstruck, angry, disillusioned.

"What I had to do," she murmured, gulping for air. "They would have killed you."

"Damn it, you've put my ship at risk, as well as your sister! You didn't have to tell this filth anything! Why'd you do it?"

Her eyes were silver-gray with a fathomless anguish. "Don't you know?"

He looked blank, then shocked, then wondering. He caught her hands. "Miri . . . ?"

"What is your will, my Lord Palu?" the Dutchman asked. "How do you suggest we dispose of these two annoyances?"

Before the sultan could reply, there was a disturbance at the opening to the *pendopo*. Lord Palu scowled at the hurried approach of a liveried minion. With a start, both Miranda and Tony recognized Ishta, the sultan's servant.

"What audacity is this?" Lord Palu demanded.

Ishta made a deep *dodok*. "Your pardon, O Mighty One. A rider just arrived with word Virat Amang attacks the southwest gate!"

Lord Palu hefted his bulk from the bench and started off the dais. "Vile spawn of a toad! Prepare my charger and sound the call to arms! I will destroy this vermin myself!"

"My lord," Steef said, gesturing to the prisoners, "what of these? Should I kill them now?"

The sultan's black eyes narrowed, almost disappearing in his plump face. "I may yet have use for them. Ishta, lock them up."

"Master," the servant said, "it is done."

"We are not finished, Englishman," Steef growled.

Tony's mouth curled in contempt, and he gave a mock bow. "I await your pleasure, sir."

With a gesture, the sultan swept from the chamber, taking his entourage and the disappointed Dutchman with them. Ishta barked rapid orders, his betel-blackened teeth bared in a feral smile. Chilled, Miranda instinctively stepped closer to Tony.

"It appears our friend hasn't forgotten his insult," he commented wryly. "At least his grievance is not as bloody as the Dutchman's."

"It's all my fault," she wavered. "What shall become of us?"

"Courage, my sweet." Raising his arms, Tony looped them over Miranda's head and crushed her to his heart. With a sharp command, Ishta ordered the guards forward. Dipping his head, Tony kissed Miri hard before they were torn apart and dragged in opposite directions.

"Tony!" Struggling, Miranda fought a profound fear that she would never see him again.

"Make your offerings, my little witch," he called as the guards hauled him roughly from the room. "Our best hope is a victory for Amang!"

Their hopes were not to be realized.

For two endless days, time for Miranda was marked only by the muezzin's high call at morn and eventide, summoning the faithful to the sultan's mosque for prayers. After countless prayers of her own, she was finally released from her confinement in a stifling room in the women's quarters, and again escorted to the *pendopo*. Her eager questions were met with monosyllabic replies from her stoic guards, but she gleaned enough to fill her with dread.

The prince's attack at the *kraton*'s perimeter had not been successful, and the revolutionary forces had been forced back into the jungle. Of Tony's fate she could learn nothing, and guilt, fear, and loneliness ate at her heart with equal fervor. Though trepidation made her quake with each step, she forced herself to stand erect and walk through the halls with composure. Having sacrificed her honor for the man

she loved, all she could do now was meet her fate with
dignity.

But her composure deserted her when she reached the
airy *pendopo*, for the first face she saw was Rija's.

Chapter 9

"Sister!"

Rija flung herself into Miranda's arms, then dissolved into tears. Oblivious to everything and everyone else in the *pendopo*, Miranda comforted her as she had when Rija was a little girl, crooning and smoothing back the inky strands of hair from her damp cheeks, at once overjoyed and profoundly dismayed.

"I thought never to see you again," Rija sobbed. "Praise Allah, you're alive!"

"Rija! Sister, hush!" Miranda whispered. "Are you unharmed?"

Rija gulped and nodded, her dark eyes liquid with emotion. "No one hurt me, but the Dutchman's men found us in Bantam. The Englishman's ship was taken, many sailors killed, and Sahib Angus lost overboard . . . Oh, Miri, I fear the old one is dead, just like Noppa!"

"Oh, no." Grief and guilt made Miranda's stomach lurch. Her desperate gamble to save Tony from torture or mutilation had only succeeded in making matters worse.

When he heard of Angus's and the *Mirage*'s fate, could he understand the selfish choice she'd made and forgive her? Knowing her actions had resulted in Rija's capture, could she forgive herself?

"Quite a touching reunion," boomed Lord Palu from his dais. Today the sultan's robes were the yellow silk of celebration, and under the golden parasol his scowl was replaced by a smiling, almost beatific expression. "Wouldn't you agree, Dutchman?"

From his place beside the throne, Steef van der Djink nodded, his narrow, ice blue gaze fastened in ill-disguised covetousness on Rija. Miranda shuddered uncontrollably, and she gently loosed Rija's clinging hands.

"Quiet now, sister," Miri said in low, stern voice. "Show them how a royal princess conducts herself in a time of trial."

Rija took a deep breath and squared her slim shoulders. "Yes, Miri."

"Is is not a joyful thing when sisters love each other?" the sultan remarked, his smile jovial. "Come, my ladies."

Rija and Miranda glanced at each other, then slowly approached the dais. The room was filled with nobles, dignitaries, and the sultan's wives and concubines, who watched them curiously, their attitudes expectant. The two sisters performed the ritual *dodok* in graceful unison, then rose again.

"You see I have restored your sister safely to you, lady," Lord Palu said to Miranda.

"I am grateful, my lord," she replied uneasily.

"Then show your gratitude by bestowing your blessing on the union of the Princess Rija and my regent."

"My lord, you know my objections." Miranda swallowed hard. "I regret that I cannot do your bidding."

The sultan clucked softly, as though chiding a stubborn child, but still his good humor did not fail him. "I have no doubt you will be persuaded."

Raising a plump hand, he signaled a guard, and a group of onlookers crowding a pillared opening melted back, allowing two muscular soldiers to drag forward a shackled man whose rusty auburn curls framed a badly battered face.

"Tony!" Miranda's horrified cry ripped from her throat, and she started toward him, but was brought up short by her guards' crossed spears and menacing stares. The soldiers released Tony at the foot of the sultan's dais, and in slow motion, he sank to his knees, swaying with weakness. Pressing the back of her hand against her lips, Miranda fought a wave of nausea.

He'd been beaten, repeatedly, by someone who knew how to inflict pain without killing the subject too soon. His left eye was surrounded by purple flesh and swollen nearly shut. His lower lip was split and puffy, and dried blood from his mouth and nose matted his strawberry stubble. Miranda's gaze slid down Tony's bare torso, taking in the bluish bruises and fiery red abrasions overlacing his half-healed wound, and as she noted each mark, there was an answering quiver of pain in her belly. Lifting her anguished gaze again, she met the slate blue gleam of Tony's good eye. Unbelievably, he winked at her.

Lord Palu studied the Englishman with interest. "I see your fine hand in this work, Steef."

"It was necessary to ascertain what the English dog knew about Amang, sire," the Dutchman said with a negligent shrug. "It was not much, but you see I did not kill him—yet."

Lord Palu turned back to Miranda. "Now, lady, perhaps you will reconsider your decision? Or would you rather chose which portion of your lover I'll feed to the crocodiles first?"

Despair burned through Miranda's veins, followed by a deadly calm. "The world will proclaim your wickedness, my lord, for giving me such a choice that is no choice at all. I will give you no answer, for you will kill us at any rate."

"How little faith you have in my mercy!" laughed the sultan. "Come, the princess must have the blessing of her family to appease the spirits."

Again, Miranda weighed the realities, balancing Tony's

life against her honor. "If I do, will you let the Englishman go free?"

"He must pay for his own crimes."

"It appears he has already paid too well for them," Miranda said, her voice wavering.

"You may yet save him some suffering, if you but will."

Miranda shook her head, her expression resigned, yet defiant. "You think I am powerless before you, my Lord Palu, so you torment me heedlessly, and torture an innocent man. Yet hear me well, for I know the *dukun*'s ways. If you give the princess to your regent, the union will be fruitless, the gods of your forebears vengeful at such an indecency, your line barren because of the inequity of the act."

Her words amounted to a curse, and they brought an uneasy hush over the assembled throng of nobles. At Miranda's side, Rija stifled a gasp of dismay.

"This whore defies your will yet again, my lord," Steef said, his beautiful face contorting with anger. "She lay with the Englishman in the house of your enemy! Under the law of Islam, is not her life forfeit?"

The sultan looked thoughtful. "An excellent solution."

Tony caught Miranda's eye. "What are they saying?" he croaked, painfully hoisting himself to his feet.

"Deciding my fate." She swallowed harshly. "I wronged both you and Rija with my weakness."

She told him Rija's report, dying inside as Tony's mouth grew grim.

"I'll not believe Angus gone until I see it myself," he pledged. "He's a tough old bird. Hard to kill." He grimaced painfully. "Like me."

Miranda's eyes filled. "What have they done to you?"

"Looks far worse than it is," he wheezed. "I'll have a debt to collect from that damned Dutchman when this is over, but never mind that now. Finish telling me what that fat slug plans to do!"

Succinctly Miranda repeated the gist of the sultan's words. "It's easier to kill me than deal with a stubborn female." Her lip trembled. "How could I choose between you and Rija? So I've failed you both."

"Widgeon! Only you would accept all the blame." His cheek flexed in a crooked half smile. With a swiftness that belied his earlier stiffness, he stepped boldly forward, grabbing the royal interpreter by the arm. "Speak to the sultan for me! Tell him I challenge his ruling. Say it!"

The startled courtier's eyes bulged, but he jabbered obediently.

"By the laws of Allah, even the sultan cannot punish a woman who belongs to another," Tony continued. He turned to Miranda and took her hand. "I claim a husband's rights over this woman."

Miranda stared, amazed and befuddled as the interpreter repeated the message. The sultan began to chuckle, his Buddha's belly shaking under the brilliant yellow robes like a saffron cake. He spoke, and the courtier turned back to Tony.

"Lord Palu asks how you make such a claim, Englishman."

"We were betrothed the night of the Lotus Moon. By English custom, I hold all the rights and privileges of a rightful husband excepting the formality of the wedding. Her life is mine, so stay your hand. No one may punish her but me!"

Lord Palu's delighted grin grew even broader when he heard this. With a sharp clap of his hands, he issued commands right and left, and the throng visibly relaxed, laughing and smiling. Only the Dutchman scowled, bowed stiffly, turned on his heel, and marched out. Rija pressed her hands to her mouth to hide a smile of joy. Tony turned his swollen face to Miranda, muttering under his breath.

"What is it? What's happening?"

In a daze, she shook her head. "You are too clever by far, Anthony Benedict!"

"You mean he accepted my argument?" Tony tried to smile, but it hurt too much.

"Oh, yes, he accepted it," Miranda choked. "It was just

the excuse he needed to proclaim a *selamatan* to mark his
victory over Prince Amang.''

Tony gave a relieved sigh. ''Well, it's a reprieve at
least.''

''Not exactly,'' she said, stifling the urge to giggle wildly.

''Why?''

''Lord Palu has decreed there must also be a wedding.''

Tony's expression darkened. ''Not Rija and Steef!''

Her pale cheeks blazed, and her voice shook. ''No, Englishman—you and me.''

He was silent, his expression hard to read under the swelling and bruises. Thinking him dumbfounded, Miranda tried
to swallow, but her throat was thick with misery.

''I'm sorry, Tony. Lord Palu toys with us like a tiger
tormenting its prey before finally devouring it. A moment
ago I thought he'd execute me, but now it suits his humor
to play us thusly.''

''When will this wedding take place?'' Tony croaked.

''Immediately. See,'' she said, indicating two approaching groups, one of nobles, the other of their wives, ''they
come to act as substitute families by taking us to be prepared.''

''Mayhap I can expect better treatment from these than
I got from Steef,'' Tony muttered.

''A ceremony and a feast will distract the sultan's dis-
pleasure from us, at least for a while. If we go along with
it, mayhap there will be a chance later to escape this madness.''

Her expression was uncertain, but the tittering assembly
of women was upon her, urging her with touches and ges-
tures to return with them to the women's apartments to
prepare for the unexpected treat of the newly proclaimed
festivities. Harried now as the women drew her away, Miranda hastened to reassure him of her motives, calling over
her shoulder.

''A wedding will be meaningless without our consent.
Do not think I mean to hold you to any vows pronounced
under coercion. I fear your generous lie bought you more
than you bargained for.''

"Nay, my lovely pagan." Surrounded by nobles, Tony watched her departure with eyes that smoldered, and his voice held an odd inflection. "I rejoice to find the truth has gained me my heart's desire."

Hours later, after Tony had been bathed and shaved in perfumed water, pampered with soothing balms and ointments, dressed in silver-embroidered *bajoe* and sarong of emerald silk, then led through the *kraton* with the other male guests to the mosque to repeat the holy words of the Javanese wedding ceremony—certainly it was an oddity to him that no woman was ever allowed at her own wedding!—they finally brought him to the hall where his bride awaited.

Double rows of excited women guests in a rainbow array of dress sat in attendance. From out in the courtyard came the oddly rhythmic cadence of bells and drums from the *gamelan* orchestra. The floor could not be seen beneath the pastel carpet of fresh flower blossoms, and their heady sweetness rose to mingle pungently with the spicy fragrance of incense. But Tony's eyes were drawn to the figure sitting as though carved from stone underneath a glittering golden canopy in the center of the hall. At his entrance, she raised her silvery gaze, and his breath stopped.

Miri.

His pagan angel. His bride. His wife now, according to the laws of this land. And she was the most beautiful thing he'd ever seen.

She was dressed as she had been the night they'd met, with bare arms and shoulders and a flowered headdress of jessamine. Her sarong was cloth of gold with a drapery of gold-woven silk, and her sash and breast cloth were dark green, growing lighter from the center out so that the gold beneath it glinted through. Her girdle was gold and ornamented with jewels, and their glitter was echoed on a neck collar and the pins of the diadem that held her hair in a coil the shape of the crescent moon. Bracelets graced her slender wrists, and bands shaped like serpents with dangling gold chains circled her upper arms.

But it was her expression that set his blood to thundering

in his ears—at once innocent and knowing, vulnerable yet unafraid, proud but giving, the duality that was the eternal Eve. And she was his. At last.

Almost in a daze, Tony, escorted by the two senior nobles, walked across the carpet of flowers to meet her while she rose and stepped forward, with Rija supporting her on one hand and the sultan's eldest wife on the other. A few feet apart, they stopped, then at the urging of their mentors, exchanged rolled-up siri leaves filled with flowers.

Miranda's eyes were wide with apprehension. "I—I feel as though I'm in a play," she whispered under her breath as they made the exchange.

"A *wajang* play," Tony agreed in a low voice, "and the sultan is the puppeteer, our lives merely a passing amusement. What do we do next?"

"Sit now." Miranda knelt down, sitting back on her heels, and Tony followed suit, sitting cross-legged across from her.

"You're a lovely bride," he said, his voice suddenly thick.

Blushing, she shook her head. "Remember, this is only an illusion."

"No." Reaching out, he took both her hands in his, oblivious to the *gamelan* music and the watchful eyes surrounding them. "It's real, Miri. I've been in love with you from the moment we met. I may have said my vows in a foreign tongue, but I meant them in my heart, no matter that fate, or God, or some maniacal puppeteer orchestrated this moment."

Shaken, her hands trembled in his. "But this is all so absurd . . ."

"Granted, but isn't it a continuation of the magical events that brought us together? Absurd or not, you're the only woman I've ever wanted to tie myself to, and I'll joyfully marry you in the name of whichever god you like, if only you'll have me." His mouth twisted ruefully at her astounded expression. "I haven't a thing to offer you but myself, and even that's not as pretty as it was, so can you blame me if I seize this moment to make you mine forever?"

"Oh, my dear," she murmured, her pale eyes searching his battered features, "can you never stop your teasing? Even bruised, you are beautiful in my sight."

"Then tell me what you feel." The words seemed wrenched from his very core, revealing a man with every human doubt, every vulnerability, every need. "Do you care for me at all?"

"I love you beyond telling," she said simply. "You complete me in ways that I can neither explain nor understand."

"Then marry me, Miri. Make it real with me." His hands tightened on hers and his voice was earnest. "You told me once that we should take the happiness we find. I would have preferred other circumstances, but I swear we'll come through this and make a life together."

She was breathless, her head spinning and her heart pounding with the impossibilities of it all. Dared she believe even for an instant that she could dream the dreams of other women? That she had found a heart-mate to bring her love, a home, children?

"You're sure this is what you want?" When he nodded, she knew, impossible or not, her decision was made. Tremulously she smiled. "How can I deny that which my own heart yearns for so ardently?"

"Then before our Christian God, repeat the words," he said urgently. "I, Anthony, take thee, Miranda..."

"I, Miranda, take thee, Anthony..."

"...to be my lawfully wedded wife..."

"...husband, to love, honor, and cherish..."

"...in sickness and in health..."

"...from this day forward..."

"...as long as we both shall live."

Tony gently cupped her face in his palms and smiled. "Kiss me, wife."

She obliged, taking care of his split lip, shaking beneath the utter tenderness of his mouth on hers and the warmth of emotion that filled and enveloped them, at least for a moment, in love's protective circle.

Tony raised his head, still smiling, then glanced around

at the curious seated onlookers. Behind Miri, Rija stood
quietly, her face wreathed in a happy smile. "Are these
people waiting for something?" he asked humorously.

"Oh!"

Blushing and bemused, Miranda placed her hands beneath
her chin and made a *dodok* to her new husband. Sliding
forward on her knees, she bent and kissed his right knee,
ignoring Tony's startled scowl. For the first time she noticed
he wore his own old, stained breeches beneath the emerald
sarong, and she grinned inwardly, imagining the ruckus he'd
no doubt caused while explaining an Englishman never willingly gave up his pants! At least he'd exchanged his worn
boots for a pair of velvet slippers. Coming back on her heels
again, Miranda made a final *dodok* and smiled.

"What was that for?" he demanded.

"It is a token of your new wife's loyalty and loving
submission, a Javanese symbol of Christ's instructions."

He grinned. "I like the sound of that, but judging by
your stubbornness in the past, I fear you may have trouble
following such a precept."

"Oh, dear!" She gave a tiny laugh. "Will my husband
always tease me unmercifully?"

His eyes darkened. "Not always."

Miranda's cheeks flushed with rosy color. "Come, now
we must lead the procession into the banquet hall."

Rising, they walked hand in hand into another large *pendopo*, followed by the chattering guests and the tinkle of
the *gamelan* on the warm and fragrant breezes. The sultan
awaited them there, his round face creased with a satisfied
smile. Miranda and Tony were shown to a place on a mat
set apart. The men and women sat on the floor in segregated
camps while a multitude of servants moved among them
serving the *sambels* and rice mountains for the *selamatan*.

Miranda sat in a demure posture, ignoring the plates of
rice and sweetmeats placed before them. As the honored
couple, no one made any demands on them, and she began
to relax, relishing the luxury of being close to Tony—to
her husband, she amended, amazed at the miracle. To her
relief, she saw that several of the sultan's wives were speak-

ing quietly to Rija, their attitude protective, almost maternal. Perhaps if Rija explained her plight, there might be one among them who could help her . . .

"Quite a celebration," Tony remarked dryly, settling down at her side.

"It is a minor ceremony compared to the usual rituals, which may last several days," Miranda replied, "but Lord Palu is no fool. Though his people will celebrate any occasion, this shows the world he is not concerned with Prince Amang's threat."

"Perhaps he should be," Tony murmured.

She glanced at him sharply. "Have you learned something? Tell me."

Tony took her hand in his, massaging her palm with his thumb in a provocative manner. "When Steef wasn't 'interrogating' me, I made good use of my pidgin Javanese among the other prisoners. There are those within the *kraton* who have no more love for this sultan than we do."

She caught her breath, both from the sense of his words and the delicious sensation of his touch. "How do you know?" she managed on a strangled breath.

"I traded my boots for some information and, if we're lucky, maybe some help when we need it."

"Your boots!" She laughed softly, then bit her lip. "What else did you trade? Not the lotus—"

"Never that." Automatically he touched his hip pocket where, beneath the sarong, rested the jade snuffbox. "That charm brought me to you. I'll never part with my talisman."

"You are a fanciful romantic, Anthony Benedict," she accused in a shaky voice. All the same, she was glad he'd held on to the little box. Despite her practical nature, she was halfway convinced it had a magical quality, too. "Now, tell me. What did you learn?"

"Despite what the sultan wants everyone to think, Amang's forces nearly breached the walls during the attack. He wasn't pushed back; he chose to retreat."

"What does that mean to us?"

"That we must be ready at all times to take advantage of any situation."

"You don't think Lord Palu will release us, do you?"

"Not until you let Rija wed the Dutchman." *And perhaps not even then*, he added to himself.

Miranda sought out her younger sister's dark head, shuddering at the thought of this child in Steef van der Djink's hands. All that she could expect was a life of unspeakable horror. "We've got to find some way to take her away from this place."

Tony pulled Miranda against his shoulder, hugging her, and his tone was wry. "I wouldn't mind that myself."

"We've got to find a way," Miranda repeated. Her lovely fantasy was fading quickly in the face of harsh reality, and a creeping sense of fear flooded her veins.

"We will, my love. I promise." They huddled in a bubble of privacy, virtually ignored by the ocean of guests, who were dining and watching the graceful and intricate performance of a trio of *wajang* dancers. But holding Miri this close made Tony impatient for her. "In the meantime, do you suppose Lord Palu intends to extend the usual courtesies to a newly married couple?"

"What?" Bewildered, she looked up into his face, and her mouth went dry at the hunger that burned behind his eyes. "I—I don't know."

"I pray so. Do you know how badly I want you?"

Her words were barely a whisper, and there was a swift and surprising flare of green in the silvery depths of her eyes. "I can only guess that it matches my own need."

He groaned inaudibly. "God, when you say things like that, you drive me mad. Sweet Miri, when we get back to the *Mirage*, I'll probably lock us in my cabin for a month!"

"You are a shameless rogue," she said, laughing while the hot color rushed up her neck.

"Maybe for the entire voyage back to England," he growled softly.

She jumped slightly. "Oh. I hadn't thought—"

"You're coming home with me, wife, so be obedient to me in that. And we'll bring Rija as well. You know that neither you nor she will be safe in this land as long as Lord Palu reigns."

"Yes, I know."

Beneath his battered features there was a sudden boyish animation that wrung her heart. "You'll love Fairhaven as much as I do, Miri. It's truly the most beautiful spot in England. And there's a glade I want to show you, a special place I loved as a boy. Mother will adore you. She's been after me for years to take a bride and produce a grandson for her. And then there's London, and the theater, and—"

She pressed her fingers against his lips, cutting off the flow of words. "Lovely, all of it, I'm sure, but nothing if I can't be with you. I love you, Tony, and God willing, I'd love to bear you many strong sons and daughters."

Her soft declaration moved him deeply. Somehow, the miracle had happened, and she loved him with no pretense, just for himself. He knew there could be no greater joy, and vowed to make himself worthy of her trust. Perhaps he should begin by telling her the truth about his heritage.

"Miri—"

"My Lord Palu directs you to come," a voice interrupted,

They looked up to find Ishta gesturing to them. Tony helped Miri rise, then they followed the smirking servant to stand before the sultan's gilded settee.

"My felicitations to you both," Lord Palu said, his jovial face alight with mockery. He hefted his ponderous bulk to his feet. "Come, it is my duty to escort you to the bridal chamber."

Miranda couldn't meet Tony's eyes for the hot waves of embarrassment and excitement coursing through her. Her breath came short at the thought of being alone at last with her husband. The sultan could have as easily ordered them both back into separate confinements. Her estimation of his mercy was due for reevaluation, she decided, then, with growing hope, began to wonder if not some other choice for Rija could be selected that would suit Lord Palu just as well. Mayhap in private discussion they might reach an agreement.

With the sultan's guard and Ishta in attendance, Miranda and Tony followed the sultan from the hall, down several long corridors, then into the main gardens. Dusk was falling, and the crickets and night birds chanted their soft and rhythmic litanies, seemingly in time with the high and chiming harmonies of the now distant *gamelan*. Tony took her hand, and she met his heated gaze timorously, her loins liquifying, knowing he was thinking, as she was, of their first meeting here in the lush and perfumed confines of these gardens. But there was still Rija to consider, and she might not get another opportunity.

"My Lord Palu, I beg a word," she said. "Your generosity today has made me reconsider my stubbornness."

The sultan checked his pace a bit, lifting one thin black eyebrow in question. "So, lady? Speak."

With a warning glance at Tony's puzzled expression, she silently begged him to hold his peace, then continued to Lord Palu. "I realize Princess Rija must be wed, but is there not another among your followers who would do as well as the Dutchman? Though I hate to lose my sister, I would have to welcome an honorable man of her own nationality."

The curve of the path they followed had at last revealed a small stone summerhouse surrounded by feathery palms, the openings of its high windows completely covered by plaited bamboo panels for privacy while allowing the free-flowing passage of every breeze. Now the sultan paused on the track of small white stones in front of the hut.

"You bargain with me now, lady?" he asked with a grunt. "It is too late."

"For a wise man, an honorable compromise to an awkward situation never comes too late," Miranda countered boldly.

"Too late for traitors who plot against me in my own house!" the sultan snapped, then smiled thinly. "Am I not correct, Dutchman?"

Steef van der Djink materialized out of the shadows, holding a large basket of bamboo splints. His sculpted features were slack with satiation, his cool blue reptilian eyes unnervingly soft. "Much too late, my lord," he agreed pleasantly.

"I—I do not understand you, my lord," Miranda said nervously.

"It is simple, lady," Lord Palu replied, his black eyes alight with malicious mischief. He pushed open the door to the house, revealing a luxurious interior softly lit by coconut oil lamps. His open-handed gesture invited them inside. "I am a merciful lord. You may lie with your husband this night. Enjoy all the pleasures of the flesh, for at dawn you both shall join your ancestors."

"What?" Miranda breathed, going white with shock.

"Tell me what this overgrown hoodlum said," Tony demanded, unable to follow the rapid exchange.

"The sultan means to execute you both at dawn," Steef drawled lazily, shifting his basket in a gesture that could almost be described as loving. "Beheading is the usual way here."

"The devil you say! On what charge?" Tony demanded.

"For all the usual crimes of a traitor and a traitor's whore," Steef replied. "Conspiracy, plotting against the throne, bribery—"

With great aplomb, he set the basket down beside the path. Miranda gasped, her shocked brain refusing the believe the message of her eyes.

Fists clenched, teeth gritted, Tony jumped the Dutchman, catching him on the ear with a mighty blow that knocked him backward into the palms. "Damn you, you sick bastard!"

The guards caught Tony, shoving him into the house in an out-of-control sprawl, then thrusting Miranda in after him. The sound of the bar sliding home across the heavy door mingled in Miranda's ears with a high keening sound. Hands balled against her mouth, she knew only remotely that the screams she heard issued from her own throat. She wasn't conscious of Tony's hands on her shoulders, nor the sound or sense of his garbled words, nor of anything but the chilling sight that made her mindless with horror.

All she could see was the image of Tony's leather boots lying in that awful basket. And protruding from them, the severed remains of two human feet.

Chapter 10

~~~✑✑~~~

She hadn't really believed she might die until that moment. But the horror in Steef's basket brought that fear home with grisly force, reducing her to an animal-like mindlessness, her screams her only defense against raging insanity. Tony's voice barely penetrated the fog of terror.

"Miri! For God's sake—"

A stinging slap caught her across the face, and her scream ended in a gasp of surprise. Jaw slack, she stared up at Tony's ashen countenance, and her eyes filled. With a look of pure anguish, he caught her to him.

"God, Miri! I'm sorry. I never meant to hurt you . . ."

Her chest ached with the weight of her tears. "He means to kill us, doesn't he?"

In the colorfully exotic, almost obscene opulence of their gilded prison, his silence was answer enough. Distraught, she clung to him, her tears spilling over soundlessly, the hot, salty drops staining the emerald silk of his *bajoe*.

"I'm sorry. Tony, I'm so sorry. None of this would have

happened if I hadn't come to you that night. Dear God, what have I done?''

"Shh. Dearling, shush," he soothed into her ear, and the little white jessamine bells of her headdress bobbed fragrantly against his lips. "Do you think I regret that night?''

"You should! You should curse the day I involved you in my troubles. The price of my selfishness is your life! Forgive me . . .'' She wept against his massive chest, her fingers digging into the strong muscles on either side of his spine.

"We all have our own guilts to bear,'' he said thickly, haunted by the knowledge that he'd been the unwitting cause of an innocent man's death. He rubbed soothing circles on her back and shoulders with his hard, callused palms, needing comfort as much as she did. "Don't question what brought us here. My need for you is so great, even death is a price I'm willing to pay.''

"Oh, you great, golden-tongued fool!'' she half laughed, half sobbed. "You lie like a devil to save my feelings, charming to the last! How can I be worthy of such devotion?''

"Simply by loving me.''

"I do!'' She touched his face. "Before God, I do. And it kills me to think my love may be your undoing.''

"Don't despair. We're far from dead yet,'' he muttered, turning his head so that his lips grazed upon her sensitive palm. "We have all night to plan our escape.''

Her breath shuddering like a child's, she let her gaze roam around their luxuriously appointed cage, despising the silken hangings, the plump cushions and pillows, the flickering oil lamps that cast shadows into every corner. With all her heart, she wished they'd never left the bare and primitive tower room of their first meeting. Even if they could somehow break free of their confinement, they'd still have to deal with the guards outside.

"Escape?'' she echoed in disbelief. "How?''

"We'll find a way.'' Bending slightly, he brushed a reassuring kiss over her parted lips, hesitated, then returned again to deepen it. Groaning deep in his throat, he spoke into her mouth. "Oh, God, Miri . . ."

"Yes," she murmured. "Yes!"

Coming up on tiptoes, she flung her arms around his neck. With death so near, it seemed inevitable that she should crave the elemental reaffirmation of life itself with the man she loved. A desperate flame kindled within her, a primal, primitive need to mate and somehow to survive.

"Miri?" His head swimming, he asked the question.

"You're my husband. Don't make us wait. Don't let me go to my grave regretting I didn't share this with you once more," she begged.

Flaming with a need that matched hers, he pulled the pins from her crown of flowers, dropping them unheeded on the woven mat where they stood. The headdress and diadem followed, and the silvery waterfall of her hair dropped to her waist, covering his forearms in a silken whisper. He looked down into her upraised face, his blue eyes burning into her very depths.

"If this should be my last night on this earth," he said huskily, "then I can't ask more than to spend it in paradise with you."

Swinging her into his arms, he covered her mouth with his, taking her lips with fervent hunger, feeding on her response as a man dying of famine and suddenly set before a banquet of ambrosia. His tongue was rapacious, sweetly demanding, sweeping the moist contours of her mouth, sliding over the edge of her teeth, tugging gently at the fullness of her lower lip. Her fingers curled into his hair, and the sweet, liquid rush of desire poured through her veins and pounded in her temples with an undeniable urgency.

Somehow, he found the low cot and lay her gently into the nest of silken pillows, his mouth ardently seeking the taste of her skin at every point—taut jawline, velvety earlobe, sensuous arch of her neck. Her fragrance filled his nostrils, the sweet odor of frangipani and sweeter woman, and restraint was left behind as heat hardened his loins and gilded his bronzed skin with moisture.

He removed the bold collar of her necklace, then, with

the air of a man opening a long-awaited gift, carefully
tugged the long breast scarf and unknotted her glimmering
sarong, freeing her from their confines. His breath stopped
as he gazed at her with fevered eyes, delighting anew in
her slimness and the delicacy of her bones, the pale beauty
of her ivory skin and rosy, cockled nipples, the mysterious
triangle of soft fair curls protecting the dewy petals of her
womanhood. When he raised his eyes to hers again, he
found her languorously watching his examination with a
small, satisfied smile. It quickly faded, replaced by a look
of breathless hunger and bold invitation.

She spoke his name and held her arms out to him. Ripping
off the *bajoe* and sarong with scarce attention to the delicate
fabric, Tony shrugged out of his breeches and came to her.
Touching, stroking everywhere, their hands communicated
their need. Rolling the voluptuousness of one breast under
his hand, he covered its pouting peak with his lips, taking
it deep into his mouth. She arched against him, her heels
digging into the cot, her fingers tangling in the fiery mass
of his curls to urge him closer still.

"Witch," he mumbled around the sweetness of her flesh,
"you undo me with your magic."

"Touch me," she whispered, pulling his beloved, battered face up to hers, covering his jaw, the cleft in his square
chin, the curve of his mouth, with tiny nips and feather
kisses. "Love me, Tony."

His fingers slid between her legs, tormenting her with
tantalizing touches until she writhed beneath him in frustration. Her hands scooped out the hollows at the base of
his spine, smoothed the flexing muscles of his hard buttocks,
and finally closed boldly on the erect evidence of his arousal,
wringing a deep groan from his throat.

"Now," she urged with hands and lips, frantic to know
his most intimate touch again. "Tony, please . . ."

Forearms braced beside her head, he kneed her thighs
apart, the throbbing tip of his tumescence probing the slick
entrance to her feminine depths. His hands tangled in her
hair, and he paused. Hearts pounding, labored breaths min-
gling, he hovered over her, his expression intense.

"Do you love me?"

"Yes!" She gripped his shoulders, arching against him.

"And know that I love you. Beyond life, beyond death, beyond eternity itself, you are mine."

And with those hoarsely spoken words, he thrust home, taking them both fully into forgetfulness with one silken plunge into her velvet mysteries. Lips melded in a fiery kiss of reunion, and what began as a denial of death became a paean to life.

Running his palms down her breasts, her ribs, he found her rounded buttocks and lifted her higher. Gasping against his mouth, she locked her heels in the small of his back, crying out with the heat and passion of his fierce possession. Her head thrown back in abandon, she arched against him, reaching, reaching . . .

And the heavens exploded, dissolving her core on waves and waves of exquisite pleasure. He smiled, feeling the rippling throes of ecstasy course through her, then his smile became a grimace as his own climax overtook him. With a hoarse shout of triumph, Tony spilled his life into his woman, and together they stormed the gates of paradise.

Night sounds flowed softly from the gardens, and in the weak and guttering light of a single lamp, Tony watched Miri sleep. Naked, she lay on her side, an ivory silhouette among the brightly colored cushions, one knee bent, her arm drawn up under her ear, her features relaxed and replete with his loving. While denied a similar peace, he still could admire the curve of her breast rising and falling with her steady breathing, one rosy crest winking and peeking at him from behind her outslung wrist. Sitting on the floor beside her cot, he watched her, and his fingers nimbly worried the sculpted outline of his lotus talisman to the rhythm of his desperately racing thoughts.

Time.

There wasn't enough of it. Not enough to savor the miracle of the woman before him and rejoice in the goodness of their joining. Not enough to figure out how to get the hell out of this mess. Maybe only enough to take the coward's way out.

Tony jammed the snuffbox back into his pocket and reached for the object that had once been Miri's neck collar. By dent of repeated effort, he'd managed to bend the heavy brass crescent, and finally break it, leaving a sharp, ragged edge. A strip off a satin pillow now wrapped the weapon's crude handle. It was a clumsy *kris*, but he understood better the Javanese notion that a weapon fashioned by the owner was endowed with special magic that could be called forth in time of trial.

Lips twisting wryly, Tony decided this was certainly such a time. Weighing the weapon in his hand, he nodded. It wasn't much—a surprise if nothing else—but he felt better for being armed, however rudely. But who should feel the touch of the blade? his tortured soul asked. Some nameless sultan's minion . . . or Miri?

Perhaps the sultan's executioner would be swift and merciful. But Tony feared the Dutchman's penchant for cruelty and the sultan's capricious mood. The possibility that Steef might amuse himself at Miri's expense made cold sweat pop out on Tony's brow, despite the humid oppressiveness of the cell. And he looked at the woman he loved and wondered if his love was strong enough to save her from suffering with a deed that would damn his soul to perdition even as he followed her into eternity.

Lost in cataclysmic contemplation, Tony jerked his head up at a distant echo. Uncertain whether the sound was real or the fevered workings of his brain, he listened, hardly breathing. High on the night breezes wafted the faint chimes of temple bells, and the fine hair on the back of his neck and forearms quivered.

Damn you, not again, he thought, clenching his fist on the hilt of his rude cleaver.

He'd had enough of mischievous demons and unpredictable monarchs, and longed for England for the first time in a great while, for a place where the portals of the next world did not stand so near to the earth. He had not Miri's abilities to see beyond the boundaries of human existence, to feel

the currents and eddies of forces invisible and unknow-
able—nor did he want them. Yet he could not deny that
something had given them a knowledge of each other long
before they met.

Miri gave a quiet, breathy sigh in her sleep, and Tony
smiled, ignoring the stiffness of his facial muscles. It was
for her that he'd been born into this life, and her for him.
And he knew then that what he contemplated was impossible. Life burned too brightly in Miri to cut it short by even
one precious moment of their allotted time, no matter how
merciful his intentions. If their fate was to meet death together, then so be it, but it did not mean that they had to
go quietly, and if there was a way to survive, he vowed to
find it. Resolutely he set aside the crude knife, then bent
over her, settling a soft kiss on the curve of her hip as if
to beg absolution for his doubts and fears.

The salty-sweet taste of her flesh tempted him, and he
nibbled the inner region of her elbow, then flicked his tongue
along the bridge of her shoulder. She stirred sleepily, and
blood pounded in Tony's loins. Stripping out of his
breeches, he lay down beside her, knowing that if they were
fortunate enough to live a hundred years together, he'd never
grow tired of this.

Rubbing his palms warmly across the shallow indentations of her ribs, he tasted and tested the texture of her skin
along her collarbone, sipping the dew from the hollow of
her throat, where her pulse jumped in a new rhythm.

"T-Tony?" she murmured, sliding her hands along his
biceps, sightlessly tracing the path of blue veins.

"Hmm?" His exploration led him down her breastbone,
and his thumbs on either side of her hips rubbed and explored
the area just north of her delta. He tasted the sweetness of
flowers, the salt of her perspiration, and maybe a bit of
himself, and the heady combination only made him yearn
for more. Pushing her gently to her back, he let his lips
roam at will.

"Tony!" With a gasping groan, her lashes fluttered open,
and she stared down her own body at the glint of coppery
curls moving over her. His tongue, hot and wet and raspy,

laved the quivering inner flesh of her thighs. "What—what are you doing?"

"Learning every beautiful inch of you, wife. So relax, and let me enjoy my lesson."

"No, I—ah!" Her fingers tangled in his hair, but he had brought her from slumber to mindlessness in an instant, and she had no will before his relentless pleasuring. The heaviness in her center ignited, and soon she was shuddering, shattered by his loving assault.

Shaking, she reached for him, drawing him up and taking him inside her still-quivering flesh. His kiss was redolent with her own flavor, and with matching groans, they rolled among the cushions, Miri straddling him. With hands on her hips, he showed her how best to please him, and her hands and lips were everywhere as she moved to his urgings, showering his bruised flesh with soothing kisses and tenderness.

Unbelievably, his thrusting undulations set off new chords within her, and she looked down into the flushed and strained face of her husband and exulted that it was she who could bring him to such heights. When he groaned and crushed her tightly against his chest, his spasms rocketed her after him into new dimensions of delight.

Collapsing together, they lay panting in the guttering lamplight, foolish smiles and gentle laughter chasing away all the hovering clouds . . . at least for a short, timeless interval.

Rocking her in his arms, he sang her praises as lovers are wont to do. "Madam, that was wonderful. As a wife you are without parallel."

She whispered shyly, "I'm glad you woke me."

"So am I, though you needed the rest." He kissed the top of her head and sighed. "And now I do."

"I didn't mean to sleep at all. Did you?"

"A bit. But mainly I watched you so that you would not melt away into thin air again," he teased.

"Would that we could both disappear." Her swallow was audible. "It's almost dawn."

"I know." Raising up on his elbow, he gently smoothed

the silky skein of her moonlit hair back from her flushed face, and his expression was suddenly serious. "You must promise me something."

"What?"

"That if a chance presents itself, you must make every effort to escape."

Her voice was tremulous. "What do you mean?"

For answer, he reached over her, retrieving the makeshift knife from the floor beside the cot. She stared at it, then back at him, her eyes wide silver pools.

"You have a plan?" she asked.

He shrugged. "Not much of one."

"I won't go anywhere without you," she said softly, and there was a pout to her lower lip and a stubborn glint in her gaze.

"Damn it, Miri!" He sat up, running an agitated hand through his hair, then reached for his breeches. "I can't do what I have to if you don't give me your word."

"What do you have to do?"

"Give us options somehow. Make us some sort of chance."

"How?" Rising to her feet, she swept the weight of her hair over one shoulder, then, unself-conscious as a goddess, went in search of her own clothing, arranging the green sash and golden sarong with a few deft twists.

Tony frowned, half in and half out of his silver-threaded *bajoe*, muttering, "I don't know how. You'll have to trust me."

"But—"

The scrape of the bar at the heavy door interrupted her protest. Swiftly Tony stuck his crude knife in the small of his back, tugging the *bajoe* into place over it, then pulled her protectively behind him.

"Promise me!" he hissed, squeezing her arm. "Our lives may depend on your obedience."

She licked her dry lips uncertainly, then nodded. With a sigh of relief, Tony turned to face the door. A querulous voice scolded the unseen guards, the Javanese words falling like pebbles in a muddy puddle.

"Insolent fish! Am I not the sultan's servant? Am I not sent to do his will?" the strident voice demanded. "Even the condemned must eat! Now, begone, butterflies!"

Tony and Miranda stared at the grossly fat figure that filled the opening, continuing to harangue the guards with ill-tempered words, a large, flat basket of fruit settled comfortably on one rolling hip. Swathed in voluminous folds of batik, wearing a coolie's bamboo hat, the man—or woman? It was too soon to say—lumbered forward. With buttocks the size of an ox's rear and a belly to match, the servant executed a *dodok* that was an amazing sight.

"Come, children," the obese lackey said, ignoring the curious eyes of the trio of guards watching from the doorway. "Come and choose from my bounty."

Casting Tony a muddled glance, Miranda shrugged and moved closer. "Thank you, most honored elder. You are kind to the lowly."

"Choose, choose, daughter of the moon," the servant urged, offering the tray.

Miranda's hand hesitated over the array of pomegranates, mangosteens, bananas, and passion fruit. Curiously she peered into the native's dark eyes, but it was as if she stared into a mirror, and a wave of vertigo rushed into her head. She swayed, and Tony caught her elbow.

"Are you all right?"

"Yes." Licking her lips again, Miranda passed a weak hand over her eyes, then reached for the luscious red berry of a passion flower.

"And your husband, too," urged the ludicrous figure.

Tony, preoccupied with the scrutiny of the guards, didn't understand the words, but shook his head at the proffered basket. "I'm not hungry."

"It would be rude to refuse," Miranda said softly.

Tony wanted to snap that he wasn't particularly concerned with the feelings of this corpulent old fright at the moment, but Miri's beseeching expression moved him to contain his irritation. Without hesitation, he picked up a berry and popped it into his mouth, and its ripe sweetness exploded against his palate.

A generous black-toothed grin shifted the servant's greasy jowls into pleased lumps of gelatinous flesh. "You have chosen well, my children. Many blessings await you . . ." His bulk swaying, he set the basket on the floor, and his voice dropped so that only Miranda heard. ". . . if you have the patience to bear the trial."

Miranda was startled; her eyes grew wide. In a similar hushed tone she asked, "What do you mean, ancient one?"

"A message from the prince, my child," the portly servant murmured. "Do not act hastily. Watch, wait, be ready."

Miranda caught her breath, but before she could frame another question, the servant backed obsequiously from the hut, loudly praising Allah, Shiva, and the Pandawas in a singsong chant of celebration. The guards smiled and nodded amiably, captivated by the rotund servant's clownish posturing.

"What is it?" Tony demanded, alarmed at Miri's dazed expression.

"Hope, my love," she choked, and repeated Amang's message.

"Wait, ask him—" Tony's instinctive movement toward the door faltered, and he frowned.

Was there something familiar about the toadlike figure happily jouncing his bulk down the path in the pearly gray predawn? With a jolt of shock, Tony realized the grotesque form was uncannily like the caricature of Semar, the androgynous Javanese demigod. At once denying the possibility, yet accepting the reality of the departing messenger, Tony took another involuntary step toward the door.

One wiry, black-eyed guard barked a warning, drawing Tony's murderous scowl. When he looked back, the first golden rays of sunrise pierced the gloom, illuminating the empty stone path. One moment the servant was there, the next, he'd vanished, an astounding feat for one of such enormous size. Tony blinked in astonishment, and gooseflesh crept along his spine.

"Who was that?" Tony's voice held a strange inflection.

"Don't question our salvation," Miranda insisted. Her

own heart beat rapidly as she met the unspoken question in Tony's eyes. "Remember, there are no absolutes, and many possibilities, in this land."

"Perhaps, my little pagan witch. But can we afford to wager our lives on your brand of magic?"

Eyes wide with desperation, she whispered, "How can we afford not to?"

There was no answer he could give, but before he could take her in his arms again, an insolent voice intruded on the moment.

"Up so soon from the marriage bed? I pray your rest was not disturbed by bad dreams?"

Swiftly and silently as a cobra, Steef van der Djink appeared in the doorway. Instinctively Miranda fell back, repelled by the man whose angelic visage could not conceal a palpable aura of evil.

"I see the vultures are up early this morn," Tony sneered. Hands clenched behind his back, his fingers twitched with the itch to use his hidden weapon.

On bare feet, Miranda glided up behind him, hovering as if seeking the protection of his body. "Not yet," she murmured for his ears only. "Remember Amang."

"Have some dignity, Englishmen. Come of your own will, or I'll have you both stripped and dragged before the sultan by force," the Dutchman promised with great relish.

Tony's jaw flexed. "Your master tugs you like a monkey on a chain, Steef. By all means, let us not keep that fat tyrant waiting."

Steef flushed, suddenly losing patience, but his smile was mocking as he bowed, extending a hand as if in invitation.

"Come, English swine. Eternity awaits."

From the size of the curious crowd of nobles, servants, and even peasants that jostled for position in the *kraton*'s main courtyard, it was clear the sultan intended to make the execution of two English renegades an example to all his people. On the next level above the courtyard, the sultan and his court waited in a *pendopo* shaded by a palm-thatched pavilion. As befitting the festive occasion, flowers were everywhere, and multicolored silken hangings on the plaited bamboo walls drifted and billowed softly in the fragrant early morning breezes.

Escorted by the Dutchman and his henchmen, Tony and Miranda mounted the steps to the upper level, then stood before Lord Palu. For once, Miranda did not make the traditional *dodok*. With her hair hanging loose and straight down her back, she lifted her chin in silent defiance. She would not humble herself before the man who meant to murder them.

At her side, Tony flicked assessing glances over the cordon of heavily armed guards, cursing himself for not taking whatever chance he and Miri might have had at the summerhouse. The weight of his makeshift knife in the small of his back was scarcely reassuring considering the bristling array of spears and swords, and he called himself every kind of fool for placing credence in the so-called message from an obviously demented servant. If Prince Amang couldn't even mount an effective offensive, how could he be expected to rescue them?

Tony's blue eyes narrowed as he measured a muscular, turbaned native waiting impassively beside a large marble block, a menacingly curved scimitar balanced over his crossed arms. The sultan's executioner, Tony decided grimly. When Miri followed his gaze, she gasped at the man's foreboding visage, and Tony reached out and took her hand, giving it a reassuring squeeze.

But his own head was filled with far from reassuring images, and he knew that he would not meekly submit to this fate. They might kill him, yes, but he'd go down fighting, not led to the slaughter like a lamb. His muscles were tensing in preparation for the end when the sultan spoke.

"Was your wedding night all you hoped, Englishman?" The royal interpreter rapidly translated, not bothering to wait for a reply from Tony. "Lord Palu reminds you of his mercy, but now your death must show that his justice is swift and sure for all who defy him. Have you anything to say in your own behalf, Englishman?"

Shaking his head, Tony drew Miri closer to his side.

"Nothing for myself, but I ask you show your great wisdom by releasing my wife."

"A traitor's whore must share a traitor's fate," Steef said, his graceful body at ease, his attitude languid. The interpreter worked rapidly, and Lord Palu nodded his assent to the Dutchman's words.

"It is, unfortunately, as my regent says. Have you nothing more? No last-minute confession to ease your soul?"

Angrily Tony clenched his jaw, the sultan's taunt setting fire to a burning inner rage. He gave a sharp, negative shake of his head.

"Wait! I beg indulgence!" Surging through the line of nobles, Princess Rija threw herself on the floor at the sultan's feet.

"Rija!" Miranda cried, aghast. Would the sultan brutally require her sister to witness the execution?

"Remove the child," Lord Palu ordered.

"No!" Rija surged to her feet, a slim but defiant figure in a red flowered sarong and *kebaja*. "Hear me, my lord! These two stand condemned for my sake. My stubbornness must be punished, not theirs."

"What do you ask of me, child of my heart?" the sultan demanded.

"Let them go in peace, and I will wed your regent without further dispute," Rija said. "Further, I will use all my influence with my people to accomplish yours and the Dutchman's will."

"You promise to be an exemplary, obedient wife?" Lord Palu demanded, a slight smile rounding his cheeks into dusky apples.

"Yea, my lord," Rija said, a flicker of hope in her black eyes.

"Sister, no!" Miranda's heart sank. Rija could not be allowed to make such a sacrifice. At Tony's insistent, questioning stare, she murmured, "Rija barters for our lives with her own."

But the Dutchman was having none of Rija's plans, and protested vigorously. "My lord, the princess is in no position to bargain!"

"A willing maid is always better," Lord Palu pointed out slyly, "especially if she will sway her peasants to labor for us peacefully."

"I have ways of dealing with recalcitrant women," Steef replied. His icy blue gaze flicked over Rija's slim form in avid anticipation. "Reject this desperate plea. These two must die."

Though young and slight, Rija took on the cool, regal hauteur of a queen, ignoring the Dutchman's outburst, concentrating on convincing Lord Palu of her determination. "Consider well, my lord. If they die, then I will, too—and then you will have nothing."

Her voice calm, she drew a glittering serpentine *kris* from the waist of her sarong and placed its point beneath her breastbone.

"Dear God! Rija, no!" Miranda cried, starting forward.

Steef's curses rent the air, and he, too, jumped to disarm the defiant princess. Tony intercepted him with a slashing sidearm blow, and the Dutchman's curses changed to screams of agony. He fell to his knees clutching a cheek scored into bloody tatters by Tony's makeshift *kris*.

Lord Palu surged to his feet, screeching orders to his stunned guards. The *kris* Rija held wobbled, and Miranda jerked it from her sister's grasp as the three of them faced off against overwhelming odds.

But in the blink of an eye, the odds changed.

A slim young man dressed in a peasant's grab and wielding a sword leapt onto the balcony wall. Miranda's breath stopped, and she mouthed a silent cry of recognition: Prince Amang!

The prince brought his sword down through the air and shouted a battle cry that was instantly taken up by other peasants within the crowd below. In the space of a second, fighting between armed peasants and the palace guard filled the courtyard. Shrieking pandemonium broke out among the assembled nobles and their women. More of the prince's men surged up the stairs and clambered over the restraining wall toward the sultan, and his soldiers turned to confront this new threat.

Tony took one look at the melee and pushed Miri and Rija toward the balcony wall, shielding them with his body, feinting with his inadequate weapon to keep the confused soldiers at bay for the few precious seconds they needed. Near the sultan, the wounded Dutchman struggled to his feet.

"Get out of here!" Tony said to Miranda. "Go over the wall. It's your only chance."

"But, Tony—"

A sudden series of explosions to the rear of the *pendopo* and outside the *kraton* walls drowned out Miranda's protest. Hands pressed to her ears, Rija cowered and screamed in fright along with the panicky nobles and the fleeing crowds below. Miranda's mouth hung open in amazement, but Tony's blue eyes shone with a fierce light, and suddenly he laughed out loud.

"Cannon, by God! Miri, do you know what that means?" He shoved her and Rija against the balcony wall and answered his own question as Prince Amang leapt down into the fray. "It means Amang got to the *Mirage* after all! I knew Tassel and Angus and the rest wouldn't stand for defeat! Hellfire, woman, we've actually got a chance! Now, go!"

He set Rija onto the wall, then turned back to defend them. One of the sultan's guard unwisely rushed at the trio, but Tony barreled shoulder-first into the surprised man and stabbed him with the makeshift knife. Miranda pressed a hand to her mouth to control the threatening rise of gorge. All around them the scent of fresh blood and carnage mingled obscenely with the perfume of flowers. Reflexively her fist tightened on the handle of Rija's *kris*.

Tony bent to retrieve the dead guard's sword, and beyond him, Miranda saw Amang nimbly dispatch an enemy soldier at the foot of the sultan's throne. Lord Palu turned to flee from the vengeful upstart, and with a swift flick of his wrist, Prince Amang sent his own *kris* winging to lodge fatally in Lord Palu's thick throat. The sultan gave a gurgle, then toppled into a flaccid, fleshy heap.

A shout went up among the attackers, but now, with

nothing left to lose, the sultan's guard redoubled their efforts, and swords clashed and clattered metallically in a flurry of offensive and defensive maneuvers. With a roar, the Dutchman came fully to his feet, swinging his sword, the right side of his face a crimson flag, his blue eye milky and blind beneath a slashed lid. His remaining eye latched murderously onto Tony and the women.

"Go," Tony instructed harshly, his eyes narrowing at the Dutchman's approach through the throng. Grabbing Rija by one wrist, he lowered her over the side as far as he could, then dropped her. She landed, unharmed, twelve feet below. Except for a few sprawled bodies, the lower courtyard cleared rapidly as the hysterical crowd poured through the open gates.

"You next," he said.

Miranda stuck the *kris* in her belt and swung her legs over the ledge, but her silver eyes were frightened at the thought of leaving him. "Tony—?"

"Take Rija to safety, my love."

He knew exactly how to ply her with her duty to make her do what he wanted, a distant portion of her thought peevishly. But at the fore of her mind, she knew his honor demanded he face the Dutchman and join Amang's fight now. Knowing he needed no other distractions, she prayed inwardly for his safety, squelching her woman's fears by valiant effort.

Nodding only, she said, "Yes. Be careful."

His wonderful grin flashed, showing the devastating slash of a dimple she loved, and he brushed her parted lips with a hasty kiss. "Always. Now go. Look for my crew. I'll find you."

Without further ado, he lowered her as he had Rija, gave her a final jaunty smile, then disappeared behind the ledge. Turning, Miranda grabbed Rija's hand, cast a swift, assessing glance over the courtyard, then plunged into the shouting, weeping, pushing fold moving toward the *kraton*'s gates.

Thankfully, no one paid them any attention. Cannon fire continued to rain down on the panicky hordes, but the fighting remained on the upper levels. After a few desperate, claustrophobic moments when they were in danger of being trampled, they pushed through the gates and spilled gratefully onto the dusty main highway.

Dazed, a bit unsure of their next step, Miranda paused, wondering if she should head for the artillery emplacements or straight across the rice paddies into the relative safety of the jungle.

"Lassie!"

Miranda whirled, coming face-to-face with Angus Pratt, his strawberry pate as grizzled as ever. Her cry was joyous. "Mr. Pratt!"

"Sahib Angus!" Rija echoed. "Allah be praised! You're alive!"

"I'm too mean to kill, lassie," the old salt answered. He led a small, well-armed group of English sailors. "And a body can nae take the *Mirage* and live to brag about it! You ladies all right? Where's the cap'n?"

"There!" Miranda pointed at the *kraton*'s upper terrace, just visible over the walls. "Hurry! They need your help."

"I'll have one of the men take you to safety," he began.

"Never mind us!" Miranda snapped, giving him a push. "Tony needs you now! The fighting . . . Dear heaven! They've fired the *kraton!*"

They all turned at her horrified cry. Hot yellow curls of flame leapt up from various points around the *kraton*, and blinding black smoke billowed into the cerulean sky. Bamboo and palm thatch and flimsy silk hangings ignited, victims of hot shrapnel and of the determination of Amang's men to raze the hated monarch's abode.

"Find a safe place and wait for us, lass!" Angus barked. "Come on, men!"

They jogged off smartly, heading through the now empty gateway. The cannon fire ceased, and Miranda's ears rang with the sudden silence.

"Sister, we must go," Rija said, tugging at Miranda's arm and sending apprehensive glances at the hordes of natives still streaming past them, some of them now laden with articles looted from the flaming palace. "Not all will look on us with kindness for this day's work."

"But Tony! Dear Lord, where is he?" Miranda's expression was anguished with worry. Her gaze never left the battlements, searching for signs of Tony even while Rija frantically tugged her down the roadway.

There! On the highest terrace! Two figures dueled with swords, and in a country of black-haired people, the glints of gold and copper she saw could only identify two individuals—Tony and the Dutchman!

It was a testimony to each man's strength of will that, injured as they both were, the battle had lasted this long. Miranda took a hesitant step forward, straining to see, but an angry voice suddenly brought her attention back to earth.

"Daughter of a serpent! My master is dead because of you!" Ishta, the sultan's servant, stood before Miranda, his turban askew, his dark eyes shimmering with hate. A *kris* glinted in his hand. "You will pay!"

"Run, Rija!" Miranda cried, backing away from the little man and his deadly blade.

Rija screamed and bolted down the road after the disappearing peasants. Ishta merely smiled, his expression vicious, and stalked Miranda with deadly purpose. She watched him warily, backing away step by step, trying to give Rija time to reach the safety of the jungle's fringes. Nerves stretched taut, cold fear knotting her gut, she felt her courage finally snap, and sprinted for safety.

With a hoarse cry of hate, Ishta sprang, slashing the air with his blade, and the point sliced across the top of Miranda's bare shoulder. She gasped and stumbled to one knee, a fiery brand of pain searing her. With a cry of triumph, the enraged servant wrapped a fist into the flowing fairness of her long mane, jerking her head back.

Terrified, Miranda knew he meant to cut her throat and she struggled wildly, reaching for her belt. Ishta raised his *kris*, smiling evilly at her fearful expression. With a laugh, he struck—lopping off a silvery hank of her hair just at her nape, then raising it to the sky like an offering.

Miranda sagged forward on her knees, but Ishta grabbed

her hair again, intent on finishing his mission now that he'd tormented his prey. Roughly he swung her around to face him, then stopped with a soft, surprised exhalation. Eyes widening incredulously, he stared down at the handle of Rija's *kris* protruding from his stomach.

Sobbing for breath, Miranda scuttled backward away from him, horrified at the result their combined actions had produced. Her hair still clasped in one hand, his blood-stained knife in the other, Ishta crumpled forward, dead before he reached the roadbed.

Shaking uncontrollably, Miranda staggered to her feet. Her shoulder burned, and blood seeped in crimson ribbons down her bosom to soak the green and gold breast cloth. The breeze felt cool and unfamiliar on her half-shorn nape. Some part of her knew that Rija was coming back, accompanied by a group of peasants. Some of Prince Amang's men, she thought vaguely, but the only thing she could focus on through her pain and shock was Tony. Where was he? Why wasn't he near when she needed him so badly?

"Sister! You're hurt!" Rija fluttered at Miranda's side, stripping off a bit of fabric to staunch the wound, but Miranda tried to brush her off. Rija mopped at the blood, her voice frantic. "Stop, Miri! Where are you going?"

"I've got to find Tony." Miranda's voice was plaintive. "I'm going back."

"You can't! The palace is ablaze!"

Streams of smoke-blackened and coughing soldiers now stumbled from the bowels of the flaming citadel, neither side able to continue the bloody confrontation in the face of this all-consuming monster. One man with a sooty face led a group to safety through the gates, then caught sight of Rija and Miranda and hastened toward them. The layer of ash could not conceal a white grin of victory on Prince Amang's patrician features.

"Victory, my ladies! The day is ours. Come, I offer you my protection, but hurry, I must regroup to rout the rest of Palu's vermin!"

Miranda blinked at the young monarch's hasty declaration, fighting to make sense of the words through the woozy haze that clouded her brain. The only thing that mattered was Tony.

"My lord," she said, grasping his grimy *bajoe* between desperate fingers, "where's the Englishman? Where's my husband? He and the Dutchman were up there . . ."

Her gaze again returned to the upper reaches of the *kraton*, and at that moment the wind shifted, lifting the black billows of smoke like the curtain on a stage. With a terrified gasp, she pointed. High on the uppermost terrace, silhouetted against a glowing orange backdrop of flame, two figures stood locked in mortal combat.

But before Miranda's shocked brain could even register the images, there was an earsplitting roar. Like a volcano consuming itself, the entire *kraton* collapsed inward. A shower of red sparks and black ash plumed a hundred feet into the smoky sky, and the two figures were gone, the interior palace regions reduced in seconds to a twisted pile of smoldering rubble.

"Tony!" Miranda screamed for her husband, trying to reach him, but Rija and the menservants held her back. She fought them with savage, frantic strength. "Let me go! He needs me! I've got to go to him—"

"Come away, sister. We aren't safe here." Tears poured down Rija's exquisite face, and she looked with anguished appeal and adoration at the young prince. Amang's dark eyes glistened with compassion, and he laid a restraining hand on Miri's arm.

"Desist, lady. You cannot help him now. No one survived that."

"Of course he did," Miranda denied, frenzied. Her voice rose in a scream of uncontrolled hysteria. "I know Tony! Let me go, damn you! Tony!"

Rija hugged her stepsister tightly. "You must be brave, sister. He's gone."

The world spun on its axis in dizzying circles, and unbearable sorrow launched Miranda's soul into the blackest, coldest regions of the universe. Fighting like a mad thing, she screamed her fury and her grief to the heavens. It took all the menservants and Rija and the prince besides to drag her away from the scene of her heart's destruction.

In a state of utter collapse, she hid her blinded eyes behind fingers she could no longer feel, and repudiated a reality she could no longer endure with screams she could not hear.

"Oh, God, no . . . NO!"

Part II

"*A*nd so, in a fit of rage, the wicked king changed his daughter into ulnar sawah, *the little snake of the rice fields*," Teacher said, her voice end-of-the-day soft, her lined face shadowed by the faint glow of the oil lamps.

"*The daughters in this land fare poorly*," Sister said as she rocked a drowsy Tiktik in her arms. "*Did not a jealous stepmother enchant another princess with a disease so hideous that she wandered until she finally flung herself into the sea?*"

"*And so she became the Goddess of the Southern Sea, restored to beauty and the bride of sultans, rewarded for her patience and long-suffering.*"

"*I hate snakes,*" Tiktik murmured suddenly from the haven of Sister's arms. "*They're ugly. And they scare me.*"

"*In her snake form, the goddess Dewri Sri protects our harvest from rats and marauders so that her people do not go hungry,*" Teacher explained. "*So you see, my daughters, out of the appearance of evil, it is always possible that good will come . . .*"

Chapter 11

England
April 1722

It was a matter of petticoats, she decided.

Miranda Langford Benedict peered morosely through the crack in the window shade of the lurching coach and shivered. Outside, pewter gray skies dripped freezing precipitation over the brown English countryside, while the blustering wind whistled through the crevices in the floorboards and up her skirts. The driver's oaths rang in her ears, punctuated by the crack of his whip and the sound of the horses' hooves as they sucked sickeningly through the viscous road mud. They were late, and it would be later still before they reached their destination on this inclement afternoon.

Miranda shivered again. Her feet were icy in her clumsy leather shoes, and she could hardly feel her fingers despite the fact she wore two pairs of gloves and huddled miserably under a secondhand camlet cloak and hood. The chill ate into her bones and gnawed at her entrails, but she stoically ignored her discomfort and fatigue. She'd hadn't come this far to give up on the last leg of her pilgrimage.

Yes, she thought again wistfully, petticoats. Not the tropical-weight cotton garments she wore that had been the only European garb available in the shops of Dutch Batavia, but nice woolen ones to keep her warm in this bitter and barbaric weather. She realized now she should have stopped long enough in London to make some sensible purchases, but what did it really matter? Inside she'd been nothing more than a block of ice since the day they'd carried her away, screaming, from her husband's pyre.

"Where'd you say ye're bound, ma'am?"

Miranda gladly wrenched her thoughts back to the burly farmer seated across from her. He and a country vicar now drowsing under his furs in the opposite corner were the only other passengers this dreary evening.

She'd caused some raised eyebrows when she'd boarded the coach alone, but Topaz, her half-caste maid who'd accompanied her from Benkulen, lay ill and feverish with ague a half score of miles back at the Millford village inn. Driven by a compulsion that had pushed her halfway round the globe, Miranda had left Topaz in the hands of the kindly innkeeper's wife, determined to complete her journey despite weather or illness or deprivation. She owed it to Tony.

The vicar, however, having made up his mind about the type of woman who would dare to flaunt convention and travel alone, had studiously ignored her from behind his prayer book most of the afternoon. But now that he and his disapproval slept, the farmer seemed more disposed to friendly conversation. So Miranda answered his question politely.

"Fairhaven," she replied. "I'm going to Fairhaven."

Her gray eyes softened at the name that had become a beacon of purpose in the dark night of her soul. At Fairhaven, perhaps she could find the peace for which she'd yearned. But more important, she could complete the sorrowful duty she'd set to herself the day she'd finally donned her widow's weeds.

"Can't say I know the place right off." The farmer scratched his stubbly chin, making a puzzled moue of his wide mouth. "But then, I ain't from around these parts. I'm Squire Knolly, from Shiredale Pond."

"Mrs. Miranda Benedict." They shook hands formally. "I'm pleased to know you, Squire Knolly. The driver said he'd make a stop for me at the turn to Fairhaven, so I'm not worried."

"Ye've ne'er been to this Fairhaven yerself, then?"

"No." She shook her head, then reached to secure a hairpin that had slipped from the loose knot of fair hair on her nape. Eight months after Ishta's shearing, her hair again reached her shoulders, but she wasn't adept at styling the shorter strands.

"Got relatives there, have ye?"

Miranda couldn't take offense at the farmer's friendly curiosity, so she smiled and tugged her black skirts closer against the draft. "Yes. That is, I think so. My late husband's people."

"Ah, then you'll find a welcome, no doubt."

"So I hope."

She'd pictured this homecoming in her mind a thousand times during the long sea voyage from the East Indies. Sometimes Fairhaven was a prosperous farm, sometimes a cozy cottage, but even if it should be the meanest hovel, she knew she would find comfort in the home that Tony had once loved. She pictured Mrs. Benedict as a plump matron, and although she hated the pain her news would inflict, Miranda knew there was someone who could mourn with her for her beloved Tony. For Tony's sake, she vowed to look after her mother-in-law, to see to her comfort and care for her as he would have wanted.

Miranda looked up to meet the farmer's gaze again and tried to throw off her melancholy for the sake of the conversation. "And you, sir?" she asked. "Where are you heading?"

"Going up to Haselton to fetch a prize bit of horseflesh I bought off some gent who went bust during the South Sea Bubble."

"South Sea . . . ?" Her brow puckered in puzzlement.

"Ain't ye heard tell of all the trouble back a year or so's

ago? Stock speculations, it was. Why, they sent the exchequer himself to the Tower for fraud, and it's whispered even the royal family got their fingers burned. Yes, sir, plenty what thought they'd make themselves a fortune lost everything!''

"How unfortunate," she murmured.

"Maybe for some, but that's how I got such a bargain on this stallion. Many's the gent who's had to sell off his cattle quiet-like to pay his debts since that bit of mischief. Had better sense than to get involved myself," he confided. "Maggie, I says to the missus, what do I know about stocks and finance and such? And it's glad I am I stayed clear of that mad folly. It's a wonder you ain't heard the talk."

"I've only recently returned to England from the East Indies," Miranda explained. "I left when I was just a girl, and I'm sadly ignorant in many respects about the country of my birth."

"Well, imagine that!" Clad in sensible, unostentatious garments of allapine wool, the squire perched his felt tricorne on his knee, and regarded her with brown eyes alight with interest. "Been gone a long time, have ye?"

"Yes."

"And I daresay seen a bit of the world, too," he guessed, his expression a tad envious. "Have ye seen London-town? Now there's a sight!"

"Just a bit. I'll admit I got quite lost." Miranda's lips twitched at the memory.

She'd gone to see her father's lawyer, The Honorable Silas Poole, and found the old gentleman charming as ever, though a bit daft with his advancing years, and deaf as a post. Although his directions were as muddled as his thoughts, he willingly agreed to act as her agent and to forward any correspondence from Rija. This accomplished, she and Topaz had left the city for Fairhaven within an hour of their arrival. But Miranda hadn't counted on weather and illness extending their journey by nearly a week. Now she was fairly bursting with frustrated impatience to reach her destination.

"How queer everything must be to you after all this

time," Squire Knolly commented. He leaned across the space separating them with a confidential air, growing expansive with a revelation of his own. "I may look worldly, ma'am, but ye see, this is the farthest I've ever been from home. But what wouldn't I give to see some wonders! Maybe Spain, even Africa!"

"Home is just as wondrous, sir, if you haven't seen it for a while," Miranda replied with an understanding smile. But then another chill racked her, and she pulled her cloak closer. "But I vow I don't recall it being so c-cold."

"I reckon ye're right about that, ma'am! Hardest winter and the latest spring we've had in ten years!" The squire gave a rueful chuckle, cast a furtive glance at the sleeping parson, then reached into his coat pocket. "But I've got just the thing to chase the chill away, if you'll pardon me for being so bold."

He produced a rustic stoneware flask, deftly pulled its cork, then offered it to her.

"What is it?" she asked curiously.

"I'd like to say it's my wife's apple brandy, ma'am, but the plain fact is it's gin. I ain't got the niceties of a cup, but if you'll try just a dram, I guarantee it'll warm your cockles."

Miranda hesitated. She didn't like to offend the bluff but kindhearted gentleman, and besides, she was damnably cold. Gingerly she accepted the flask, sniffed cautiously, then took a tiny sip. Fire burned down her gullet, tears sprang to her eyes, and she gasped for breath.

"Harrumph!" The vicar stirred in his corner, disturbed from his nap by her involuntary reaction, and his beady eyes glowered at Miranda in patent disapproval.

The stuffy prelate's intolerance pricked her. The gin was no more potent than Noppa's palm wine, but it was clear the churchman considered her action one step away from eternal damnation. With the first real flare of life she'd felt in a long time, Miranda took another defiant swallow. Coughing and choking, she passed the flask back to the squire.

"Thank you," she said, wiping at the moisture stinging her eyes, her voice liquor-hoarse.

The squire nodded, sheepish and red-faced now that the pastor had turned his baleful stare his way. He recorked the bottle without partaking himself, slipped it into his coat pocket, then settled back with a huge sigh, folding his arms and closing his eyes as though sleep could not be denied another moment.

Miranda stifled an inward giggle, keeping her expression bland as she met the vicar's glance. Muttering under his breath about shameless bawds, he, too, looked away. With the gin warming her pleasantly, and a sense of having proven some subtle point, Miranda shifted into a more comfortable position and resumed her perusal of the dripping landscape.

She was faintly amazed at herself. Where was her quiet, ladylike reserve? On the other hand, where was the beaten, broken woman of these past months? Perhaps the closer she came to Fairhaven, the more she regained of her old self, her old strength. She knew that for a time, Rija had feared for her sanity. In her mind, she heard again her stepsister's concerned admonitions . . .

"Sister, please! You must not be up," Rija had said, trying to keep Miranda from rising from her bamboo cot.

They'd found refuge deep in the jungle at the *dukun*'s hut during the first confused days after the razing of Lord Palu's *kraton*. Half-delirious with the pain and fever of her shoulder wound, Miranda clung tenaciously to a gossamer thread of hope.

"I've got to go back," Miranda said, pushing painfully to a seated position. Her eyes held the wild wariness of a trapped animal. "Tony may be hurt . . ."

"Miri, do not torture yourself like this," Rija murmured, gently smoothing the short, damp strands of Miranda's now chin-length hair from her flushed face. After Ishta's bob, they'd clipped the remaining locks so that it was all one length, and now Miranda scarcely recognized herself, neither physically nor mentally.

Somehow, the sisters' roles had been reversed, and now

it was Rija who cared for Miranda, making the decisions to go or stay, consulting with the wizened *dukun* over the proper herbs to heal Miranda's wound, nursing injured soldiers and dispensing calming words to the confused and worried villagers with all the dignity and wisdom of a queen.

"But I've got to find him," Miranda insisted. "Angus will help me. Have you seen him? What about Mr. Tassel and the rest of Tony's crew? They'll help; I know they will."

Rija's piquant features grew solemn, and she sat down on the low cot beside Miranda and gently took her hand. "They're all gone, Miri. Prince Amang says the *Mirage* sailed soon after the *kraton* fell."

"I don't believe it." Beneath Rija's soothing touch, Miranda's fingers twisted in agitation. "Angus wouldn't leave without his captain!"

"Miri, you must understand there was no one here for him to leave," Rija said. "They'd done all they could. There was no reason for them to stay any longer."

"How can you be certain? Did you see them? Talk to them? Someone has to search the ruins." Miranda's voice rose with her desperation. "Oh, Rija, there's a picture in my head that won't disappear. I feel it. He's there, trapped and hurt, suffering . . ."

"May I enter?" Prince Amang stood in the hut's open doorway, a sword strapped to his side.

His aristocratic features were haggard from lack of sleep, but satisfaction and triumph etched a new maturity into his expression. He and his men had routed the remnants of Lord Palu's forces, pushing them into the jungle, but the work of reconstructing the sultanate had just begun. It was a challenge that sat easily on the prince's slim shoulders. His black eyes met Rija's in a silent question, and she shrugged in a slight, helpless gesture. But Miranda greeted his arrival with renewed hope.

"Your Highness, I beg your help. My husband . . ."

"My lady, I owe you both a debt I cannot repay."

"Then help me find him!" Miranda cried.

Again, the prince caught Rija's eye in unaccustomed hes-

itation. Moving into the small, shadowy room, he abandoned his dignity, hitching up his sarong and squatting so
that he was on Miranda's eye level.

"What is it?" she asked in alarm.

"Your sister has conveyed to me your anxieties, lady.
So great is my affection for you both, I personally took men
into the *kraton* this day and combed the ruins for any sign
of your valiant spouse."

Miranda's breath caught. "You found . . . ?"

"Only ashes. And this."

He opened his hand, revealing the charred remains of
what had once been a lotus blossom cunningly carved from
the finest jade.

Miranda's heart plummeted into an abyss of despair.
Though she'd prayed for possibilities, here was proof of a
reality she could no longer deny. Hands shaking, she took
the brittle and blackened object from Amang and clutched
it to her shattered heart. Only in death would Tony have
been parted from his talisman, and she knew then beyond
hope or doubt that he'd perished in the conflagration.

She heard Rija's and Amang's voices from far away, her
grief a cocoon that enveloped her, separating her from the
world and the world's consolation. Her sorrow was beyond
tears, and so she did not weep. Vaguely she knew the ancient
dukun pressed a cup to her lips, and she drank obediently,
without question—for what did anything matter without
Tony?

"It is a draft of forgetfulness, my daughter," the *dukun*
whispered kindly. "Sleep and let the healing begin."

Pressed back down onto the cot by loving hands, Miranda
sought the relief of oblivion, but she soon learned to hate
the need for slumber, for when she woke again the pain
was always there.

After that day, time was a blur, all her energies focused
within on her withered soul while her body slowly healed.
Inconsolable, Miranda was hardly aware that day by day
Prince Amang consolidated his army and his power. Within
weeks, the charismatic young man had reclaimed his rightful
heritage as well as captured Rija's affections.

It was when the young prince took Miranda aside one day and formally requested Rija's hand in marriage that she finally forced herself to bury her depression and attend to her sisterly duties. The new sultan had accomplished much—assembled his court and set up his household in the *desa* where she and Tony had first met him, restructured the system of nobles and accepted their tribute in return for amnesty, and received a Dutch representative of the Company and signed a new, more liberal trade agreement to assure a fair price for his subjects' rice and coffee production. And during all this, he'd found time to woo and win a princess.

Even in her own pain, Miranda could see that Rija was deeply in love. Her young stepsister had grown up during their ordeal, taking on the robes of adulthood in ways that continually surprised Miranda. Certain that Rija knew her mind and could accept the responsibilities of wife of a monarch, Miranda gladly gave her consent to the marriage. The wedding was a bittersweet experience, recalling her own brief marriage as she relinquished the responsibility for her sister's care to her new husband. Miranda felt adrift and purposeless for the first time since she'd come to Java.

It was shortly after Rija had become the new Sultana of Preanger that Miranda broached the idea of returning to England. Despite Rija's loving objections and Amang's assurances she would always have a place in their household, she knew the young couple needed to find their way together with no interference from an older widowed sister. Further, she had reached the point where she could no longer stand the pitying looks they cast her way when they thought her unaware.

But the real reason she latched on to the idea with such fervor was that duty had always been her driving force, and finding a new role was essential to her sense of self. With Tony, for the brief span of time they'd shared, she'd become caught up in her own happiness, a selfishness that had ultimately cost Tony's life and now plagued her with guilt. If she could fill the emptiness of her existence by becoming a dutiful daughter-in-law, it was a selfless task that reiterated her inner image, gave her direction, and someday might assuage a portion of that guilt.

So after a tearful leave-taking with Rija, she'd undertaken the arduous voyage, gifted with a small but adequate purse from her new brother-in-law's meager treasury and earning her passage by working as interpreter for the merchant captain. And the closer she'd sailed to England, the greater her eagerness had become to reach . . .

". . . Fairhaven. Be ye coming or not?"

Miranda came aware with a faint start. The driver stood impatiently at the coach's open door, the freezing drizzle slanting down through the darkness into his cold-mottled face.

"Oh! Have we arrived?" She scrambled for her small satchel of belongings.

"Aye," the coachman grunted, then stepped back so she could descend.

"Good luck to ye, missus," Squire Knolly said from the other seat.

Miranda flashed him a smile that reflected her excitement. "Thank you, sir, for all your kindness."

Pulling her hood into place, she stepped carefully down, and her shoes sank instantly into the road's icy quagmire. One look at the bleakly empty and dismal landscape and she gasped with dismay. The tired coachman slammed the door, then slogged wearily back to the front of the coach.

"Wait, sir!" Miranda struggled after him, the rain stinging her face, the coach lanterns' flickering light poor help in the rough terrain. "What place is this?"

"Fairhaven Cross." He pointed to a track cutting the highway at right angles. "Go right to the village, left to Fairhaven House."

Miranda gaped in the directions he pointed. The track disappeared into the darkness on either side, the eerie shadows of hedges and bare trees marking the path. "How far?"

"Not far." He climbed into the high seat.

"Wait! Will you take me? I'll gladly pay you." Licking

the rain from her lips, she fumbled with the money pouch tied securely inside her pocket slit.

"No time. 'Tain't far." He lifted his whip, then paused somewhat grudgingly. "Climb back in if you want. There's a posting house at the next stop. You can come back tomorrow if the roads ain't too bad."

Miranda hesitated, already wet through her cloak. Perhaps what he suggested was prudent, but she was so close! She shook her head. "I'll go on, thank you."

"Suit yourself, ma'am." With a shout and a crack of his whip, he set the team in motion again. Miranda watched it disappear into the darkness, then determinedly set off down the left-hand track.

The going was harder than she expected. She sank into mud up to her ankles with each step, and so tall were the hedges in places, it was difficult to see the highway at all, forcing her to move forward strictly by feel.

Not far, he'd said. Shivering wretchedly, she wondered what that meant. Not far on a warm summer afternoon? Or impossibly far in a freezing downpour?

At last, when she thought her strength would desert her, the track made a wide turn, suddenly topping a bare hill, and Miranda saw squares of lighted windows in the distance. With something to focus on, she increased her pace. The road leveled out, passing through rolling open meadows on each side. Gravel crunched wetly beneath her heels, replacing the mud, and the going was easier. As she drew nearer the well-lit establishment, her mouth hung open and water dripped off her cold nose as she stared in amazement.

This was certainly no cottage! Stretching into the darkness, the massive manor house rose to three stories. Its elegantly simple facade was pierced by evenly spaced windows ablaze with light. Coaches, carriages, and grooms came and went through the circular drive before the portico of the front entrance, while to the rear, the stables were in a tumult of activity. Despite the miserable weather, Fairhaven House appeared to be in the midst of some grand entertainment.

At a loss, Miranda pulled her hood lower over her face

for protection, considering what Tony had told her about his mother. It was precious little, she realized. Was Mrs. Benedict the housekeeper here? A servant or nurse for some great nobleman? She wished she'd made more inquiries regarding Fairhaven, yet she knew nothing would have stopped her from coming to find Tony's mother. A massive chill racked Miranda, and she realized it didn't matter. If she stood out in this weather much longer, she'd die of exposure, and she hadn't come all this way to fail now. Gathering her resolve along with her muddy hems, she made her way up the drive and climbed the wide marble steps.

With hands numb and clumsy with cold, she lifted the heavy brass knocker and let it fall. Almost immediately the massive door swung open, and a blast of warm air redolent with the scents of beeswax candles, tantalizing edibles, and sweet perfumes rushed to meet her. Music and the giddy hilarity of a crowd of invisible guests swirled around her, so alien and yet so familiar that she took an involuntary step backward, blinking into the face of a liveried footman.

"Yes?" he demanded haughtily.

"M-Mrs. Benedict, if you please," Miranda responded, her voice faint.

The footman scowled, then spoke over his shoulder. "Mr. Tweedale, you'd better deal with this."

The footman was replaced by the head butler himself, an older man dressed in impeccable black, not a hair of his peruke out of place, who scrutinized Miranda in her bedraggled state as if she were some particularly exotic insect. Hesitantly she repeated her request.

"Impossible. Domestic help may apply at the kitchen entrance tomorrow." He began to push the door shut.

"Oh, sir, please!" Miranda stumbled to the door, throwing back her hood, convinced Tony's mother was employed here. Fair, silvery tendrils of damp hair wisped about her distraught face. "You misunderstand me. I'm not asking for a job. I must see Mrs. Benedict." She hesitated, struck by a thought. "She does reside here, does she not? She has—had a son named Anthony."

"Yes, that is correct," the butler replied, "but she cannot be disturbed. Good evening."

"It's a matter of extreme urgency," Miranda persisted, pressing her hands against the broad panels of the door in a feeble attempt to resist its closing. "I know she'll see me. It's about her son."

"I don't believe—"

"I won't take a moment, if you'll only let me speak to her!" Miranda promised.

"Your name?"

"Miranda Langford Be—" She broke off. How could she break the news of her brief marriage so brutally? "Langford," she finished. "Mrs. Langford."

"Well, Mrs. Langford, as you see, with her ladyship's festivities, your visit is most inconvenient."

Her lower lip trembled. "Please, sir. It's extremely important, and I've come so very far . . ."

Perhaps it was something in the lambent quality of her distressed gray eyes, or the fact that her speech revealed her as a gentlewoman, or perhaps it was the gigantic sneeze that shook her in the next moment, but Mr. Tweedale relented.

"Very well," he said, reluctantly opening the door again. "I'll see what I can do. Come this way."

Mumbling her thanks, Miranda scurried inside before he could change his mind. She found herself in a huge entry hall tiled in squares of black and white marble. A broad staircase led to a square upper gallery, where a set of double doors marked the ballroom, from which poured music, laughter, and the deep hum of many conversations. Statuary in the Greek style stood on pedestals and in carved niches, while paintings of heroic battles and distinguished men and women of earlier generations lined the walls.

But she scarcely had time to register more than the briefest of impressions before Mr. Tweedale led her rapidly to a small side door, down a narrow hall, and up a steep servants' staircase. On the next floor, he ushered her into a small, delightfully feminine salon.

"Wait here," he instructed firmly. "I'll bring Madam to you when I can."

Gravitating to the fragrant applewood fire burning in the carved marble fireplace, Miranda managed a small smile. She placed her hands beneath her chin and bowed in an abbreviated *dodok*. "Thank you, Mr. Tweedale. You're very kind. Allah will bless you."

The butler's impassive expression wavered, and he frowned, puzzled by her words. "Ah, nevertheless, do not leave this room."

"Of course."

As the door closed behind Mr. Tweedale, Miranda chewed her lower lip in growing apprehension. Now that the time when she would meet Tony's mother was almost upon her, she was aflutter with nerves. What should she say? Would Mrs. Benedict like and accept her? Might there be a place and perhaps a job for her here in this great house, too? Or was forging maternal bonds with her unknown mother-in-law just another dream?

Shivering suddenly, Miranda set down her bag, removed her gloves and then her dripping cloak, laying it over the back of a delicately carved and painted chair near the hearth. The tall gilt mirror over the fireplace reflected her face, too wan and pale, the cheekbones too prominent from grief and lack of appetite. With a small sound of disgust, she turned her back on her reflection, hastily smoothing back her hair, jabbing the pins into her chignon haphazardly. She knew she looked far from her best, but then, widows were supposed to be haggard, she supposed.

Facing away from the fire, she lifted her skirts slightly to catch the warmth, sighing with pleasure as the heat ran up her cold legs, and the damp fabric of her unbecoming black gown began to steam dry. As she warmed herself, she admired the pretty salon, the walls covered with daffodil satin, the luxurious rugs dotting the polished floor, the dainty chairs and sofa embroidered with wreaths of pastel spring flowers so real, they looked ready to pluck. Whoever lived here had exquisite—and expensive—tastes. Surely Mrs.

Benedict must be a favored employee to be allowed the use of such rooms.

As the minutes ticked by, the warmth coupled with her exhaustion made Miranda drowsy, but she hesitated to take a chair, afraid she would disgrace herself by falling fast asleep if she became too comfortable. Pacing back and forth, she tried to meditate for calmness in the manner of the Buddhist monks, but nothing could have prepared her for the blond termagant who burst through the salon doors just moments later, followed at a respectful distance by a stone-faced Mr. Tweedale.

"Well, what do you want?" the woman demanded.

"I—I beg your pardon, madam," Miranda faltered, taken quite aback by the sparkling vision before her.

The woman was of that fortunate, indeterminable age that only hard work and a magician for a lady's maid could explain. Her cornsilk yellow hair, bunched in curls about her ageless face and twisted high in back, was shaded with just a few strands of silver that accentuated its fairness rather than detracted from it. Her gown of white sarcenet silk shot with silver would have seemed too virginal and ludicrous on a larger woman, but she was petite and dainty, swishing her wide hoops with just the right amount of dash to be called daringly coquettish rather than blatantly provocative. Her nose was short and straight, her mouth a perfect rosy pout, her eyes the color of gentians, and she oozed sensuality with each step.

Miranda was totally intimidated.

"I'm waiting for Mrs. Benedict," she explained weakly.

The tiny woman drew herself up, her chin high and haughty, her blue eyes cold. "*I* am the Marchioness of Bentley."

"Oh. My lady, pardon me," Miranda said, sinking into an awkward curtsy. "Mr. Tweedale bade me wait here for Mrs. Benedict."

An exasperated frown marred the perfection of the Marchioness's alabaster brow. "Are you addled, girl? Here I am."

Now Miranda was confused. "But I wish to see Anthony Benedict's mother."

"Tony? What about him?" The Marchioness's expression narrowed suspiciously and grew hard. "What business have you with my son?"

"Your—?" Miranda pressed a hand to her throat, and her eyes widened in shock. She groped her way to a chair, holding on to its back for support, and her voice was breathy and strained. "He never told me."

"Told you what?"

Miranda gestured weakly around the room. "About all this. About you." Her gaze turned inward, considering, remembering. "I wonder why . . ."

But she knew. He'd been a victim of a small boy's insecurity, wanting to be loved just for himself. And oh, she had, she thought, fighting tears. She truly had. Compassion poured forth from her heart, and she took a hesitant step toward Tony's mother.

"My lady, I fear I bring you sorrowful news. You must prepare yourself to be strong. Tony is gone."

"Gone? Gone where?"

"Killed in battle, my lady, on Java. He died for an honorable cause."

Incredulous, the Marchioness laughed, then as quickly sobered. "You are quite daft! And I've heard enough of this twaddle! Mr. Tweedale, remove this person!"

"You must believe me, my lady," Miranda said urgently. "I was there. I saw it. It pains me eternally, for I loved him, too."

"This is the biggest pack of nonsense I've ever heard!" the Marchioness snapped. "And you are either a deluded liar or an adventuress, but either way, I will not let you spoil the most important night of my life! Throw this baggage out, Tweedale!"

"Yes, my lady," the butler responded stoically, moving toward Miranda.

"Lady Bentley," Miranda pleaded, "you must hear me—"

The salon door crashed open, interrupting her.

"God's wounds, Mother!" bellowed a voice. "What's keeping you?" A tall man in a dandy's exquisite purple coat and creamy lace cravat stalked in on red-heeled shoes, waving a crystal goblet while voicing loud and drunken complaints. "Colleton's nigh chewing my ass off to have this over, and I can't find a decent bottle of champagne to celebrate—"

Miranda's sharp, wordless cry ended his tirade, and he noticed her for the first time, turning to face her fully.

"Jesus," he whispered. Beneath his expertly coiffed and powdered periwig, his face went white. The stem of the delicate glass snapped between his fingers and fell unnoticed to the floor.

Miranda couldn't breathe, and the blood rushed in her ears. She fought the insensibility that threatened her mind with darkness. She knew him.

Tony! But not Tony. How could it be? Her frantic mind beat for an explanation like a bird trapped behind a window glass. Kit, then! Was this Tony's brother? Or dared she wish for a miracle? Against all hope, she breathed the one word she could manage.

"Tony?"

With the grace and power of a jungle cat, he moved in one fluid motion to close the distance between them. He caught her upper arms, his slate blue gaze piercing her to the core. "Miri! My God!"

As one, they spoke. "I thought you were dead."

As one, they drew in ragged gulps of air to feed their blasted senses.

As one, they laughed in a delirium of joy.

"How . . . ?"

"I don't know . . ."

"Did you . . . ?"

"Angus . . ."

"Rija . . ."

"The knife . . ."

"The lotus . . ."

"Your hair . . ."

"Only ashes . . ."

"Burned . . ."

"Hurt . . ."

"Lost . . ."

"They told me you were dead."

She touched his face, praying that if this were a dream, she'd never wake again. There were too many questions, but that could come later. For now, all she wanted was to look at him, touch him, and know that her miracle was reality. Even his mother's strident demands for explanations did not penetrate Miranda's bubble of euphoria. Looking up at Tony with her heart in her eyes, she silently begged for his kiss.

Groaning, he bent closer. "My little pagan."

A trilling feminine laugh flitted through the moment, splitting it asunder. A lovely young woman with eyes and hair the rich color of chocolate sailed into the room in a shimmer of amber silk. She gave Miranda a brief look, then dismissed her, coming up beside Tony and tugging playfully on his sleeve.

"Darling, you must come now," she said.

Without releasing his hold on Miranda, Tony looked up at the dark-haired beauty like a man waking from a deep sleep, and his voice was a hoarse rasp. "Catherine?"

Again her laugh was gay. "Don't tell me you've forgotten already. How very bad of you! Now, do come. Uncle Colleton is most impatient to announce our engagement."

Miranda felt Tony wince, and her own mouth dropped open.

"That's impossible," she blurted. *"I'm* Tony's wife!"

Chapter 12

❝**Y**ou lying bitch!❞
    Tony's mother landed a stinging slap across Miranda's face with such force, she staggered backward out of Tony's grasp.

"Mother, no!"

Tony positioned himself between Miri and the shrieking Sylvie. Adrenaline poured through his bloodstream, lifting the champagne-induced fog from his brain, leaving him cold sober and shaking with reaction. A ghost had just walked back into his life, a ghost who touched the red stripes on her assaulted cheek in stark disbelief and looked at him with accusing silver eyes.

"Anthony, I'll have no more of this nonsense!" Sylvie raged. "Whoever this woman is, I want her out of my house at once!"

"What does she mean, your wife?" Catherine demanded with all the righteous indignation of a spoiled seventeen-year-old. Her dark eyes were bright with suspicion, and twin spots of hot color rouged her cheeks. "Who is she?"

213

"Miri. Miranda," Tony murmured, swallowing harshly on a swell of emotion that threatened to unman him completely.

"It doesn't matter what the slut's name is!" Sylvie shouted. "The conniving harlot is obviously trying to spoil the announcement. Well, my girl, it won't work!"

"Mother, please!" Tony croaked.

With a final glare, the Marchioness gathered her composure. Forcing her perfect features into a soothing expression, she turned to the bewildered brunette. "Lady Catherine, ignore the ranting of a spurned mistress. It signifies nothing. I'll deal with this impertinent wench."

"I'm not his mistress!" Miranda's voice shook with distress.

"Certainly not," the Marchioness agreed with a nasty laugh. "My son has better taste than to choose such a drudge."

"Then who is she? What does she want?" Lady Catherine's voice rose to a shrill pitch.

"This is all some sort off misunderstanding. Nothing to be concerned about, I'm sure." Lady Sylvie laughed indulgently. "Men must have their pastimes, and my wastrel son is no exception."

Catherine's dark eyes flashed. "Not while he's betrothed to me! My Uncle Colleton—"

"Here, my child," boomed a robust man from the open salon door. In his sixties, the powerful Lord Colleton still cut quite an imposing figure in his mulberry brocade coat and gray full-bottomed wig. "What is all this tumult? Come, Bentley, Catherine. Everyone's eager for the announcement of your marriage."

"There won't be any announcement."

Tony's words cracked across the conversation like a pistol shot. There was a moment of stunned silence, then protests flew from all directions.

"I demand to know your meaning, sir!" Colleton blustered.

"Anthony, have you taken leave of your senses?" Sylvie gasped. "We have two hundred guests waiting—"

"What did she mean your *wife?*" Catherine wailed tearfully.

"I won't stand for another minute of this farce!" Lady Sylvie cried. She pointed an imperative finger at Miranda. "Tweedale, take this troublemaker away immediately!"

"Enough!" Tony roared. He caught Miri's arm in a possessive grip. She stumbled against him, her expression a mixture of dazed mortification and flustered discomposure. "Stay where you are, Tweedale. Miri isn't going anywhere, but the rest of you are. Now, get out! All of you!"

Lady Catherine burst into tears and dashed out of the salon.

Colleton swore darkly. "I'll have your head for this outrage," he said, and followed his niece.

"Anthony, how can you do this to me?" Sylvie cried. "You're ruining everything I've worked for over this . . . this strumpet!"

Tony took a deep breath. "Mother, I can explain everything."

Fury burned in Sylvie's blue eyes. "I'm not the one who needs explanations! You'd better find a way to set things right, or we're ruined, I tell you. None of your charming airs will keep us out of Newgate after this!" Turning on her heel, she swept after the others. "My Lord Colleton, wait!"

"Jesus, that's certainly burnt my bridges," Tony muttered.

"What does it mean?" Miranda gulped. "What's happening?"

"It doesn't matter."

"Doesn't matter?" she cried. "You blackguard! You're engaged to that girl!"

"Mother's doing, not mine. Catherine means nothing to me."

"You obviously feel enough to consider bedding her."

Tony groaned. "For God's sake, Miri! I thought you were dead."

"You left me behind."

"Angus swore he'd seen you killed!"

"My congratulations on your speedy recovery from your tragic loss." The icy quality of her words could not conceal the hurt. She stared stonily at his chest, then her eyes widened incredulously at the quail's egg pearl sitting atop the pin in his lace cravat. "Rija's pearl!" she gasped.

"What?" He glanced down, disconcerted.

"You have the utter gall to sport the prize you took from me while you pledge yourself to another woman!"

"How could I begrudge myself my only reminder of you?"

"Pretty words from a liar and a thief!" she flung.

"Be reasonable, Miri!" he snapped, exasperated.

"My lord—"

Tony whirled about, snarling. "What is it, Tweedale?"

"Your presence is required," the butler said from the door.

Tony muttered an oath. "All right, I'm coming. I'd better make my apologies."

"Not on my account!"

Provoked past endurance, Tony grabbed Miranda's shoulders and bodily pushed her into a chair.

"Not another word from you!" he roared. "Sit down, stay put, and hold your shrewish tongue if you can!"

Her chin flew up at a defiant angle. "I'll thank you not to shout at me, Captain—" She broke off, horrified by a sudden conclusion. "My God, you're not a mere ship's captain, are you?"

Tony's long cheeks flexed with tension. He nodded stiffly and gave her a mocking bow. "Anthony Benedict, Marquess of Bentley, at your service, madam."

"And all this?" She made a vague gesture indicating their surroundings.

"Mine. For a while, anyway." He drew a deep breath, and his forbidding expression relented slightly. "Please, Miri, bear with me while I prevent a riot. Then we'll talk, I promise."

Chin wobbling, she dropped her head to stare at her clenched hands. Tony sighed again, wanting to take her in his arms but knowing instinctively her hurt pride and confusion made it a dangerous course. His mind whirled like a dervish in a trance, still overwhelmed by the miracle of her resurrection, and he knew she must be feeling the same shock.

Looking at her closely, he realized she was exhausted, cold, wet, and probably hungry. What had she endured to come halfway around the globe to find him again? There was so much to consider, so many questions to answer. But perhaps they both needed a few moments to assimilate these events into some sort of manageable cogency before hasty words proved their undoing. And in the meantime, he had to deal with the complications her arrival had precipitated.

"Bring some tea or something," he ordered the butler. "Anything she wishes, understood?"

Tweedale's impassive expression never faltered. "Yes, my lord."

Tony reached out to touch Miranda's hair, but she pressed against the back of the chair, skittish and resentful. With a knot of tension jumping in his jaw, Tony let his hand fall away again. Patience, he told himself. First he must deal with the world, and then he'd deal with his wife.

The world was in an uproar.

His mother intercepted him on the gallery, leaving a clump of distinguished guests the moment she spotted him. A calf-eyed young man whose dandified attire rivaled Tony's followed her, calling her in a petulant voice. "But Sylvie, my love . . ."

"Not *now*, Cecil!" she snapped, then paused to pat his cheek, much as she would have soothed her favorite cocker spaniel pup. "We'll talk later," she promised.

Placated for the moment, Lord Cecil Edmund bowed and was rewarded with a smile. Then Sylvie hurried after her son. Only Tony knew how brittle her smile really was.

"Have you disposed of that woman?" she hissed, pausing before the doorway leading into the overflowing ballroom just as the orchestra struck up a gay country dance. Women in sparkling silks and glittering gems took their places across from their partners, and the men were even more resplendent in gold and silver lace and jewel-toned satins. Tony's gaze fell without interest on the scene.

"That woman is my wife."

Sylvie sucked in an outraged breath. "What is this ridiculous prattle? You cannot be tied to such a pitiful creature! What is it? Have you the wedding jitters? You may lie to Catherine, but you may as well tell me the truth!"

"Then believe what I say." Tony's mouth hardened with resolve. "Where is Catherine? I'd best explain."

"In the library with her uncle. And you may also explain how we'll survive without Catherine's dower portion!"

"I'll find a way," Tony answered grimly, striding toward the library.

Lady Sylvie sniffed disdainfully and glided after him. "Tell me how. You haven't come up for air since you returned from that useless voyage!"

Tony's eyelids fluttered at the barb. It was futile to deny her charges. Believing Miri dead, there'd been no reason to strive, no reason to care about anything any longer. Hurt and ill, he had no memory of portions of the voyage home. Upon his arrival back in England, he'd learned that his Free Indies Shipping Company was on the verge of bankruptcy, his assets reduced to almost nothing, the family lands heavily mortgaged because of Sylvie's greed and his steward's mismanagement during the South Sea Bubble affair. All that had merely seemed a fitting ironical footnote to the many failures of his life.

In his despair, he'd fallen back into his wastrel ways as the only method he knew to mask his pain. He'd tried drowning his sorrow in a bottle, hiding from it in the rounds of the fastest crowds, losing it in nights of gaming. Nothing worked. Forced gaiety had only reiterated his agony. But now fate, or God, or whichever of the exotic deities Miri invoked had given him a second chance. The woman he loved was restored to him, and by all that was holy, he would make himself worthy of her.

"I'll find a way," he said again. That vow ringing in his ears, he entered the paneled library.

Catherine sat on a tufted leather sofa, delicately sniffling into a lace-edged handkerchief while her uncle hovered protectively nearby. Tony wondered in brief irritation how she managed to weep without altering her beauty one whit. Miri looked dreadful when she cried, the end of her nose red, her lovely skin mottled, but there was something real about her emotions that was not present in Catherine's artificial distress.

And Tony realized with relief that although Catherine did not deserve this turn of events, her upset was more out of feminine pique than any real attachment or affection for him. She'd felt a certain amount of pride for landing the infamous Wastrel Lord over all the other contenders, choosing to forget Lord Colleton's sizable dowry had been the determining factor when Tony had finally acquiesced to the match under Sylvie's incessant prodding. An easy solution, he'd thought, especially apt since nothing really mattered anymore.

With a start, he recognized how unkind and callous his attitude had been, how he'd reeked with self-pity. But now purpose in the form of a silver-eyed goddess was back in his life, and it was past time to have done with apathy.

"Lady Catherine, may I have a word?" he asked formally.

"Bentley, you scoundrel!" Lord Colleton began, his silver brows lowered in a thunderous scowl, "I'll—"

"Uncle, please," Catherine interrupted in a soft, injured tone. "I'll hear his lordship."

"Thank you, gentle Catherine." Tony knelt beside her and took her hand. "I've caused you pain and I regret it, but we have all received a severe shock this night."

"Then that girl really is . . . ?"

Tony knew a pang of guilt at Catherine's pallor, but he answered the only way he could. "My wife, Miranda."

"This is unforgivable, sir!" Colleton said between clenched teeth. He turned a baleful glare upon the Marchioness. "I should never have listened to your assurances, Sylvie! Once a blackguard, always a blackguard!"

"My lord, I'm as shocked at you," Sylvie protested. "I

had such great hopes to unite our families, but now this—!''

"Both my mother and I are innocent of malice in this astonishing circumstance," Tony insisted. "Miranda Langford and I were married last year by Eastern rites on Java. I had no idea until I stepped into that salon tonight that she was alive."

"How could you not know?" Catherine demanded, her lips swelling in a pout.

"Witnesses told me she'd been brutally murdered during the Java uprising, and brought what I thought was certain proof." A grimness clouded Tony's blue eyes, turning them gray with the remembrance of how he'd howled his grief like a madman when they'd brought him a silvery skein of blood-stained hair.

"Why didn't you tell us this before?" Colleton asked.

Tony flicked him a glance that was coolly distant and, releasing Catherine, stood again. "I thought her dead, and my grief was private."

"But now she is not dead at all," Catherine said with a petulant shrug. "How inconvenient."

"Perhaps the situation is still salvageable," Sylvie interjected. "Who is this Miranda person? Obviously no one of consequence. It should be a simple matter to arrange an annulment."

"Nay," Tony ground out in a rusty tone. "She is my wife in every way."

Sylvie clutched desperately at straws. "Your word against hers? No? Then a divorce. Discreetly, of course. The wedding would only need to be postponed . . ."

"That's enough, Mother!" Tony snapped. "Miranda is my wife, and you must accept that."

"And I must accept it also?" Catherine asked angrily. "You have played me for a fool, sir. What shall I tell all our friends? How shall I ever show my face again after such a public humiliation?"

"Be thankful the truth was known now, instead of after the wedding," Tony replied impatiently. Catherine's shocked gasp made him temper his next words. "There's no need to say anything, since we made no formal announcement. Or, if you wish, you may say you cried off yourself, having discovered what a bounder I am. That will be easily believed, and you will be applauded for your great good sense.''

"You care not that you have shattered my heart," Catherine said in a forlorn voice, dabbing at tears again shimmering down her cheeks.

Tony stifled an impatient snort at this playacting, letting her have her moment. "Of course I care, my dear, but it would be unfair to offer any hope, knowing now that I am not free."

"Oh, but how shall I live without you?" Catherine cried dramatically.

"Come, come, child," Tony said with a faint smile, "you will be breaking new hearts in no time at all and have quite forgotten an old man like me."

Catherine raised her dark eyes in a way calculated to show their tear-washed beauty and her undying adoration. "No, never."

"Even so, we must both put on a good show," Tony said, his manner encouraging. He pulled his kerchief from his pocket and gently mopped her face. "Now, come. You shall dance with me, and flirt with all the other young men, and everyone will decide your are teaching the Wastrel Lord a lesson I richly deserve. You will find it amusing, and in the meantime your uncle will have leisure to select a suitor far more suitable than I could ever be."

He could see Catherine considering the prospect of having the world believe she'd turned the tables on him. She nodded at last, and he exhaled in relief, grateful the idea appealed.

"All right, but you must dance with me several times before I spurn you," she warned.

Though Tony chafed to return to Miri, he smiled in agreement. "It will be my pleasure."

"These childish games are no compensation for the insult you have paid my niece," Colleton said with a snort of disgust.

"Come, my lord," Tony cajoled with a charming smile,

"we must all be reconciled to the inevitable. Let us part friends. I have no desire to see my blood spilled on the dueling fields!"

"Certainly not!" Sylvie agreed. She forced a bittersweet smile and took Lord Colleton's arm. "Come, my lord, we must all stifle our disappointment over this unfortunate predicament."

Tony was leading Lady Catherine toward the door and looked back sharply at his mother. "Hardly unfortunate, Mother. We are in the midst of a miracle, for you have gained a daughter, and I, my Marchioness."

There was no mistaking the stricken look that paled Sylvie's cheeks. "Y-yes, of course, Anthony," she faltered. "I confess in my shock I had forgotten that."

The look in Tony's eyes was stern. "See that you do not again."

For the next three-quarters of an hour, Tony forced himself to laugh and play the part of gracious host. If there were some curious looks from his guests when no announcement preceded the call to supper, he chose to ignore them. Catherine meanwhile flirted outrageously, and with a daring that surprised even Tony, walked into supper on the arm of a Jamaican planter while ignoring Tony completely. This snub was the object of the dinner conversation henceforth, and Tony thought it entirely in character to stalk from the room at this point.

Hurrying down the corridor to the yellow salon, Tony felt his heart quail with trepidation and eagerness. Hopefully, Miri was in a frame of mind more conducive to communication now. How eager he was to cast off his facade as the Wastrel Lord and just be himself! She brought out the best in him, and he wanted to pour his love into her heart forever, to feel alive again after so many months of grief and loneliness. He wanted to talk to her, hear her voice, touch her, hold her, carry her to the huge bed in his room and not rise for a week. His heart raced at the thought, and his smile appeared like the sun coming out from behind a storm cloud.

He erupted through the salon doors in a burst of boyish impatience. "Miri!"

Her name echoed in his ears, and the clouds descended again.

The salon was empty.

Bristol was a city that smelled of the sea. No matter where you were, Miranda decided, the salt and the fish and the tar permeated every plank and brick, every pore and follicle. Even the stale water she poured from a cracked pitcher into the washbowl reeked faintly of fish.

When she'd reached the city late the previous night, she'd been grateful to find any kind of shelter. Now, in the early light of day, she was sure The Hand and Garter hadn't been the wisest choice of accommodation. Holding her breath, Miranda used the icy, odoriferous water to wash her face, then hastily dried it with the hem of her thin petticoat, considering the preceding evening's events.

When the coach had stopped under the weather-beaten sign of a woman's hand holding a coffeepot, the squalid character of the street hadn't concerned her. At that point, she'd been too exhausted by her flight from Fairhaven to look for other lodging or to care overmuch about the impression she made. Her request for a private room produced nothing more than a disinterested grunt from the slovenly innkeeper, though she'd received several leering, speculative glances from the roughly garbed seamen, stevedores, tradesmen, and the drabs and serving wenches who made up the coffeehouse trade this close to the docks. Two seconds after she'd thrown the bolt of her cold, tiny room and fallen onto the coarse bed, the carousing and ribaldry rising from the taproom below her had ceased to matter.

Now, her morning ablutions complete, Miranda brushed the worst of the dirt and mud from her black gown, then pulled it over her shift. Her mind shied away from the memory of the scene of two nights before that had provoked her impetuous flight, but like a sore tooth one couldn't help touching, her thoughts returned to it again and again.

Shame, chagrin, and an overwhelming and panicky sense

of having lost all control had made her bolt just moments
after Tony's departure from the yellow salon. No one had
expected such action from the female fortune hunter, of
course, so retracing her steps out of the great house and
bribing a greedy groom to take her to the next village had
been swiftly and easily done. Though now her cowardice
made her blush, at the time she'd been too shocked and
dismayed to worry about dishonor. It had seemed a fortui-
tous omen that a west-bound coach, delayed by the weather,
had come along just then, and a voice from heaven that had
planted the seed of an idea along with Cousin Letty's name
in the whirlwind of her thoughts.

Giving her hair a final pat, Miranda swept on her camlet
cloak, picked up her bag, hesitated, then set it down again.
If her search for her only living blood relative proved fruitless, then she'd need a place to stay again tonight. Locking
the room securely, she placed the heavy key in her pocket,
then crept downstairs, wrinkling her nose at the heavy odors
of many years accumulation of smoking grease, stale ale,
and unwashed bodies.

No one was about at this early hour except a surly potboy
cleaning the ashes from the cold fireplace. Since the custom
room appeared even more unsavory by day, she did not
bother him for breakfast, but tipped him a ha'penny to
inform the landlord she wanted to engage the room for
another night.

"Aye, missus!" he agreed, a grin lighting his grimy face.
"I'll see to it meself!"

Once on the misty cobbled street, Miranda breathed in
the salty air with relish, deciding its fishiness was preferable
to the inn's seamy odors, and the thin fog a decided im-
provement after days of rain. Straightening her shoulders,
she went to hire a chair, a curious contraption of enclosed
box supported on poles carried by two porters. The expense
seemed warranted, as her porters would surely know more
about the city than she did, and thus quickly aid her in
locating Cousin Letty.

By midafternoon, however, both Miranda and her porters
were heartily discouraged. On applying at the address on

the last piece of correspondence her father had received
from his cousin, Miranda was informed Miss Letticia Sutherlin's services had been terminated when the youngest son
had left the nursery for school some eight years back. They'd
been referred to a succession of establishments after that,
following Cousin Letty's varied employments as nurse,
housekeeper, companion, nanny, seamstress, and tutor of
young ladies from one household to another, up and down
the canted streets. Finally, on the advice of an elderly cleric
for whom Cousin Letty had copied sermons and devotions,
they came to a tall attached house at the top of a gloomy
alley in a dismal lane.

Miranda felt a sense of déjà vu when she raised the heavy
brass knocker, but she was too disillusioned by her experience at Fairhaven to hope for anything, forcing her mind
into a state of Eastern acceptance. It was hard to believe
this dank doorway was not just another dead end. She let
the knocker fall again.

The handle rattled, and the door swung open to creaking
hinges and irritable mutterings. A plump matron of fifty,
wearing a ruffled mobcap with dangling lace lappets on her
gray hair, and a patched apron over a serviceable brown
gown, appeared on the threshold.

"No need to wake the dead with your knocking! 'He
maketh the deaf to hear!' Yes, what it is? Speak up, miss,
I've got—" She broke off with a startled gasp. "Richard!"

Despite her best intentions, Miranda's heart jumped with
hope. "Cousin Letty?"

Hazel-green eyes speckled with gold ranged up and down
over Miranda. "My dear! Could it be . . . ? Of course it is!"
she answered herself, and reached for Miranda with both
hands outstretched. "Little Miri Langford! I'd have known
you anywhere. You have the look of your dear father, the
same fey eyes, looking always at dreams. Oh, I can't believe
it! Come in out of the chill. My dear, you must tell me
everything—"

Taking Cousin Letty's hands, Miranda got caught up in
a warm, enveloping hug, and she laughed in relief and
delight. "May I? You're sure?"

"You don't appear on my doorstep like a Lazarus risen from his tomb and expect to get away from me so easily, do you?" Letty demanded. "Come in now. You look half-frozen."

"I'll tell the porters to wait."

"You'll do no such thing! No use paying them to stand still, and I'll not let you out of my sight until I've heard the news behind this miracle. I'll send Dame Octavia's scullery girl after another chair if need be."

"Very well."

Moments later, after paying off the porters and giving them each a hefty tip, Miranda sat in a musty parlor decorated with moth-eaten tapestries and heavy Jacobean furniture while Letty plied her with tea, crusty bread, and pots of clotted cream and rhubarb jam.

"Atrocious old pile, isn't it?" Letty asked cheerfully, catching Miranda's surreptitious glances at her surroundings.

"Have you lived here long?" Miranda briefly recounted her difficulties in locating Letty's whereabouts.

"I've been Dame Octavia's companion almost a year now, and glad I was to get the position, even though she's a demanding, spiteful old termagant, and her stingy son won't spare an extra penny for his mother's comfort or mine."

A strident tapping erupted from the ceiling, then as quickly subsided. "What . . . ?" Miranda began.

"Dame Octavia. She loves to pound her cane to make me run up those stairs a hundred times a day." Letty continued to sit, complacently sipping her tea, and a mischievous twinkle appeared in her eye. "She's bedridden because she chooses to be, you see. It's a battle between us. Will she get up and beat me for not coming quickly enough? Or will she wear herself out with tapping and fall to sleep again?"

Letty glanced up again as the tapping repeated, slower now, then stopped. "Naptime, it appears." She flashed a sweet smile. "Don't look so appalled, child. It's not such a bad life for a maiden lady from a genteel upbringing, and one does what one must to survive.''

"Yes, I understand that," Miri murmured, setting her cup down, "but don't you want more?"

"Oh, I have my dreams, too. A little cottage with a thatched roof and a rose garden, and perhaps someone to scold for crossing my clean kitchen floor with his muddy boots on. Silly dreams for an old woman like me." Letty shrugged, then smiled again, making her plump, rosy cheeks as round as apple dumplings. "Good, the hot drink's brought your color back. Now, tell me everything."

And for the next hour, that's exactly what Miranda did, leaving nothing out except some of the more personal encounters with Tony that would have shocked a virtuous spinster like her cousin.

"I didn't know what to do, so I ran to you," Miranda finished, staring down at the tea long grown cold in her cup. "I don't know what I would have done if I hadn't found you."

"Survived, as you have so admirably up to now," Letty said staunchly. "It's a Langford trait."

"Yet I thank all the many heavens that you're here. I don't wish to burden you with my woes, but I felt so alone."

"My poor child!" Cap bobbing, Letty patted Miranda's hand reassuringly. "You aren't alone any longer, and praise the Lord, neither am I. 'Whither thou goest,' as Ruth said. But this tale is nearly unbelievable!"

"It seems like a dream at times to me, too," Miranda said with a strangled laugh, "but I assure you it's the truth."

"You cannot leave this so unsettled. Imagine! You and the Wastrel Lord. Oh, there are such tales . . ."

"What sort of tales?" Miranda asked uneasily. "What wickedness earned him such a terrible name?"

"I cannot say, but 'judge not, that ye be not judged.' Believe only what you know of the man, not what his enemies or even his friends say about him. Besides, such vainglorious boasting is often exaggerated, you know, especially by the envious."

"England is a curious place indeed if wickedness is a virtue to be aped," Miranda replied tartly.

Letty chuckled. "Sinners are more fascinating than ordinary folk, my dear. You aren't the first woman to fall for a man with a bit of the devil in him, and I'll wager you won't be the last! At any rate, you'll have to face the Marquess again and resolve the situation."

"Yes, I know," Miri said in a quiet voice. "But not yet, not until I know my own mind. I was so glad to find Tony alive, yet he is not the man I thought I married." She buried her face in her hands. "I'm so confused..."

"And worn to a frazzle with it, no doubt," Letty said, her voice laden with compassion. "Don't worry, Miri, things have a way of working out for the best. Now, you must stay here with me until this is all settled."

Miranda lifted her head. "Is it possible? I wouldn't want to jeopardize your position. At any rate, I retained my room at the inn for tonight."

"Pooh! What position? I may offer my own cousin my hospitality, if you can stand this dingy dungeon. Besides, neither Dame Octavia or her son need know."

Miranda smiled at Letty's feisty attitude. "I'd like that, at least until I find a position of my own."

"That's settled then. At which inn did you stay?"

"The Hand and Garter. I must go pick up my bag—"

"Oh, dear, this won't do at all! Miri, that is not a respectable establishment for a young gentlewoman."

"It certainly wasn't at all clean," Miranda admitted, puzzled by Letty's frown, "but I had no trouble."

But Letty was already on her feet. "I'll have Ellie go for a chair, and Cook listen for Dame Octavia. You and I will go get your things, for the sooner you've shaken the dust of that establishment from your feet the better!"

Warmed by Letty's determination, concern, and her unconditional welcome, Miranda agreed, musing ironically at the contrast between her reception at Fairhaven and here. With this industrious and indomitable woman firmly in her corner, Miranda decided, she might be able to somehow resolve her dilemma with Tony.

Within a short span, they alighted from a sedan chair, bade the porters to wait, and entered The Hand and Garter together. While Miranda settled with the landlord, Letty glowered at the roisterous crowd, placing herself as a shield between Miranda and any untoward attentions. Faintly amused by Letty's actions as self-appointed chaperone, Miranda finally led her up the smoke-blackened staircase to her room.

"I haven't much with me," she explained, inserting the key. "I left most of my things in Millford with Topaz."

"We'll send for her, too," Letty said firmly. "Now, hurry, dear. There's much to do."

"You are too kind," Miranda murmured, newfound affection making her voice thick. Pushing open the door, she started into the room, then came up short with a strangled gasp.

Tony lounged with boneless grace in a straight wooden chair, smoking a long-stemmed clay pipe, his boot heels propped on the edge of the sagging bed. From the evidence of his coat and wig lying on the bed, his rolled-up shirt sleeves, and the thick haze drifting against the ceiling's dark beams, he'd been there for some time.

"Come in, sweeting," he said in a voice that was too quiet. With thin blue-gray trails of smoke drifting from his nostrils, and his blue eyes blazing with rage, he looked like Satan himself.

"Go away." Fighting a wave of vertigo, Miranda heard her words come out faint and shaky. "I have nothing to say to you now."

Tony's heels hit the floor with a thump, evoking an involuntary squeak from Letty. Eyes fastened on Miranda's defiant countenance, he set aside his pipe and rose to his full height, his movements slow and deliberate, as though if he moved too fast, he might fly apart altogether.

"On the contrary, my dear, you should have plenty to say." The low fury in his voice raised the hairs on the back of Miranda's neck. "And you may start by telling me why I find my wife in a goddamn brothel!"

Chapter 13

"**M**ust you be so disagreeable?" Miranda complained. "I know this place isn't much—"

Tony gave a disgusted snort. "You don't believe me? Even as we speak, the landlord thinks the Wastrel Lord has come to meet his latest mistress."

Miranda's cheeks burned, but she lifted her chin defiantly. "Then he'd be wrong, wouldn't he?"

"Not by much," Tony growled. "Don't you know what a woman's hand on the sign means?"

Miranda's expression faltered, and her breath wheezed from her lungs. "Not . . . a place for women of injured morals? Oh, dear."

"I didn't like to say it," Letty murmured, wringing her hands, "but this establishment is as infamous as Gomorrah."

Tony's attention settled on the plump older woman. "Who's this? Your accomplice in depravity?"

"Don't be ridiculous!" Miranda snapped, bristling. "As

usual, your temper gets the better of your sense! This is my kinswoman, Miss Letticia Sutherlin.''

"My lord." Wide-eyed as an owl, Letty bobbed a hasty curtsy.

"I had no idea of the true nature of this place," Miranda continued.

"Shall I extol your innocence or curse your ignorance?" Tony's voice dripped sarcasm. "God's blood, woman! Anything might have happened!"

Miranda straightened her shoulders under her cloak and made her tone cool. "It didn't. And since I'm leaving now, there's no harm done. Not that you should concern yourself in the slightest. Come, Letty."

Before she could reach for her bag, Tony grabbed her, thrusting her roughly down into his vacated chair.

"You're not going anywhere," he ground out, looming over her like an avenging angel. "Not until I've had some explanations."

"I owe you nothing, sir."

"Blast it, Miri!" he exploded. "You're my *wife*, and by God, I'm taking you home, where you belong. Any other man would flay you alive for the hell you've put me through these last days!"

Guilt prickled her conscience and made her voice small. "How did you find me?"

"By scouring the countryside. It wasn't easy, but I have my methods," he said dryly. A frantic scratching and an abrasive yowl from the corridor made him grimace. "Here's one of the search party now."

Someone rapped, and as the door swung open, a furry black shape dashed through the crack, followed by a wiry old salt in a fearnought jacket and a striped stocking cap.

"Ach, Cap'n! She's here somewhere," Angus Pratt announced. "Lookit this daft animal—" He broke off, his rheumy gray eyes lighting up. "By Old Nick! Ye found her!"

"With yours and Beelzebub's help," Tony replied, the corner of his mouth twitching.

The victim of a gleeful pouncing, Miranda peered around

a purring armload of black cat and smiled weakly. "Hello, Angus."

"Ach, lass! Praise be, ye're really alive."

Miranda rubbed Beelzebub's tattered ears, amazed they'd used the feline as a bloodhound. She couldn't even recall why she'd once disliked him, though Letty's horrified expression gave her some clue. Smiling at the old sailor, Miranda battled the urge to laugh and cry all at once.

"Yes, Angus, it's really me."

There was a suspicious gleam in Angus's eyes, too, and his voice was gravelly with emotion. "It's time for me to retire when I start seeing things like this. It's my fault the cap'n thought ye were dead."

"It was a confused time," Miranda murmured, her tone oblique. "Many mistakes were made."

"That palace burnt down around our ears while we dragged the cap'n free, but one of the mates heard you screaming." The old sailor shook his grizzled, sun-faded strawberry head at the memory. "By the time we got the cap'n out, grievous hurt, there weren't no sign of ye, except for that bloody knife and a hank of hair. I knew there wasn't another woman on that isle with hair like yours, lassie."

"Hurt?" Miranda's heart leapt painfully, and her gray eyes went bottomless with well-remembered fear. "Tony was hurt? Badly?"

"Ach, we like to lost him then and there," Angus answered before Tony could object. "Had to cut his burnt clothes off him, we did."

"I see." A deep trembling set off spasms of emotion within Miranda. So that was how he'd come to lose his talisman. The pieces of the puzzle, the coincidences and choices, fell into a pattern so neat, it was hard to call it mere accident. Miranda shivered as though an unseen hand brushed her neck with icy fingers. What forces pushed them along their appointed paths?

"Save your pity for the Dutchman, Miri," Tony interjected on a harsh note. "He might have won our duel if the *kraton* hadn't collapsed when it did. There wasn't anyone to pull him out of that inferno."

"Good," Miranda said fiercely. "A man so evil deserves no pity."

"There weren't a sign of him, that's for sure," Angus added. "But we had our hands full with the cap'n, him passing in and out, cursing and howling to go after you. He'd have killed himself for sure if I'd let him, so we dosed him with opium and headed for the *Mirage*. Forgive me, lass. With no hope left for you, all I could do was try to keep the cap'n alive as best I could."

"I understand."

"By damn, you'd better," Tony said, scowling. He scooped Beelzebub from her lap and handed the hissing cat to Angus. "Get him out of here, and take Miss Sutherlin, too. I want to talk to my wife alone."

Angus obediently took Letty's arm, but she jerked free, searing him with a fulminating glance.

"Unhand me, you ruffian!" Ignoring Angus's astounded expression, she turned back to Tony, her lappets flapping against her plump chin, a stern frown pleating her brow. "My lord, I must object! As Miranda's closest relative, I have a right to know your intentions."

"My intentions?" Tony glowered at the older woman, a high color rushing to his cheekbones. "By God, I intend to make her live up to the vows we took. Like it or not, she is my wife, and I will have her at my side."

"You still think like a spoilt child!" Miranda snapped, jumping to her feet again. "It's only *I* want this or *I* want that. But my wishes play a part in this, will you or no!"

"You cannot think you can reappear in my life, then leave again without a word," he said angrily.

Miranda's fury matched his, and her hands clenched at her sides. "What choice have I? I've played the sorrowing widow while you've been easing your grief in the arms of another woman!"

"I told you about that!" he gritted.

Miranda's breasts rose and fell with her sharp, angry words. "Why should I believe the promises of the Wastrel Lord?"

"Child, child! This acrimony will bring you naught,"

Letty interrupted in a chiding tone, watching the two of them warily.

"The lady's right," Angus interjected. "Don't let a squall turn into a hurricane over a wee misunderstanding."

Letty eyed the old salt with a mixture of approval and irritation.

"Have you some solution then?" Miranda asked, bitterness coating her words.

Letty nodded hesitantly. "There's only one thing you can do, 'for it is better to marry than to burn.'"

"Letty!" Miranda looked askance.

"Since the Marquess declares he will treat you honorably, as his lawful wife," Letty continued stubbornly, "you have a duty before Our Lord to cleave unto him."

Miranda gaped in shock at Letty's defection, but Tony's expression cleared, and his smile was radiant with gratitude.

"Thank you, Miss Sutherlin. 'Tis Miri's duty, is it not? I appreciate your candor. And of course, as my wife's nearest relation, you are always welcome in our household."

Letty's jaw dropped, and her hazel-green eyes sparkled with sudden eagerness. Miranda ground her teeth at this blatant bribery. Of course Letty would be willing to give up her penurious job for a position of honor in a lord's establishment! Miranda felt a pang of guilt. Could she be so selfish as to deprive Letty of a chance for a life of comfort and a contented old age? Something of her dismay must have shown on her face, for when Letty noticed it, she instantly shuttered her gaze.

"Of course, my lord," Letty said in a demure tone, "that would depend entirely on Miranda."

"As does so much," Tony returned sourly. Bracing one forearm on a low overhead beam, he gestured toward the door. "Miss Sutherlin, will you be so kind as to wait in my carriage with Mr. Pratt? Miri and I have things to discuss."

"It will do no good!" Miranda hissed, suffocating under a sense of hurt betrayal. "Nothing you say can change the truth."

"Hear him out," Letty urged, giving Miranda's hand a

quick, encouraging squeeze. "Remember, 'cease from anger, and forsake wrath.' Well, Mr. Pratt? Are we going to stand here all day?"

Angus blinked. Muttering darkly under his breath about domineering women, he tucked Beelzebub under his arm and allowed Letty to precede him from the room, firmly shutting the door behind them.

Miranda clamped her lips shut, folded her arms, and stared mutinously at her husband. Tony pointed his long index finger at her nose, and spoke clearly and deliberately, as if to a thimble-witted child.

"For the last time—Lady Catherine Salter is a simpering miss, and I thank God that there's no need to wed her, bed her, or sire insipid children with her. The betrothal's broken off completely, and Mother will get over her disappointment as soon as we produce her a grandchild."

His arrogance took her breath away. "You assume too much, sir!"

Tony's blue eyes narrowed into ominous slits. "Do I?"

"Yes! This is unworkable, and you know it."

He took a step closer. "Why?"

Swallowing nervously, Miranda backed up. "Because . . . because you deceived me from the start, letting me think all this time you were someone other than who you are."

"I suppose I did. Just as you did the night we met." He laughed softly at her revealing blush. "So now we're even."

"I'm not a part of your world and I never could be," she said desperately, backing away until her calves bumped the forgotten chair. "And I'm obviously not needed or wanted. The only sensible thing to do is petition for divorce."

"Goddamn you, no!" Roaring his fury, he whirled around, slamming his fist against the wall so hard, it split the plaster.

Shocked by the sudden explosion of violence, Miranda sank down into the chair, her mouth open, staring up into Tony's black countenance with the first real glimmerings of fear. Breathing hard, oblivious to his scraped and bleeding knuckles, he stalked toward her with a curious stiff-legged gait as though a pain twisted his belly.

"I won't let you leave me again." Bending over her, he released the clasp of her cloak and roughly pushed it from her shoulders, then plunged his fingers into her hair, painfully tugging it free from its confining pins to wash like moonlight over her shoulders.

Frozen, Miranda watched the play of emotions cross his lean face as he sifted the fair strands, so much shorter now than he remembered. Kneeling in front of her, he smoothed the contours of her shoulders beneath the coarse black gown, as though learning her again by touch, then slid his hands lower to the fullness of her breasts. The tension in his jaw was so keen, it made the cleft in his square chin flatten to nothing.

Fearful apprehension and a deeper excitement mingled within Miranda. Shuddering uncontrollably, she wondered if she'd provoked him too far—and wondered with a blinding flash of honesty if she'd done it intentionally.

"No divorce," he repeated hoarsely, blue eyes smoldering.

Hard fingers cupped her chin, and he took her mouth, kissing her with a fierceness that revealed his desperation, bending her back against his arm and ravaging her lips so fully, she could neither reject him nor respond. Breaking the kiss, he groaned from his depths, then buried his face in her lap, holding her around the waist, his bent shoulders shaking violently.

It took her a moment to realize what the quakes that racked him meant. Then another long, awestruck moment passed as she tried to comprehend the forces that had made a man of Tony's strength weep. It was impossible.

"Shh," she whispered, her hands hovering over the froth of sunset-colored curls. She touched the familiar softness of his hair and was lost. Collapsing over him, her cheek on the top of his head, her palms scoring the muscular expanse of his silk-clad back, she murmured incoherent words of comfort. "Oh, don't, don't . . ."

"God, how you torment me!" His voice was strangled

with despair. "Appearing and vanishing like a will-o'-the wisp, stealing my soul each time you go. No mortal woman could hurt me this way."

"Please, Tony . . ." Her choked voice matched his.

"You're really a *Pontianak*, aren't you? I lost my talisman, so the spiteful spirit is trying to kill me for my love. Well, it's working."

"Don't say that." Her fingertips trembled against his face, baptized by the heat of his tears. Closing his fist over her wrist, he pinned her with the pressure of his fingers, raising her up as he tried to peer into her averted face.

"Look at me," he ordered.

Reluctantly she lifted her eyes to his. He made no attempt to wipe his cheeks or hide his emotional nakedness. "I pray to God I never treated any woman with such careless cruelty as you have me," he said hoarsely. "If I did, perhaps this is my just punishment."

Her expression was anguished, torn. "I don't want to hurt you."

"How can you not if you deny me my salvation? For that's what you are."

She shook her head. "Don't make me more than I am."

"You're everything," he said simply. "Didn't you know?"

"Oh, Tony . . ." Her hand slid down his forearm in a helpless gesture, and she caught her breath on a soft gasp. Beneath her fingers lay the raised pink ridge of a scar, the remnants of a burn. The thought of his suffering made her go pale. "You were hurt, near to death, Angus said. I—I saw it all. Dear God, Tony! Why did you stay too long?"

"The flames surrounded us before I realized, and Steef gave no quarter. He was crazed, blocking off our retreat." Tony shook his head at the memory of the conflagration. "I jumped finally, and a falling beam knocked me into the open. It probably saved my life, for Angus found me there, but it left its marks on my back and legs."

"Oh, my God," she whispered, stricken with compassion.

He scowled. "It's not pretty, but I function well enough."

"You make light of your pain to spare my guilt," she accused in a shaky voice, then impulsively bent and pressed a soothing kiss on the scar of his forearm.

Tony swallowed, and his words grew thick. "The worst pain wasn't physical. You don't know what I went through! The guilt—if only I hadn't been so damned set on taking my revenge on the Dutchman, then maybe I could have protected you better."

"We both did what we thought was best," Miranda protested. "You could not know Ishta would attack me."

"Ishta!"

She looked away. "I—I killed him. Noppa taught me well the uses of a *kris*."

"My poor Miri." He brushed a strand of fair hair back from her cheek. "You've suffered, too."

"When the *kraton* fell, I went a bit mad. Rija and the rest had to carry me away. It was natural for Angus to believe I'd been killed. Don't blame him too much."

"I don't. I never did. Your death was my fault. Why was I spared while you had perished? I knew it wasn't right, that I had to pay. Mayhap that explains why I haven't given a damn about anything ever since, and why I've been hell-bent on the road to destruction." Self-revelation clouded his expression momentarily, then his earnest gaze came back to her. "But, Miri, all that changed the instant you came back into my life! You can't leave me bereft again. Don't send me back to a living hell."

Visibly shaken by the rawness of his confession, she bit her lip. "You—you're stronger than that."

"Not without you. Never without you."

"But the two people who fell in love on Java don't exist anymore."

He pressed her palms to his cheeks, letting her skin soak up the residue of his tears. "They're right here," he contradicted softly.

Her lower lip trembled suddenly, and her eyes filled. A single silver tear slipped from her lashes and drifted down her face. "They were part of a terrible, lovely dream, but dreams don't last. Those people don't fit in this reality."

"You're making this too hard," he said, suddenly impatient again.

"I'm trying to be sensible, Tony." Unconsciously, her thumbs stroked the hard bones of his face, the sensitive pads rasping over the red-blond stubble of his beard. "What can I be to a man in your position?"

He smiled, shifting so that he could drop a shivering kiss into her palm. "My wife. My love. The mother of my children."

Panic flickered behind her eyes. He was so determined, yet so naive. How could she make him see the problems? "I have no dowry, no position, no training, and I—I never bargained for the life of a titled lady."

His mouth hardened, became stubborn. "That's too bad, because that's what you've got."

"Against my will?"

He winced. "Do you wish me to beg, Miri? I have no pride left where you're concerned."

"No, I don't want that, ever. But . . ." She broke off with a shuddering breath.

"But what? Tell me."

With a little sob, she pulled her hands free and covered her streaming eyes. "If I allow this to happen, someday you'll realize you made a mistake, and I won't be able to bear it."

"Miri," he murmured tenderly, "It won't happen. I love you."

"Are you certain?" she asked, wiping her cheeks and lifting her chin valiantly. "Don't say so unless you're sure."

Tony's jaw flexed. "Perhaps you no longer care for me. Is that the problem?"

"How do I know what I feel anymore?" she cried. "I want to believe I love you still, but is it really you, or an illusion? Circumstances and people change, and that was made abundantly clear to me at Fairhaven."

Frustration etched deep groves next to his mouth. "I moved heaven and earth to find you again. What else must I do to convince you? You're coming with me, and that's final!"

"What about society, your family? I'll never be accepted."

"Hang them all!" he shouted. "What difference does it make to us?"

"A world of difference if you come to hate me."

"Your fears are without foundation!" In exasperation, he ran his hands through his hair.

Miranda chewed her lower lip worriedly. "But your mother—"

"Will accept you for my sake. All she wants is to see me happy in my married life." Rising, he drew her to her feet. "You know you have no choice. You gave your vows as I did. Your cousin Letticia is absolutely right. It is your duty to live with your husband."

"But you're a stranger to me. I do not know the Marquess of Bentley!" she protested. "You can't expect me to . . . to . . ." she broke off, blushing hotly.

Tony's countenance grew thunderous with suppressed anger. "To make love with your own husband? Hell! What do you want of me, woman?"

"Time," she answered promptly. "Time to become reacquainted before we resume intimacies, to see if we should really suit before we make another sort of mistake."

"Damnation! You don't want much!"

She looked down at the floor. "It's the only way I'll come willingly."

Muttering curses under his breath, he glared at her bent head, rubbing the throbbing tendons in the back of his neck. He wanted her so badly he ached, but he wanted her in all ways, not just in bed. Though he did not share it, he understood her caution. If she needed a little time to sort through her feelings and ascertain the depths of his devotion after that sordid little scene at Fairhaven, then he had no choice but to give it to her.

"All right," he said suddenly. "You have my word, my lady. I will not demand a husband's rights until you're ready to give them to me freely."

"And all I must do is return to Fairhaven?" Miri's head

jerked up, her eyes shimmering with a mixture of surprise
and suspicion. "It's a poor bargain for you."

His slow smile heated her blood. "I have every faith that
my patience will be amply rewarded. Besides, it will be a
novelty to woo my *own* wife."

A reluctant, rueful laugh burbled from her throat. "You
are ever the rogue."

Catching her hand, he nibbled tiny kisses over her knuckles, watching her expression through his sandy lashes. "And
a scoundrel, so beware."

"Yes, that, too." Her words were short and choppy as
her breath came faster.

"But you'll never be bored," he promised. "Or unloved.
So, you'll come?"

Miranda hesitated, tempted by a promise of paradise, yet
afraid. The task of becoming a Marchioness was certainly
daunting, while the thought of facing Lady Sylvie again
made her blood run cold, not to mention Lady Catherine
and her uncle. But most of all there was this too familiar
stranger who called to her in a lover's well-remembered
voice. Selfish desire battled with duty. Duty warred with
self-preservation. Would the first step off this precipice
plunge her into despair or raise her to paradise?

"Come, my little pagan," Tony urged softly, "be brave
for me. You were ever my stalwart companion, and gods
and goddesses are your champions. After coming so far,
you can't fail me now. Or yourself."

"I must be bewitched," she said half to herself.

"It was ever thus with us, from the very first." Tony
pulled her gently into his embrace and nuzzled her temple.
There was a smile in his voice. "How can you deny what
Semar himself ordained?"

She could not. Closing her eyes, she took the first step.
"Yes," she whispered, "I'll come."

"I think our first family dinner went fairly well, don't
you?" Tony asked Miranda cheerfully several evenings
later.

If one likes humiliation for an entrée and mortification for dessert, Miranda thought miserably.

They strolled down the long corridor toward Fairhaven's master suite, but her sensibilities were too frayed for her to admire the lavish carved moldings or the gracious proportions of the hall.

"I probably shouldn't have disagreed with Reverend Fromme about Hindu doctrine," she said instead, nervously smoothing the stomacher of her ill-fitting gown. Beside Tony's peacock blue coat, she felt dowdy indeed in the castoffs of an earlier generation, all that could be found for her since her arrival. "I'm sorry. I certainly never meant to upset him."

"Nonsense! The old relic had no business pontificating on like that. Besides, his expression when you said he'd had another life as a cow was priceless."

"Not a cow, a Brahman."

"Isn't that Indian cattle?"

"Yes, but it's also the name of the highest caste reserved for the priesthood. I meant it as a compliment. Neither you nor Lord Edmund should have laughed so hard."

"Impossible," Tony said with a grin, "especially when young Cecil accidentally spewed his wine over Mrs. Moothy's bodice. I thought the squire would die of apoplexy on the spot."

"Don't remind me, please," Miranda moaned. "I've disgraced myself."

"Not you—Cecil. Why Mother allows that puppy to hang around, I'll never know. Sighing after her and writing endless reams of bad poetry—what a bore!"

"Lady Bentley is quite beautiful. It's not surprising the young man is enamored of her."

"There's always one or two like him somewhere close." Shrugging, Tony paused outside the paneled door to Miranda's chamber. "I suppose having a trained lapdog handy to escort her when she goes to Bath for the waters is a convenience."

"I'm afraid I didn't make a very good impression on your

guests,'' Miranda said, swallowing. "And Mrs. Moothy
appears the kind to spread the details over the countryside."

"I depend on it," he said wryly. "No quicker way to
announce our marriage."

"Ohh . . ." Her pulse throbbed painfully in her temple,
and she rubbed it dejectedly. "Everyone will know what a
poor match you've made with an eccentric spinster! It is
too humiliating, and now your mother truly hates me."

"That's unfair. This was all a shock to her, too, remember? I think she's doing admirably well adjusting to your
return, so don't take any coolness on her part too much to
heart, for that is just her manner. When she knows you
better, I'm sure she'll come to love you as I do."

Miranda bit her lip to keep from voicing her reservations.

All during that miserable meal and afterward during the
evening's casual entertainments of cards and music, she'd
felt Sylvie's enmity radiating toward her in icy waves.
Worse, she'd sensed her mother-in-law's satisfaction that
Miranda's social ineptitude had been displayed so openly.
She knew without doubt that Sylvie was at this moment
hoping Tony was taking his new wife to task for her blunders
or at least was having serious second thoughts about her
acceptability.

She certainly wouldn't blame him, Miranda thought,
sneaking a surreptitious glance at her tall husband. Was he
hiding his annoyance behind that mask of joviality? Or was
he really as unconcerned as he appeared? Nerves stretched
tight, she felt as though she balanced on a razor's edge,
never knowing if she could trust her own feelings, wondering if what she saw and felt was real or the shadowy
movements of some mystic puppeteer.

"You will bear with Mother, won't you?" Tony asked
somewhat anxiously when she didn't answer. "I'd like you
to be friends. Promise you'll try."

"Yes, of course." Miranda nodded, trying to smile. "I'll
say good night now."

She reached for the knob, but Tony forestalled her with
a hand to her arm. "Are you so eager to leave my company?" he murmured.

Miranda's pulse jumped. How could she tell him that avoiding him was the only way she could combat the fire that burned in her blood when he was near? Licking her dry lips, she stammered, "I—I'm quite fatigued."

He stared at her for another long second, then, with a sigh, placed a chaste kiss against her brow and released her. "Of course. But should you become lonely during the night, you know where I'll be."

A rosy tint colored Miranda's cheeks. "I, ah—" she gulped inanely. "G-good night."

Inside her chamber at last, she pushed the heavy door closed behind her.

Yes, she'd been extremely aware these past nights that Tony lay just beyond the connecting door between their chambers. His mother had tried to establish her in other apartments on the opposite wing of the house, but Tony had been adamant, insisting Miranda have the sumptuously appointed room next to his as befitted his Marchioness. But true to his promise, he had never attempted to breach the barrier between them, leaving her at her door each night to seek her rest innocently alone and guilty that it was so. But it was better this way, she told herself firmly, as least until they both were certain . . .

Letty sat drowsing in a deep wing chair by the ornately carved fireplace, and she awoke with a start at the muffled click of the latch.

"Oh, there you are!" Yawning widely, Miranda's cousin bobbed to her feet. "And a good thing, too. You've looked so white these past days, an early night would not come amiss. Let's get you out of that dreadful gown. La, you'll be glad when the new things his lordship ordered for you arrive!"

Miranda was already unlacing the stomacher. "Letty, you aren't here to be my servant. Topaz can help."

The tiny Sumatran woman dressed in a plain European-style gown and her own native head shawl appeared from the wardrobe closet and made her obeisance, her dark eyes huge as a doe's in her brown face. At Miranda's request, Tony had sent to Millford for her, but she still was not entirely recovered from her illness. Now she hurried to help Miranda, chattering softly in her native dialect.

"I don't mind helping you, child," Letty protested, watching as Miranda slipped from her gown, petticoats, and hoops, and Topaz carried them away. "Lord knows there's not much for me to do about this place. It's quite well run, you know, though I daresay you'll want to place your own stamp on the way things are done."

"Not right away," Miranda said hastily, pouring water from the pitcher to wash her face. Slipping out of her shift, she donned the plain linen night rail that Topaz brought her, thanking the woman in her own language and dismissing her for the night. Topaz gave a little bow, then discreetly disappeared through the wardrobe room and up the tiny staircase that led to the servants' quarters on the floors above. Miranda frowned after her, then turned to Letty.

"Does Topaz look all right to you? I'm afraid this wretched weather will induce a weakness of the lungs. I'd offer to send her home, but as a half-caste, her existence was a miserable one. She was eager to come with me for the little I could pay."

"There's always a risk involved in building a new life," Letty replied. "But we must be as the apostles, who 'thanked God and took courage.'"

The comment, though equally true for all three women, struck Miranda on a raw spot. Was her caution with Tony mere cowardice? Where was her certainty? Her spirit? Had the harsh English climate sucked it from her as easily as it had stolen Topaz's health?

"I think Topaz will throw off her malaise once the summer comes," Letty continued, "and from all appearances, with training, will make an able lady's maid, but for that heathenish tongue of hers! I'm trying to teach her a bit of English."

"Trust you to find something practical to do!" Miranda said with a smile, and something that had been coiled tight in her began to relax.

Letty's prescription for Topaz could hold true for her, too. The depression and turmoil she felt now would no doubt vanish as she grew accustomed to her situation and spring arrived. With training, she, too, might be able to squelch her awkwardness and put on the patina of a Marchioness that would make Tony proud of her and win her mother-in-law's respect if not admiration. She had only to be patient with herself and take the chance Tony so generously and gallantly gave her. Her heart swelled with emotion as she thought of him, so handsome, so gentle, so understanding.

Just a little more time, she thought as a tender ache built within her, *and then . . . and then . . .*

Somewhat soothed, she settled cross-legged on the poster bed and began to brush her hair, transferring her attention back to Letty. "I thank you for befriending Topaz, but as I said, you mustn't think you're here to work. You must enjoy yourself as well."

"Faugh! I have no stomach for useless amusements," Letty snorted. "I've become too pinchpenny over the years to gamble at piquet or whist every night. But never mind, I've made the housekeeper's acquaintance, and she's most desirous of obtaining my rhubarb jam recipe. In fact, we were having quite a cozy chat this evening until that uncouth Mr. Pratt interrupted us. How his lordship can abide that skulking individual, I'll never know."

Miranda hid a smile. "Under his rough seaman's exterior, Angus is one of the kindest men I've ever known. And he saved Tony's life."

"Well, I suppose I can be civil," Letty said grudgingly, "for his lordship's sake."

Miranda's pleased nod was interrupted when the hall door swung open suddenly and Sylvie swept into the room in a cloud of cloyingly sweet perfume. Astounded, Miranda rose, standing uncertainly beside the bed. "My lady?"

Sylvie pointed her painted fan at Letty. "Leave us."

Letty's plump cheeks quivered at this rudeness and her mouth cinched tight, but she obediently bobbed a curtsy. "Yes, Your Ladyship."

As the door closed behind Letty, Miranda licked her lips nervously. "Can I be of service, my lady?"

"Only if you've decided after this evening's fiasco to

pack your miserable belongings and get out of my son's life,'' Sylvie said pleasantly. She drifted over to stand in front of Miranda, examining her suddenly pasty face with interest, nodding to herself as if a judgment had just been confirmed. "You are a plain girl."

"So I've been told," Miranda answered meekly. Sylvie's verbal blow had landed directly on her battered self-esteem, scattering her wits and her defenses. It seemed the kid gloves were off.

"So mild!" Sylvie's blue eyes narrowed. "But I won't underestimate you, my dear. You are sly enough and mercenary enough to have trapped my son, something a thousand others could not accomplish."

"I never intended to trap anyone," Miranda protested faintly, but Sylvie was already moving away, idly examining the meager collection of pins and notions on the polished dressing table, then letting her gaze roam over the velvet drapes, embroidered chairs, and gilt moldings crowning the walls and carved cornices.

"Do you like this chamber?"

Disconcerted, Miranda blinked. "It—it's very beautiful."

"It was always too old-fashioned for my taste," the older woman admitted with a negligent shrug. "But I'd advise you not to become accustomed to it, as I'm sure you know your residency in it will be a limited one."

"Lady Bentley—" Miranda began.

"My son is destined for greatness," Sylvie interrupted, turning to pierce Miranda with her cold stare. "His place will be even greater than his father's. No nameless, wheyfaced chit is going to spoil his chances!"

"I would never do anything to hurt your son, my lady," Miranda protested. "We are both bound by a common goal—Tony's happiness. I'd hoped that united in that sole endeavor, we might become allies, even friends."

"Presumptuous imp! Think you can best me in this intrigue?" Sylvie tapped her fan against her palm in an irritated tattoo. "It is a game I have won many times."

"I play no games, my lady."

"Then you are a fool," Sylvie said in disgust. "I can squash you like an insect, while gently pointing out to my son what a desperate mistake he's made, and how totally unsuitable you are. It will not be pleasant for you. You can spare yourself much if you will but leave again. And this time, with my help, you may run where Anthony cannot find you."

Deliberately she withdrew a small purse that clinked of coins from the lace at her décolleté and waved it invitingly.

Holding on to the tall carved bedpost, Miranda stared at Sylvie with a mixture of dismay, disappointment, and resignation. But she had faced execution at the sultan's hands with dignity, so now she straightened her spine and ignored her pounding heart. She would not let this woman intimidate her further.

"It is unwise to warn an enemy of your intentions," Miranda said softly. "Keep your bribe. I won't be bullied or bought, my lady. Whether I leave or stay, it will be my choice, not yours."

"Foolish mewling bitch!" Sylvie hissed, angrily slipping the purse back into its hiding place. "You will regret this."

"No doubt," Miranda said tiredly.

"You have nothing that can hold my son—not fortune, nor looks, nor even wit!" Sylvie flung viciously. "A man of Anthony's sensual nature must have diversity. It won't be long before he casts you off for another, and you will have nothing. I have only to wait until he comes to his senses."

With that final sally, Sylvie stormed from the room. Miranda's quivering knees gave way, and she sank down on the bed. Despite her bravado, she was shaken to her core.

Deep inside her soul, something that might have been the first green shoot of hope had shriveled, nipped by the hard chill of Sylvie's hateful words.

Chapter 14

"**W**hy do you decorate these coconuts?" Tiktik asked, solemn with the dignified weight of a full thirteen years.

"Teacher takes Ciweo to the river today for the Bath," Sister said, drawing another fine line on the coconut with her kris. It was a duty only recently relinquished by the old woman to her most apt pupil, and Sister performed it carefully under the old one's watchful eye. "You know Ciweo will have her baby soon. Today seven old ones, all happy and fruitful, will pour water over Ciweo and her husband from seven different directions to ask for happiness and well-being for her child."

"But what are these?" Tiktik persisted.

Teacher lifted the two coconuts. "You know this hero. He is Arjuna, one of the five Pandawas, the warrior-heroes you see in the wajang stories. And this is his most beautiful wife, Sumbadra, who is meek, ladylike, and loyal. After the Bath, I will drop them through Ciweo's sarong as a symbol of an easy delivery."

Tiktik examined the coconuts curiously. "Did not Arjuna have another wife as well?"

Teacher laughed softly. "You have not forgotten Srikandi, have you?"

"She fought a knight for her husband and could debate with the teachers."

"Independent, strong-willed, and lively," Sister agreed with a smile. "Arjuna must have had a time with her."

"I want to be like Srikandi," Tiktik announced.

"That would lead to trouble for both you and your husband," Sister scolded gently. "Sumbadra is a better choice."

"Too dull!" Tiktik made a face at the coconut.

"But Tiktik—"

"What you must both learn," Teacher said, interrupting the squabble, "is that a good wife should have the qualities of both."

Tony swallowed the last bitter dregs of his coffee, then, with a grimace of equal distaste, set aside both his cup and the latest missive from his London man of business. Watery sunlight poured through the long sash window of the Small Salon, where of habit he took his breakfast. He squinted against the glare, thoughtfully considering the ironical fact that if he'd been able to secure a shipment of coffee from the Dutchman, he'd not now be at the mercy of the contents of that letter.

"Bad news, darling?"

Tony glanced up as his mother glided into the salon, artfully arranged in morning undress of loose cream-colored satin sacque gown, a delicate lace cap resting atop her blond locks. A footman instantly brought her a cup of chocolate and discreetly withdrew again.

"Not even two weeks have passed since calling it off with Colleton's niece, and already my creditors are beginning to snap at my heels," Tony said in disgust.

Sylvie sipped her chocolate like a well-bred kitten, examining her son over the rim of her cup. "Without the prospects of Colleton's fortune, what else did you expect? I tried to warn you."

"I'll have to go to London soon," he mused, inwardly calculating which pieces of property could be disposed of, which favors he might call in, and if the situation was desperate enough to risk the gaming tables.

"You don't intend to take her with you, do you?" Sylvie asked.

Tony frowned across the table. "*Her* name is Miranda. And I haven't decided."

Sylvie licked the film of chocolate from her short upper lip, and looked regretful. "I wouldn't recommend it."

"Oh?"

Setting down her cup, Sylvie gave a little annoyed shrug at his chilly tone. "Don't lift your eyebrows at me, Anthony. I'm thinking of you, of course, but Miranda as well. She would only be an embarrassment at this point, to you and herself. New gowns won't hide the fact that she's hopelessly provincial and simply not ready for polite society . . . and may never be."

"You're too hard on her," Tony protested, a muscle jumping in his jaw. "Of course her adjustment to her new position will take time."

"Yes, but at what price? Your wife should be a help to you, but I fear she has too many outlandish ideas ingrained in her head."

"What ideas?" Tony asked.

"Like that foreign jabber she speaks to that Nubian maid of hers. Half the servants are afeared of witchcraft because of it, and the other half are complaining of the extra work caused by her strange penchant for bathing every day."

"Topaz is Sumatran," Tony corrected mildly, "and speaks no English as yet. And lazy servants can be replaced. Miri may call for hot water a dozen times a day if it pleases her."

"That's just an example," Sylvie responded in exasperation. "Haunting the library for musty old tomes—as if society lauds an educated woman! And that busybody cousin of hers pokes her nose into every corner as if *she* were the new mistress of Fairhaven.''

Tony concealed a rueful smile. Angus had voiced much the same complaint in recent days. He and Letty hadn't passed a single pleasant word between them. Angus's temper was uncertain at best, partially because the old salt missed the sea but stubbornly stayed on with Tony, and partly because he hadn't a notion how to deal with a female of Letty's caliber or bright-eyed outspokenness.

"I'm sure Letty is merely trying to be helpful," Tony said.

"That old hen hasn't a notion of fashionable behavior," Sylvie sniffed. "And poor Miranda! Though her looks are improving with the aid of my lady's maid, she would be treading in deep water indeed if you took her into Society now. Why, she doesn't even know needlework and is useless at cards. And as for conversation—well, you remember what happened the evening Reverend Fromme was here!"

Tony chuckled openly. "Scandalous deficits in a Marchioness, eh, Mother?"

"There are other deficits, as you call them, that are more worrisome," Sylvie snapped. Then her expression became the same as when she produced a trump card at piquet. "Why does she deny you her bed? How can a man of your appetites tolerate such a situation? Or have you already engaged another mistress?"

Angrily Tony pushed back his chair. "That is no concern of yours, Mother."

"I'm not blind! There is little that happens at Fairhaven I do not know. What I fail to understand is all this fuss and bother over a woman who cannot or will not fulfill a wife's most basic duties! I'm trying to be charitable, but I'm concerned for your happiness. What hold has she over you?"

"You wouldn't understand," Tony muttered, stuffing his letter into the pocket of his fawn-colored riding jacket.

"You think not?" Sylvie's rosebud mouth flattened into bitter lines. "Your father taught me much about obsession. Rosalind—"

Tony cut her off with a sharp gesture. "Enough, Mother. Put the past behind you forever."

Her expression was puzzled. "I do not understand this change in you. After all you suffered from your father's whore and her bastard, where is your hatred?"

"Neither Father, nor you, nor I were entirely blameless," Tony said in a strange, tired voice. "It is a waste of energy to pursue it, that's all."

"You lost more than your senses in the East Indies," Sylvie said, her voice cutting. "Where is your manhood? Did your wife slice that out of you as well as your heart?"

"Leave Miri out of this," Tony grated.

Sylvie looked instantly repentant, her gentian blue eyes suspiciously bright, her lower lip trembling. "Forgive me, my dearest. Truly, she is a sweet and admirable girl, and if she is the right one for you, then I applaud your choice, of course. It's just that I want your happiness above all else."

Tony sighed, then bent and kissed her white brow. "I know. But you must let me find it in my own way. Excuse me now. I'm going to exercise Horatio."

By the time he reached the stables, Tony's mood was as sour as his stomach. He pulled on his heavy gloves and tricorne against the brisk wind, for though April progressed, winter's sere hand still lay upon the dormant countryside. Mounting his favorite roan stallion, he gave the animal his head down the winding drive between Fairhaven's geometrically landscaped gardens, but even that release scarcely lightened his tension, nor the sense of frustration that had been growing since he'd brought Miri back over a week ago.

Nothing was going as he'd planned. Though he'd shown Miri nothing but courtesy, and hadn't pushed for a renewal of physical intimacy as he'd promised, she'd grown more distant every day, retreating into a shell so that she resembled nothing so much as the dried-up spinster he'd once thought her.

Oh, she was utterly polite, commenting correctly on everything he proudly showed her around the great house and estate, making careful, stilted conversation over dinner, acquiescing amiably to the demands of seamstresses and mantua-makers, ladies' maids and serving women, as Sylvie "took her in hand" at his request. But the warm, continually surprising woman he'd known on Java seemed as distant as that green island, and he missed her dreadfully.

Perhaps it had been a mistake bringing her back to Fairhaven to be overwhelmed by the title, the house, and his mother. Perhaps it had been another mistake to agree to this ludicrous cessation of marital rights. They'd always communicated physically before any other way, and now, while his veins hummed with need, his vow stymied him from reaching her by the most elemental method. So he'd dampered his frustration by riding hard each day, not returning until both he and Horatio were lathered with fatigue, but even this regimen offered little relief. Though he realized Sylvie's motives weren't the purest, she was right to be concerned. He was almost at the end of his tether.

Tony turned Horatio back across the stubbled hayfields toward Fairhaven, and tried to find the serenity this place always brought to him. He knew every nook and cranny, and even in the height of his wastrel days, always found refuge at Fairhaven. More important than the title, it was the Bentley lands that nurtured his soul in the long, lonely growing-up years, but today the peace he usually felt eluded him.

He caught sight of a slight, cloaked figure tromping through the bare apple orchard that adjoined the field. He knew who it was at once. In his precarious mood, it angered him that she'd come out without maid or groom, so he dug his heels into Horatio's sides, slicing a diagonal course across the patch to intercept her at the stile in the rock wall.

Walking eyes to the earth as if in deep meditation, Miranda did not hear his approach until he was nearly upon her. She looked up, startled at first, then laid back her hood and waited with a calm patience that somehow infuriated him.

"Well, madam?" he said, drawing Horatio in beside her. "You're about early."

"As are you, sir," she replied, eyeing the blowing, snorting animal uncertainly. "Did you enjoy your ride?"

"As well I might, considering," he muttered. "I dislike your coming out unescorted."

She looked surprised, her gray eyes wide and guileless. "Am I not safe upon my husband's land?"

"That's not the point."

"If I'd wanted company, I'd have arranged it," she said simply, then glanced away. "I suffocate from an abundance of attention in the house."

"Including mine?"

She looked back sharply. "That's not what I said."

"You haven't had to these last few days. Where I hoped to draw you closer, I feel you pulling away."

"I only wanted some air," she protested faintly, dismayed at his glower. Shivering, she tugged at the edges of her cloak. "It's cold out. I should go in."

He noted the rosiness in her cheeks and the way she stamped her feet in her new leather shoes beneath the heavy woolen petticoats he'd paid for. Over them she wore a silly gossamer apron that was all the fashion, but he thought he'd never seen a less flattering or less domestic ensemble. It was as though she'd purposefully chosen uncomplimentary garments in an effort to be unobtrusive. Where was the woman who'd worn only a sarong with such aplomb?

Leaning down, he offered his hand. "Come," he said gruffly, "We'll ride back together."

"I—I've no experience with such large horses," she faltered.

"Then we'll change that. Come."

Biting her lip, Miranda took his hand, fit her toe into the stirrup, then allowed him to pull her up onto the saddle before him. He dragged her back against his chest, noticing how she shook with a chill.

"You are cold," he murmured. Settling her cloak about her, he circled her waist with his left arm. "Too many years in warm climes. Your blood will thicken eventually."

"Sometimes I fear spring will never come," she admitted softly, her voice a shade forlorn.

On impulse, Tony turned Horatio away from Fairhaven. "Then I'll show you something."

She looked back over her shoulder at his face, shadowed by the tip of the tricorne, trying to read his expression. With a brief smile, he pulled her even closer, leaving her no option but to snuggle against his warmth.

Luxuriating in the feel of her, Tony did not hurry, merely letting Horatio pick his way through the bracken into the forest. The flowery scent of frangipani that was a part of Miranda rose to his nostrils in heady waves, and he drank in her nearness, the blood pooling heavily in his loins. After a long, silent interval, he reined the horse to a halt in a little cove created by the curve of a brook and a bank of evergreen hedges, dismounted, then caught her by the waist and helped her down.

"Look," he said, pointing at a mossy bank.

Miranda caught her breath in delight. "Oh, Tony! Violets! How did you know?"

"They always bloom here first," he said, smiling at her pleasure.

She hastened to the edge of the stream, stooping to pick a few of the velvety purple blossoms from their carpet of heart-shaped leaves, carrying them to her nose to inhale their sweetness. Treading carefully, Tony plucked a handful more to add to her nosegay.

"How lovely," she cooed, her eyes shining as he placed them in her gloved hands. "I do so miss the flowers at home."

With an effort, he refrained from reminding her that this was now her home. Instead, he said, "There's an old orangery behind the stables. I'll fill it with ferns and orchids and all manner of exotic flora so that you'll always have flowers."

She smiled uncertainly at the offer, then cast another look around. "This is your glade, isn't it?"

"You remembered." He nodded, pleased. "Yes, I spent many an hour here, hiding from my tutors to avoid a caning or sulking after a row with my father."

"You don't speak of him."

"I loved him." Tony shrugged. "We rarely saw eye to eye, except about Fairhaven and keeping it intact whatever the cost. Although we both loved it here, we were not a happy family."

"I'm sorry." She frowned, confused. "But your brother?"

"For many years, I thought he was dead. Don't speak of him to Mother. Someday I'll tell you why." He smiled. "But not today, when you have violets to remind you of spring."

"Yes." She dipped her nose again into the fragrant bouquet. "Thank you for sharing this with me."

"Ah, Miri," he murmured, brushing the pale, fair strands of flyaway hair from her cheek, "there's so much I wish to share with you—if only you'll let me."

"I'm trying," she whispered, her eyes huge.

"I feel your unhappiness here, and I so wanted you to feel at home. Sometimes I've felt it's the only place I truly belong, and I wanted to give it to you, too."

She made a little helpless gesture of denial. "It's just that everything is so new. And I feel like a . . . an usurper . . . as though I've stumbled into the midst of someone else's fairy tale."

Tony slipped his hands beneath her cloak to clasp her waist. "This is your rightful place. I know you're overwhelmed, but things would be easier if you'd let me help you."

"I just need a little more time."

"Time," he said huskily, tugging her inexorably closer. "Fate gave us another lifetime. Why waste a moment of it?"

Bending, he fit his mouth over hers, softly wooing, gently persuading. She was as sweet as nectar, as rich as cream, and he was starving for her taste. Deepening the kiss, he held her against his pounding heart, feeling the hard coins of his silver coat buttons pressed between them. Gasping, she broke the kiss, turning aside, her hands palm-down on his chest.

"Stop, Tony. Please, you promised . . ."

Involuntarily his hands tightened on her in angry frustration. "You're entitled to some happiness after all that's happened. Why won't you let me give it to you?"

"This isn't all there is to a good marriage," she said a bit wildly.

"But it's a hell of a good place to start! And you've got to start somewhere, Miri." His eyes blazed, and his voice was throaty with earnestness. "You're in limbo now, caught between two worlds, belonging to neither. Everyone senses your uncertainty, the lack of commitment despite our marriage vows. How can you hope to win their respect? Even Mother knows we aren't sleeping together!"

Miranda's face blazed, but her mouth pressed into a stubborn line. "We had an agreement."

"I'm not an honorable man," Tony warned, his eyes narrowing. "You know that, so don't push me. You can't walk this tightrope indefinitely."

"Are you threatening me?"

"Call it what you will. I want my wife, but you're too busy playing the martyr to notice my patience is running out."

"What a despicable thing to say!" Miranda struggled out of his grip, glaring at him.

"You're terrified of experiencing all life can offer with me, and so you hide behind your talk of duty and purpose."

"That's not true!" she cried, wounded to the quick. "Just because I'm trying to be sensible—"

"Were you sensible in Java?"

"No, but look what it got us."

"I was never so alive as those days I spent with you," he said. "If you're honest, you'll admit it, too. Life was too precious to waste in endless, futile deliberations. But you've fulfilled your duty to your sister, and you're free. Don't you see? Self-sacrifice and denial can't shield you forever from the duty you owe yourself. You can choose to be happy—if you dare."

"I'd expect such a selfish philosophy from the Wastrel Lord, but that does not mean I can adhere to it!" she snapped, a cornered light in her eyes. "Without ideals and loyalties, we're no higher than the animals."

"Don't hide behind high-minded words, my sweet. Life isn't that tidy. It's raw and messy and complicated and glorious, and there are no guarantees."

"I know that fully as well as you!" She swallowed harshly. "And knowing that makes me even more certain I can't possibly be the kind of wife you need."

"When did you become so craven? You're looking for excuses not to live. Do you know what I think?" Tony's mouth grew hard and his eyes flinty. "I think you were disappointed to find me alive."

His brutal words pierced her, and with a ragged cry, she flung her little nosegay in his face. Whirling, she ran, not caring of the direction, but Tony caught her with a steely arm from behind, jerking her backward to slam against the hard wall of his chest.

"It would have been so much easier to live out your life as the dutiful widow, wouldn't it, Miri?" he grated, his voice rough as crushed glass. "Doing good deeds, going to church on Sundays, and seeing after your aging mother-in-law. Then there'd be no inconvenient demands from a flesh-and-blood man who wants you in his bed, his home, his heart, and there'd be no reason to question that pinched and sterile existence you call a life."

"Bastard!" she hissed, crying a little, struggling a lot.

"True enough. Now be still," he ordered against her ear. "You'll hurt yourself."

"Let me go!"

"No." His tone was implacable, but the words were wrenched from his depths. "I can't."

Her head spinning, Miranda slumped in defeat and confusion. After a long moment, Tony swung her into his arms, carried her to Horatio, and lifted her into the saddle. The ride back to Fairhaven was accomplished in grim silence. They'd stepped over an invisible line in their relationship, but neither could guess the outcome.

Tony watched his wife carefully over the two o'clock dinner and afterward during the evening's entertainments,

mentally cursing his rashness. A cold ache grew in the pit
of his stomach at her overt coolness. She spoke only in
awkward monosyllables to him while easily carrying on an
animated conversation with that fop, Lord Edmund. He
resisted the jealous urge to thrash young Cecil soundly only
by imbibing more port than he wanted. When Miranda retired for the night, he followed her with his eyes and asked
himself for the hundredth time if he'd gone too far.

He's gone too far, Miranda told herself for the hundredth
time. Her husband was arrogant, selfish, and—completely
right.

Perched on the edge of her vast empty bed, her shoulders
slumped beneath her shapeless night rail as the sustaining
anger drained out of her. Her quivering fingers closed over
the charred remains of the jade lotus blossom.

"Coward," she accused herself. "Poltroon!"

On the small bedside table sat a nosegay of violets that
had mysteriously appeared during her absence. The sweet
aroma tickled her nose, no heavy, exotic perfume, but a
subtle and charmingly English scent that was just as be-
witching. Hesitantly she tucked the posy behind her ear,
having no doubt of its origin. *He* was not afraid of risks.

She remembered the first time she'd gone to Tony. Then,
duty had driven her and given her the courage she needed.
Now his words taunted her. Did she dare face her duty to
herself? But what if she took the chance he offered and then
failed? Would that be worse than never trying at all?

From deep within the recesses of her memory, there came
the sound of temple bells and a whispered call to the heart.
Clutching the lotus, she rose, and the night rail puddled
about her feet.

Wearily Tony resigned himself to another aching, sleep-
less night in the velvet-hung bed that had seen generations
of Benedicts conceived and born, saving he and Kit. The
taper on his candle stand had guttered down to a stub when
the door connecting his chamber to Miranda's creaked open.

Tony sat up slowly, covers pooling at his waist, mesmerized by the slender shape hovering like a wraith in his
doorway. Miranda drifted forward into the golden circle of

the candle, her fair hair loose about her shoulders, her feet bare on the icy floor. She wore only the familiar patterned cloth of a batik sarong and a knot of purple blossoms in her hair.

Tony felt the hot surge of desire flood his veins, and he croaked her name. "Miri? What is it?"

"I—I've been thinking about what you said." Reaching him, she lay a hand upon his bare shoulder. Her sweet, flowery scent enticed him. "We have been too long apart, husband."

"Damn right," he said on a strangled note. His flesh shuddering beneath her butterfly touch, he held on to his restraint by the merest silken thread. "Please don't tell me you're here because it's your goddamn duty."

"No. I—I've come to return your talisman."

She opened her palm, revealing the charred lotus snuff-box. Protruding from the broken lid was a new lock of fine silver hair. It was a symbol, freely given, of his power over her, and hope flared inside him.

Tony took the tiny box, swallowed hard, then set it aside. Cupping her nape, he drew her closer so that he could stare into the luminous depths of her moon-silver eyes.

"There won't be any going back. You'd better be certain."

Miranda quivered. Tony's painfully probing words of the morning had plucked chords within her she'd never heard before, and now, for the first time in her life, she made a choice that went against all the inner precepts by which she'd lived. Selfishly she chose Tony, and damned the consequences.

Folding her hands under her chin, she inclined her head in an abbreviated *dodok*. "Englishman," she whispered tremulously, "I must have you."

"Then come closer, love," he murmured tenderly, slowly unveiling his slash of a dimple, "and show me what you mean."

With a small soft cry, she flung herself against him, her arms circling his neck with a hungry desperation. "I'm not too late?"

Pulling her across his lap, he moved his mouth hotly against the pulse pounding in her throat. "No, never."

"I've been so stubborn, so foolish," she said, her tone husky with remorse. "I want to be your wife in every way." She swallowed, making a difficult confession. "You were right, I am a coward, afraid of failing you or disappointing you."

"You could never do that," he said with conviction.

"What if I disgrace you? I don't know how to be a proper Marchioness."

The corner of his mouth quirked wryly. "You think that matters to me? I've always been on the outer edges of propriety myself. My reputation for dissolute living is notorious, and many will wonder and point at you as my spouse. But, Miri, none of that is important. I want only to live with you and grow old with you. As long as you're with me, the rest of the world may go to the devil."

"You have such faith in us, it makes me ashamed of my weakness. Can you forgive me?"

"With ease." Threading his fingers into her silky hair, he spilled the violets across her shoulders and into the rumpled covers. "You see, I love you."

"Tony." Choking with the swell of emotion that flowed from her heart, she dotted tiny fervent kisses on his cheek, his brow, the upper curve of his lips. "I love you so much! Whatever happens, you must believe that."

"I know. I've always known." Rolling her across his body, he pressed her down into the flower-strewn bed-clothes, nibbling the elegant curve of her jawbone. "And what could happen, now that we're together again?"

Shivering with cold and with the delicious sensation of his warm breath on her skin, Miranda tried not to think about that, for too many possibilities rose to mind. But if defying Lady Sylvie and learning to be a Marchioness was the price she had to pay for loving Tony, then she'd never really had any choice at all. Caressing the strong tendons in his neck, sinking her fingers into the softness of his curls, she sought his kiss.

"Make love with me," she whispered against his mouth.

"Make the world disappear as you did the night of the Lotus Moon."

"Ah, Miri-mine," he said, laughing softly, "the heavens and the earth conjoined that magic night, but I'll certainly do my best, tonight and all the nights to come."

Spreading her hair upon the pillows, he kissed her gently, one long finger trailing from the hollow of her throat to the top of her sarong and back again. Then he found the small place at the top of her shoulder.

"Miri, what—?"

"Ishta's work."

"Christ!" He shuddered at how close she'd come to death.

"It's over. Don't think about it. Kiss me again."

With a groan, he obliged, the tip of his tongue teasing the seam of her lips. She opened gladly, shivering at the fiery dragon's flick of tongue on tongue. Moaning low, she ended his teasing, tugging his head down and hotly demanding a thoroughly intimate exchange that made her move restlessly beneath him. Breathing hard, Tony raised his head, running his fingers insinuatingly under the upper edge of her simple Javanese garment, brushing the swelling mounds of her breasts with his knuckles.

"You are so mysteriously exotic in this thing, like no woman I've ever known," he muttered. Untwisting the tucked edge, he began to loosen it. "And it makes my blood run hot to think of what's under it."

"I wanted you to remember other times."

"Shameless! You intentionally tried to seduce me," he accused with a grin. Tugging the sarong free, he gazed down at her slender form, her silky skin gilded by the golden candlelight, and swallowed hard. "Madam, it worked like a charm."

Rescuing a single violet that clung to her hair, he touched it to the crown of one rosy nipple, watching ardently as the hard bud tightened. He repeated the action, neither of them breathing quite steadily, senses heightening with each breathy stroke of the bruised blossom. Finally, when he could stand it no longer, he bent his head and drew the tip into his mouth. Miranda gasped and arched against him, clasping her arms around his back, sighing her pleasure. But then her fingers found a hard ridge of tissue low on his back, and she gave a sharp cry.

"What is it? Did I hurt you?" he asked anxiously.

"Oh, Tony!" Her fingers fluttered over the small of his back, his taut buttocks, the hair-dusted backs of his powerful thighs. "Your poor back!"

"'Tis nothing."

She slipped free of his embrace. "Let me see."

"It's not pretty."

"Roll over and let me *see*," she insisted, pushing at his shoulders. "I'm your wife. I have a right."

Tension in every muscle, he did as she bade, throwing himself down on his stomach and burying his face in his folded arms. He held himself stiffly for an interminable span. "Satisfied?"

"Oh, my dear . . ." Kneeling beside him among the tumbled bedclothes, she gently pressed a kiss to the largest band of raised pink tissue, outlining it with sorrowful sighs and soothing kisses. "How you must have suffered . . ."

Moving down his body, she continued her ministrations, delineating each parallel ridge of scarring with fingers and mouth, murmuring her sympathy from spine to buttock to ankle while the rhythm of Tony's breathing became more and more labored. Finally, his control to the point of snapping, he rolled to his back, carrying her with him so that she sprawled against his chest.

"You would tempt a saint, woman!" he gasped, cupping her breasts within his large hands, playing the nipples with the edge of his thumbs.

"You were very lucky," she said solemnly.

He hesitated, his jaw working, and his hands grew still. "Most women would find my scars abhorrent."

His insecurity touched her deeply, and with a tender smile, she hastened to reassure him.

"I regret each and every one for the pain it caused, but how can I abhor the fact that you were alive to suffer them and not dead as I feared? Scars and all, you are beautiful to me in every way.'' She lightly traced the path that Steef's bullet had left on his side, and her smile grew impish. ''Besides, each mark tells of your varied and interesting career.''

Relaxing imperceptibly, he caught her nape, kissing her deeply, gratefully, and with growing passion. His mouth ravaged hers expertly, and when he raised his head again, they were both struggling for breath.

''As much as I enjoyed your examination of my defects,'' he said in a strangled tone, ''you will be remiss in your wifely duties if you don't notice there is a certain part of your husband that needs your further attention.''

''Is there?'' She undulated against him, then boldly stroked the hard, velvety length of his manhood, wringing a groan from his throat. ''I wonder what it could be?''

''Witch!'' Laughing, he tossed her onto her back, struggling with the tangled covers and smiling down at her.

As one, their matching smiles died. Miranda licked her lips in an unconsciously provocative gesture, feeling the flames of desire settle in her core. Weakly, her bent knees fell open, disclosing her feminine secrets for his heated perusal. His gaze grew lambent, and, reaching out, he stroked her dewy folds, finding her ready for his possession.

Dragging the coverlet over his shoulders, he covered her body with his own like another blanket, taking her mouth in a heated exchange and plunging himself into her creamy depths.

''Oh, God, I've wanted this,'' he said in a voice gone raspy with passion.

Her hands clung to his hips, and she rose to meet him, shuddering with the impact of his penetration, filling her, stretching her, touching her in ways that surpassed the merely physical. ''Oh, Tony . . . Tony!''

His powerful thrusts rocked her, and she gave herself up to the freedom of knowing this man loved her and would never knowingly hurt her. Abandoned, she strove with him, giving herself freely, wantonly taking of his generosity, sharing all they felt in an elemental communication both basic and sublime.

With a soft gasp, she fell over the edge, pleasure radiating from her core in a sunburst of warmth that filled her being. Aftershocks racking her, she felt Tony's powerful completion and wrapped her legs around his thighs, holding him close and closer still as he groaned from his soul. Together, they exploded into another universe filled only with the two of them and the power of their love.

After a very long while, when they could both breathe again, Tony kissed her tears away, instinctively understanding the powerful emotional release that had caused them, for he had shared it, too. Still joined, he rolled them to their sides, pulling twisted covers over them and enveloping them both in a cocoon of warmth.

"It's probably illegal for a man to feel about his own wife as I do about you," he murmured, kissing the tip of her nose.

Giggling giddily, totally sated, yet curiously refreshed, she curled her fingers into the reddish-blond thatch on his chest. "Will the magistrates object?"

"If they knew, I'd be carted off to Tyburn double-quick. Such lusty thoughts are inappropriate for old married men such as I."

She snuggled sleepily against him. "Then we'll have to keep it our secret, for I am loath to lose you again."

"Alas, all the world will soon know I've retired my wastrel name, for I'm determined to take you off to London to show off my beautiful wife."

"London?"

"Business calls me hence, and I refuse to leave you behind at Fairhaven, especially now. We'll open up the Leicester Square house and make the fashionable rounds together. What do you say?"

The idea of leaving Lady Sylvie's venomous sphere far outweighed any trepidations Miranda felt over meeting Society as the Marchioness of Bentley. "It sounds grand. But will I be able to stand the wails of all your disappointed ladies? And are you prepared to withstand their charms?"

"No one can outshine my lotus girl," he promised tenderly. "I will be the most faithful of husbands, my love, as long as you are mine."

She raised one eyebrow. "Have I reformed the rake?"

"Without regret, I admit it."

Kissing him mischievously, she slid her hand down his flat stomach to the point where they still met. "Reformed, yes. But not too much, I pray."

The were both surprised by the results her teasing touch produced. Laughing quietly, joyously, Tony pulled her beneath him again. "Nay, not too much—thank God!"

Chapter 15

"I'm not ready for this."

"Of course you are," Tony insisted, pushing aside the strap of Miranda's low-cut shift to kiss the curve of her shoulder. He smiled at her shiver of pleasure, raising his eyes to meet hers in the gilt looking glass hanging over her dressing table.

"But we've only been in London a fortnight," she said, biting her lip anxiously. "Please, Tony, do I really have to go?"

" 'Tis the Princess of Wales's birthday celebration, my love. Now that our marriage announcement has appeared in the papers, I'm counting on you to enchant my friends, intimidate my enemies, and charm my business associates into forgetfulness. Besides, everyone of import will be at the Princess's masquerade."

Miranda buried her face in her hands and groaned. "That's what I'm afraid of!"

Straightening, Tony laughed indulgently at her nervousness, his chuckles echoing throughout their high-ceilinged bedchamber. A huge four-poster bed dominated the luxuriously appointed room, while a glass-fronted case displayed the best of his snuffbox collection and a plump chaise stood near the window overlooking the rear gardens. "Stage fright, dearling. Don't worry, you'll be glorious."

"I'm more nervous than when we met Lord Palu," Miranda admitted.

"Perhaps this will take your mind off things." Tony pulled a small object from his waistcoat pocket, then slipped a circlet studded with a pearl the size of a quail's egg over Miranda's ring finger.

"Tony—what? Oh, it's Rija's pearl!"

"No, it's your wedding ring." He kissed the ring and then her palm. "I realized I'd been remiss in gifting you with a token of my esteem. 'Tis your dowry, after all. I hope you like it."

"It's magnificent," Miranda breathed, admiring the shimmering gem, now surrounded by a circle of diamonds. "Though I hate to deprive my stylish husband of his favorite cravat pin."

"I'd rather it on your hand to remind you that you've belonged to me since the night of the Lotus Moon." Smiling, he kissed her lightly. "Now hurry and dress or we'll be frightfully late, and don't forget your domino. I'm anxious for you to meet Their Majesties so that I may be the envy of every man present."

A smile curved her lips. "Anthony Benedict, I swear you could charm the birds from the trees!"

Tony urged her to her feet, pressing her scantily clad form against himself provocatively. "Or a pagan angel into my bed?"

"Yes," she laughed, "that, too, you rogue! I confess I've long since lost all my defenses where you're concerned."

"Yes, but are you happy?" Despite his smile, there was an anxious gleam in the depths of his slate blue eyes.

"Delirious!" Miranda flung her arms around his neck, taking care not to crush his lace cravat, and kissed him soundly.

In the days since their reconciliation, Miranda had never known such joy. The luxury of being with Tony, touching him, and hearing his conversation filled her with delight. He was everything she could want in a husband and lover— tender, demanding, infinitely exciting. Even the rough trip to London had been a pleasure with Tony at her side to ease her way.

The only dark cloud that marred an otherwise spotless horizon was the fact that Lady Sylvie had also decided to spend the season in London, "to be of service to Miranda." Fortunately, she'd chosen to stay at Lavender House, a small place of her own near St. James Park, while Tony had brought Miranda to the Bentley town house on fashionable Leicester Square. While Miranda remained wary of her mother-in-law, Sylvie had not repeated her threats, and Miranda hoped now that it was clear she and Tony were husband and wife in all ways, his mother was reconciled to her son's marriage at last.

At length, Tony lifted his head, breathing raggedly, and gave Miranda one last regretful peck. "Madam, I suggest you refrain from further demonstrations of affection or we may never leave the house this evening!"

"Mmm," Miranda purred, her gray eyes slumberous with desire, "there's a thought."

"Shameless hussy!" He laughed, giving her an affectionate slap on her rounded bottom. "I'll be certain to remind you of it later. Now, get dressed!"

"What are bully you are," she complained with a soft smile. "Very well, my lord. Will you send Letty to me?"

Minutes later, Letty bustled in carrying a gown wrapped in muslin, flustered with the importance of Miranda's toilette.

"Imagine! The Prince and Princess! Surely you'll see the King as well," she burbled. "And look what just came! The Dowager Marchioness herself has sent you a surprise, a gown her seamstress made to your measurements for this special occasion."

"Of all things . . ." Wonder touched Miranda's expression. "Do you suppose it's a peace offering?"

Eagerly she and Letty laid the gown on the bed and pulled the muslin covering away. They stared at it for a long moment of horrified silence.

"I can't wear *that!*" Miranda managed at last.

"I should say not!" Letty agreed indignantly, fingering the garish orange and aqua dimity with distaste.

Miranda's dismay focused on the sheerness of the bodice and its plunging lines, a design that would leave nothing to the imagination. "I cannot attend a masquerade dressed as a tart!"

Letty snorted. "A poor joke, and an expensive one, I'd say."

"I can't begin to guess the Marchioness's purpose," Miranda admitted. "Never mind. Where's Topaz? Due to Tony's generosity, I have several suitable gowns."

Unfortunately, Miranda's confident words came too soon.

They found Topaz in tears in the small dressing room set off the bedchamber. She was futilely trying to scrub sooty smears that looked suspiciously like paw prints out of all of Miranda's new gowns while Beelzebub hissed and glared at her from the top of a tall armoire.

"That wretch, Angus Pratt!" Letty stormed, surveying the damage. "Him and his devilish beastie! See what they've done!"

"Don't blame Angus," Miranda began.

"Carelessness, that's what it is! I'll give that purse-mouthed rogue a piece of my mind!"

Sighing, Miranda turned to Topaz and tried to calm the weeping, lamenting woman. "No, I know it isn't your fault. No, I'm sure no one is trying to drive you away. It's all right, don't worry. They'll wash, I'm sure."

"But not in time for you to go tonight! How could this have happened?" Letty demanded.

"I'm sure it was just an accident," Miranda soothed, then coaxed Beelzebub down from his perch. She rubbed the skittish cat's tattered ears, then frowned, puzzled. "Old fellow, did you roll in the fireplace? And how did you get in—" She broke off with an indignant gasp, unwrapping a scrap of thin cord from the feline's back leg. "Look, he's been tied!"

"Someone did this deliberately," Letty said darkly, "and I'll wager I can guess who's responsible!"

"Not Angus! Why—?"

"Of course not him. That Scotsman may be a dolt, but he's loyal. No, I see the fine hand of the Dowager Marchioness in this nasty bit of business."

A pleat appeared in Miranda's brow. "So either I miss this event altogether and disappoint Tony, or I wear that sluttish gown and humiliate him before his friends," she mused out loud, then scowled. "Lord, what an insult—to be thought so stupid!"

Firing orders in Topaz's dialect, Miranda and the maid quickly dragged out the battered trunk that had accompanied them from Java.

"What will you do?" Letty asked, wringing her hands.

Miranda paused over the open trunk, gave the pearl on her finger a quick rub for luck, then let a slight smile tilt her lips. "Someone wants me to make an indelible impression on Society tonight. I shan't disappoint them."

"Ah, Bentley! Just the man I wanted!"

The anteroom at Leicester House was crowded with costumed and masked guests, and Tony had to examine the crush closely to find the voice who'd hailed him. His lips twitched at the sight of Lord Peter Ingram bulling his way between two draped and plumed dowagers waiting to be escorted into the ballroom.

"My dear man, you care little for your life to risk a pummeling from Lady Redmond for such rudeness," Tony said, laughing at his friend's flushed face. "I'll wager she could best you with her cane inside a minute."

"I give as good as I get," Peter replied cheerfully from behind his mask. He straightened his wig and tugged at his crumpled waistcoat with the air of a man having bested an enemy in single combat.

To the despair of his valet, Lord Ingram sported a rumpled air at all times, a fault forgiven by the Earl's many friends,

who admired his sunny disposition and unfailing good humor if not his fashion sense. Wide of mouth and long of
nose, Lord Ingram had a ruddy complexion that spoke of
his expertise as an outdoorsman and sportsman, and his
advice was avidly sought at Newcastle during the racing
season, at the boxing matches, and at the hunt. Only a select
few knew, however, that he was just as clever with finances.

"What luck to find you alone," Peter began.

"My wife is removing her cloak and attending to her hair
or some such female nonsense," Tony said, idly sliding a
mother-of-pearl snuffbox between his fingers in a practiced
gesture.

"Spoken like a true husband!" His friend chuckled.
"Forgive me for not having called on the two of you before
now to bespeak my congratulations. Dashed busy I've been
and all."

"I'll be happy to introduce you to Miranda."

Lord Peter took Tony's elbow and drew him slightly
aside. "About that small matter we spoke of last week . . ."

Tony tensed imperceptibly. "Yes?"

"Damned sorry, old man, but it's no go. Fallowit was
all for offering his capital to invest in the Free Indies Company, but he cried off this morning with some feeble excuse."

Tony tamped down his disappointment, feigning boredom
as he made a production of putting away the snuffbox.

Another door closed in his face! Since his return to London, he'd been quietly attempting to shore up his finances,
but it was clear that he had to have a new infusion of capital
or be forced to sell off property. Since he couldn't dispose
of any assets of the shipping line without Kit's approval as
silent partner, and he absolutely refused to contemplate sub-
dividing Fairhaven itself, he'd racked his brains and Peter's
to come up with a scheme to bail him out before his creditors' screams sent him to debtors' prison.

He'd kept his worries from Miri, of course, wanting nothing to disrupt their newfound happiness. But it would be a

damned fine mess if now that she was finally his again, he found he couldn't support her with all the luxuries she deserved!

Peter's expressive mouth twisted with regret, but he shrugged philosophically. "Fallowit got cold feet, I guess. Seemed queer, if you ask me."

Tony frowned. "How so?"

"As I said, all enthusiasm one minute, then nothing."

"I wonder if anyone else got wind of the proposal," Tony said thoughtfully. "I don't doubt there are one or two who'd relish spoiling my plans."

"Old enemies, eh?" Peter asked with a mischievous twinkle. "Jealous husbands and scorned mistresses have long memories, my friend. As do jilted fiancées."

Tony stiffened, his irritation plain in the cool timbre of his voice. "Keep such speculations to yourself, *my friend*. I will not have Miranda embarrassed."

"I meant no offense, Bentley!" Peter exclaimed, amazed. Then he grinned. "God, you are besotted, aren't you?"

Cheeks burning, Tony was grateful for the partial coverage of his half mask. "Am I so transparent? I beg your pardon, Peter. I—"

"Say no more. I'm delighted with this turn of events. But where is this paragon of a wife who can keep even the Wastrel Lord on a short leash?"

"Tarrying as women are wont, I suppose, to make me even more eager for her return," Tony said with a wry grin. "Meanwhile, I'll ask you to learn what you can of Fallowit's defection. I'd rather know who my enemies are."

"Of course. I'll—" Peter broke off with a startled gasp. "Lord, who is that angel?"

Tony turned curiously, then stared. "Good God—Miri!"

Miranda walked toward him, her silver eyes a trifle anxious behind her domino. The crowd melted back as if by magic, awed by the exotic nature of the costume that had been hidden beneath her voluminous cloak until now.

It was the emerald and cloth-of-gold sarong she'd worn

on their wedding day, and Tony was shaken by the powerful resurgence of emotions evoked by the sight of her dressed in this fashion. The only difference was the addition of a Javanese-styled *kebaja* crusted with gold embroidery that covered her shoulders. She'd knotted the sarong at her waist, and the hem brushed the floor and fell into a train, modestly hiding all but the toes of her satin slippers. Her slender silhouette contrasted to the wide hoops of the other ladies, and with the addition of another jeweled brass collar, armlets, and the curved handle of a *kris* protruding from her sash, she was a startlingly beautiful and mysterious shock to the senses.

"Will I do?" she murmured when she reached Tony's side.

He swallowed, delighted and appalled at the same time. "My God," he repeated.

Lord Ingram's bright hazel eyes shone with admiration. "Exquisite, madam. Introduce us, Bentley!"

"Isn't it the custom at masquerades for identities to remain a secret until the unmasking?" Miranda asked with a coquettish smile. She extended her hand. "For tonight, I'm the Emissary of the Sultana of Preanger."

"Delighted, I'm sure," Peter chortled, making a sweeping bow and pressing his lips to her knuckles.

"Perhaps we'd better get this over with," Tony said in a strangled voice. Taking Miranda's elbow, he led her into the ballroom.

The picture they made as they joined the dancing—the tall, elegantly tailored nobleman and the gracefully exotic *houri* on his arm—created an instant sensation. Despite the abundant variety of costumes turned out for the event, the shepherdesses, fairy queens, and Grecian heroines paled when compared to Miranda's beguiling garb and the severe elegance of the intricate coif into which Topaz had fashioned her moonlight-colored hair. Behind every lady's fan, envious questions were asked and whispered scraps of gossip repeated, while gentlemen gazed on with admiration, some with more than casual speculation.

Anger had buoyed Miranda thus far, but all the avid eyes

upon her and Tony made her question her actions for the first time. Had she let her temper get the better of her and made a terrible mistake? The orchestra took up the strains of a stately saraband, and she took her position beside her husband.

"Are you angry?" she murmured, taking his hand but not looking at him.

"Amazed. What did you once tell me? Something about taking up English attire to remain unobtrusive?"

Miranda blushed, but pride kept her chin at a defiant angle. "If I am to be notorious, it will be on my own terms."

"Meaning?"

She shook her head. "Later. Right now, I've no choice but to brazen this out."

"That happens to be my specialty," he remarked with a surprising smile, then swept her into the first forms of the dance.

Miranda's memory of the remainder of the evening was a blur of music and an endless stream of partners, but several incidents later glittered in her mind like the diamonds in her new bridal ring.

She remembered her surprise when she found His Highness, King George, wasn't stout at all, as she'd imagined him, and how no one in the company seemed to regard the presence of his mistress, Melusine, Duchess of Kendal, as anything out of the ordinary. Then there was her astonishment when Tony explained the King's legal wife had been safely locked away in Hanover for her indiscretions years before the accession.

She'd felt an instant affinity for pretty and acerbic Lady Mary Wortley Montagu, who announced to all who'd listen that she, for one, was glad there was another eccentric female in the city for the broadsheets to lambaste in doggerel verse, as she was tired of being their only amusement!

The quiet and friendly graciousness of the Princess of Wales impressed Miranda when Tony presented her after the unmasking, and Caroline of Anspach drew her into the conversation, unmasking Miranda in a different way by discovering her linguistic skills so that for nearly half an hour Miranda had conversed with Georg August, the Prince of Wales, in his native German.

But Miranda's crowning moment came when across the ballroom she caught Sylvie's resentful blue eyes upon her, and she gifted her mother-in-law with a brilliant smile that was pure triumph.

"How does it feel to be a leader of Society?" Tony asked some days later.

"Oh, pooh!" Miranda said, tossing a handful of invitations onto the pile overflowing the inlaid top of her drawing room desk. "Just because I had the audacity to wear a sarong, I'm suddenly a leader?"

"I can't plow a path across my own parlor most evenings for the glittering company come to pay you homage," Tony mock-complained. "The press and gossip sheets compare your beauty to the moon, your wit to a rapier, and your ability to break hearts to Helen of Troy. And if it's not the opera, it's the theater, or Ranelagh Gardens with a horde of new friends."

Miranda swiveled on her delicately carved chair and surveyed her husband with dismay. "It is too much, isn't it? Perhaps we should retire to Fairhaven for a while. I'm sure it's beautiful there in the summer—"

Tony burst out laughing and walked to her side. "Nay, sweeting. Never mind my teasing. I'm delighted in your success, though hardly surprised. Where else can there be had lively conversation, gracious hospitality, a sparkling array of literati, musicians, eccentrics, and even statesmen!"

"Mr. Walpole is most charming," Miranda said severely, "and I know he came expressly to see you."

"Nay, they all come to see that most rare of occurrences—a true love-match."

"You are too cynical, my lord," she said, giggling. "If you feel my salons are getting out of hand—"

"No, I want you to enjoy yourself." Touching the ruff of lace edging the square neckline of her French-inspired sacque dress, he spoke in a husky voice. "Just so long as you find time for me occasionally."

"As I did last night?" Rising from her chair, Miranda caught his hand and gently urged it lower, shivering at the touch of his fingertips on the swell of her breasts. Her smile was loving but provocative. "You are welcome to all the time you care to take, Englishman."

Sliding his fingers even further beneath her bodice, Tony teased the pebbled nub of her nipple, then bent and nuzzled her neck, his voice high with feigned shock. "In broad daylight, madam? Shocking!"

She drew back to make some quip, but their gazes locked and grew hot as their pulses jumped with the flame of desire. Taking his caressing hand, she threaded her fingers between his and tugged him toward the door. They crossed the foyer sedately, but halfway up the stairs they chanced another glance, and suddenly they were laughing, racing the rest of the way, slamming their chamber door and falling onto the bed like children whose only concern was their pleasure.

"See what you've done," Miranda complained sometime later following a healthy sexual romp that had left them both replete. Lying rosily naked in their bed, her cheeks and breasts lightly abraded by Tony's beard stubble, she tugged at the twisted wreck of her chignon. "And after Topaz worked so hard to make me presentable."

The Sumatran maid worked doubly hard these days, as if to make up for the misfortune of the wardrobe, even though Miranda assured her she didn't blame her. And while for a time Miranda had considered taking up her suspicions about his mother's involvement in the event with Tony, everything had turned out for the best, so it seemed rather mean and petty to mention it.

Tony tugged on his last stocking and reached for his shoe, grinning like a well-contented cat. "It is one of the great joys of my life to undo Topaz's work. But Sims will likely go into spasms should he chance to see what you did to my cravat before I make my escape."

"I wish you didn't have to go," Miranda murmured drowsily.

"Business, my love." He kissed her once more, reveling in her taste, then reluctantly made for the door. "Have a rest. I'll be back before dinner."

"I may take a chair to the shops later," she said lazily.

At the door, Tony frowned. "No, order the curricle. And take Letty with you, and a couple of footmen, too. I don't want a repeat of yesterday's near-accident."

She came up on one elbow, amused and touched at his protectiveness. "The chair wouldn't have overturned but for the rowdiness of that unexpected mob. No harm was done, and I'm sure it won't happen again."

"No, for you'll take the curricle, as I said, or abide at home, madam," he said sternly.

Miranda blinked at his vehemence. "Very well, Tony, if you feel so strongly. I only thought to save you the expense."

He was at her side in an instant, dragging her up by the shoulders and pressing her against him. "I waited all my life to find the one woman who could fill me, body and soul. Do you think I'd risk your safety for a few pennies?"

Miranda had never felt so cherished, so loved. She traced the hollow in his cheek with her fingertip, then set her thumb in the shallow cleft of his chin. "I am truly the most fortunate of women, Anthony Benedict. What I did to deserve you, I'll never know."

"That's easy," he said, kissing her tenderly. "You loved me."

Tony's mood was still euphoric when he reached Lavender House an hour later. Optimism made his blood hum, and he whistled cheerfully under his breath as he waved the footman aside and bounded up the stairs to Sylvie's private sitting room. He knocked on her bedroom door.

"Mother? Are you up?"

Sylvie slipped through the door a few moments later, hastily tying the sash of her dressing gown while firmly pulling her bedroom door shut behind her. She shoved her silvery-gold locks out of her face, which was paler than normal for lack of her usual paint, and gazed at her tall son with a mixture of irritation and maternal concern.

"What is it? Has something happened to your wife?"

"No, of course not." Tony frowned. "She's fine."

Sylvie exhaled in exasperation and dropped onto a dainty French settee. As always, her taste in interior decorations was exquisite and the very best money—hers and Tony's—could buy. "Then why have you disturbed me at this ungodly hour?"

Tony drew up a matching dainty chair, perching gingerly on its edge. "Simply this. I must find out if Colleton holds a grudge large enough to thwart every financial enterprise I initiate."

"'Tis possible." Sylvie yawned. "And no more than you deserve for what you did to Catherine's pride."

"She'll recover," Tony said carelessly, "but we may not if I cannot identify the bastard who checkmates my every move! Thrice now it's happened, just when I thought to dig us out of this hole. But I'm being stymied by ghosts who leave no tracks. If it's Colleton, I may be able to reason with him. If 'tis someone else, then I must know who. So call in your favorite dogs, Mother, and see what they can learn. Otherwise, I'll be forced to liquidate some of our holdings, beginning with the Dower House."

"Absolutely not! That's mine!"

Tony sighed. "And the debts left over from the South Sea Bubble are yours, too, even though the stock has made some resurgence in recent months."

Tears sparkled in Sylvie's gentian blue eyes. "You can't mean to deprive me of my security. The Dower House has always been meant for my old age. Sell the Leicester Square house. That should bring a tidy sum."

"The Dower House is unused practically all the year, and Miri and I are quite comfortable where we are. She's had so many changes lately, I am loath to make her endure yet another."

"I should have known your young wife would persuade you to set aside your mother," Sylvie said bitterly.

"Surely you can't believe that!"

"Oh, it's always the way," Sylvie said, dabbing delicately at the corner of her eyes with a lace-edged handkerchief. "A son takes a viper for a wife, and jealous of her new position, she wants no reminders around of his previous life and loyalties. Oh, an ungrateful child is a bitter portion, indeed!"

"You're stretching this all out of proportion. No one's trying to turn you out!"

"Your wife hates me. She'll drive me out of your affections with her insinuations and gibes."

Tony stood up with barely suppressed irritation. "I see you still can't be reasonable about Miranda. Nevertheless, I ask your help in my investigation because it concerns us all. If we lose Fairhaven completely, the style of all our lives will change for the worse. Good day, Mother."

Tony turned abruptly on his heel and stalked through the door. Sylvie sat for a moment, chewing her lip, lost in thought. Her bedroom door creaked open.

"All done, m'love? Devilish bad timing. Come back to bed."

"Leave me alone, Cecil."

The slender young man tugged his dressing gown over his white legs and, coming up behind Sylvie, began to nuzzle her nape. She swatted at him absently like an annoying fly.

"It's that little bitch, putting him up to this," she muttered.

"Hmm? Don't worry, Sylvie, my precious. I'll take care of you."

Slowly Sylvie turned around to stare at the brown-haired youth. Though his chin lacked character, and the fine lines of dissipation were beginning to appear around his brown calf's eyes, he was comely enough and a grateful as well as energetic lover. Which were exactly the reasons she was bored with him.

And there had been a man at last evening's variety performance who'd made her curse the custom of going masked, for she'd felt his intense regard from across the theater. Baron something-or-other from one of the German principalities, someone had said, and a sender of exotic nosegays if the wilting posy on her dresser was any indication. A little thrill trickled down her spine at the thought of a new chase.

Refocusing on the young man watching her anxiously, Sylvie's thoughts returned to the problem at hand. Perhaps this puppy still had his uses. "You do care for me, don't you, Cecil?"

He reached for her eagerly. "Immensely!"

Like a queen granting a boon, Sylvie allowed him to kiss her, smiling. "Then I know that I can count on you to do me a small favor . . ."

"This is absolutely the last straw!" Letty said angrily. She stripped off her gloves and the jacket that matched her new seal brown gown, and then plopped down on the settee in the main salon. "Something's got to be done!"

Miranda cast her indignant cousin a cautionary glance. "We'll take our tea in here, Wexill," she told the waiting butler.

"Yes, my lady," the wiry, chubby-cheeked young man replied. Recently promoted, Wexill did his best to hide his relative youth behind a severe expression, resulting in a face that always looked as if it had just made a visit to a pickle barrel. Sucking in his round cheeks, Wexill bowed out, drawing the paneled double doors closed behind him.

At the click of the door latch, a fit of trembling overtook Miranda, and she sat down abruptly in the tapestry chair across from Letty. The May afternoon was sunny, and the windows were open to admit a balmy breeze that rustled the china bowls of daffodils and phlox scattered about on the polished tables and carved mantelpiece. But despite the welcome, pleasantly warm weather, Miranda shivered uncontrollably beneath the lilac silk of her gown.

"Are you all right?" Letty demanded suddenly, the lappets of her lace cap flapping about her plump chin. "You're as white as Lot's wife."

"Delayed reaction, that's all," Miranda replied, forcing a weak smile. "It's not every day I'm nearly run down in the street."

"Irresponsible hooligans! I'd wager those ruffians on

horseback were members of the infamous Mohocks so notorious a decade ago! Sons of the quality out to terrorize
innocent folk just for the sake of amusement—reprehen-
sible! My heart nearly stopped when that rider knocked you
down.''

"It seems city living can be more dangerous than I expected," Miranda replied with a short laugh. "But it was
only a glancing blow, and I didn't fall hard."

"You don't intend to go to Lady Hamilton's musicale
after this shock, do you?"

"I'll send her a note with my apologies. My nerves are
a bit more shaken than I realized," Miranda admitted, ac-
knowledging the weakness in her knees. She looked up at
the knock on the door. "Here's our tea. I'll be perfectly all
right just as soon as I've had a cup."

Letty poured out, making certain Miranda had two spoon-
fuls of sugar in hers. "First the sedan chair, then a falling
flagstone nearly flattens us, and now this! I declare, Miranda, you've had so many mishaps lately, I'm beginning
to think you're jinxed!"

Miranda nearly choked on a swallow of tea, trying to
suppress a superstitious quiver. She told herself to be sensible, but years of the *dukun*'s instruction had taught her
not everything was as it appeared. Still, a few unlucky
incidents was hardly proof she was cursed. "Oh, I'm sure
that's just your imagination," she replied.

"Well, did I imagine someone ruining your dresses?
What about the things that have come up missing from the
laundry? And those invitations that went astray? We had
enough food for fifty people and only ten showed up! And
don't tell me I imagined the man that followed us at Ranelagh! Gave me the willies, it did."

"You know you can't avoid the curious at Ranelagh.
That's part of the entertainment, watching the gentry at play.
As for the rest . . ." Miranda shrugged. "Accidents hap-
pen."

"Well, *I* think it's the work of the Marchioness again.
'How long shall the wicked triumph?' " Letty bit into a
cake, chewing vigorously. "It'd be an easy matter for her

to bribe a servant or two. Mark my words, she's out to make things either so unpleasant or mayhap even so frightening, you'll get fed up and leave.''

"Nothing could induce me to do that,'' Miranda said firmly. "I love my husband too much.''

Letty smiled indulgently at the soft look on Miranda's face. "Nevertheless, you must tell his lordship about all this so he can do something.''

Miranda set down her empty cup, her normal equilibrium somewhat restored. "I hate to bother him with such trifles when he's so busy. He's consulting with Lord Ingram and the Free Indies supervisors nearly every day. Something's worrying him, Letty, though he assures me it's nothing. And besides, what would I say? Minor annoyances have convinced me your mother is trying to drive me insane? He'd think I was truly demon-touched at such silliness.''

"Well, I say that blond witch is jealous of your success and your place in his lordship's heart.'' Letty wagged an admonitory finger at Miranda. "Beware the evildoer, my girl.''

"She resents me, but I don't think she'd do me any real harm, and sooner or later something will make her realize I'm here to stay.''

Something like her first grandchild, Miranda thought hopefully. She knew that Sylvie loved Tony in her own peculiar, obsessive fashion, so perhaps a child of his body would go a long way toward healing the breach of his having brought home an unsuitable wife. And maybe she'd even learn to tolerate the mother of that child.

Surreptitiously Miranda pressed her palm against the place where she hoped a child might be growing even now, though she knew it was too soon to be certain. On Java, women desiring children sacrificed to Dewri Sri, the goddess of rice and fertility, and with an inner smile, Miranda wondered if anyone would understand her urge to do so, too. Only Tony, she realized, and resolved to laugh with him later over this pagan inclination.

Letty was spreading rhubarb jam on a biscuit, still muttering under her breath about the Marchioness, when a knock interrupted them.

"Ach, pardon me, lass—er, my lady," Angus Pratt said, peeping around the door.

"Angus, you're just in time to join us," Miranda said, delighted. "Letty, pour Mr. Pratt a cup of tea."

Angus cast a cautious glance at Letty and shook his grizzled head. "Nay, I couldn't impose, lass."

"Nonsense! Do come in," Miranda insisted.

Out of deference to his place in the household of a Marquess, Angus wore black knee breeches, a white shirt and plain stock, and a wine wool jacket. He looked remarkably handsome, Miranda thought, and a glance at Letty proved she was not alone in that observation.

"This just came for you, is all," he said, walking forward with his rolling seaman's gait, a cloth-covered box in his hands. A high, excited chattering came from the package.

"What on earth . . . ?" Miranda quickly unwrapped the box, and gave a delighted gasp. A tiny, bright-eyed monkey with a fine leather collar and velvet jacket chittered at her from inside a bamboo cage. "Oh, look how darling!"

"Ugh, horrid!" Letty said, waving her handkerchief. "Mr. Pratt, how could you bring that ugly, smelly creature to her ladyship? What if it bites? Take it away!"

Angus's expression became mulish. "Ugly is a matter of opinion, I ken."

"Oh, stop, you two!" Miranda admonished, releasing the lid and reaching for the tiny creature. It scrambled up her arm, and she laughed. "Isn't he adorable? Oh, it's just like Tony to give me a pet like this! Is there a card? Do sit down and drink your tea, Angus."

"Here's the card," Angus replied, passing her a heavy cream-colored envelope. "And I ain't got time for tea, thank you all the same."

"Hmmph," Letty sniffed. "What makes you too good to drink tea with her ladyship, I ask?"

"I ain't good enough for some, I guess," Angus sneered.

"Poppycock! If Lady Bentley says you are, then you are!" Letty poured out a cup of tea and rapidly filled a plate with an assortment of cakes, then shoved both into Angus's hands. "Now sit, and not another word!"

Suppressing a smile at their squabbling, Miranda handed her new little friend a cake and eagerly ripped into the envelope.

"You wouldn't take a meal with me exceptin' her ladyship ordered it," Angus grumbled, balancing his cup on his knee.

"Much you know!" Letty sniffed again.

"Well, I'd wager you wouldn't take tea with me at Ranelagh on a Sunday evening."

"Well, you'd be wrong," Letty snapped, glaring at him.

"You mean you would?" Angus asked with a belligerent air.

"Er—yes. Why not?" Letty looked surprised.

Angus scrubbed his jaw with his fist, hiding a satisfied smirk. "Well then, Miss Sutherlin, I'll wait on you this Sunday. Unless you ain't a woman of your word."

"I am, Mr. Pratt," Letty replied haughtily. "And I accept your invitation, clumsy as it is."

Angus snorted. "Figure I may as well see the sights anyway. I'm thinking to go back to the Colonies with the *Mirage*."

"Of all the ridiculous notions!" Letty scoffed. "You're too old to go to sea again."

Indignant, Angus beat on his barrel chest with his fist. "What! Why, I've the heart of a man half my age! There's life in me yet, woman!"

Since the conversation was fast getting out of hand, Miranda decided that it was an opportune moment to interrupt. She waved the note. "How curious. This little fellow isn't from Tony after all. I can't quite make the signature out. Can you, Letty?"

Letty drew her eyeglasses out of her pocket and set them on her pert nose. "What a deplorable scrawl! Whoever wrote this must have toes for fingers!" She examined the missive. " 'With gratitude to the author of my intent,' it says. Signed—Boot? Foot?"

Miranda frowned. "I don't recall meeting anyone by that name."

"What's that supposed to mean?" Letty asked.

"Just a flowery compliment," Miranda dismissed. "I'll inquire around so that I can thank my benefactor since I do intend to keep this clever chap."

"Oh, Miri, must you?" Letty said, grimacing.

Miranda laughed, letting the tiny animal play with the ribbons on her bodice. "He reminds me of home—Java, I mean. It's said the little men of the forest have special powers and bring good fortune. To hunt one is very bad luck indeed. Help me decide on a name."

"Ach, I'm nae good at such as that," Angus said, shaking his head. "He's no bigger than a mouse, is he?"

"If we're not careful, that's exactly what that black devil of a cat may think, too," Letty said tartly.

"Beelzebub would never—" Angus spluttered.

"Would you help me secure a sizable cage, just so we can avoid such a tragedy?" Miranda asked sweetly.

"Sure, lass—er, my lady. Won't be no trouble, then we'll button him right up."

"That's a perfect name—Button!" Miranda placed the tired animal back in the small cage and handed it to Angus. "Perhaps you can put him on a leash for now and let him have a run in the garden?"

"Of course, I—"

The salon door opened and Wexill hurried in, his round face so flustered, he'd forgotten to suck in his cheeks. "Pardon me, my lady, but there's a guest—oh, madam! You must see for yourself!"

Alarmed, Miranda hurried to the door, followed by Angus and Letty. A tall man and a dark-haired woman stood in the foyer. They both turned at Miranda's quick steps on the black and white marble squares. Miranda opened her mouth to form a question, then gasped softly, taken aback by a face both familiar and new.

Slate blue eyes under sun-bleached brows.

A long, handsome face with a slash of a dimple.

A strong, square chin with the hint of a cleft.

"Oh, hello!" Miranda's face lit up with the joy of recognition, and she rushed forward, both hands outstretched in eager welcome. "You must be Kit!"

Chapter 16

"**C**hristopher Ryan, at your service, ma'am."

A quizzical smile hovered on Kit's mouth as he took Miranda's hands. Dressed in a worsted coat and breeches of excellent quality and understated elegance, his pristine stock immaculate and faultlessly knotted, he was every inch the cultured colonial merchant-planter.

Breathless with delight, Miranda squeezed Kit's fingers, then cast a glance at the green-eyed, raven-haired beauty at his side cuddling a shawl-draped bundle in her arms.

"And Lexa, too," Miranda said warmly. "I've have known you both anywhere! Oh, welcome! Tony will be so pleased."

"Then we have not come amiss. When I said I wanted Lord Bentley, your butler looked at me as if I were daft," Kit said with a grin.

"Poor Wexill! He thought it strange Tony should be asking for himself!" Miranda said with a laugh.

"Understandable, I suppose," Kit replied, his mischievous grin growing even wider. "But, madam, *you* still have me at a disadvantage . . . ?"

"Oh! Yes, of course! How could you know?" Blushing, Miranda explained. "I'm Tony's wife, Miranda."

"What!" Lexa's mouth formed a perfect O of amazement, then she began to laugh, her slim shoulders shaking under her stylish daffodil silk traveling gown. "Oh, that scoundrel! Wait until I get my hands on him—keeping such a secret from us! We come to present his niece, and he trumps us with a bride!"

"And such a beautiful one!" Bending, Kit kissed Miranda's cheek. "You must be special indeed to have captured the heart of my wayward brother. I hope he makes you happy."

"Oh, sir, I am the fortunate one," Miranda demurred, then her gaze strayed back to Lexa. "But did I hear aright? You have a daughter?"

"Here she is." Lexa folded back the shawl, uncovering the sleeping form of a little girl just over a year old whose milk white skin and dark curls were the mirror of her mother's. The child rubbed a chubby, dimpled fist against her retroussé nose, yawned, and opened eyes that were a dark Benedict blue.

"Oh, she's beautiful! What's her name?" Miranda gravitated instantly into the cherub's sphere, captivated. "She has Tony's eyes!"

"Kit's eyes, too," Lexa corrected with a droll twist of her mouth. "And his sense of mischief. Her name is Rose, after their mother."

Rose scrambled in her mother's arms, flashed Miranda a dimpled grin, then turned suddenly bashful and buried her face against Lexa's neck.

"How delightful," Miranda murmured, faintly puzzled, but before she could ask about Rose's name, Kit gave a great shout.

"Angus, you old sea dog!" Kit clamped his broad arms around the bandy-legged old man, and they took turns pounding each other's backs. "God, you're a sight for sore eyes!"

"Ach, Cap'n!" Angus's voice was suspiciously husky, and all he could manage after that was a rusty "Laddie!"

Kit held the old sailor away, examining him. "So you're still all in one piece, are you?"

"'Tis been a near thing a time or two," the Scotsman said with a shrug.

"I want to hear all about it!" Kit turned back to Miranda. "And all about my new sister-by-marriage as well."

"Oh, pardon my manners," Miranda said, flustered with excitement. She ushered them through the foyer, chattering animatedly. "You must be fatigued. Come into the salon. When did you arrive? This is my kinswoman, Letticia Sutherlin. Letty, order some fresh tea for our guests, please. Where are you staying?"

"We're just come from the ship," Kit explained as they all made themselves comfortable. "Tony will roast me completely when he learns I've been sent as Carolina's representative to the Plantations and Trade Ministry. Entirely too respectable for a reformed privateer, he'll say."

"Nonsense, Kit!" Lexa objected. "The Assembly knew you were the only man for the job. And since I could not bear the thought of so long a separation, and we'd planned to commission London furnishings for Bonaire anyway . . ." She shrugged, the expression on her diamond-shaped face impish. "Here we are."

"I apologize for arriving unannounced, Miranda," Kit said. "We were under way almost as soon as the decision was made, and a letter would have arrived with us. In fact, with Tony's wanderlust, I'd scarcely hoped to find him in England at all, and I'd thought to inquire about a house—"

"Oh, no, you must stay with us," Miranda interrupted. "Please, I insist. We've more than enough room, and it would mean so much to my husband. Tony speaks with such affection of you both."

Lexa dimpled charmingly, holding on to one of Rose's hands as she wobbled around the circle of her mother's skirts, exploring and prattling quietly to herself. "Yet he may not approve of your filling up his house in such a manner, especially when you see all our trunks and this moppet's gorgon of a nurse.''

"I can't think of anything we'd both like more," Miranda insisted.

A maid appeared with a fresh tea tray just then, and a large black shadow streaked into the room. With a strident yowl for attention, Beelzebub stalked toward Lexa. Miranda made a move to stop the headstrong animal, but Angus grinned and touched her arm.

"Ach, watch this, lass."

"Beelzebub!" With a cry of delight, Lexa gathered the cat into her lap. "Oh, you dear black monster!"

Beelzebub broke into a loud, rumbly purr, rubbed the flat of his battle-scarred head under Lexa's chin, then curled into a contented ball in her lap.

"They're quite old friends, ye see," Angus explained, shooting a wry glance at Letty. "Takes quite a woman to charm an old sailor like Beelzebub."

Letty "harrumphed" and looked away.

"Well, that certainly settles it," Miranda said with an amazed laugh. "Now you absolutely have to stay here! Tony will tell you so himself as soon as he returns from the Free Indies office."

"Oh, ho! This is a change," Kit chuckled. "Dare I say married life is transforming Tony into a responsible businessman? If so, then we are much more indebted to you than you can know."

"He works very hard," Miranda said, her gray eyes sparkling, "but I have no wish to change him. He should return soon. Please, tell me all about your trip."

Over the tea tray, Kit recounted the comparatively uneventful voyage, bragging that his precocious daughter had inherited her father's sea legs and thrived during the journey. Miranda narrated an abbreviated account of her and Tony's adventures in Java and subsequent reunion in England, much to Kit and Lexa's amazement.

As cakes and biscuits and great quantities of tea disappeared, a fast friendship formed. It was fascinating for Miranda to listen to and watch Kit, so like Tony yet so different.

Lexa embarked on a merry tale of how the two of them had once totally confounded her with disguises as Squint, an old sailor, and the Dandy, a flamboyant buccaneer—until she'd solved the confusion by nearly twisting the mole off *her* twin's right ear!

Miranda found Lexa warm and intuitive, and little Rose entranced her so much, she abandoned her dignity, such as it was, and settled down on the floor amid her hoops, drawing her new niece onto her lap to play patty-cake and run-Johnny-run while Angus and Letty carried the rest of the conversation.

Much to Miranda's chagrin, that was how Sylvie found her.

Sweeping into the salon before poor flustered Wexill could announce her, the Dowager Marchioness was the epitome of aristocratic arrogance, a ruff of lace perched atop her golden curls. Her still youthful figure was smoothly encased in an eye-catching creation of creamy silk and pink ribbons, and a pink ruffled parasol dangled from her wrist by a matching cord. Her smooth face was hard with rage, however, and had she known it, the Marchioness would have been even more annoyed, for her expression destroyed the ingenue effect she and her maid had worked so hard that morning to accomplish. Spotting Miranda sprawled on the Turkish carpet, she curled her lip in contempt.

"Where is my son?" the Marchioness demanded imperiously. "Lord Russell had the gall to approach me about purchasing the Dower House, but I distinctly forbade Anthony—" She became aware of the tall blond man slowly rising to his feet, and inhaled on a sharp hiss. "What are *you* doing here! How dare you!"

Kit's features were carefully blank and still, his blue gaze hooded. Hostility vibrated in the air. He inclined his head just a fraction past insolent. "Lady Bentley."

Angus stirred uneasily, and Letty's eyes bobbed from face to face, trying to read the nuances sizzling through the charged air. Bewildered, Miranda scrambled to her feet, passing Rose to her mother just as Sylvie whirled on her with an inarticulate snarl.

"You traitorous bitch! Where is your loyalty?"

Too late, Miranda recalled Tony's caution about his mother and Kit. There were things here she did not understand, and she felt as though she'd stepped into murky water filled with hungry crocodiles. Berating herself for not having questioned Tony further on the subject, she licked her dry lips and tactfully attempted to tread through the situation.

"My lady, I don't understand—"

"Stupid as well!" Sylvie snapped. "Ignorant trollop! You welcome your husband's deadliest enemy into his home!"

Truly dismayed now, Miranda gaped incredulously, and her stomach flopped like a dying fish. Had she made a mistake? But no, she'd heard Tony speak of his brother in terms that could not be misinterpreted. Pulling her scattered wits about her, she tried again.

"My lady, please, won't you sit? I'm sure there's some mistake."

"Yes! The one Anthony made when he thought with his member instead of his brain and married the likes of you!"

Little Rose whimpered at the angry tone of Sylvie's voice, and Lexa's expression grew as cold and haughty as the Marchioness's. Sylvie pierced them both with a brief, dismissive stare, then suddenly paused, disconcerted. She mapped Rose's face with her hot gaze, seemingly taken aback by the baby's unblinking blue eyes, then visibly shook off whatever notion had struck her and resumed her harangue at Miranda.

"Tony will never forgive this piece of treachery! If you know what's good for you, girl, you'll throw this bastard out on his ear—and his whore, too!"

"Enough!" Kit growled, starting forward, his brow thunderous.

But despite the chill Miranda felt, she knew her duty, and she quickly intervened, placing herself between Kit and Sylvie.

"I confess my ignorance of this matter, but I know my husband would never allow anyone to insult a guest in his home," she said in an even tone, though her insides quaked.

Whatever hopes she had of winning her mother-in-law's acceptance withered under Sylvie's baleful gaze, but she continued doggedly. "I must ask you to excuse us now, Lady Bentley."

Sylvie's pale complexion blazed red with rage, and her knuckles went white on the ivory handle of her parasol. "What? You—you harlot! Jezebel! You'd dare such impertinence?"

"Wexill," Miranda said, "please show Her Ladyship out."

The butler's Adam's apple bobbed convulsively, and his eyes bulged like a frog's, but he did as his mistress bid. "This way, Your Ladyship."

Incensed, Sylvie swung her parasol at Miranda, but Kit moved like a striking cobra, grabbing its pointed tip and tearing it from Sylvie's grip. His voice was deadly. "I said enough."

Something like fear flickered behind Sylvie's eyes, but she instantly controlled it, her gaze turning glacial. She grabbed up her skirts as if to avoid contamination, and her contemptuous sneer burned through Miranda.

"I knew Tony shouldn't have trusted you. You'll regret this, I swear it!" Then she hissed at the unfortunate Wexill, "Well, idiot! Show me out!"

As Sylvie disappeared through the door, a wave of light-headedness washed over Miranda, and she swayed drunkenly on her feet. The reaction of the others was instantaneous. Kit tossed aside the parasol and helped her to a chair. Lexa patted her hand and offered her perfumed handkerchief. Letty nodded to Angus, who went to the sideboard and poured a hefty shot of brandy for her. One sip of the powerful stuff, however, and Miranda's stomach lurched alarmingly. She pushed it away, vainly trying to reassure them all while ignoring the painful heaviness that centered low in her belly. It took a full ten minutes before she could convince any of them she was quite all right. She was still making protestations when another figure appeared unannounced in the doorway.

"I should have known!" Tony greeted the cluster of backs

bunched around his wife. A wide, mocking smile lit up his lean face. "The Dandy and his Duchess arrive, and of course, all hell breaks loose!"

"Jimmy!" Kit met his brother halfway across the room, and the two men exchanged handshakes and masculine bear hugs.

"Leave it to you two to disrupt my entire household!" Tony said with a laugh, catching Lexa up to kiss her soundly, then chucking Rose under her double chin. "Lexa, you're gorgeous! And is this cherub my new niece? Miri, are you overwhelmed? Or did Kit just scare you with his ugly countenance?"

Miranda shook her head at his teasing, biting her lower lip to control its tendency to tremble. "Forgive me, my lord, but I have done something dreadful. Your mother . . ." She swallowed, unable to continue.

"What?" Tony frowned, taking in Miranda's pallor for the first time. He dropped down to one knee before her chair and caught her trembling hand. "Mother was here?" At Miranda's nod, he muttered, "Oh, hell!"

"She came and said the most awful things to . . ." She gestured at Lexa and Kit. ". . . and . . . and I sent her away. I'm sorry, but I didn't know what else to do and—"

"Calm yourself, love," Tony said, moved by her obvious distress. "It's of no import."

"But I don't understand! Why was she so angry with Kit?"

"You mean you haven't told her?" Lexa demanded suddenly.

Tony looked away from the confusion shining in the depths of Miranda's silver eyes. "Not everything."

"Then it's time you did," Lexa said firmly, shifting Rose, who was becoming restive, from one hip to the other.

Listening to one side, Angus nodded in agreement. Beside him, Letty frowned her puzzlement, but when she whispered a question, Angus touched his gnarled forefinger to his lips and shook his grizzled head to silence her.

"Your wife should know," Lexa repeated.

Increasingly anxious, Miranda looked at each of them in turn. "Know what? I don't understand."

"It's difficult to know where to begin," Tony said, his mouth grim.

"Aye, it is." Kit sighed deeply. Folding his arms across his broad chest, he met Miranda's bewildered glance. "Sylvie hates me because I'm not her son. As her late husband's bastard, she always saw me as a threat to Tony."

"And while Mother does love me," Tony said, squeezing Miranda's hand, "you have to know that I'm not really her son either."

Miranda inched back in her chair, staring at the two men incredulously. "This riddle rivals the tale the *dukun* told of the quest of Semar's heroic masters."

"Why must men convolute a simple story?" Lexa demanded, her dark curls swinging in exasperation about her piquant face. "Their mother was Rosalind, their father's mistress. Sylvie raised one twin as Charles Benedict's rightful heir, while Rosalind raised the other."

"Yes," Miranda said, nodding, "I know they were separated as children."

"We believed we were half brothers," Tony explained, "separated by two sides of the blanket."

"And we hated each other's guts," Kit said cheerfully. "Had a hell of a time revenging a lot of imaginary and not-so-imaginary wrongs."

"Only through Lexa's persistence did the truth come out," Tony said, picking up the narrative. "And, like the hardheaded Englishmen we are, we pounded the pulp out of each other and then settled our differences."

"You see," Lexa said, "my father helped Sylvie destroy Rosalind's relationship with Charles many years ago, a fact that once caused me much pain. But I alone had the Cathay pearls and proof in my grandfather's diary that 'the Dioscuri are Rosalind's.' "

"Ah, Jove's sons, the Gemini!" Miranda said, understanding and, at the same time, envious. "What a wonderful gift to give them both, Lexa!"

Lexa settled into the curve of Kit's arm, her smile wry.

"Though the trial was arduous at times, it has had its re-wards."

"Minx!" Kit murmured, pulling his wife and daughter closer, his expression loving.

"But then your mother knows nothing of your reconcil-iation?" Miranda asked Tony.

He looked faintly chagrined, and rising, began to pace. "Only that I've given up the fight, not why. When I first came back from the Colonies, I was too angry to confront her. Later, it seemed to serve no purpose. Hell, what was I to say to her anyway? I always believed my father betrayed her with another woman, and that was certainly true enough, even though that woman was in fact my natural mother! Who can say who was totally wrong or right after all these years?"

"When loyalties are divided, there is no easy path," Miranda said softly, her gaze compassionate.

"I cannot say that I totally forgive Lady Sylvie for the suffering she caused our mother," Kit said slowly. "But I understand your moral dilemma, and I regret the trouble I've caused between Lady Bentley and Miranda by waltzing in here bold as brass without any warning. You ought to have me keelhauled for such an asinine stunt, Jimmy."

Tony rubbed his hand across the back of his neck in a tired gesture. "Mayhap 'tis time to have it all out anyway. To heal some wounds, only a cauterizing fire will serve."

"No." Miranda rose, steadying herself on the arm of the chair. "If you act hastily, you may sever your bonds with the Marchioness permanently. You must be certain that is what you want. For all she did not carry you in her womb, she has been your mother, and you owe her more than that."

"I will not have Mother thinking ill of you because of this situation," Tony said staunchly.

"Her opinion of me is already sealed," Miranda retorted, her tone dry. "Reflect before you act, my love, and a happy resolution may well be achieved. I can be patient with your mother's annoyance since it is nothing new."

"Wise as well as beautiful," Kit said in admiration. "You chose well, brother."

"Ah, but that's where you're wrong, Kit!" Tony said, chuckling. "You see, 'twas Miri who chose *me*."

"My husband is a great tease." Miranda flushed and wiped a faint sheen of perspiration from her upper lip. With an effort, she made her tone businesslike. "Now, we must get Kit and Lexa settled. They can have the blue suite, don't you think, Letty?"

"Oh, yes," Letty agreed, her head bobbing in agreement. "And the one connecting it for that sweet babe."

"Fine. Angus, tell Wexill to send the carriage to the docks and—oh!" Miranda stopped in her tracks, a peculiar look on her face.

"Is everything all right?" Lexa asked.

Miranda forced a smile. "Certainly. This has been a most eventful day. I—" With a small cry of pain, she bent double.

"Miri!" Tony was at her side, supporting her, her hand in his. "What is it?"

Her eyes were wide and fearful. "I—I don't know." She could not contain another low groan.

"Miri!" Tony's blue eyes held a frantic gleam.

"Oh, no," Miranda whispered, glancing downward. "Help me upstairs, Tony. I—I am unwell."

Tony followed her gaze, and his face grew grim. Without another word, he scooped Miranda into his arms and bounded toward the stairs, but not before the rest of the group had seen what he'd seen—the bright circlet of red staining her skirt.

"She wasn't far along," Tony said. "A few weeks at most. But she grieves as though she'd carried the babe full term."

Kit laid a comforting hand on his brother's stooped shoulder, and they both stared out the long window overlooking the Thames at the Ministry of Finance. In a few moments a clerk would show them in to see Sir Robert Walpole, first lord of the treasury and chancellor of the exchequer, but for the moment the business of colonial trade was the furthest thing from both their minds.

"You must give her time," Kit advised. "We men can never fully know the secret sorrows of a woman's tender heart."

"But it's been weeks! From Letty's sighs, you'd think Miri's on her deathbed, though the doctor says she's recovered physically. Miri seems so lethargic and distant, not like herself at all, and she has some damnable notion I'm disappointed in her!"

"Are you?"

"Confound it, no!" Tony gave his brother an irritated glance. "Saddened, of course, for her sake, but these things happen. Miri always expects too much of herself, more than I'd ever ask. She sees this as just another reason why I shouldn't have married her. And I'm damned tired of her doubting my devotion! Why doesn't she understand I love her unconditionally? If children are denied us, then it's a burden we'll bear together."

"You should be telling her this, not me."

Tony's expression was haggard. "Don't you think I've tried?"

The appearance of the clerk forestalled any reply from Kit. "Sir Robert will see you now, gentlemen."

Minutes later, Tony introduced Kit to the canny financier who'd turned the South Sea Company's troubles around and stabilized national credit. Fiftyish, short, and ruddy, Walpole greeted them warmly, his Norfolk squire's accent unchanged by his years in the King's service. He raised one eyebrow when Tony introduced Kit as his brother, for anyone with half an eye could see their resemblance, though Tony's garb was more dandified than Kit's colonial dress, but diplomatically, the chancellor refrained from commenting.

"It is always a pleasure to work with you and your family, Lord Bentley," Walpole said, indicating chairs to them. "Last evening I visited at the opera with your delightful mother."

"Handel's *Rinaldo* is a favorite of hers," Tony said in a noncommittal tone. Since Kit's arrival, he'd not heard from Sylvie, and he'd been too worried about Miranda to give his mother's surprising silence much thought except to assume he was out of favor for harboring an erstwhile enemy. Sylvie was one problem that would have to wait. "No doubt she was attended by Lord Edmund?" he commented.

Walpole frowned, considering. "Actually, I believe she has a new admirer. Baron Foote, a German—no, a burgher from Holland, a curiously shy chap behind his domino."

Tony shrugged. "My mother collects admirers as other women collect fans. But I know you are pressed by your duties, Sir Robert, so to the point."

The three launched into a discussion of colonial and domestic trade, tariffs, and taxes. Since King George's speech before Parliament the year before, domestic prosperity and peace were the highest priorities, and Walpole was too astute a statesman to neglect the concerns of these two men whose shipping enterprises stretched throughout the known world. Kit related the Carolina colonists' dissatisfaction regarding the policy of shipping goods first to England before dispersal abroad. Tony reported on the markets he'd seen to the east and the dangers of trade restrictions through granting monopolies.

"Well, gentlemen," the chancellor said, showing them out nearly an hour later, "you've given me much to think on. Mr. Ryan, you can assure the colonists that I am working assiduously on new tariffs. I promise advantageous rates for anything that promotes domestic prosperity, especially raw materials, lumber, naval stores, and the like."

"Sir Robert, we certainly desire to expand our markets," Kit agreed, but added a warning. "Do not think we Carolinians can be relegated to just that role, however, for we desire to develop our own manufacturing in due time."

"Prosperity in the New World can only aid our endeavors at home, Mr. Ryan," the chancellor said. "I think a compromise can be reached to allow colonial products to be shipped abroad directly as long as British ships continue to be used."

"Indeed," Kit said, "that would go a long way toward ending many grievances."

"Good." Walpole nodded, then turned to Tony. "Lord

Bentley, your interest and support of these polices is certain to win a considerable number to our favor. I'll have a draft of proposed legislation ready soon. Are you prepared to introduce it in the House of Lords?''

Startled, Tony protested. ''Sir, I'm honored, but I don't think I'm the most suitable choice.''

''Nonsense, you have great presence, just the sort of thing to make a grand impression on the introduction of new and sweeping policy changes. Further, your interest, commercial experience, and adventures abroad will offer much insight to us more pedestrian types. I must insist, for the welfare of our nation.''

Still dubious, Tony bowed in acquiescence. ''In that case, how can I refuse?''

''Excellent! I'll have my clerks send the draft around as soon as possible. Good day to you, gentleman.''

''Amazing,'' Kit mused, giving his brother a wry glance when they again reached the humid, muggy street and retrieved their horses from the waiting groom. ''One moment a wastrel, the next a leader of Parliament.''

''I shall fall flat on my face and Walpole will regret ever having had such a notion!'' Tony grumbled.

Kit laughed, then sobered. '''Tis the shipping office for you now?''

''Unfortunately, yes.'' Tony swung himself into his saddle. ''Peter and I are juggling accounts again. I despise dealing with moneylenders, but Peter assures me consolidating the debts will relieve some pressure. At any rate, pray the three Free Indies ships that are due in arrive soon, for if we disburse the cargo promptly, I just may be able to stay out of Fleet Street debtors' prison. Otherwise, I will be joining our friend, General Sir Woodes Rogers.''

''It's a damned shame so gallant a soldier should be hounded for debts he incurred out of his own pocket to support the Nassau colony,'' Kit said, a muscle in his jaw twitching angrily. They kicked their mounts into a trot, threading their way through Whitehall's busy thoroughfare.

''That it is. You will assure him of my support when you

speak to him directly? I still have influence in some circles, and I will wield it in his favor if I can.''

"I'll tell him, though he'll say to rescue your own hide first, I'm sure. I still say we could sell the *Mirage* to cover your most pressing debts," Kit said.

Tony scowled. "No! I can't let you do that. I won't compromise yours nor Sir Percy's interest in the Free Indies line. After all, you both have families to provide for now."

"But, Jimmy—"

"I have my pride," Tony said quietly. "You of all people must understand that. I'll get out of this tight spot in my own way. Besides, I've got a tender place in my heart for that ship. She'd didn't come home from Java loaded with coffee as I'd hoped, but while I lay ill, Angus managed to pick up a few bolts of silk and hogsheads of rice, and that's been what's made the difference. I'd like you and Lexa to take the *Mirage* when you return home."

Kit grinned. "It would bring back fond memories."

"No doubt." Tony's answering smile was wry. "And by the time you reach Charles Towne, I'm sure Rose will have a brother or sister well on the way."

"If God wills. And for your bride as well."

"Yes," Tony said, looking inward to a distant place, *"Insya Allah."*

They separated soon after, Kit going off toward the rough Fleet Street district to visit the incarcerated general, Tony heading for the Free Indies Shipping Company office located near its riverfront docks and warehouses.

He skirted the edges of the most squalid areas to avoid the desperate, gin-soaked inhabitants of London's East End slums. The dregs of society were found in the leaning, rat-infested tenements. Cutpurses, prostitutes, highwaymen, and murderers roiled in a caldron of poverty and misery that erupted into violence day and night, and where, for a modest price, any manner of wickedness could be arranged. Only the foolhardy ventured into this den unaccompanied, with the river on one hand and the line of rotting warehouses to the other, but something even more malignant nagged at the edges of Tony's thoughts. Little by little, his preoc-

pations with Miri and his business troubles were pierced by
a growing sense of uneasiness.

Loaded wagons, burly longshoremen, drunken sailors,
and peddlers of knives and vegetables and black coal plied
the narrow streets leading to the docks, but looking over
his shoulder, Tony could see nothing amiss. No eyes
watched from behind broken shutters; no stealthy figures
followed him. Rather, a deep sense of "unrightness" permeated him, a black-tentacled anxiety arising from no
known source but so powerful that at last he stopped his
horse dead in the middle of the street, unable to make
himself go any farther.

Breathing hard, Tony fought down the inner flurries of
unreasoning panic, his mind spinning with thoughts of insanity and devil-possession. Had his worry over Miri finally
muddled his brain completely? He didn't even hear the
curses of the wagoneer behind him, nor the ribald comments
of the slattern selling her wares on the corner. His heart
lodged in his mouth, and he knew something was terribly
wrong—but what? Though he'd never have called himself
a spiritual man, and he'd never believed in intuition, Tony
focused his thoughts inward, searching . . . and found a certainty that drenched him in a cold sweat.

"My God—Kit!" Jerking the reins, Tony wheeled his
mount about and kicked the animal into a fool's headlong
gallop. "I'm coming, Jimmy! I'm coming!"

Chapter 17

❦❦❦❦❦

"**F**rom the way you're studying it, surely that is the most spectacular view in London."

Miranda woke from her reverie at the sound of Lexa's voice, blinking at the rather banal prospect of the rear garden below her bedroom window—a row of flower beds, a shell path, and the square top of Button's cage Angus had built beneath an apple tree. She sent a weak smile at the dark head peeking around her door.

"Letty is of the opinion sustained contemplation of nature will aid my recovery."

Lexa wrinkled her nose at that notion. "Your cousin is an admirable nurse, I'm sure, but I'd prefer you out in that sunshine rather than merely looking at it. May I come in?"

"Yes, of course." Miranda pushed aside the forgotten book in her lap and nodded to Lexa. Button, who'd been curled in a ball at the foot of Miranda's longue, as disinterested in the prophylactic efficacies of the view as she was, scampered up the drapery fringe. He chittered excitedly from the vantage of the cornice board as Lexa opened the door and walked in with Rose.

The little girl was dressed in a lacy, ruffled confection that made her look sweet as a comfit. Miranda winced at the sharp pang that sliced through her heart. Rose babbled in delight at the monkey as she hung on to her mother's finger. In a sprigged muslin day gown, Lexa herself hardly looked old enough to be the babe's mother, making Miranda feel all the more worn and dowdy in her night rail and dressing gown.

How can she do this? Miranda thought miserably. How could Lexa flaunt Rose in her face, a living symbol of Miranda's loss and failure?

"You needn't look like that," Lexa said in a matter-of-fact voice.

"Like what?" Miranda croaked, her throat constricting.

Lexa's smile was understanding. "It's for your own good, you know."

A bit dismayed that Lexa could read her thoughts so clearly, Miranda leaned back against the pile of ruffled pillows Letty had thoughtfully plumped for her. Sadness, guilt, and black depression washed over her in waves, leaving her floundering, helpless. "Lexa, please . . ."

"We've got something to show you, haven't we, sweetheart?" Lexa asked the baby. "All right now, show Auntie Miri what a big girl you are."

Rose dimpled, her pink cheeks rounded like tiny apples, then she chortled something unintelligible, let go her mother's finger, and took exactly six tiny steps all by herself right to the edge of Miranda's couch before she plopped down on her bottom.

Without thinking, Miranda scooped the little girl up into her lap before she could cry. "Oh, that's marvelous. Walking, you are! Your papa must buy you a pair of red shoes so that we may show you off to the world!"

Crowing her agreement, Rose reached for the end of Miranda's silvery-fair braid, then tugged at the bit of blue ribbon that secured it. Her sweet baby smell filled Miranda's nose, and her plump little person invited cuddling. With a sigh, Miranda surrendered, luxuriating in the pleasure-pain of holding the child and kissing her dark, fluffy curls.

"See?" Lexa said, looking quite pleased with herself. "You can stand it, and I'm not nearly so cruel as you thought."

Miranda tickled Rose's nose with the tip of her braid, evoking a giggle and a sneeze. "I see that now."

"You're stronger than you realize, and Tony's missing you. He's the sunny one, you know, but he's been the mask of doom since you lost the baby. Do you think you can make an effort to put this behind you, for his sake?"

"I know I must," Miranda whispered, moisture prickling her eyelids. "But, oh, Lexa, it's so hard. I've disappointed him so often. He must blame me. If only I'd been more careful, perhaps I wouldn't have taken that fall, or if I'd been more composed, Lady Sylvie wouldn't have upset me so much, and—"

"Rubbish!" Lexa interrupted, seating herself on the end of the longue. "You're an intelligent woman. You know as well as I that probably none of those things had anything to do with your miscarriage."

"In my head, perhaps, but I can't seem to shake off this awful blue mood. I know it's wicked, but I don't even want Tony around. His comfort only makes me feel even more guilty!" Her lower lip trembled. "I'm perverse and hateful to him, but I can't help it, and I'm so afraid I'm driving him straight to another woman!"

Lexa's incredulous laughter pealed merrily. "What nonsense! My Lord Anthony may once have had a certain reputation, but one look tells me he's absolutely wild with love for you."

Miranda glanced down at Rose and smoothed her baby-fine curls. "I sometimes think I shall wake to find myself back in Java and this all a miraculous dream. Tony feels everything with such passion and depth, and I know my hesitation has disappointed him in the past, but it's just that I can't understand what he sees in *me*."

"I understand full well, for I feel the same about Kit," Lexa replied with a soft smile. "We've been blessed with

remarkable men, you and I. They've both had their share
of suffering, so when they give their love, it's wholeheart-
edly. Tony understands all you're going through. Believe
me, holding yourself apart from the man you love is the
worst thing you can do.''

Just then, Rose tugged Miranda's hair ribbon completely
free and tossed it on the floor. Button rattled down the
drapes, grabbed it up, then dropped it back in her lap.
Delighted, Rose threw it down on the floor again, and both
women laughed. The freedom of the sound startled Miranda,
but she felt the steel bands around her heart begin to loosen
for the first time in weeks.

"You're good for me," Miranda told Lexa. "And I'll
try to take heed of your advice. I know we've had little
time to get to know each other, but I hope we can be good
friends.''

"We are already," Lexa said firmly, her emerald eyes
sparkling with warmth. "Besides, it's time you were up so
that I may enjoy a few of these glittering affairs Tony's
been telling me about. For example, you received an invitation to hear Handel play at a Lady Mary Montagu's
tonight.''

"She is quite a delight—a true eccentric and an educated
woman. You'd enjoy her.''

"See, you're feeling better already to even consider it.
We must make plans, but first, tell me, do you know anything about indigo?''

Intrigued, Miranda sat up, holding Rose so that she could
continue her game of fetch with Button. "Indigo? A little.
They grow it in certain areas in Java. Why?''

"Your field may be languages, but mine is botany," Lexa
explained. "I've been looking for some other cash crop we
may grow in the Carolinas along with our rice. If I could
import some slips, and find someone who knew how to
grow and then process it . . .''

"Why, you'd be famous!" Miranda cried eagerly, taken
with the notion. "And rich, too! There was a man in our
desa who grew it. I could write my sister, the sultana . . .''

A sudden disturbance from below interrupted their discussion, and a tattoo of footsteps raced down the corridor. Letty burst through the bedroom door, her cap askew, her lappets flying.

"There's been an accident," she gasped. "It's the master!"

Swiftly passing Rose to Letty, Miranda flew from the room, followed closely by Lexa. They reached the marble-floored foyer just as a ragged tangle of villainous-looking ruffians carried a dirty, blood-streaked figure through the doorway. Curses peppered the air, the most virulent issuing from the throat of the party being so roughly "rescued."

"God's bones, you jackals! Put me down!"

Miranda's mouth hung open. "Tony?"

"No!" Lexa gasped, rushing past her. "It's Kit!"

"Well enough, good fellows!" Tony's voice boomed over the cacophony, and Miranda spotted him in the middle of the throng. Like Kit, he was disheveled and dirty, but thankfully, looked to be unharmed. With a cry, Lexa flung herself through the rowdy group and reached her husband.

"It's not as bad as it looks, Duchess," Kit said in a placating tone, then winced as he tried to put his weight on his left foot. With a murmur of distress, Lexa slipped under his arm to support him and pressed her handkerchief to his bloody cheek.

"Here's for your trouble, mates!" Tony said, pulling a purse from his pocket. "You, Mertle!" He tossed the purse into the hands of a scabrous, stoop-shouldered individual with a large hooked nose who seemed to be the leader of the group. "See that's shared with your friends."

"Aye, m'lord, thankee!" Mertle weighed the purse with satisfaction, then winked and saluted smartly. "An ye ever need us again, just say the word!"

"Wait!" Miranda hurried forward, oblivious to her state of undress, intent only on taking her place at Tony's side. "Please, sir. Won't you and your friends come round to the kitchen for a bite to eat? It's the least I can do to repay your kindness."

Mertle's ugly face was a comic picture of disbelief. In

awe, he scraped his ratty cap off his balding pate. "Oh, m'lady, we'd be right pleasured."

"Wexill," Miranda called, "will you see these gentleman to their meal? And bring a bottle of port from the cellar, too."

With a ragged hurrah, the rescue squad followed Wexill from the foyer. The duties of hospitality discharged, Miranda turned to her husband, anxiously searching him again for signs of damage. "What on earth happened?"

Tony dragged his coat sleeve across his sweaty brow. "God, I'm not really certain even yet."

"Nor I," Kit said. "One moment I'm leaving Fleet Street Prison, the next, I've got an impressment gang on my neck, trying to paddle my brains into mush and throw me on a ship bound for Africa! If Tony hadn't shown up when he did, that's likely where I'd be! How the hell did you know I was in trouble, Jimmy?"

Tony looked blank. "I don't know. I just did somehow."

Miranda nodded gravely. "Your spirit sensed Kit's need. The *dukun* says twins share a bond that connects them over time and space."

"Don't start mumbling about magic," Tony protested. "We left all your sprites and demons behind in Java!"

"Did we?" Miranda asked with a quiet smile. "Sometimes I'm not so sure."

"Well, whatever the reason for your inspiration, many thanks," Kit said with a roguish grin. "Nothing like a good brawl, eh? We really whipped the scoundrels, just like old times."

"Yes, but I found it odd you seemed the only victim of that gang," Tony commented. "Almost as if you were their target."

"But who would want to do such a thing to Kit?" Miranda demanded, then broke off suddenly. Only one person hated Kit enough for such drastic measures—Sylvie.

"Why should we assume it was Kit they wanted?" Tony countered.

Though he'd followed Miranda's train of thought, he could not believe his mother would go to such elaborate lengths. No, her methods for dealing with her enemies were more subtle. Besides, there were other possibilities, considering Colleton's enmity over his jilted niece and the virulence of several of Tony's creditors.

"Since we're so similar in appearance," Tony said, "mayhap they made a mistake. If revenge was their motive, it could just as easily have been me they wanted."

"That's absurd! Surely it was just a random thing," Lexa said, dabbing at the bloody scrapes on Kit's cheekbones. "But to be brutally accosted on the streets in this day and age—how absolutely outrageous!"

"Ouch!" Kit grabbed Lexa's handkerchief. "Stop fussing, woman! I'm all right, I tell you! Do you want me to dance a hornpipe to prove it?"

"You—you cabbage!" Lexa snapped, but her anger wasn't really directed at Kit, and they both knew it. Hauling her close, Kit touched his forehead to his wife's, murmuring private reassurances while she clung to his neck.

Tony's mouth tilted at the scene, and he and Miranda exchanged indulgent looks. Suddenly he frowned, focusing on Miranda in concern. "You shouldn't be up."

"Of course I should, when my husband needs me," she said softly, and slipped her hand into his.

Tony searched her face, and his hand tightened convulsively. "Miri . . ."

"Come," Miranda said, drawing him toward the stairs. "Sims will have a fit when he sees what you've done to that suit. We must get you and Kit cleaned up. Lexa wishes to attend Lady Montagu's rout, and I think it would do us all a world of good to get out this evening. Don't you agree, Lexa?"

Snug in Kit's arms and smiling again, Lexa nodded. "If our wounded warriors feel up to it."

Kit stifled a groan. "I'd almost rather take on the impressment gang again as posture and bow at one of these affairs, but for you, Duchess, I suppose I can make the sacrifice."

"And you, my lord?" Miranda asked Tony.

For once, no easy, charming reply came to Tony's lips.

Instead, he merely squeezed his wife's hand and smiled around the lump in his throat.

Later that evening, during the interval between musical pieces in the Montagus' drawing room, the conversation among the glittering array of fashionables ranged from the cost of the King's annual visit to Hanover to the difficulty of obtaining good French port to Locke's latest treatise. But the most earnest talk was among the group of women surrounding their hostess as she espoused her controversial opinions on the matter of the prevention of smallpox.

"Why, the Princess of Wales herself had her two youngest inoculated on my recommendation," Lady Mary Wortley Montagu said. "And neither they nor my son have suffered any lasting ill effects from the procedure."

"You say the Turks have been using this method for years?" Lexa asked. Elegantly attired in emerald brocade, she wore a magnificent triple strand of pearls at her throat and a pensive expression.

"Absolutely," Lady Mary replied. Her longish nose was balanced by a pair of fine dark eyes, and she sported a twist of silk in her hair, turban-style, with such flair that one received an impression of vivacious beauty though her features were in truth unremarkable. "When my husband served as ambassador, I had many occasions to observe its effectiveness."

"How marvelous to at last be able to protect our children from such a dreadful scourge!" Miranda commented, waving her tasseled fan. The accessory was a gift from Tony to remind her of a special night, and its painted violets matched her gown and the purple velvet ribbons threaded through her upswept hair. "But I fail to understand why physicians do not sound the call of this miracle to one and all."

Lady Mary snorted disdainfully. "Ignorance! Sheer ignorance and male pride! They feel women are fit merely for ornaments or diversions, so such an idea from one of our sex cannot have merit!"

"Public opinion may be one thing," Lexa said, "but I

intend to discuss this with my husband, for if Rose can be protected, I will let nothing stand in my way.''

Several of the other women in the group nodded, murmuring in agreement, but others looked dubious. Lady Mary drew Lexa aside, promising to arrange an audience with the Princess of Wales and the doctor who had inoculated the young royals. Listening with interest as the conversation continued, Miranda felt a touch on her arm. Her polite smile died on a wave of surprise as she turned to face the exquisite person of Lord Cecil Edmund.

"How good it is to see you so well, Lady Bentley," Cecil said, bowing over her hand with a wave of his lace handkerchief. His large brown eyes held a flirtatious light. "I often think of our conversations at Fairhaven, but alas, I fear your wonderful success in London causes you to forget old friends.''

"You are always welcome to call, of course," Miranda replied. She cast quick, surreptitious glances from side to side, but in the crush of the crowd, could not locate a single familiar face. "Do you escort the Dowager Marchioness tonight, my lord?''

"Unfortunately, she took the headache just a short time ago over the presence of—er, certain guests and left in a fit of temper. I, of course, was loath to miss Master Handel's performance, so I remained." He tucked Miranda's hand into the crook of his arm and graced her with his best smile. "But I welcome the opportunity to assure you of my respect and admiration. Taking on Lady Sylvie as a mother-in-law is a formidable task, and I have no doubt you will win her over.''

"What a surprising thing to say! Especially coming from you, sir," Miranda said, too amazed to temper the blunt nature of her words. But Cecil wasn't offended, chuckling instead.

"Think you I'm blind to the Marchioness's faults? Nay, my lady, but Sylvie is a powerful woman, and I have a career to consider. But let me assure you that if you ever need a comforting shoulder or someone to listen to your woes, I'm at your service.''

Miranda's silver eyes frosted over. "My husband serves those needs quite well, Lord Edmund."

"Now I have offended you, and that was not my intention!" he cried with a mock pout. "Indeed, I feel only the warmest friendship for you, my lady. I merely meant Sylvie and her son share many qualities and—well, he wasn't known as the Wastrel Lord for nothing! So if you ever need help or simply commiseration, who better to come to than another victim of the Benedict brand of love?"

Inwardly seething at the impudence to her and the insult to Tony, Miranda set her teeth and bit back angry words. Only someone of Cecil's supreme and unfounded self-importance could presume so, but there was also no use protesting, for he was of a breed who could never accept an avowal of complete indifference. It was simpler to let the buffoon have his say.

"I will remember that, Lord Edmund," she said coolly. "Now, pray excuse me, I must find my husband."

"Of course." Cecil bowed, his words offhand. "I believe I saw him go into the small library a short while back."

Murmuring her thanks, Miranda gratefully made her escape. If Sylvie had to put up with much of Cecil's posturing, no wonder she'd developed a headache. Rubbing the throbbing place in her own temple, Miranda made her way though the crowd, greeting new friends and acquaintances, sharing a brief smile with Kit as he spoke with Lord Peter Ingram, neatly sidestepping the crowd around the eminent musician and composer George Frideric Handel, whose performance of his *Harpsichord Suite* had produced both sighs and shouts of appreciation.

Finally, with a sigh of relief, Miranda slipped into the relative quiet of the main library. The empty room smelled pleasantly of leather bindings and musty paper, and the low sound of voices coming from a side room drew her forward into the doorway. Tony's name froze on her lips, and she gasped sharply. Only one fact registered through her shock—her husband was kissing another woman!

Catching sight of his wife's white face, Tony felt his heart plummet to his feet. Frantically he tugged at Lady

Catherine Salter's clinging arms, wrenching his mouth free, cursing his luck.

Damn it! Not Miri, not now! he thought.

Cecil was right about the wastrel! Miranda thought, dazed.

I've ruined everything! Tony groaned inwardly.

I drove him to this! she cried silently.

God, she'll never believe me!

I can't believe it!

Tony wondered how many times in his sketchy past he'd found himself in such a situation, cornered by an irate mistress or jealous husband, and merely laughed it off. Now he heartily regretted each occasion with a bitterness that choked him. Had fate decreed an ironic punishment for those misdeeds by turning the tables on him?

"Miri," Tony croaked aloud. Throat working, he took Catherine's hands and roughly broke her grip around his neck. "For God's sake, Catherine, stop it!"

Her youthful bosom heaving, Catherine turned to confront Miranda, her chocolate brown eyes defiant, but the hand she raised to her mouth trembled.

Miranda quelled her first impulse—to run away from what she'd inadvertently witnessed like the traditional wronged wife—and forced herself to seek the inner serenity of a Buddhist monk and look beyond the physical as the *dukun* had taught. What she saw was a frightened, shame-faced girl hiding behind a bravura that was only skin-deep, and a man whose dismay plainly stated his innocence, no matter how incongruous it seemed.

"Anthony, dear," Miranda said with the glimmer of a smile, "may I help? You appear to have your hands full."

Tony swallowed, cleared his throat, swallowed again.

"Indeed. Ah—"

Gliding forward, Miranda placed a friendly arm over Catherine's shoulder and began to usher her toward the door. Although she sympathized with the circumstances of Catherine's jilting and had no wish to humiliate the girl further, she was determined to make her message clear.

"Only a cad would refuse such a generously given kiss,

Catherine, but not all men are as honorable as my husband."
It was an effort not to laugh at Catherine's bewilderment.
"Tony may once have been the very devil with the ladies,
but no longer, and it is very wrong of you to place him in
such an awkward position."

Catherine's cheeks flushed with embarrassment, and she
dropped her gaze to the floor. "I'm s-sorry, Lady Bentley.
Someone told me—that is, I thought Tony still had a *tendre*
for me. I had to know for sure . . . I see I was mistaken."

"I'm fond of you as a friend, Catherine," Tony said in
relief, finding his voice at last.

"And friends are a treasure we both cherish," Miranda
said kindly, "but you see, dear, he has a wife, and I'm
willing to fight for what is mine. Now, we'll say no more,
and do promise me you'll come to the dinner we're planning
for next week."

Catherine's lower lip trembled. "I—I'd like that, if you
truly mean it."

"Of course we do!" Miranda assured her, strolling arm
in arm with Catherine back into the party throng. "And,
Tony, don't you think it's time you introduced Catherine
to Lord Ingram? He's *such* a likable young man, and *so*
clever . . ."

Hours later, in the privacy of their bedchamber, Tony
watched Miranda remove the violet ribbons from her hair,
and shook his head in amazement.

"Peter's completely smitten. Never saw a man fall so
fast. And those cow's eyes Catherine made at him! How
did you know?"

"Female intuition," Miranda replied, curling the ribbons
around her fist and neatly storing them away in a covered
china dish. Tony caught her shoulders, his large hands gentle
on the delicate bones covered by her blue satin dressing
gown, and turned her to face him squarely.

"No," he said softly, "I mean, how did you *know*?"

"That Catherine had thrown herself at you?" She caught
his chin between thumb and forefinger and mischievously
wagged his head back and forth, watching the candlelight

catch the red highlights in his curls. "Because of the guilty look on this handsome face."

Tony shuddered and gathered her close, whispering into her hair. "I've never been so terrified in all my life."

"Not even when you fought the Dutchman? Or faced Lord Palu's executioner?"

"Only when I thought I'd lost you, but this was even worse."

Miranda snuggled against his chest, nuzzling her nose into the reddish-blond thatch revealed by the opening of his silk shirt, inhaling the warm, musky scent of his skin. "I've given you little reason to believe in my love of late. I'm sorry. You have my faith and my loyalty forever, even when I don't show it."

"I thought I loved you as much as possible, but every day you make me love you more," he murmured, bending his head to kiss her tenderly. "Witch-woman, magician, caster of spells—how do you do it?"

"When we share our love, it grows," she said, her expression solemn. "So share with me as your equal, Tony. Tell me what's been troubling you."

"You. The baby—"

"We'll have lots of babies, *insya Allah*. It's something else, too, something to do with the shipping company and Fairhaven, isn't it?"

Tony released her, rubbed the back of his neck in a gesture that was fast becoming as familiar to her as his everlasting worrying of his snuffboxes, and began to pace. "It's nothing for you to worry about."

"Tony, don't shut me out, please." She flopped on the edge of the bed in exasperation. "Perhaps I can help."

He deliberated silently, then nodded. "At least you deserve to know the truth."

Briefly he outlined the troubles at the Free Indies Shipping Company, the help Peter had given him, the adamancy of his creditors, the hope of arriving shipments. There was also the continuing debt from the South Sea Bubble and his mother's refusal to sell the Dower House.

"So you see, it's not totally hopeless, though we're hanging on by the skin of our teeth," he said at last.

"It seems the world contrives against us." Miranda sighed. "Am I wrong in thinking we've had more than our share of mishaps?"

Tony's jaw hardened. "It would be easy to blame some shadowy and sinister force for my position, but I must accept that it was my own neglect and wastrel ways that brought me hence. My enemies have good reason to wish me misfortune."

"But no longer, for I see how hard you work," Miranda protested, then bit her lip, hesitating. "Your mother's hostility toward Kit and me has not helped. What nearly happened to Kit today and Lady Catherine's little exhibition this evening are too coincidental to believe. Do you think . . . that is, your mother—?"

"I know." Tony stood with his back to her, gazing into the tall glass-fronted case that held his dandy's collection of precious snuffboxes. His gaze locked on his most prized piece—a charred jade lotus—and he felt a shiver of foreboding. "It's possible."

"Then you owe it to Kit to resolve things with Sylvie before something more serious happens."

"It's difficult to know how to broach the truth without her blaming Kit even more." He shook his head. "Her intrigues are nuisances now, but they're nothing compared to the trouble she's capable of."

"I know you'll find a way," Miranda returned staunchly.

Tony spun on his heel, his mien serious. "Well, until I do, I want you to stay away from Edmund. He's involved in this mischief."

Miranda wrinkled her nose. "With pleasure. He's such a conceited twit! He acts as though any woman should be delighted with his attentions. Rather like someone else I know," she teased.

"Sprite! I'm trying to be serious and practical here," he groused, but his lips twitched. "Or hadn't you noticed?"

"Of course. I have every faith you'll resolve these financial worries," she soothed.

"But if the unthinkable happens, I could still lose everything." Tony looked into the distance, and his voice dropped. "This place, Fairhaven itself."

"Is that all?"

Miranda's relieved laughter startled him, and he stared incredulously at her merry expression.

"Is that all?" he repeated. "Don't you understand? I want to give you everything, every comfort, every luxury. Now it seems an impossibility."

"I'd care, of course, but only for your sake," Miranda explained, pulling the last of her pins from her hair so that it tumbled in a fair pale sheet about her shoulders. She went to him, hugging his trim middle and leaning back so that she could smile up into his eyes.

"A simple country life would suit me splendidly, Tony. We'll take the *Mirage* back to Java and work in the rice paddies, or you may sail as ship's captain again and I'll be your interpreter. In all our trials haven't we learned that one lesson? Nothing else matters as long as we're together."

Tony sank his fingers into the fine strands of her hair and pulled her against his broad shoulder. "I love you."

"I know." She sighed and smiled as he urged her gently toward the huge bed, but then her gaze focused on the tall case behind her and she stiffened suddenly. "Wait, Tony."

"Hmm?"

"Your snuffboxes. Some are quite valuable, aren't they? We'll sell them."

"It wouldn't help much."

"But every pound counts," she insisted. "And my ring! You can't tell me Rija's pearl won't bring a handsome price!"

Tony scowled at her. "Madam, that's your wedding ring!"

"You may buy me another when we can afford it."

"This is most unsentimental of you," Tony complained.

"I'm the practical one, remember? You must do it. Tomorrow, I insist!" Smiling at his sour expression, she slipped her hand beneath his shirt, stroking the hard chest muscles, drawing a gasp when her thumb flicked the bronze coin of his flat male nipple. "Besides, what need have I of keepsakes when I have the genuine item in my arms?"

"All right, you win," Tony groaned. He scooped her up and fell with her into the bed. "We'll sell everything tomorrow. The paintings, the furniture, the buckles off my red-heeled shoes. I'll even hock Angus if you want!"

"Idiot," she giggled. "I do love you."

"Good," he mumbled, nuzzling the frangipani-scented curve of her neck. "I could not abide life if you did not."

Miranda buried her fingers in his hair, and smiled as his eager hands loosened the tie of her dressing gown. Then he hesitated and drew back, frowning.

"I'm a lustful, selfish cad," he said, swallowing harshly. "I'm sorry, dearling."

"What is it?" she asked in dismay.

Rolling onto his back, he tucked her against his shoulder, shuddering as he brought his passion under control. "It's too soon. Perhaps we shouldn't—"

"It's all right." His tender concern filled her with warmth. "The physician assured me we could resume intimacies."

Turning his head, he raised a hand to her temple, threading his fingers through the fair skein of her hair. "You're certain?"

"Yes," she whispered, transfixed by the tenderness in his eyes. "Always."

With a groan of need, Tony kissed her, molding their mouths as if he couldn't get enough of her taste. Slowly, with utmost care, he wooed her with hands and lips, stripping them of their garments, testing the sensitivity of her skin in her most secret places. Miranda responded, showing him her love and need in the same manner.

Their lovemaking had always been basic and exciting, but this time they experienced a tenderness and caring that evoked their deepest emotions. Every look, every touch, every murmur, bound them closer. When Tony slipped within her depths, Miranda sobbed with the supreme pleasure of their joining, the ultimate communication of two separate beings who became one soul in this act of love.

Skillfully Tony drew out their pleasure, neither wanting
it to end, but at last, bound by the ties of human flesh, their
desire flared out of control. Thrusting deeply, Tony braced
himself on his elbows and watched the flickers of ecstasy
overtake his mate and knew that he'd never seen anything
so beautiful as the woman he loved dissolving in his arms.
When she stiffened and cried out his name, his own cataclysmic release catapulted him into a new realm of perfection beyond paradise. Clinging together, they laughed, and
their joy echoed with the heavenly sound of temple bells.

Sylvie screamed, climaxing under the sweaty rutting of
her new lover's final impalement. She fell back into the
bedclothes, blind and blinking in the pitch blackness of the
chamber, her flesh shuddering. He drew away abruptly, but
she didn't mind. She'd been right. Even her jaded appetites
had been aroused to fever pitch by the Baron's unmatched
ferocity, her senses titillated by his macabre demands for
the anonymity of darkness. She shrugged, unconcerned at
whatever fantasies he'd played out in his head during their
frenzied coupling. It was a rather mild eccentricity compared
to the varied perversities she'd encountered during her career.

But the forgetfulness of passion quickly dissolved, replaced by the angry frustration and fear that, in a fit of
recklessness, had finally driven her to accept the Baron's
overtures. As pounding heart and ragged breathing returned
to normal, she clenched her fists in the bedclothes and
ground her teeth.

"That bitch! It's all her fault," Sylvie muttered. At her
side, the Baron grunted, and that was all the encouragement
she needed to continue. "I know it's Miranda's doing that
Ryan and his whore stay on. She emasculates my son and
turns him into the spineless, impotent fop his father was!"

"A disappointment, surely." The Baron's accented
words were faintly amused.

Sylvie rolled onto her side and glared into the darkness.
"Laugh if you will, but what do I have left if my son
abandons me? And it may be only a matter of time. Ryan's

whore—I know her now. Phineas Howard's whelp. And she wore the Cathay pearls tonight! My God, that the Wicked Earl should return to haunt me thus! What does she know? What lies might she tell Tony? And like a fool, that bitch Miranda welcomes them into my son's home.''

"Do old sins lash a guilty conscience, my lady?''

"Regrets are for fools,'' she returned in her chilliest tone. "Besides, 'tis no concern of yours.''

Sitting up, Sylvie jerked at the sheets in her agitation, but before she could leave the bed, rough hands slammed her back down and the Baron's shadowy form loomed over her.

"A woman with the black fire of vengeance in her heart excites me like no other,'' he growled in wry amusement.

"I will make the bitch rue the day she stole my son from me. Now, release me—oh!'' Sylvie gasped as the Baron unerringly found her nether mouth with one hand and cruelly pinched her nipple with the other.

"There are subtler ways to destroy one's enemies.''

His boldness incensed Sylvie while the uncontrolled savagery of his touch ignited her anew. Flirting with the danger of a man she could not govern produced a sense of heady intoxication that was addictive. Looping her arms around his neck, she purred, "Are there? Tell me more.''

"Many ways, of exceeding cunning and finesse.'' His skillful hands wrung a gasping groan from the woman in the bed. "Pray, my lady, let me be of service to you . . .''

Chapter 18

"I can't do any more," nine-year-old Tiktik wailed. Her ironwood rice mortar lay idle in the hollowed stump, a pitiful amount of husked rice lying at the bottom. *"My arms are tired."*

"Hstt!" Teacher chided. *"Don't be like Loro Djong-grang, Slender Maiden. She, too, was a lazy princess. One day at her loom, she dropped her shuttle and promised to marry whoever brought it to her. That's how she came to wed her dog!"*

Tiktik giggled and smiled at Sister, who was moving her own mortar up and down, up and down, pounding like a steady drum.

"She was not a clever maid," Sister said.

"Not then," Teacher agreed in her age-cracked voice, *"but once she told an unwelcome suitor she would marry him if, in a single night, he could build her a temple with one thousand statues."*

"But that's impossible!" Tiktik said, picking up her mortar again.

"Unless you have magic to do the work," Teacher replied. *"But when Slender Maiden saw what was happening, she called all the maidservants to pound rice just as you do now, and the noise woke up all the roosters, so the wicked suitor thought the sun had risen and only finished nine-hundred and ninty-nine statues."*

"I will work hard and wake up all the roosters, too!" Tiktik announced, returning to her task with a renewed will.

"Slender Maiden's tale sets a good example," Sister murmured.

Teacher shrugged. *"I will tell you the rest of the story so that you may judge that yourself."*

"The rest?"

"On learning how he'd been tricked, the wicked suitor unleashed his fury on Slender Maiden and turned her into stone. You see, she is the thousandth statue in her own temple."

"Walpole was right."

Tony pulled his gaze away from the bustle of activity on the Free Indies dock and raised an inquisitive eyebrow at his twin.

"He was?"

Kit leaned his elbows against the railing of the stairs leading into the warehouse offices and grinned. "By God, you do have presence! One day I'll be able to tell your children I was there the day their father made his debut as the greatest orator in the British Empire!"

"I simply made a speech," Tony replied with a shrug.

Below them, grunting, sweating sailors used block and tackle to unload huge hogshead barrels from the hold of a ship. The gray waters of the Thames glistened in the hot July sunshine, and the humid atmosphere was fetid with rotting fish, fresh tar, and the contents of the city's chamberpots. The stench as well as the thicket of ships, barges, and boats that plied the river reminded Tony of the port of Batavia and of a certain determined spinster who'd turned his life upside-down almost exactly a year earlier.

Kit laughed at his brother's humble reply to his compli-

ment and clapped Tony's shoulder affectionately. "Your
modesty becomes you, brother. But in every English coffeehouse and club, men speak only of the Marquess of
Bentley's eloquence before Parliament. What a triumph! I'd
say those tariff and trade reforms will pass easily, thanks
to you."

"It wasn't hard to speak on behalf of legislation in which
I firmly believe, but doing something for the benefit of the
nation . . ." Tony flashed a grin that was half wonder, half
pride. "It felt good, Kit. Damn good."

"The King has need of able statesmen. Mayhap your
future lies along that path?"

"Me, a politician?"

"Who better? You have the position, the contacts, and
the native wiliness to match Walpole and Townshend move
for move. The strategies of the never-ending chess game
must surely appeal to you."

"You know me all too well," Tony admitted. "I confess
I've considered it, and now that it appears my financial
salvation has arrived, perhaps I'll give the idea more
thought. But if you don't mind, I'd like to see the *Evening
Star* unloaded before you appoint me Prime Minister."

Kit chuckled. "Very well, my lord. I must admit I'm
glad to see your good humor restored."

"And why not? Her cargo of ivory and sugar will save
my striped ass and give you and Percy a tidy profit as well.
Now, if only there was word of the *Morning Sky* or Morgan's
Revenge . . ."

"They'll turn up in time."

"Peter's got merchants ready to make a quick turnaround
on whatever arrives, so—" Tony broke off, frowning.
"What the devil?"

Below them, sailors slacked their ropes and walked off
the dock, bringing the unloading to a standstill. They could
see Angus gesticulating vigorously, though they couldn't
hear his words, then he and Mr. Tassel consulted, looking
up to the landing where the two brothers waited.

"Now what?" Tony muttered, starting down the stairs.

Angus met them halfway. The old salt's ruddy counte-

nance was brick red with heat and fury, and he carried a
paper bunched in his bony fist.

"You're nae going to like this, Cap'n," Angus said without preamble.

"What's the trouble?" Tony demanded. "It's imperative
we get that cargo unloaded as quickly as possible."

Angus shoved the flimsy broadsheet at him. "You better
take a look."

Perplexed, Tony unfolded the cheap, creased paper usually reserved for advertising or political purposes. With Kit
peering curiously over his shoulder, Tony scanned the badly
printed contents, and his expression grew darker with each
line of doggerel.

In poorly rhymed language of the most vulgar sort, the
poet blasted the new Marchioness of Bentley's reputation
with hints and innuendo, denouncing the exotic mistress of
Fairhaven's Wastrel Lord as a whore, a sorceress, and
worse. By the time Tony reached the last verse, his curses
blistered the air.

"Goddamn the slanderous bastard who penned this cal-
umny! What piece of villainous tripe would attack me
through my wife? Is this why those crewmen left, Angus?"

"Seamen are an ignorant, superstitious lot, Cap'n," Angus said, his disgust thickening his Scots burr. "Afeared
of curses and the evil eye, they be."

"Blast their cowardly bones!" Tony shouted furiously.
"To hell with them, then! Angus, hire more laborers. Anyone who'll do the work, no matter how mean. Mertle will
help if you can find which gin mill he's graced with his
trade today."

"Aye, Cap'n. But it ain't no guarantees. The sailor what
showed me this trash says they're posted all over."

"Jesus!" Tony gritted his teeth and stared out over the
deserted dock.

"All over?" Kit repeated, his blue eyes narrowing. "You
don't suppose Miranda . . ."

Tony's face blanched. "Oh, *hell!* Give Angus a hand,
will you, Kit? Maybe it's not too late to spare her this
indignity."

But the white sheets were posted from Whitehall to Leicester to St. James on gates, fences, trees, and lamp-posts. Tony's mouth was a flat, grim line by the time he entered his front door. Tersely he ordered the footmen out to retrieve as many of the offensive sheets as could be found, but any hope of keeping this attack from Miranda died when he heard the barrage of feminine weeping coming from his drawing room. Steeling himself, he went in.

Sodden, wailing, red-eyed, Letty left off crying for a moment at Tony's appearance, then plunged into another paroxysm of despair while Miranda tried vainly to calm her.

"What's to be done, my lord?" Letty wailed. "My poor Miri! 'A good name is rather to be chosen than riches.' What a calamity!"

"Letty, please! This does no good," Miranda begged, her face pale with distress. "Go upstairs and lie down. Have Topaz bring you a cool compress. All will be well. Please, for my sake."

"Yes, of course," Letty gulped into her handkerchief. She staggered to her feet and made her exit, muttering. "My poor innocent! So brave, so brave . . ."

"I gather you've seen it?" Tony asked hoarsely.

Miranda sank wearily into her chair, gesturing weakly at the blizzard of torn envelopes and papers that spilled from her desktop onto the polished floor. Beneath the desk Beelzebub and Button, fast companions now, batted at crumpled balls of paper.

"Letty was helping me with the post. Someone very thoughtfully sent several copies, so I would be certain not to miss being immortalized in verse." Miranda clenched her fists in the fine spring green muslin of her skirts, and her silver eyes glinted with an ironic emerald fire. "I suppose being named a gin-swilling prostitute shouldn't be a surprise since, unfortunately, 'tis true you found me in a Bristol brothel, but certainly I have no powers that would make me into a witch."

"Do you make light of this slander?"

Miranda's lower lip trembled, then her chin firmed as she

controlled the tremor. "If I do not, I will surely melt into a puddle twice the size of Letty's."

"Damn it, Miri!" Tony rubbed his neck in exasperation. "Don't you understand how serious this could be?"

"Why? Because I speak a heathenish tongue to my maid? Because I set out ritual offerings by the light of the full moon to honor the woman who taught me her lore?" Her voice was haughty with angry disdain. "Oh, and don't forget I also have a black cat for a familiar and a monkey who steals hair ribbons!"

"Don't be ridiculous," he snapped. "But such talk only makes new fodder for those looking to find fault. No one has dared bring open accusations, but it hasn't been many years since such as this could place you on the end of a gibbet, or the very least, a dunking stool!"

Miranda jumped to her feet and glared at her husband.

"Charming, I'm sure! We English are an intolerant lot, aren't we? Anything different, we disdain as improper or inferior. Well, I've done nothing improper, and I refuse to be made to feel inferior because my beliefs and education have given my mind and soul more scope than can be tolerated in this pedestrian, uncivilized backwater!" With a toss of her fair head, she picked up her skirts and swept past him.

"Miri, listen to me!" Tony caught her shoulders to stop her, staring intently into her angry face. "I'm telling you what you once told me. You're in my world now, and you must let me be your guide, for all our sakes, but especially for your own safety."

Dumbfounded, she caught her breath. "My safety? That horrible scandal sheet destroys your wonderful new reputation, o'ershadows your triumph as a brilliant orator, and you're worried about me?"

"Of course. What else?"

Her head drooped like a flower on a too slender stem, and she dropped her forehead against his chest, shuddering silently. "I'm a fool to take my anger out on you when it is really myself I hate for failing you yet again."

"Hate? Sweet pagan, you are always too hard on yourself."

"Not when my differences make you a target for someone's poison pen and Society's contempt! I knew something like this would happen eventually, that I would hurt you somehow." Her voice broke. "I can't bear it."

"Hush, love. You are too quick to accept blame," Tony murmured into the shell of her ear. "There are tigers in my world, too. But there are ways to avoid claws and teeth. This broadsheet is but a trivial matter, someone's weak attempt to cause trouble. There are new ones each day. We will smack this tiger on his nose and send him running for cover by ignoring the entire event."

Lifting her head, Miranda laughed, but the sound was without genuine humor. "Brazen it out again?"

"Absolutely."

"Then prepare yourself, my lord, for it's obvious you've forgotten we've invited thirty guests for supper this evening."

Tony smiled, showing the slash of a dimple she loved so well. "A perfect opportunity to prove we aren't afraid of that pathetic rubbish."

Foreboding crowded Miranda's senses, obscuring the brilliance of Tony's smile and making her shiver. "Hold me, Tony."

He gathered her close, pressing her against his chest, molding her contours with his hands. "What is it?"

"It seems as though an evil genie haunts us," she said with a tremor. "If we take two paces forward, something or someone forces us to take ten paces back."

"You don't really believe in that demon, Semar, do you?"

"N-no."

"You don't seem certain."

"Sometimes I don't know what to believe," she admitted.

Their happiness had not been unmarred by trial, but deep down, Miranda still feared she somehow didn't deserve the bliss they'd shared. Events kept chipping away at their contentment, and all her old doubts and feelings of unworthiness rose to haunt her. But how could she tell Tony that she felt the oppression of invisible storm clouds gathering, or express the nameless dread that made her fearful of things more dire than half-truths and lies printed on a piece of cheap paper?

Her fingers knotted in the fabric of his coat, and she clung to him as though some force were trying to tear her from his embrace. "There are powers beyond our comprehension that at times shape and move our lives like the puppeteer behind the *wajang* screen."

"Nay, sweeting. I refuse to accept a destiny in which we have no part. We'll come through this because we're determined to do so." Tony raised her chin with his knuckles and smiled at her pensive expression. "So when you doubt, just believe in this," he whispered, then took her mouth in a lingering kiss.

As Miranda gave herself over to the magic of his possession, she prayed that Tony's faith would sustain them and that love would be enough. Later that evening, as she looked miserably over her nearly empty table, it was clear that for pride's sake, she had no other recourse but to pretend it was.

Of all the guests invited, only Lord Ingram and Lady Montagu had appeared as expected. Lady Catherine Salter had been the only one with sufficient courtesy to send around a note of apology, explaining her uncle had forbidden her attendance but sweetly expressing her outrage and disbelief in the defamatory broadsides. Miranda had also been asked to pass on Lady Catherine's private message for Lord Peter, whose morose face had instantly lightened on receiving the perfumed missive.

In order to fill out the table, Miranda had pressed Letty and Angus into delaying what had become a customary evening airing in St. James Park to join the sparse company. With Lexa and Kit, it made a tolerable party of eight around the supper table, which would have done well enough, except for the awkwardness of the stilted conversation about everything saving that which was most on all their minds.

By the time the pudding had been removed and the port and cheese appeared, Miranda could stand it no longer.

"Wexill, take that away and bring champagne instead," she ordered, interrupting Lord Peter's desultory comments on a recent horse race.

At the other end of the table, Tony quit toying with his gilt snuffbox and lifted one sun-bleached eyebrow. "My dear?"

Deliberately Miranda set down her silver spoon and laced her fingers beneath her chin. The ornate painted ceiling medallion and intricately carved panels of the dining hall formed a perfect setting for her pale blond beauty, set off by a sky blue satin gown with huge puffed sleeves and square neckline, but her brittle smile could not hide the unhappiness in her gray eyes.

"This company is far too gloomy," she said. "You mustn't tiptoe on eggshells on my account, you know."

"Now, Miranda . . ." Letty began, shaking her gray curls in warning. She caught Angus's attention across the table, but he merely shrugged and tugged uncomfortably at his stock with a gnarled finger.

Miranda's mouth firmed stubbornly. "I mean what I say. 'Tis been quite an interesting experience going from the toast of Society to pariah overnight. If Society snubs me and my long-suffering husband on the basis of the hogwash we encountered today, then it's their loss. Frankly, it's a relief to know who our true friends are, and I think that is cause to celebrate. Wexill, the champagne, if you please."

The butler bowed, sucked in his cheeks in apparent approval, and went immediately to fetch the wine.

"My stars, how refreshing—a freethinker!" Lady Mary Montagu said with an appreciative laugh and nod of her turbaned head. "And a very clever attitude, my dear. 'Tis been my experience Society fawns over those who care least what King Mob thinks—as has been proven so often in the past by the popularity of the Marquess himself!"

"I have to agree," Kit said, grinning at his brother. "Never gave a tinker's dam what people thought, did you, Tony?"

"Only certain people," Tony responded dryly. "But if all one needs is originality to woo the crowds, then my lady wife's place is assured, for she possesses a host of unusual ideas."

Miranda blushed and laughed softly, relieved to have the subject out in the open. "Perhaps to salve my wounded pride, I should start a club that permits only females with outrageous ideas," she suggested lightly.

"Sign me on," Lexa quipped, her green eyes sparkling. "I should not like to miss such fun!"

"Nor I," Lady Mary added. "And you, Mistress Sutherlin? Do you care to become notorious with us?"

To everyone's surprise, Letty's cheeks grew bright pink, and her hazel-green eyes darted to the man across the table for guidance. "Well, I . . . that is . . ."

Angus cleared his throat and slowly stood up. "Seeing as how this is somewhat a celebration, I got somethin' to say." He twisted his napkin into a knot and swallowed hard at the curious expressions surrounding him.

"Yes, Angus?" Miranda prompted.

"Ach, it's like we was all family here, ye see. And so 'twould be best to say it among friends, as it were . . ." The grizzled old sailor gulped, then blurted, "Miss Letticia and me, we're going to splice our lines."

Across the table, Letty threw up her hands in disgust. "Just like a Scotsman to be so stingy with words! Why not just say we're getting married?"

There was a split second of stunned silence, then everyone converged on the beaming couple in an excited flurry of questions, good wishes, and felicitations.

"What? Retiring from the sea to take a wife? Gadzooks, it must be love!"

The bonniest lass this side of Edinburgh.

"You old sea dog!"

"Purchase an inn in Bristol? Near the water, of course? What a wonderful idea!"

"A certain success. Congratulations!"

"Only if you promise to take good care of our Mr. Pratt!"

*So kind, and such tales! Always knew a sailor would steal
my heart.*

"Oh, Letty! You'll have your own kitchen at last. And
a rose garden, too!"

Wexill's arrival with the champagne met with hurrahs,
and glasses were filled and toasts drunk. The warmth of
true affection and a contagious gaiety replaced the earlier
heavy mood. When the four men joined in a chantey to
serenade the ladies, Miranda smiled around the lump of
emotion in her throat and knew that it was times like these
that counted in the pages of one's life, not the empty, false
glitter of fickle Society's favor. What did it matter as long
as she had the ones she loved around her?

Even after Lord Ingram and Lady Montagu made their
departures much later, the euphoria did not diminish. In one
corner of the drawing room, Kit, Tony, and Angus rem-
inisced about their seagoing exploits, while in another, the
three ladies bent their heads over the very pleasant task of
planning a wedding. They'd gotten as far as discussing the
advantages of silk taffeta versus Chinese brocade for Letty's
wedding gown when a clatter of hooves in the street and
the sound of someone beating on the front door interrupted
them.

Miranda's heart began to pound, and she lurched to her
feet, intuition screaming. "Tony?"

But he'd heard it, too, and met Wexill at the drawing
room door.

"My lord, you'd best come. There's a fire—"

"Where?" Tony barked, but as the others gathered
around, he knew the answer before Wexill spoke it.

"My lord, 'tis the Free Indies wharf."

The sound of voices, low and husky with exhaustion,
broke through Miranda's self-imposed stupor. She left the
darkened drawing room, where she'd kept her unhappy,
anxious vigil through the wee hours, and paused uncertainly
in the doorway leading to the lamplit foyer.

Tony and Kit stood there in their shirt sleeves, their two
heads bent together in earnest discussion, the bright gold

hair of one and the coppery gilt locks of the other both
tarnished by sweat and ash. Their faces bore black smudges
of soot, and their stained and torn garments reeked of smoke,
but those were small matters because—thank God!—they
were both safe.

"Is it over?" she asked, her words tremulous.

Tony's head jerked up, and she quailed before the bleak-
ness in the blue depths of his smoke-reddened eyes. "Aye,"
he said heavily, "it's over."

Miranda walked toward the two men. "How bad?"

"Bad," Kit said, flicking a worried glance at his twin.
"One warehouse, all the cargo, and the *Evening Star* itself
burned and sank at the dock."

"Oh, no," Miranda breathed in disbelief. "Everything?"

"By the time we arrived and got the fire brigade out, it
was already too late," Tony said, the muscle in his jaw
working beneath a layer of grime.

"I'm sorry, but are you both unharmed? Was anyone else
hurt?" At the negative shake of their heads, she gave a sigh
of relief. "That's a blessing, at least. How did it start?"

"There were three or four outbreaks at about the same
time, so it's clear they were set deliberately."

"But who would do such a thing? Why?" Aghast, she
faltered, struck by the horrifying truth. "It—it's that witchcraft thing, isn't it? Oh, God—"

"Shut up, Miri!" Tony snapped. "Aren't things bad
enough without you taking credit for it? All I know is that
if someone set out to destroy me tonight, they did a damn
fine job!"

"Easy," Kit cautioned, then sent Miranda an apologetic
grimace. "It's been a hell of a night."

Miranda swallowed the sudden lump of guilt clogging
her throat and forced herself to speak with some semblance
of normalcy. "Yes, of course, and I just stand here blath-
ering. What can I get for you? I sent the staff to bed, and
Lexa went up a bit ago to settle Rose back down, but if
you're thirsty or hungry—"

"Nothing, thank you, Miranda," Kit said wearily, then
headed for the stairs. "I'm going to wash, check on my

women, and fall into that bed. And, Jimmy, I suggest you
do the same. A clear head is what you need, and the morning's soon enough to see if we can salvage anything."

Tony snorted softly, and his voice was bitter. "Then stay
in bed, Jimmy, for there's no chance of that!"

Without another look at Miranda, Tony stalked through
the drawing room into the library, heading straight for the
decanters of spirits that stood on the polished sideboard.
Uncertainly Miranda followed him, watching with mixed
emotions as he poured himself a generous dram, splashed
it to the back of his throat in one gulp, then repeated the
procedure. Hesitantly she laid a hand on his arm.

"Don't!" he ordered sharply. "You'll spoil your gown."

The glands under Miranda's tongue and down her throat
prickled with her need to cry. What did she care for a gown,
no matter how lovely, when all she wanted was to lend
comfort to her husband? But he rejected her overture so
coolly . . .

"The hounds Peter and I've managed to hold a bay will
be snapping at my heels again come morning," he said, his
voice hollow.

Futility and impotent rage burned through Tony, its path
even more scalding than the brandy he'd just drunk. And
that was what he wanted to be: drunk and oblivious to the
fact that he was the biggest fool and the greatest failure in
all of England. Why hadn't he set more guards at the warehouse? Why couldn't he put a face to the enemy who per-
secuted him so handily?

"I'll have to sell Fairhaven."

Miranda caught her breath. "Tony, no."

With a sudden, vicious motion, he hurled his empty glass
across the library. It shattered on the mantelpiece below the
accusing portrait of Charles Benedict, the father he'd never
been able to satisfy in life and now had failed so miserably
in death.

"*Who the hell is doing this to me?*"

The sight of Tony's pain stole Miranda's speech, but her
brain screamed the silent answer. *It's me! I'm the cause of
your misfortune. I was selfish enough to believe I could have*

you, that the world couldn't touch us, and now look what my cursed arrogance has done!

Still, she knew her wifely duty. "Come to bed," she murmured in a voice throaty with unshed tears. "You're exhausted."

"I *must* find out who's behind this," he gritted. Ignoring her suggestion, he strode to his desk and began pulling down ledgers and account books. "By God, there's got to be a clue here somewhere. Some thread, something! Mayhap Mertle can help, and Peter knows every gossip in London. The coward attacks us by stealth, but if 'tis a fight this poltroon wants, he'll find the Wastrel Lord can give him one. A man this determined has got to leave tracks of some sort—unless he's a damned spirit!"

Seeing him so desperate tore at Miranda's heart. Knowing that he had only to look up to find the true cause of his difficulties ripped it asunder. "Tony, please, you've done enough tonight."

He seemed to come aware of her for the first time in many minutes, and his handsome face drooped in haggard lines. "Go to bed, Miranda," he said gruffly. "I need to be alone."

Though he'd never admit it, gentleman that he was, Miranda knew in her heart how badly her husband must regret his involvement with a woman whose troubles would deprive him of his legacy. His distance only reinforced her feelings of inadequacy, so she gave him the only thing he wanted of her—her absence.

"G-good night, then," she managed, stumbling from the library before she totally disgraced herself. In the privacy of their chamber, she undressed and threw herself down into the bed pillows to smother the sound of her wracking sobs. Exhausted by her misery, she fell into a restless sleep plagued by dreams of demons and banshees.

At dawn she woke with a gasp, her heart pounding in fright, uncertain whether it was her nightmares or something else that had awakened her. Holding her breath, she listened in the pearly light of a foggy sunrise, then realized that she was still alone in the great poster bed.

A wave of apprehension crashed over her, thrusting her to her feet. She threw a soft woven shawl over her shoulders, her brain in tumult. Tony! He'd not come to bed at all. Where was he? What—?

She came up short at the dressing room door. Tony lay on the small cot sometimes used by Topaz, his elbow bent over his face, his long limbs in a dead-to-the-world sprawl. Miranda bit her knuckle to stifle an involuntary cry of pain. Nothing could have spoken with more eloquence of her husband's acceptance of her guilt in this disastrous situation than his choice not to share her bed.

Agonized, she stood frozen, then jerked, the hairs on the back of her neck standing at attention at the low, mournful wail that reverberated through the still house. She recognized that it was what had awakened her, and it was likely to do the same to Tony. Knowing he must still be exhausted, she was loath to let that happen. Backing out of the dressing room, she silently closed the door, then paused to listen again.

The sound was repeated, and she realized it came from the garden below her window. Pulling back the drapes, she could see nothing but the shadowy outline of the apple tree where Angus had built Button's cage, nearly obscured by the enveloping fog. Throwing open the window, she leaned over the sill, the cool, moisture-laden air slicking her skin and making her shiver beneath the thin stuff of her night rail. The sound came again, and this time she caught momentary sight of the outline of a large black feline. Beelzebub!

"Quiet, cat!" she hissed. "You'll raise the house!"

Her words only increased the pitch of the animal's cry. There was no knowing what the cantankerous old tom was up to, Miranda thought in distraction. In her unsettled frame of mind, she latched on to this mission as a drowning man would a lifeline. If she was good for nothing else in her husband's service, at least she could insure that his much-needed rest was undisturbed!

Sprinting on bare feet, she raced down the rear stairs, through the vestibule, and out into the deserted garden.

Milkmaids' chants and the clang of the butcher's wagon wheels on the cobbles drifted over the enclosing wall of the quiet, flowery oasis. The gravel path hurt the soles of Miranda's feet, so she stepped into the dew-dampened grass, wetting her toes and soaking the hem of her gown as she moved through the mist toward the apple tree.

"Beelzebub?" she called softly. "Come now, and we'll ask Cook for some nice, fresh cream—"

The tattered old warrior crouched in the grass in the shadow of Button's cage, his yellow eyes gleaming, his teeth bared in another sibilant screech.

"What is it, puss?" Miranda frowned, glancing about uneasily. It was easy to believe no one else in the world existed, wrapped as she was in the muffling cocoon of misty silence. A square of white on an overhanging apple branch caught her eye, and she took an angry breath.

It was another of those infamous handbills, pinned on a twig, and crudely printed across it in black was the message: "Death to the witch! Death to her consort!"

"Damn them!" she choked. Wasn't she safe from this torment anywhere? Furiously she snatched the paper free, and strangled on a cry of absolute horror.

Beneath the paper, in a gruesome parody of a Tyburn execution, Button's poor little corpse swung at the end of a hangman's noose.

Chapter 19

It was a warning, loud and clear.

Fighting panic, Miranda removed Button's tiny body from the branch, wrapped him tenderly in her shawl, and buried him in the soft soil of a flower bed, instinctively sensing that to reveal this atrocity now would only produce hysteria within the house. In Java, to kill a little man of the jungle was the most dire of evil omens—especially for the killer—and she had lived there too long to shake off a superstitious foreboding of imminent disaster.

Shocked to the core by the sick brutality of her tiny pet's death, Miranda knew a soul-deep certainty that Tony's life was at risk because of her. Not only had she failed miserably as an ideal wife, but now her presence was a real threat to him, the venom directed at her spilling over to menace her husband, and this she could not abide. If the phantom that had perpetrated this horror was so bold as to come unseen unto their very doorstep, what might he try next?

She covered the new grave with a stone while Beelzebub cried pitifully and curled around her bare ankles, and her

blood ran chill with absolute fear. Tony was in danger, and
it was all her fault. She had to do something, but what?

The answer took form with each step back to the house.

No one else was up at such an early hour, but the pall
of disaster hung over the house in the wake of the fire, the
servants moving about as if there had already been a death.
As she dressed in a day gown of peach muslin and ecru
lace, moving quietly to avoid waking Tony, her choices
became increasingly clear. And as she forced down the cup
of black coffee a subdued maid brought her in the drawing
room, she could no longer ignore the obvious conclusion.
Miranda shuddered at the bitter taste of the coffee and the
bitterness of her decision.

To protect Tony, she had no choice but to do something
she'd sworn never to do again. She had to leave him.

Miranda prayed that he would understand her motives,
that a separation for his safety was essential, at least for a
time, at least until this dangerous situation could be resolved. She would take a coach, disappear into the country,
and remove at least one threat from Tony's worries.

She set down her cup with a grimace, trying to ignore
the painful gnawing of her conscience. Her practical nature
could see no other course, despite the fact that for her to
desert Tony yet again might do irreparable harm to their
relationship. Still, her decision not to tell Tony her plan,
only to send word after the fait accompli, was not so much
out of concern that he'd argue and try to stop her, but, after
last night, out of fear that he *wouldn't*. And that would truly
be too much to bear.

Sitting down at her desk, Miranda dipped a quill into her
inkstand and tried to pen a letter to her husband that would
explain the necessity of her action. She was on her fourth
clumsy attempt when a messenger arrived. As Wexill
showed the servant into her presence, Miranda shoved the
inadequate and awkwardly worded missives into her desk
drawer, then rose to accept the square of heavy vellum.

"I was told to wait for a reply, my lady," the liveried
footman said respectfully.

When Miranda unfolded the letter, she was astonished to

find the note came from Lord Cecil Edmund. She was even more astounded at its bold contents. *Madam*, it began.

> I know who is behind your husband's many troubles. I leave for the Continent tonight, my heart shattered by that betraying bitch who sends me away bereft as well as penniless. Should you see your way clear to fund my departure (perhaps with the bauble you wear on your finger?), the reward for your generosity would be great. You may trust my man with your token. When and where may we meet?
>
> In desperate haste, .   Edmund

Miranda's brain spun frantically, and she pressed her hand to her flushed cheek. Cecil on the outs with Sylvie at last? 'Twas indeed possible he might know something important if he'd been privy to her plotting. Though certain Sylvie's mischief had been directed at *her*, Miranda could not overlook the possibility that this might be the thread Tony desperately needed to uncover his real enemies.

With a little gulp of grateful relief, Miranda knew she couldn't leave just yet, not without learning what Cecil knew. The depth of her gratitude made her realize how reluctant she had been to follow that course at all, no matter how logical. It might still come to it, but here was a chance to help Tony without sacrificing all they'd built, and she accepted it with all the fervor of a condemned man receiving a stay of execution.

"Do you know what this says?" she asked the waiting servant.

"No, my lady. Only to bring a reply."

"Wait, then."

Miranda reseated herself at the desk, took a new sheet of paper, and wrote: "St. James Park. One hour."

When she went to remove her ring, she hesitated, then steeled herself against the pang of regret. After all, she'd intended for Tony to sell it all along to help them out of their straits, which, after losing the *Evening Star* and her cargo, were more dire than ever. Now, if Rija's pearl could buy the answers Tony needed, she hadn't the right to be squeamish. Resolutely she pulled the ring from her finger, folded it into her note, and sealed it with wax. Rising, she handed the packet and an extra coin to the footman.

"Take this to your master immediately."

"Very good, my lady." Bowing, the servant withdrew, wondering if there was time for a quick pint before he returned to Lavender House.

The message on its way, Miranda found herself in a state of agitation that did not dissipate one whit during the ensuing wait. The internal debate she conducted with herself regarding whether or not to tell Tony of Cecil's possible information was decided for her when Tony and Kit passed through the foyer on their way to the Free Indies Company wharf. The fact that her husband did not seek her out plunged her into another slough of despondency, but she bit her lip and decided it was just as well.

It would serve no purpose to get his hopes up for nothing, and she wasn't at all certain she could have presented a serene facade, considering the state of her overstretched emotions. The possibility that his own mother was responsible for, or at least involved in, his problems was a ticklish subject she could only deal with when she knew something concrete. If she was lucky enough to glean information of real value from Cecil, she meant to use it to restore Tony's regard, whether it was at Sylvie's expense or not.

After allowing sufficient time for her message to reach Cecil's dwellings, Miranda had Wexill order a sedan chair, but her departure was delayed when Letty appeared on the stairway.

"Going out?" Letty asked, astonishment lifting her brows. "Are you certain that's wise after all that's happened?"

"I—it's just a short errand," Miranda replied, edging toward the door. "I won't be long."

"Wait then, you need a wrap. Doesn't look as though this damp fog is likely to burn off. Like to suffocate a body, it does, when it's so thick and dark of a summer's day."

"I must go." Miranda looked distracted. "I've misplaced my shawl."

"Take mine, then," Letty offered, bustling down the rest of the steps to tuck Miranda neatly into her woven wrap. "Mustn't have you catch a chill!"

"Yes. Thank you." Miranda dropped a quick kiss on Letty's plump cheek, then gratefully scurried out to the waiting chair, missing Letty's puzzled frown.

Within a short time, the sedan chair porters had brought her to the spacious, tree-lined concourses of St. James Square. She was beginning to wonder just how she would find Cecil, so dense was the mist curling off the river, but then a rather shabby carriage drew abreast of her, and Lord Cecil's boyish face popped from behind one of the leather curtains. Until that moment, Miranda had been halfway afraid he wouldn't come, so when he gracefully alighted and invited her to join him within the coach for a more private place for discussion, she readily agreed, allowing him to pay off the porters.

"You'll be able to take me back, won't you?" she asked.

"Oh, assuredly" was his amiable reply as he handed her into the coach. He settled into the seat opposite her, re-closing the curtains as the coachman set the carriage in motion. At her curious look, he explained, "We'll ride a bit around the square while we talk, shall we?"

"As you please, Lord Edmund. Now, what have you to tell me?"

Cecil laughed, waving a languid hand and displaying an inordinate amount of lace at his cuff. "My, such impatience, my lady!"

"When it comes to my husband's welfare, I do not suffer fools gladly. I gave you what you asked. Was I the fool to do so?"

"You were extremely generous," Cecil said, almost kindly. Leaning forward, he sandwiched her hand between his, squeezing it earnestly. "So generous, kind, and beautiful—and altogether too trusting."

Miranda shot him a look of disgust. "Then you know

nothing? Why, then, this play? If 'twas money you wanted, you had only to ask outright!''

"Would you have given it to me?" He laughed again at her irate expression. "Don't answer that, my lady. At any rate, 'twas the pearl we wanted, and what makes you think I haven't got the answers you wish?''

Confused, Miranda jerked her hand free and glared haughtily at him. "I weary of this game of cat and mouse, sir! Explain yourself at once.''

"All in good time.''

"That commodity is at a premium at the moment!" she snapped. "Lord Edmund, if you are privy to information that may help us, I beg you to tell me. Even now, my husband's enemies may be plotting some new mischief! My ring is certainly worth what you know, but I will go to any lengths to help Tony.''

"That is exactly what we counted on.''

"Who is this 'we'?" she demanded.

"Why, Sylvie and myself, of course.''

Miranda's gaze narrowed suspiciously. "Your note said you'd broken with the Marchioness.''

"A necessary fabrication.''

"Necessary for what? I thought you were leaving London tonight. What is going on here, sir?''

"There's been a slight alteration in plans, my lady. I do plan to leave London, you see. But I'm taking you with me.''

The absurdity of his calm statement made Miranda laugh. "Don't be ridiculous!''

"Sylvie and I have planned it all very carefully. It's nothing personal, you know, but I couldn't bypass an opportunity that will assure me a life of comfort on the Continent for some time.'' The swaying coach drew to a halt as he spoke. "Ah! St. Crispin's. It appears we've reached our destination.''

Shocked, Miranda dragged back the leather window curtain and stared at the hazy outlines of decaying warehouses, rickety tenements, and the destroyed spire of an abandoned church. Releasing the curtain as though burned by the sight of such squalor, she shrank back against the leather cushions, her nerves trilling alarms. "I—I don't know what you mean."

Cecil's look was pitying. "No, I don't expect you do. But you will. Now, come."

"No."

Cecil grabbed her arm. "Don't be difficult, Miranda. You'll only make it harder on yourself."

"What is it you want?" she cried, resisting, but she was no match for his strength and he pulled her from the coach as though she were a recalcitrant child. Her slippers sank into the evil-smelling mire of sewage and offal clotting the cobbles of the narrow lane that fronted the river's edge, but he'd chosen the ghostly place well, for there was no one about to hear her cries except the apathetic coachman who never once looked her way.

"Tell me what you want, damn you!" she raged, struggling vainly.

Smiling, Cecil dragged her toward the black, gaping maw of a ruined warehouse. "I think you know."

"Is it ransom?" Propelled through a littered maze of fallen beams and years of accumulated filth, Miranda choked on the odors of rat droppings and rotting wood. "Tony will pay you—"

"He hasn't two farthings to rub together, my lady, and you know it." Cecil dragged her to a halt before an arch whose iron-hinged door was still miraculously intact. "Not that it makes any difference. You see, Sylvie is determined to be rid of her daughter-by-marriage, and since fair means were never her forte, then foul means will have to do."

Miranda swallowed and licked her dry lips. "You mean to keep me here?"

"For a day or two only, my sweet."

"For what purpose? I don't understand!" she cried.

"For what purpose do lovers ever disappear?" Cecil asked dramatically.

"You mean . . . ?" Her silver eyes opened wide with incredulity. "You and I are supposed to be . . . and you think Tony will believe such a lie?" Her laughter rang merrily, causing Cecil's heretofore placid expression to darken. "You, sir, are a much greater buffoon than I thought!"

"He'll believe it when he sees your ring." He smiled as her laughter ceased abruptly, then chucked her under the chin. "Besides, by the time you and I are done, you'll be so completely ruined that not even the Wastrel Lord will want you back."

Shivering at his touch, Miranda drew back, making her glance as cold as ice. "'Tis to be rape, then, my lord? The Javanese have a name for men like you. Loosely translated, it means excrement eater."

"Sylvie warned you wouldn't be cooperative," he said with an aggrieved sigh.

"She was right." Whipping off Letty's shawl, Miranda threw it at Cecil's head, momentarily distracting him. Turning, she took two steps toward freedom, and nearly collided headlong with the barrel of a horse pistol pointed straight at her head.

Her heart froze, then pounded double-time. Miranda warily raised her terrified gaze to this new assailant, a tall figure in a domino whose steadiness of grasp never wavered. He jerked the pistol once, and she took his meaning instantly, retreating cautiously until she was backed up against the broad planks of the archway door.

"So glad Sylvie provided for every expediency," Cecil remarked.

"She must truly hate me," Miranda croaked, unable to look away from the pistol still pointed at her forehead. "Do you intend to kill me?"

Cecil feigned a hurt look. "Nothing so uncivilized. After a few days here, no doubt you'll welcome my . . . attentions. After that, I think we'll travel to the country for a time before we part company. Come on, Miranda, be a good sport. We'll have quite a lark together."

Defiance flashed a spark of green behind the silver of her eyes, but her voice was flat. "Never."

"You disappoint me." Cecil pouted. "Perhaps I should let my friend here sample your wares first?"

Miranda's breath caught. Staring past the barrel of the

pistol, she searched the black, blank eyeholes of the man's
domino for any flicker of compassion. Finding none, she
felt despair course through her veins. The round end of the
pistol barrel seemed as merciless as those staring holes behind the mask.

"Well, Miranda, what's it to be?" Cecil asked. "It's
rather tiresome to jolly you along like this. I do hope you're
going to be reasonable."

"You'll have to kill me," she whispered, then jumped
at the sound of the pistol being cocked.

The gunman drew a bead on the bridge of her nose, but
before she could close her eyes to meet her Maker, the shiny
barrel swung in a wide arc. A shot exploded, and Cecil
crashed to the littered floor and lay still, a circle of crimson
blossoming on his chest.

Miranda pressed her hands to her mouth to stifle a bleat
of horror. The stillness of Cecil's form made her gorge rise,
and she swung her gaze back to his assassin. Despite her
shock, a tiny ray of hope filtered into her battered mind.
"Sir? Why . . . ? Who *are* you?"

Wordlessly the man dragged off his domino. The blood
drained out of Miranda's cheeks, and a mindless scream
pushed past the clog in her throat. Blessed oblivion overtook
her, dragging her down into the darkness, mercifully obscuring the sight of a face that had once been as beautiful
as an angel's.

A northerly wind blew up at sunset, dissipating the last
of the clinging mists that had plagued London that day, and
leaving behind a wealth of clean, summer-fresh scents
blown in from the northern dales and a clear, starlit sky to
welcome the rising moon.

The Marquess of Bentley, however, was in no mood to
appreciate the uncommonly fine evening. After spending
the day trying to salvage the unsalvageable at the Free Indies
wharf, Tony was certain his situation couldn't be any worse.
His assumption proved unjustified the minute he, Kit, and
Angus returned home.

Letty intercepted Tony in the foyer. "My lord, we were just after sending for you!"

Kit and Angus excused themselves to clean the grime and smoke soot from their persons, but Letty positioned herself in front of Tony and denied him that luxury until he paid her proper notice. With a shrug of resignation, Tony gave the older woman his courteous attention. "Yes, Letty?"

Letty's wrinkles seemed more pronounced, and her cheeks sagged. " 'Tis the most curious and worrisome thing..."

"What is? And can it wait?" Tony wearily stripped off his soiled coat, longing only for a bath, food, and the solace of his wife. He'd been reluctant to inflict his black mood on her that morning, but he'd missed her like hell. "Where's Miri? I—"

"My lord, that's what I'm trying to tell you—she's gone." Letty nodded vigorously. "Went out early this morn and hasn't yet returned. Isn't like her to be gone so long without telling anyone her destination."

Tony frowned. "Surely she's out visiting? Wasn't there a rout she planned to attend?"

"After all that happened yesterday? I think not, sir! And that's not the half of it. Little Rose has cried all day for Button, but no one can find him, either, and that possessed cat has wailed like a banshee and caused no end of mischief. And now, sir, your mother awaits you in the drawing room—and I must warn you I've never seen her in such a mood! Even threw a teacup at Wexill!"

Tony groaned inaudibly. "Ye gods! What next? Never mind, Letty, I'll see to Mother. In the meantime, have a couple of the footmen locate Miri. Perhaps at the Montagus'? If Miri needed a respite from this house of doom, I can't say that I blame her."

"Yes, my lord." Letty bobbed obediently, then scurried off, calling for Wexill.

Tony tossed his coat onto a tapestry hall chair and untied his neckcloth, sending it the way of the coat. He'd come a long way from a dandy's perfection, he reflected wryly, but somehow he liked the change. Squaring his shoulders, he entered the drawing room. Dressed in a gown the color of her eyes, Sylvie was using the gilt mirror over the fireplace to adjust her curls while a tea tray cooled in front of the sofa.

"Well, Mother?" Tony said, one brow lifted sardonically. Suddenly realizing he was ravenous, he picked up a cake from the tray and bit into the sweet apricot confection. "Come to offer your commiserations?"

Instantly Sylvie shuttered her expression, turning to her son with every evidence of concern. "Oh, my poor, poor boy! What shall we do? What can we do?"

Perched on the arm of the sofa, Tony reached for another cake, but he grimaced as the sweetness turned sour on his tongue. "Whatever we must, I suppose. Fairhaven is forfeit, you realize. Have you ever thought of remarrying? It may be your only recourse if you wish to preserve your accustomed style of living—"

Sylvie's blue eyes glistened with sudden tears. "You don't know, do you? What does money matter now? We are both betrayed! My son, my son . . ."

Sylvie's unaccustomed display of emotion startled Tony. "What is it?"

"The rats have left our sinking ship," Sylvie said, pathos making her voice tremble. "I know you never thought my affections were involved, but Cecil has left me for another!"

Tony threw down the remainder of the cake and straightened, disconcerted. "Oh, my dear, I'm sorry."

"Besotted fool!" Sylvie stormed suddenly. "Don't you realize? They played us for idiots! 'Tis *your* wife Cecil took, though perhaps *she* is the one who seduced him. I knew you couldn't trust the whore!"

"Miri?" Tony shook his head as if he hadn't heard aright. "That's impossible."

"Where is she, then?" his mother demanded. "Gone! Don't bother to deny it. You owe her nothing."

"This is ridiculous!" Tony rubbed his neck. "Miri's merely out. Whatever gave you such an idea?"

"All my jewelry disappeared, along with Cecil," Sylvie said, the exquisite lines of her face a picture of desolation.

"I couldn't believe it, but when I went round to the jeweler he frequented, I found he'd sold it all. Along with this."

She opened a lace-edged handkerchief retrieved from the bosom of her gown. A ring glistened on the square of linen, a quail's egg pearl surrounded by diamonds. Something twisted inside Tony's chest, and he couldn't breathe.

"Don't you see?" Sylvie demanded angrily. "Your faithless wife has eloped with my feckless lover."

"That's absurd."

"Don't be a fool! Look what I found in her desk." Sylvie picked up a handful of papers from the desktop and thrust them at him.

Beloved, he read, *forgive me, for I have no choice but to leave you—*

Tony's fist abruptly curled around the letter, and his denial was hoarse. "No . . ."

"You think you're the first man ever to be deceived?" Sylvie taunted. Triumph gleamed behind her eyes. "She's the cause of all your misfortunes. And now that you're at your lowest ebb, she deserts you. We're well rid of them both, I say! We'll come through this, and everything will be just as it was."

His mother's words slamming into him like musket balls, Tony swayed on a wave of vertigo. Miri! Was it true, then? Had she deceived him all this time, made him believe with lies that her love was real? He'd lost her before. Was it happening again? This time it would surely destroy him. The loss of Fairhaven paled in significance when compared to the loss of his love, his other self, the soul-twin who'd showed him the path to salvation and purpose.

Distant thunder rumbled in his brain, demanding notice despite the eviscerating pain that sliced through his belly. He took the pearl from his mother's hand, staring at the shimmering, luminous orb that was nearly as big as the full moon under which he'd first seen it.

Pearls . . . for tears . . .

First man ever deceived . . .

Or was he?

"No," he grated with a certainty that sprang from the

faith Miri's love had given him in himself. "It's not true. None of it."

"How can you deny the evidence before your eyes? The ring, the letters—they're damning!"

Tony's eyes narrowed dangerously, and his fingers closed around the ring with such force, the gold setting pricked the flesh of his palm. "Just as was the evidence against Rosalind?"

Startled, Sylvie faltered. "Well, er—yes."

"You have a strange obsession with this particular gem, Mother."

Sylvie made an exasperated sound. "I don't know what you mean."

"You used the Cathay pearls to prove Rosalind betrayed my father, but she was just as innocent then as my Miri is now." Tony's voice was deadly quiet.

"What?" Sylvie's eyes grew round, and there was a faint flicker of apprehension behind her gentian blue irises. "Of course not. Rosalind was a whore, just like Miranda! You know nothing of that!"

"I know everything," Tony said, the tension in his jaw muscle flattening the cleft in his chin. Deliberately he shoved the ring into his trousers pocket. "I've known since I returned from the colonies."

"You were a mere child when your father broke with his mistress!" Sylvie scoffed. "How can you know anything?"

"Lexa's grandfather recorded it all in his diaries." He stalked Sylvie, grabbed her shoulders, and forced her to look at him. "I know about the Cathay pearls, about you and Phineas Howard, about your plotting. I know Kit and I shared Rosalind's womb, and that you and Father divided us like Solomon, leaving scars my twin and I still carry. I know that your thirst for revenge was responsible for my birth mother's slow, sad death and my father's unhappiness. *And I know that now you're trying to do the same damn thing to Miri and me!*"

Sylvie's face had grown pale as alabaster during Tony's tirade. "You're wrong," she breathed.

Enraged, Tony shook her fiercely. "I'm not wrong! All

I don't know is why I was too gutless to confront you before. I guess I didn't want to acknowledge that the woman I've called mother all my life is a ruthless bitch.''

"Anthony, please listen," she pleaded.

"Damn it, woman!" he roared. *"Tell me what you've done to my wife!"*

"Nothing, I swear!"

"More lies! What a consummate actress you are." Tony thrust her away in disgust. "It profits you nothing, madam. I—"

A disturbance at the door interrupted him.

"My lord, pray pardon me." Letty stepped inside the doorway, wringing her hands in agitation. "There's a gentleman here . . . It's about Miri, he says."

Tony started forward. "What? Who is it?"

A tall, cadaverous figure in moth-eaten solicitor's robes and full-bottomed wig flapped into the room like a drunken crow.

"Most inconsiderate! No end of trouble," the elderly lawyer all but shouted, myopically peering about the room. "Hmmm. Lovely table, that. Had one like it myself—"

"Sir," Tony interrupted the wandering monologue. Gathering the man was nearly deaf, he raised his voice. "May I be of service?"

"Oh! Indeed." With a flutter of his black robe, the old man made a courtly bow. "You are the Marquess of Bentley, I presume?"

"I am."

"Married at present to one . . ." He paused, reached deep into the pocket of his robe, removed a crumpled sheaf of papers, and read at the top of his lungs. ". . . Miranda Agnes Langford Benedict?"

Tony nodded, perplexed. "My wife, yes. What—"

"Very good, my lord. Silas Poole, at your service. I take it the Marchioness is out?"

"Yes, but why—"

Mr. Poole interrupted again. "Tut, tut! Don't thank me. Think nothing of it. Would have done the same for any of my clients, though 'twas a dashed difficult time I had finding you both. Please advise the Marchioness to keep me informed of her whereabouts in the future. Apologize for the delay, you know, but the post to Bristol and Fairhaven took some time. Now, if you'll just sign here—''

"Mr. Poole!" Tony exploded. "God's blood, man! I have no time for poppycock. State your business and be gone!"

The lawyer looked down his long nose at Tony, highly affronted. "Very well, sir. No need to get huffy. I only wish to turn possession of a ship and its cargo over to you."

"What ship?" Tony asked suspiciously. At Mr. Poole's blank look, he shouted, "What ship? From whom?"

"Oh! The *Cameroon*, I believe. Sent to your wife by the sultan and sultana of Preanger Province, Java. Relatives of the Marchioness, I take it? Loaded to the yardarms with coffee, that ship is, sir! The Marchioness is an extremely wealthy woman."

"Good God." Tony's expression was incredulous. "Unbelievable!"

"I assure you it's quite on the up and up, sir! Docked at the Queen's Wharf waiting for orders regarding its disposition."

"Mr. Poole, your news is most welcome, more than you could know. That cargo is my wife's dowry, and it could not have arrived at a more opportune moment."

"Splendid!" Mr. Poole boomed, beaming jovially. "Now, if you'll affix your signature . . ."

Tony did so, then roared his instructions. "Take this around to Lord Ingram's rooms. He'll know what to do with it. I thank you again, sir."

"No need to shout, sir," Mr. Poole said, routing his ear with his little finger as he bowed out of the room. "Extend my best wishes to the Marchioness."

"That I will!" Tony lowered his voice with an effort. "As soon as I get to the bottom of what's become of her."

His lips tight with determination, he turned back to Sylvie. "Well, Mother? Perhaps in light of the fact that 'tis Miri's newfound wealth that will save us all from debtors' prison, you'd care to reconsider what you've told me."

"What difference does it make?" Sylvie demanded, her expression defiant and disdainful. "The wench is nothing! She was never good enough for you. You're meant for greater things. You mustn't ruin your life by clinging to a nobody."

"I love her. Nothing else matters."

"You utter fool!" Sylvie raged, her small hands clenching into fists. "You're just like your father—bewitched by a woman, a weakling whining after love with every breath!"

"Mayhap I am more like him than I knew," Tony acknowledged, "since it's clear we were both capable of only one transcendent passion in this lifetime. Is that why you did it? Is that what's driven you from lover to lover, from plot to plot, from manipulation to manipulation? To seek the destruction of Rosalind, then Kit, then Miri? Because the woman my father loved could never be *you*?"

Sylvie's expression was stricken, her voice hoarse. "Nay . . ."

"I pity you, even as I despise what you've done."

"But, Anthony, I love you. I want only the best for my son."

Tony's jaw flexed. "A warped and twisted perversion of love, madam, to take from me the one person on this earth who can insure my happiness."

There was desperation in Sylvie's eyes. "I told you, she's run off with Cecil! You can't hold me responsible!"

"Oh, but I do," Tony said, his voice like steel. "If the least harm comes to Miri, I am certainly no son of yours."

Sylvie gasped at the harshness of his words. "You'd deny your own mother?"

His reply was flat. "My mother is dead."

Sylvie's face crumpled, and the bubble of youth burst, leaving her no more than she was—tearful, bitter, and old. "Tony, no . . ."

"Tell me what you and Cecil have done to my wife, and perhaps someday I may forgive you."

"I only meant to show you how unsuitable she was, how her blunders would make you a laughingstock. The ruined dresses, the lost invitations—small things only." Tears

streaked the paint on Sylvie's cheeks as excuses rattled from
her lips. "But nothing went as I planned. She was even too
stupid or too greedy to leave you when I had Cecil arrange
for you and Catherine to meet!"

"Ah." Tony's visage grew stony with suppressed rage,
and Sylvie hastened on, the words tumbling out in a torrent.

"It was the Baron's idea to frighten her with the runaway
horse, and those broadsheets—who'd have guessed the
common people would panic so that they'd set fire to the
wharf?"

"Baron Foote?"

"Yes," she gulped, nodding. "I'd grown bored with
Cecil, you see, and the Baron . . . It was all his idea. Have
Cecil take her away for a while, he said, then both incon-
veniences would be gone. No one would believe it wasn't
voluntarily, a woman like her with all those outlandish ways
and pagan ideas. Cecil needed the money I offered, and of
course, the fool actually believes he's so irresistible, he can
charm her into his bed."

The pulse beat in Tony's temple, and the urge to murder
clouded his brain with red. "If he touches her, I'll kill him.
Tell me where they are."

"I don't know." She saw the killing rage in his eyes and
shrank back in fear. "I swear, they never told me the details.
Only that they had a place somewhere in the city, then
would take her into the country."

But Tony had heard enough. Roaring for Kit and Angus,
he stormed into the foyer just as Wexill closed the front
door behind a messenger.

"Find my brother!" Tony snapped, reaching for his discarded coat. "Then bring all the footmen to me, now!"

"Yes, my lord." Wexill nodded, intimidated by the aura
of violence that emanated from the Marquess. A bit diffi-
dently, he sucked in his cheeks and thrust the newly arrived
envelope at his master. "My lord, this just came."

Tony ripped open the missive, then froze as a lock of
moonlight-fair hair slipped from its folds, glittering like
fairy skeins of silver thread on the marble floor. A giant

hand squeezed his lungs and heart. "Oh, Jesus. This can't be."

At that moment, Kit rounded the upper stairway landing. At the sight of his twin's stricken face, he took the remaining stairs two at a time. "Jimmy! What is it?"

"He has Miri," Tony croaked. "Kidnapped. Bring a ransom . . . I haven't got a hundred thousand pounds!"

"What?" At the opening to the drawing room, Sylvie gave an astonished shriek. "That blackguard Cecil! That's not the way it was supposed to happen!"

"Not Cecil, madam. Look how 'tis signed." The words ripped from Tony's dry throat while panic clawed at his entrails. "You used Cecil, but your low country lover used you!"

"I don't believe it!" Sylvie snatched the letter from Tony, scanning the contents. "What is this? The Baron's hand I know, but who is this Steef?"

"Van der Djink! The Dutchman! The devil himself cheats death and seeks his revenge as Baron Foote. Ah, sweet Jesus . . ."

Tony shuddered violently, his mind filled with the image of bloody boots and the satiated smile of a evil seraphim. So much was suddenly clear—the thwarted business deals, the sabotage, the mysterious accidents. Impossible as it seemed, his nemesis had followed him to finish what had begun halfway across the globe. And now the unspeakable madman had Miri!

"I don't understand," Sylvie whimpered.

Rage and hate blazed in Tony's eyes, and he spread his hands wide.

"Madam, behold your handiwork! Like the whore you are, you took my deadliest enemy to your bed. Now Satan holds my heart, and I have no way to save her! Curse you to perdition, woman! You have destroyed both me and yourself!"

Chapter 20

The cool disk of the moon appeared overhead like the broad, shining face of a benign deity. It cast pale slats of light through the holes in the roof of the dilapidated dockside warehouse, illuminating abandoned bales, empty casks, rotting burlap sacks, and a slim, feminine figure slumped in a mound of peach-colored skirts at the base of a hand-hewn pillar.

Miranda watched the steady advance of the parallel bars of brightness across the dusty floor and for the thousandth time tested the bonds that secured her numb wrists around the upright beam behind her. They didn't budge, so she returned to the task she'd set herself, mechanically rubbing the twisted cords over a splintered place on the pillar. It was a pitifully hopeless effort, but she had to do *something* or go mad.

Somewhere close, wharf rats scuttled and squeaked along the rafters, and Miranda glanced up with a spasm of alarm. Built on piers over the river, the once proud warehouse's dangerously swaybacked galleries and rickety staircases disappeared over her head into the dark nether regions of the attics. The steady *lap-lap-lap* of the Thames beneath the decayed flooring was a rhythmic counterpoint to the uneven cadence of her heart. Fighting for calm, Miranda tried to swallow, gagged weakly on the rag binding her dry mouth, and wondered how long the Dutchman intended to keep her prisoner.

Low voices echoed hollowly in the deserted vault, and a faint golden glow blossomed in a distant corner, dispelling the shimmering silver moonbeams as it grew ever closer. Bootheels clicked on the wooden-floor, and a swaying oil lantern appeared, held aloft by a disembodied form, invisible behind the glare. Miranda quivered with apprehension.

Since rousing from her swoon many hours earlier, alone with only her nightmares to disturb her solitude, she'd known the torture of uncertainty and prayed for action—any action at all. But now, faced with the object of her nightmare, fear constricted her heart, and she regretted those foolish prayers. Whatever the Dutchman had in store, it began now.

Dressed in unrelieved black, the shadow came to a halt in front of Miranda. She squinted up the long length of black boots and trousers, noting pistol and sword at his belt, then focused on his black coat and finally the domino, vastly relieved she couldn't see his face.

A superstitious tremor shook her, and for a crazy instant she was uncertain whether this apparition was man or spirit. She forced herself to be logical, practical. That both Tony and the Dutchman had escaped the *kraton*'s conflagration might be unbelievable, even miraculous, but the truth of it stood before her eyes. And demons did not tie their captives to posts.

"Enjoying the accommodations, Miss Langford? Or should I say my Lady Bentley?" The Dutchman's accented English lilted gracefully on her ears.

Bending, he set the lantern down amidst the litter on the floor, then squatted in front of her and tugged her gag free. Sucking in great drafts of air, Miranda tried to get the words past her cottony tongue.

"You . . . should be dead . . . saw you die . . ."

"Illusion only. A shadow play."

"What . . . do you . . . want?"

"From you—nothing. In fact, I owe you a great deal."

"Me?" she croaked.

"Quite." He pulled a flask from his pocket and lifted it to her lips. "Here, drink. Your wait has left you without a voice."

Shrinking away, she shook her head, her eyes smoky with suspicion. He found that amusing.

"You don't trust me?" Chuckling, he took a long pull from the flask himself. "Nothing to fear, see?"

He held it to her lips again, gripping her chin and pouring the aromatic brandy into her mouth. She choked and gasped with its searing heat, shuddering with distaste at the involuntary intimacy while tears stung her eyelids and the spirits trickled down her chin and splattered her bosom.

"Better? I want you in good form tonight." He recapped the flask and put it away. "As I said, I'm grateful to you."

"Wh-why?" She coughed, and her voice grew stronger. "What have I done?"

"Led me to that bastard of an Englishman, of course." Squatting back on his heels, the Dutchman continued conversationally. "I'd never have guessed he, too, survived the fall of the *kraton* if it hadn't been for you. I'll admit I followed you from Java to exact retribution for all the trouble you caused. Because of you I lost my bride, my empire—but not everything. No, I had assets in Amsterdam to fall back on, means to punish my enemies. But if I'd killed you before I found Anthony Benedict was still alive—ah! It hardly bears thinking on! You have to agree it's so much more satisfactory this way."

Chills prickled Miranda's spine, and cold dismay filled her. Once again, her presence had brought potential disaster upon Tony. Teeth chattering, she defied the Dutchman's words.

"Murderer! Cold-blooded fiend! How dare you tally vengeance!" A thought struck her. "Cecil! You murder even your own cohort!"

He made a dismissive gesture. "Such a fuss. He was still breathing when my men rolled him into the river."

"Butcher!" Enraged and terrified past caution, Miranda glared at her tormentor. "You had my father killed, attacked Tony's ship, and tried to have the sultan execute us! What right have *you* to seek revenge?"

"*This* gives me every right!" he hissed, snatching off his domino.

Miranda gave an involuntary cry of revulsion and turned her head aside. He caught her face between his gloved hands and wrenched her back around.

"Look on me!" he growled, squeezing her jawbone in a painful grip.

Steeling herself, Miranda swallowed harshly and forced herself to look at the grotesque horror that was now Steef van der Djink.

The weapon Tony had fashioned from her neck collar had been ragged but lethal, deeply scoring a wicked path down one side of the Dutchman's face from eyebrow to jawbone. The eyelid was divided into two obscene flaps, the blank, opaque blue of his blind eye milky and staring. The scar had healed, but at the price of drawing the muscles into impossible contortions, dragging down the corner of his mouth, twisting the cheek into a frozen caricature more reminiscent of something ghoulish and long dead than alive and human. The disfigurement was all the more startling because the other half of Steef's countenance was un-marked. Like a combination of the masks of tragedy and comedy, the dichotomy of the Dutchman's angelic beauty and demonic heart was revealed for all the world to see.

"Well? Don't you think *this* is cause for vengeance?" Steef grated. His good eye glittered coldly. "Or this?"

He stripped off his gloves, showing her the livid pink and white scars, places where portions of digits were burned completely away, then shoved up his cuffs to prove the raised scoring continued up his arms.

"I'm condemned to spend my life making babes cry while their mothers scream, 'Dear Lord, what *is* it?' You'll allow I have the right to be peevish."

Miranda didn't flinch away, but forced herself to study his ruined face and hands dispassionately. The monstrous distortion of beauty was no doubt the supreme blow for a man of such ultimate vanity, who'd used his appearance to advance his nefarious ends. But the barely leashed, insane affinity for violent evil still radiated from him in a palpable aura, and she could feel no compassion.

"The real ugliness is inside you," she said.

He made a disgusted noise and rose to his feet. "But someone must pay, don't you see? You know who. Can you guess how?"

"N-no."

"Your lack of imagination disappoints me."

Miranda struggled awkwardly to her knees, then to her feet, leaning against the pillar for support as the blood tingled back into her legs. But the pain made no impact, for the conclusion she drew was too shocking. "It's been you all along, hasn't it?"

The Dutchman's grin was an evil, twisting grimace. "I'll admit I've spent many pleasurable evenings contemplating all the varied ways to destroy the English bastard's fortune and family. It is a simple enough thing to kill an enemy, but to first deprive him of all he holds close and dear— now, that takes finesse and skill."

"The fire last night . . . ?"

He nodded graciously. "My work. And don't you think the charges of witchcraft against you were especially effective?"

"Button," she whispered.

"I giveth; I taketh away," he said. "Fittingly biblical, don't you agree?"

"The little ones of the jungle have their own gods. You will answer to them."

He paid her no attention. "Overall, I'm well pleased with the way the game has run, though not everything went quite according to plan. The impressment gang should have exacted a much greater physical toll, but you can't always count on riffraff. If Bentley had suffered a sound beating, it would have given me more time to plan mischief, but I suppose I can't blame my men that a crazed horseman came to the Marquess's rescue.''

Miranda pressed her lips together. If the Dutchman didn't realize that it had been Kit who'd been accosted, then Steef wasn't as all-seeing and all-knowing as he'd have her believe. What other weaknesses did he have besides this tendency to megalomania? If she kept him talking, perhaps he'd reveal them.

"You've been extremely clever," she murmured.

"More than you know. How Bentley will cringe when he learns I made his mother my accomplice! Deliciously ironic. So I've taken everything . . . even his unborn child?''

Miranda gasped, confirming his guess.

"Lucky happenstance, that you should be quickening just as my horseman runs you down. A fine bit of additional drama.''

Nausea churned in her stomach, and the bitterness of bile rose to the back of her throat. "You are mad.''

"Just determined. Piece by piece, I've stripped Bentley of everything. He will understand what I've done to him before I end his life.''

Miranda's heart leapt at that threat, but she kept her tone level. "You underestimate Tony. You haven't found it easy to best him in the past, nor will you now.''

"Will I not?'' The grotesque smile appeared again. "He'll come here tonight as I directed, with everything he owns or can borrow or steal. His estate lies in ruins, but he'll bring what he can to ransom his beloved wife. And then I'll have him.''

Realization snapped Miranda's head up. The Dutchman had set his trap for Tony, and she was the bait! How could she endure the fact that once again Tony was in jeopardy because of her? There must be something she could do—escape or stall or somehow warn Tony of the danger. *Think!* she told herself, frantic with fear.

Brazen it out, a memory whispered, and from somewhere deep inside, the master puppeteer opened a floodgate, and courage flowed.

"You're wrong," she denied in a steady voice. "All

your plans are for naught. I was leaving my husband anyway, before Cecil stepped in with his fumble-fisted bum-
bling!''

"Sylvie's gambit," the Dutchman snorted disdainfully.
"As if the ruination of a reputation was payment enough!"

"Nevertheless, Tony's made it clear he doesn't want me.
You're wasting your time here. The Wastrel Lord won't
care what becomes of his inconvenient wife."

Leaning back against the post so that her hands were out
of his sight, she strained desperately at the frayed cords that
bound her. There! Had one slipped just a fraction? Keeping
her gaze and her voice even, she continued.

"You'll see. You've miscalculated on the most vital point
of your plan. I've been nothing but a nuisance. I daresay
Tony is relieved to have me gone. When I'm out of the
picture, he'll be able to marry Lady Catherine and use her
fortune to replace his losses." She laughed softly, taunt-
ingly. "You're actually doing him a favor, *Minjheer* van
der Djink! He won't come, and he certainly won't bring
any money."

The Dutchman stepped close again, leaning his deformed
face into hers. "I sent him a lock of this pretty hair, did
you know? He'll come."

"He won't," she repeated stubbornly.

"So I'll send him another message, and perhaps enclose
an ear."

She gulped, but continued to regard him stoically. "I
suppose I'll miss it on musical evenings, but it won't make
any difference."

"Then the third message will contain a slender finger."

"Entertaining though you may find such sport, the Marquess won't come."

"Oh, yes," the Dutchman whispered, touching her cheek
with the stubby remains of one finger. "Piece by piece, one
way or the other, he'll come. And I will take great pleasure
in killing him very slowly."

Miranda shuddered inwardly and shrank away from his
loathsome touch. A rising wave of desperation congealed
her blood. Above her, the full moon recalled another time,

another night of desperate chances and fateful choices. Had Semar stalked her footsteps since that night, only to have it end here with the Dutchman in the role of the God of Destruction?

Despite her lies, she knew Tony would come, ignoring the risks. She also knew that there was no way the Dutchman would allow her to live after this. Worse than that, however, was the fear that Tony would be lured to his destruction because of her. She couldn't let that happen.

A small noise came from the entrance of the warehouse, and the Dutchman drew back, frowning. "Curse those ruffians," he muttered. "I told Dikes I wanted everyone quiet—"

"Miri? Where are you?"

"Tony!" Miranda screamed, electrified by a bolt of sheer terror. "It's a trap! A trap—"

The Dutchman's scarred hand covered her mouth with such force, her head bounced painfully against the wooden pillar.

"Quiet, you bitch!" he hissed into her ear, raising his pistol. Dazed, she twisted with frantic strength. The ropes scraped painful gouges in her skin, but her bonds slipped another notch. Steef placed the pistol against Miranda's throat and pulled the hammer back. "Come out where I can see you, Benedict, or I swear I'll shoot."

"Let her go, Dutchman." The reply came from somewhere among the scattered bales and crates. "I'm here, and I've got what you want."

"Step out," Steef ordered again, pressing the barrel under Miranda's jawbone. "Or do you value her life so little?"

A tall, elegantly dressed form stepped free of the shadows of a man-sized cask and tossed a leather satchel halfway across the space that separated them. It landed with a heavy thud and the jingle of coins. "There's everything you wanted. Now let her go."

Steef's mouth twisted in satisfaction. His hand dropped from Miranda's lips, but the pistol stayed where it was. "How very enterprising of you. And you're early, too. You weren't foolish enough to come armed, were you?"

"No."

The Dutchman nodded in satisfaction. "I hadn't expected such cooperation."

"What choice did I have?"

The Dutchman laughed. "None. I saw to that. Come closer, Englishman."

Get back! Miranda thought, frantic. Drenched in cold sweat, she wanted to scream at Tony in frustration, but the sounds clogged in her throat. The golden lantern light glittered in the blue depths of his eyes as he took a step closer—and she stifled a gasp of surprise.

"Dikes! Get in here!" Steef bellowed. No response. "Dikes!"

His opponent's voice was lazily amused. "You didn't think I'd allow you to have *all* the advantage, did you? I have a friend named Mertle who delights in trouncing thugs."

"You think it matters?" Steef snarled. The pistol swung away from Miranda and aimed for the tall man's heart. "Nothing matters except that the Marquess of Bentley pays his debts."

Another voice spoke from the darkness behind Miranda. "But first you must be certain you have the right man, Steef."

The Dutchman whirled, whipping the pistol around at the second elegant figure lounging negligently against a rotting crate. Steef made a choking sound, and Miranda understood his dilemma. Dressed similarly, identical perukes hiding the slight difference in their hair coloring, Tony and Kit were mirror images of each other. Only a loving heart could tell them apart. And while Kit had appeared first, it was now Tony who faced the Dutchman's menacing weapon.

"Nay!" The sound ripped from Miranda's throat at the same instant her bleeding wrists finally slipped their ropes. Lunging free, her only thought to stop Steef any way possible, she grabbed up the lantern and pitched it at the Dutchman's head.

Then everything happened at once.

The pistol fired. Kit leaped forward. The lantern whizzed

through the air, spinning end over end, spilling oil and flames in every direction. Tony dove behind a cask and rolled to his feet clutching a sword. Tinder-dry, a pile of sacks exploded into flame with a *whoosh*, cutting Kit off behind a wall of fire. With a hoarse cry of rage, the Dutchman threw the useless pistol at Tony, then his feral blue eye caught on Miranda. Drawing his sword, he slashed at her. With a squeak, she turned and ran for her life.

Black smoke blossomed, filling the air with its choking, noisome richness. Tongues of orange flame raced from pile to pile and skittered up and across the rafters like red trailing vines. Gasping, Miri plunged through the maze of barrels and crates, twisting and turning, becoming as disoriented as she had the day she and Rija had fled through the back alleys of Batavia, and always, the sound of the Dutchman crashing after her.

"Steef! Goddamn you, Dutchman! It's me you want!" Tony shouted from some unseen nook. "Miri, where are you?"

"Tony!" Miranda turned another corner, but there was nothing before her but a blank wall and the base of a rickety staircase. She turned to retrace her steps, and her cry lodged in her throat as the black shadow of the Dutchman came out of the smoke toward her. Trapped, she took the only way out—scrambling up narrow risers into the heavy pall of smoke with the Dutchman growling at her heels.

"Jimmy! The whole place is going up!" Kit shouted from below.

"Get the hell out!" Tony roared. *"Miri!"*

"Up here!" she gasped. She stumbled, falling on hands and knees. Hands clutched at her hems, and she kicked out, evoking a howl and a curse. "Oh, God! Tony, help me!"

"Steef, you spawn of Satan! Let her go!" Tony's voice came from the direction of the stairs.

Scrambling madly, Miranda gained the wooden catwalk and a relatively clear patch of air. Fighting for breath, she backed cautiously across the swaying walkway, terrified to see how high she stood above the burning floor of the warehouse, but more terrified by the monstrous apparition still

following her. There was the insane light of murder in
Steef's pale blue eye, and the unmarked side of his face
formed half of a perfect smile.

"Don't run and I'll be quick and merciful," the Dutchman said.

"Merciful!" she spat. The rotten rail broke under her
hand, and she gasped and clutched the other side. The heat
and smoke was again suffocating, the flames leaping higher
and higher. "You have no notion of the word, even for
yourself, you monster! We still have time to flee this place
before it becomes our pyre."

"No. I'll see you and your lover in hell, then join you
there."

"Steef." Tony appeared behind the Dutchman, his eyes
reddened, his chest heaving for air. "Turn and fight me,
you cowardly whoreson! Finish what we began at the *kraton*,
if you can. Or is it too much to expect of the faceless cripple
I made?"

The gibe shot through the Dutchman like a bolt, and he
whirled around, the violence of his movement making the
catwalk shimmy and shake. "English bastard! You'll be
fish bait when I'm through."

The Dutchman thrust, and Tony parried, with a metallic
clang of swords. On the narrow suspended walkway, there
was no room for the finesse and movement of a fencing
match, so the fight took on the aspects of an ancient broad-
sword clash. Where only strength and endurance counted,
Steef's partial blindness was no handicap. Of equal height
and reach, they pounded at each other with unmitigated
ferocity while the walkway creaked and swayed, and smoke
burned their lungs. Miranda watched in horror, unable to
help, unable to move until Tony caught her eye for an
instant.

"Damn it, Miri! Go! Now!"

She stumbled down the catwalk until she reached the far
landing of the upper gallery, and only then did she realize
she was crying. The smoke was growing so thick, she could
barely see the two combatants. If only she had a knife, a
stick, anything! But their perch was so precarious, the ad-

dition of her weight again might plunge them all into the
inferno below.

Suddenly she heard a hoarse shout and saw the flicker of
silver as a blade flew through the air. Knuckles white, she
gripped the handrail, straining to see. In the garish red flare,
Steef stood unarmed, the point of Tony's sword at his throat.
Mesmerized, she couldn't breathe a sigh of relief, couldn't
guess what Tony would do.

Tony's face was hard with hate and blood lust, and for
an instant it was too bone-chillingly like the Dutchman's.
Then Tony slowly dropped the tip of the sword, jerking his
head to indicate the vanquished villain should follow Miranda.

"Go on," he said, his voice gruff. "I'd rather you live
to suffer."

"Poltroon!" Steef spat his contempt. "You don't have
the guts to kill me."

"Why do you invite death?"

"You've never understood, have you?" Steef made his
grimace of a smile. "I *am* death. *Yours*."

Like a striking cobra, Steef charged Tony, impaling himself on the lowered sword. Miranda cried out as the crimson-
coated blade appeared through the Dutchman's back, sprout-
ing like the bloodred pistil of an exotic black orchid. He
arched, but even in his death throes, his hate lived, and he
grappled with Tony, pulling them both over the railing.

Miranda screamed. The catwalk collapsed, and the
Dutchman spiraled into the flaming pit on his way to hell.
For a panicked moment, Miranda knew he'd taken Tony
with him, but then she saw a form clinging to the swaying
underside of the supporting structure.

"Tony!" With every atom of her being she willed him
strength, and was rewarded as he swung his leg over the
dangling beam, then inched his way over the chasm to
safety, rolling onto his back on the floor of the opposite
gallery. Relief made her tremble with weakness. "Thank
God."

"Miri!" Tony's frantic call echoed through the smoke-
filled space.

"I'm here!" She coughed harshly, half-smothered in the broiling atmosphere. "Are you all right?"

"Yes, but I can't reach you! You've got to find a way out. Hurry, before this place burns down about our ears. Now, run!"

"Yes. Be careful," she called. Holding the hem of her gown across her nose, she hastened across the gallery, nearly blinded by the hot haze and flying cinders. She found another stairway, but halfway down, came up short, her path blocked by burning timbers. With the roar of the growing inferno drowning out her gasps for breath, she retraced her steps, searching for another exit.

There was none.

Driven by the northerly winds, the fire climbed up every pillar and marched across the stairways, consuming everything in its path. Panic poured through Miranda even as her strength deserted her, and with a sense of déjà vu, she knew the terror Tony had experienced in the burning *kraton*. Now fate had brought them both full circle. Blind, coughing violently with each breath, she knew she was trapped.

Praying that Tony had escaped, she wobbled along the gallery, feeling her way through the enveloping black gloom. Her foot struck something, and she fell headlong, barking her shins. Flailing, she tried to catch herself and grabbed a short span of board nailed to the wall. Dazed and alone, she clung to it. Her fuzzy brain painfully sorted out the myriad sensations and came to a surprising conclusion— it was a rough ladder, but where did it lead?

Then she heard the bells.

Shaking her head to clear the cobwebs, she listened intently. The silvery sound came from over her head. Something deep and primal moved within her chest. Without thinking, acting on pure instinct, she mounted the first rough rung, then the next, forcing her shaking limbs to carry her up toward the sound.

The climb was endless, excruciating. She couldn't breathe, couldn't see, but the tantalizing call rang in her ears, and she moved without volition, knowing only that she had no other choice. Finally she sensed a subtle change, some current in the clogged air that made her reach out. An opening surrounded her, a square cut into the attic floor, and she rolled out of it onto her stomach, nearly retching with the effort.

But still the bells chimed, growing louder and louder, urging her to her feet. She blinked, realizing that the pall of smoke was less dense here, and struggled to her hands and knees. Out of nowhere, hands appeared, crushed her to a broad, familiar chest.

"Miri." Tony's voice was smoke-rough. "Thank God."

She clung to him, her heart full of gratitude and desperation. "Tony . . . I heard the bells."

"I did, too." He dragged her to her feet. "Where the devil are they coming from?"

She pointed. "There."

Stumbling together, they moved cautiously, skirting sagging holes open to the sky above and fire below that acted as chimneys, channeling the heat and smoke upward. In places, the shingles were already alight. Bending low, Tony urged them under the steeply pitched roofline, away from the leaping flames, and toward the vague outline of a lighter triangle at the end of the building.

The opening set under the eaves had once been an entrance for cargo raised by block and tackle for storage. The air was easier to breathe there, and they stood gasping, surveying the vantage of the glittering river far below. Miranda took one look and drew back hastily on a wave of vertigo, while the moon beamed benevolently on their perilous predicament.

"The church bells will bring the fire brigade," Tony said tightly, "but we haven't got that kind of time."

He stripped off his coat, then reached for the rather dubious-looking rope looped around the protruding ridgepole.

She gave him an incredulous look. "Tony . . . no."

"It's the only way, dearling. We'll be roasted long before help arrives if we stay here."

The beleaguered building creaked and groaned alarmingly as if to emphasize his words. Miranda threw herself into her husband's arms.

"I'm so sorry—for everything," she choked.

"Ah, Miri," he murmured tenderly, "when are you going to realize that you can't blame yourself for all the bad things that happen in the world?"

"I never wanted anything to hurt you." She quivered, pressing herself against him. "If it hadn't been for me, none of this would have happened."

"Listen to me!" he ordered fiercely. "You're the only good and beautiful thing in my worthless wastrel life."

"After last night, I was so afraid you didn't want me anymore," she confessed.

"Just the opposite. Wondering how I'd keep you if I lost everything." He swallowed harshly. "And then Mother's lies . . . But I'll tell you all that later. Just know this: if it all ends now for us, or a hundred years from now, I will have cherished every moment, never felt one regret. Not one, do you hear?"

Turning her face up to his, he kissed her with all the passion and love and conviction of which he was capable. With trembling fingertips she touched his face, his cheekbone, and an enormous wave of emotion flooded her being, lifting her doubts, removing the terrible weight of responsibility she'd taken on herself.

And she knew that he was right. Life held no guarantees for anyone, and she'd been foolish to think she could change the course of the world all by herself. Maybe the best one could do was to survive, to meet each new challenge with humor and courage and, if you were one of the fortunate, with love. Then, no matter what the outcome, good or bad, at the end of the journey you'd have had it all.

"No regrets," she whispered against Tony's lips. Stepping back, she reached for the laces of her gown and demanded, "Help me get out of this."

"W-what?"

"I'm counting on the fall to kill us," she said tartly, shoving off petticoats. "But in case it doesn't, I can't be expected to swim in this foolish English garb!"

Tony threw back his head and roared with laughter. "Right you are, my little pagan!" Grabbing the back of her dress, he ripped it from neckline to hem. In moments she stood only in shift, garters, stockings.

"Quit grinning at me, you rogue," Miranda ordered. "This is serious."

"I want to remember you this way in eternity," he said gravely, slinging his arm around her waist and wrapping the rope around his other hand. "I'll always love you, you know, in this life and beyond."

Miranda looped her arms around his neck, closed her eyes, and whispered, "I know."

With a whoop, Tony launched them from the top of the burning building. They swung out over the dark, glittering river, and at the end of the rope's arc, he let go.

Epilogue

The ancient dukun *stood at the doorway of her hut, her gnarled fingers clutching a coconut shell teacup. She smiled at the rising sun, letting its golden warmth bake into her wrinkled cheeks. After an anxious night of magic and demon-mischief, the face of the goddess had disappeared behind the smoking mountain, leaving behind serenity and peace for the old teacher.*

From the hillside path below her hut drifted the cheerful chatter of her visitors. The colorfully arrayed group of noble ladies was led by bright-eyed Tiktik, now Rija, sultana of Preanger, who waved eagerly from under the golden parasol carried by her servant. The dukun *lifted a hand in reply and waited for the party to climb the rest of the way.*

Soon they would speak of many things—of the certainty of an heir for the sultan come the rainy season, of the beloved sister who'd sailed away from her adopted homeland so many months ago to seek a new destiny, of the signs read under the silver light of the yearly Lotus Moon.

The dukun *looked again at the pattern of tea leaves in*

377

*the bottom of her cup, at the evidence that said the child
of her heart had passed her trials safely. There would be
much to discuss with her noble visitor. The old woman
smiled, and a distant memory quivered in her mind, then
blossomed like a lotus flower.*

*"But, Teacher, how do you know when you've found
love?" Miri's voice whispered across time and space.*

"Not all are favored, my daughter," came the dukun's
*reply, "but if the goddess smiles, in your heart you'll hear
joy like the sound of temple bells."*

The echoes of chapel bells lingered in the mild September
morning, their joyous song reprised by the merry sounds of
fiddle, pipe, and tabor. Across Fairhaven's rolling velvet
lawns, guests of every calling crowded around the linen-
covered tables to celebrate the wedding breakfast of Angus
Pratt and Letticia Sutherlin, joined as man and wife only
an hour earlier.

Miranda gave a final quiet suggestion to Tweedale, re-
flecting that even the butler's ramrod demeanor had relaxed
a fraction for the happy occasion. She paused on the white
shell path leading to the house, letting her gaze roam across
the crowd, well pleased with her efforts. Fairhaven's windows shone like crystal prisms, every dish and wine served
was perfection itself, and even the late roses had seen fit to
burst into a reckless profusion of blooms that released their
sweetness like a benediction.

"Walk with me, my lady?"

With a smile for her handsome husband, Miranda shook
out the skirts of her dusty rose bridesmaid's gown, then
took his outstretched hand. "Your magnificence makes me
catch my breath, my lord."

A slash of a dimple winked in Tony's cheek, and he
tugged at his embroidered waistcoat self-consciously.
"Kit's idea. But I have to admit, never has there been a
bridegroom with two such resplendent best men!"

"Without doubt," she said with a soft laugh, the ribbons
of her flowered headdress caressing her flushed cheek.

At the main table, Kit, clad in a brocade suit of Benedict

blue identical to Tony's, chatted with the newlyweds. Angus's ruddy face shone bright as the sun, and beneath her wedding crown of lilies and roses, Letty looked the picture of the ideal bride, flustered, happy, and young.

"Come," Tony said, tugging at Miranda's hand to draw her off a little way from the crowd. "The sound of church bells has made you pensive."

They strolled across the grass, and Miranda shrugged. "I can't help but remember . . ."

"Nor I . . ."

They didn't talk much about the night Steef van der Djink died, about the terror of falling free between heaven and earth, not knowing whether those moments were to be their last ones or not. Sometimes Miranda awoke in the middle of the night with a start, jerked awake by a dream in which she hit the river again and this time couldn't find the surface or Tony. Then Tony would hold her until she stopped shaking, reassuring her with his words and touch that they'd both survived their deadly plunge, plucked from the river's clutches by Angus and Kit with the help of Mertle's men.

Drenched, shivering, but exultant, they'd sat on the broken stoop of St. Crispin's and watched the fire brigade work. Wrapped in a borrowed cloak, Miranda had refused to leave until there was nothing left of the warehouse but a few charred piers sticking up from the river sludge like a dead man's fingers. Unlike the myth of Semar, who rose from ashes to stand again with his brother-god Shiva, there would be no return from this grave for the Dutchman.

"Yer's the lucky ones, ye are," Mertle of the hook nose had opined more than once during that vigil. "Smoke black as night. How'd you find each other, much less the way out?"

"The bells," Miranda murmured.

Tony nodded. "We owe a debt to whoever rang the alarm. It gave us something to head for in the murk. We'd never have made it without that sound to follow."

Mertle shook his head, puzzled. "Bells, milord? I ain't heard none this night."

"But you must have!" Miranda exclaimed. "They were very clear . . ."

"The church sexton must have rung them," Tony said.

"But, milord," Mertle said on a queer, strangled note. "There ain't been bells at St. Crispin's in over thirty years!"

Tony had put his arms around his wife then, and in silence they'd watched a moon as white and full as a lotus blossom disappear into the river. Now, on the grounds of Fairhaven, he squeezed her hand in silent reassurance, and she returned his smile. Whatever their part in these mysteries, what mattered most was that they were together.

A large black cat scurried past them, followed by a small, black-haired dynamo. With her flower girl's garland of ribbons and posies cocked rakishly over one blue-gray eye, Rose plowed into her Uncle Tony's legs, threw back her head, and chortled brightly. "Bub-bub!"

"After the kitty again?" Tony asked, setting the toddler aright on her sturdy legs. "There you go, mate. After him!"

Rose darted off again after the leery old black tom.

"Don't encourage her, Tony," Lexa scolded, holding her own bridesmaid's garland in place with one hand as she hurried after her wayward daughter. "You and Kit are just alike!"

To Lexa's utter chagrin, Rose chased Beelzebub under the head table and crawled in after him. Lexa dragged Rose, giggling wildly, from under the table, and with a look that said, "She's *your* daughter," passed her to Kit. On the other side of the table, Letty gave a tiny squeal of surprise, staring down in amazement as the battered old feline sought the protection of her lap. Gingerly Letty stroked him, and Beelzebub's gravelly purr sounded his approval.

"Ach, would ye look at that?" Angus demanded. He bent and kissed his bride soundly. "Yer mine for life, lass, now that Beelzebub's set his cap for ye!"

Letty turned bright pink. "Why, Mr. Pratt!"

"Aye, Mrs. Pratt. You know what the good book says: 'Whoso findeth a wife findeth a good thing.'"

His bride's hazel eyes widened in wonderment and melting affection. "Oh, Angus . . ."

Kit nudged her and winked wickedly. "And you thought all he admired was your rhubarb jam!"

Miranda laughed with the rest of the guests, then poked Tony and nodded toward another happy couple. Lord Peter Ingram only had eyes for Lady Catherine Salter, and everyone knew an engagement announcement was imminent. Even her Uncle Colleton beamed with approval. Catching Miranda's and Tony's eye, he lifted his wineglass in a brief salute. Tony smiled and bowed.

"All is forgiven at last," he muttered under his breath.

"Fortunately for everyone," Miranda replied with a laugh. Then she gave a quiet sigh. "I'm happy for Peter and Catherine, but I hate to see Kit and Lexa leave."

"Yes." Tony's look was solemn. "But their life is in the colonies, and they're eager to return, especially now that Kit's duties as representative to the Crown have been fulfilled."

Turning, Miranda smoothed the lapel of her husband's coat, and her smile was proud. "I'm sure you'll do your best to keep the colonies' interests alive in Walpole's plans and Parliament, too."

Tony chuckled. "'Tis fortunate I have a wealthy wife whose coffee trade allows me to indulge my penchant for politics from time to time."

"Oh, pooh! The arrival of your other Free Indies ships did more to restore our fortunes, as you well know, though I'll admit our trading direct with Sultan Amang pleases me greatly since I'll have more regular contact with Rija. And bringing the Dutchman a satchel of rocks and pennies instead of the ransom he demanded showed much initiative."

Tony grimaced wryly. "I'm glad you incinerated the place before he had a chance to discover my deception."

"Anthony Benedict! You promised you wouldn't tease me about that anymore!"

He grinned, unrepentant. "Sorry, sweet, but I love to see that spark of green in your eyes."

They had resumed their stroll across the lawns and now paused on a small rise to admire the view of Fairhaven.

"It would have been a pity to give up all this," Miranda said quietly. "I'm so glad it didn't happen."

"I thought losing Fairhaven would prove I was the failure my father believed I was."

"Charles Benedict couldn't possibly have thought you were a failure!"

Tony smiled. "Such loyalty. But I think I understand him better now, for I was able to achieve something he never did."

"What is that?"

Tony touched her cheek, then lifted her hand and kissed the pearl ring he'd put back on her finger himself. "True happiness. Your love gave me the strength to believe in myself, in *us*, even in the face of Sylvie's manipulations. I've been haunted by the sense that I failed Father, but *he* failed me, and Kit, and Rosalind. I succeeded where he did not, had faith where he had none. I broke his bitter legacy and kept history from repeating itself."

"And can you forgive him now?" Miranda asked softly.

"I feel"—Tony looked across the rolling park, frowning as if searching for the right word—"reconciled, as though I redeemed us both."

"Perhaps in some sphere of existence he and Rosalind feel that, too."

Tony searched her face. "You are a remarkable woman."

She shook her head, blushing a little as they found their way to a bench set in the shade of a spreading elm. "I simply have to believe that love is eternal."

Smiling, he kissed her lightly, then lifted her coronet of ribbons and flowers from her lustrous hair and set it on the bench. Running one finger around the lace ruching of her décolletage, he raised one sun-bleached eyebrow at her solemn expression. "Why still so quiet on Angus's wedding day?"

"My darling, what about Sylvie?"

Tony's mouth tightened. "Damn it, Miri! I thought we agreed—"

"To give it some time, and we have." She laid her hand on his thigh, her expression earnest. "I think the business with the Baron—the Dutchman, I mean—shook her badly. She was a victim, too."

"As far as I'm concerned, her retirement from Society and self-imposed exile to the Dower House is punishment enough, so you needn't plead her case, my softhearted spouse. I'll see to her sustenance, but that's all she can expect from me."

"Will you never forgive her?"

"She nearly cost me everything I hold dear. Forgiveness is beyond me."

"The vicar wrote me that she's so changed, Tony. Broken. Ill and old. I think you were the only thing she ever truly loved, and the fact that she was part of something that nearly destroyed you is eating her alive."

His mouth set in a mulish line. "What is it you want me to do?"

"I'm not sure, but would you at least think about seeing her?" Miranda leaned over to nuzzle the taut underside of his jaw with her lips. "Not for her sake, but for your own. Hating her will only hurt you in the end. And after all, she is the nearest thing to a grandmother our children will ever have."

Tony slid a possessive hand over the rounded swell of her abdomen. "You think she deserves to be told about this?" he growled.

"I think that seeing your offspring might be *her* redemption. People can change, my love, as we both know."

"Well . . ." He shifted uncomfortably, his expression still dubious. "I suppose it wouldn't hurt to think about it."

"I knew you'd say that." Her smile was mischievous, the hand on his thigh rather adventurous.

He tried to hold on to his irritation. "Woman, am I destined to have a wife who always takes these matters into her own hands?"

"Possibly," she purred, letting her fingers explore farther afield.

"Witch!" he groaned. He gave a swift glance at the bevy of guests still celebrating down by the house, then took her hand and dragged her out of sight behind the tree. "Now let us see you try your tricks!"

Pushing her against the massive trunk, he let his hands roam freely, nipping at her neck with his teeth, then capturing her mouth in a kiss that stirred them both.

"My Lord, you are too bold, to think to take me in broad daylight in a public field!" she mock-scolded, shivering with delight at his touch. "You are a rogue and a scoundrel and a—oh!"

She broke off with a gasp as he found his way under her skirts, stroking her sensitive folds and rubbing the rounded swell of her fecund womb.

"And you love me," he muttered thickly against the sweet juncture of her jaw.

"Eternally," she sighed.

"Wanton," he said, laughing in her ear. "And see what it's gotten you! I swear your girth increases daily. Before this babe appears, I fear you'll grow too fat for me to do my husbandly duty!"

"Although I'm certain with your imagination and experience, we will always find ways to pleasure each other, you have only yourself and your passion to blame if I grow enormous," she said serenely. "That's what comes of carrying two Benedicts."

Tony froze. He drew back and stared at her, all the blood washing from his lean cheeks. "Two? You mean—twins?"

"Of course." She smiled, and her silver eyes were radiant with joy. "I'd say it was your doing, sir. I believe twins run in the family."

"Oh, God." Tony went even whiter. He released her abruptly, then caught her close to him again with supreme tenderness, as a man holding his most fragile, precious possession. His blue eyes were dark with wonder. "Are you sure? God, how can you be sure? How do you know?"

"Remember Semar, Englishman." With the ancient, enigmatic smile of all women, she touched his face lovingly, then kissed him. "Some things you just know, right from the start."

Avon Romances—
the best in exceptional authors and unforgettable novels!

KAREN ROBARDS

THE MISTRESS OF ROMANTIC MAGIC
WEAVES HER BESTSELLING SPELL

GREEN EYES
75889-X/$4.95 US/$5.95 Can

They were swept away by a passion
that knows no bounds, and found
a love that heals all wounds.

MORNING SONG
75888-1/$4.50 US/$5.50 Can

Though scorned by society,
theirs was a song of love
that had to be sung!

TIGER'S EYE
75555-6/$4.95 US/$5.95 Can

Theirs was a passion that could
only be called madness—but
destiny called it love!

DESIRE IN THE SUN 75554-8/$3.95 US/$4.95 Can

DARK OF THE MOON 75437-1/$3.95 US/$4.95 Can